Dancing on the Edge

Shepard C. Wilbar

authorHOUSE®

AuthorHouse™
1663 Liberty Drive
Bloomington, IN 47403
www.authorhouse.com
Phone: 1-800-839-8640

Published by AuthorHouse 11/12/2012

ISBN: 978-1-4772-7180-3 (sc)
ISBN: 978-1-4772-7181-0 (e)

Library of Congress Control Number: 2012917457

Prologue

August 10,1992

The container was cold inside and rats scurried above the layer of trash. Underneath he waited, hungry and frightened. The yogurt dripping out of the cup wasn't enough to satisfy his hunger. He spit out the small amount that moistened his lips. It was so disgusting! It was one of the most unpleasant times of his life. As he felt for the duffel bag, he rubbed it and felt the wad of cash inside. That was it. All he had left. Would this also disappear?

The feel of the cold steel of the .357 Magnum under his belt gave him some sense of security. He knew there was substantial risk, but what else could he do? How did life take such a horrible turn? Where does it go from here? Or is it the end?

He had to wait in this position for hours until his chance came. Then, he shut his eyes and slipped into memory.

CHAPTER 1

November 1945

Two hours after the birth on November 2, Johnny entered the maternity ward. His excitement was high. "Franny, it's a boy. Just what we hoped for. It's exhilarating! Are you OK?"

Frances replied, "I'm fine, Johnny, but where have you been? They called you repeatedly from the front desk without any answer. Where have you been?" she repeated.

"I had a meeting tonight which couldn't be avoided." It was three a.m. "Honey, you know my schedule, and also know that I work crazy hours to support you and Chad. And now baby Nicholas Allen. That's what we named him, right?" He smelled of alcohol and his excitement seemed greater than just that. Earlier he had shot up with heroin!

"Nicholas is a fine name," Frances agreed. Frances had just gone through many hours of labor and given birth to an eight-pound boy who was now named Nicholas Allen Packard. A choice they had tentatively agreed upon months ago. Their older boy was named Shadrach after Johnny's great uncle. Chad, as he was nicknamed, was now a playful and happy two-year-old. Chad seemed very crafty at his young age, while Nick was showing extreme alertness upon birth and had a special quality. Both Frances and Johnny thought that Nick might be destined for something big!

John W. Packard, born the son of a war hero, followed a lifelong course of crime that began in childhood. As a small schoolboy he was running numbers as a delivery boy for "Lord" Barrington, a local bookie and criminal with a lucrative business. His Anglo-Saxon community had that typical English penchant for gambling.

Johnny was a quick mover and could run as fast as a jackrabbit, which saved him from trouble on many occasions. He had a knack for conning just about anyone. One time, in 1937, young Johnny convinced Guiseppi from the North End of Boston to purchase twenty-four cases of hijacked second-rate scotch, which he and his youthful clan had stolen from a truck after Johnny had held a gun to the driver's head. He charged Guiseppi a cut rate for this "high-quality" scotch and the North End crew sold it for many times its real value. This was successful because Johnny's clan had neatly changed the labels and resealed the cartons.

Guiseppi sold the scotch for a huge profit. It must have been halfway decent because no one knew the difference and no complaints were ever made! Johnny had turned a handsome profit for his clan and an even better one for the Mob. He now had an Italian paisano with whom he'd arrange other lucrative deals in the future. It was unusual talent for a thirteen-year-old. By age twenty-two Johnny Packard had attained an important position in the hierarchy of crime in America. The young Englishman had established a high level of respect from his clan and from the Italians in the North End. He holstered a .45 automatic at all times which he seldom used. It was more for effect. But if he did, his opponents suffered drastically.

The activities of his clan came to cross all lines, including hijacking, loan sharking, prostitution, and other robberies. He never worked a day in his life for anyone else, much less took orders. What stood out about Johnny, however, was the love and respect he had for his family and the pride taken in them.

Johnny hardly reflected his ancestral patterns and habits. His known ancestry had been traced forward from Thomas Packard I, who was born shortly after Columbus discovered America. Thomas was a Knight of the First Order in His Majesty's Court, and an extremely honorable man and great family protector. Thomas's son, Nicholas J. Packard, was a magistrate of the High Court in London. He lived on an estate in Sible Hedgingham, Essex, England, and lived a serene and long life to the ripe old age of ninety-two.

The first of the English Packards to sail to America was Samuel, who sailed on the Griffin in 1633. He landed and settled in Boston, but was banished from the colony to Portsmouth, Rhode Island, for being a follower of Ann Hutchinson, the religious zealot who was excommunicated from the Church of Boston by the Puritans and moved to Acquidineck Island, which Samuel had purchased from the Narragansett Indians. This island would one day include the famous Newport, Rhode Island—the area where the summer homes of the super wealthy such as the Astors and Vanderbilts were built.

Samuel became one of the richest men in America and opened the first ironworks there. He would have been listed in the Fortune 500 had it been in publication back then! The Packards made great inroads in America into politics and industrial development.

Johnny's father was named George Packard, and was a highly decorated World War I hero who had been awarded many medals, including a Purple Heart and a Congressional Medal of Honor. He lived with his wife and two children and worked in his later years as a recruiter, up until his untimely death at age forty-four, when an artillery shell inadvertently exploded at his Long Island base and instantly snuffed out his life.

In 1943, Johnny Packard tied the knot with his high school sweetheart, Frances O'Malley, an attractive Irish brunette, who was his only love ever. He had the ability to separate business and family. He never uttered a word to Frances about his business activities. Now he had two fine sons whom he vowed to steer away from crime.

In late November, after the birth of Nicholas, Johnny and his top two lieutenants went to a meeting in New York City with a crew there to divide the spoils of a major hijacking. They had done all the dirty work and were owed a major stake. When Johnny never returned Frances got paranoid, and rightfully so. They had all been taken out, and their bodies would allegedly show up years later in shallow graves located by the FBI!

CHAPTER 2

Summer 1957

The double doors below the EMERGENCY sign at Browning Memorial swung open. There first appeared a police officer, followed by a gurney being maneuvered by two EMTs. The boy on the stretcher lay motionless, his eyes staring in a deathlike gaze. The only sign of life he showed was a choking attempt to vomit. A nurse held the boy's head and shoulders up to prevent his choking. The scene was frantic as nurses and technicians rushed toward the gurney. A resident doctor took his vital signs. The boy was clinging to life.

His brother, Chad, followed the procession and seemed to be in a state of shock. His blond hair was matted against his forehead from a drenching sweat caused by the extreme humidity of the dog days of early August. His face was pale, and although Chad had celebrated his thirteenth birthday just last week, his drawn look made him appear to be well beyond his years.

An admitting secretary called to Chad, saying, "Son, please come here. We need the patient's information." Chad continued to stare off into the distance and didn't respond. He seemed almost catatonic, lost in space and time.

A third boy, Danny Levin, who was part of the group of kids bicycling back from the lake that afternoon and had been trailing Chad, stepped forward and sat in a metal chair beside the admitting desk. The secretary, a burly, middle-aged, and proper bitch with shiny brown hair pinned up in a bun, spoke in a harsh, seemingly indifferent tone.

"What's your name, young man?"

"Uh, Danny, ma'am. Levin. Danny Levin."

"Who's your friend?"

"Who? Chad or Nick?"

"The patient, son! The patient!"

"Oh, Nick. Packard. Nicholas."

"Is that Nicholas Packard, son?"

"Yes!" Danny bellowed.

The woman went on, "How old is Nicholas?"

"Eleven, ma'am."

"What's his address?"

"Pine Street. I don't know the number, but it's here in Braintree," said Danny, feeling embarrassed.

"What happened, son?" the nursed inquired.

"Well, we were riding our bikes on Pleasant Street and Nick fell off his bike while trying to show off for some girls watching from across the street. He smashed his head on the road!" Danny related with tears in his eyes.

"Thank you, Danny. Have a seat in the waiting room and we'll inform you of his condition as soon as the doctor examines him."

"Thanks, ma'am," said Danny.

Danny took Chad's arm. He was crying profusely. He knew that his brother was badly hurt. They went to the waiting room which was around a corner beyond the admitting area. After they were out of sight of the admitting desk, Danny said, "Chad, be cool. Clamming up won't help Nick now. Let's go find him. He needs us now. Be tough!"

"Yeah, OK," Chad answered. "But I just can't believe it. Poor Nick. He's such a good brother, and smart too! My brother. I love him."

He prayed out loud, begging God to please save Nick. Holding back more tears, Chad followed Danny down the corridor and they meandered beyond the waiting area. Danny stopped and asked a young candy striper for directions to the exam room where Nick was. They found the door ajar and could hear the drone of voices inside the exam room. Peeking around the corner they saw an intensive effort under way to keep little Nick alive. A doctor stood beside Nick's apparently lifeless body. A huge parabolic light hung over the exam table. A nurse constantly monitored Nick's blood pressure through a cuff on his thin little arm while another listened to his heart rhythm with a stethoscope. His labored breathing was slow and substantially restricted. Nick's mother, Frances, was holding his hand and sobbing. She had just arrived after receiving the fearsome call.

Chad whispered to Danny, "Do you think he's still alive?"

"Of course, ass wipe, do you think they'd be doing all that crap to him if he wasn't?"

Just then, a man walked into view from the corner of the room. He was a distinguished-looking man of about sixty, with a full head of white hair, and wearing a gray pinstriped suit. He was Dr. Rangely, a neurologist who happened to be at the hospital when Nick came in on the gurney.

The boys couldn't hear all the conversation over the drone from the room, but could hear "severe…brain laceration…coma…twenty percent, maybe"!

CHAPTER 3

"Chad, you didn't take out the trash as you promised. Get away from the boob tube and do it. Now! The truck will be here soon!" Frances yelled.

"All right, Mom, give me a break. I'm watching Leave It to Beaver. It's funny. I'll do it right after it's over. I promise. Ma, can I go to see Peyton Place with Danny tonight?"

"Not a chance, Chad, we have enough misery now. You don't need to see more. I hear that movie is loaded with filth and is overdone, not real." She knew better, though. "Go see The Ten Commandments. Or, more important, visit your brother at the hospital." As she spoke, tears welled in her eyes.

"Mom, do you think Nick will be OK? It's been days and he's still unconscious. He seems to move around a lot more now, though."

"Chad, pray with me." And they did, together.

Chad eventually arose from the couch and disappeared for a while, taking the trash out, while Frances forlornly watched the news. President Eisenhower came on in a special broadcast about atomic proliferation. Great Britain had tested its first atomic explosion. What followed was Gein's arrest for his rash of brutal serial killings. Frances didn't know then, but this maniac would soon become the inspiration for Norman Bates in the movie Psycho.

She turned the TV off. She didn't want to hear any more of the world's misery. She lay back and shut her eyes, then drifted off for a bit.

She awoke when Chad returned from his trash chore, clicking his heels as he walked in. He sat down beside her and put his arm around her shoulders, kissing her cheek. "Mom, I just noticed out in the garage, a gun resting on one of the tool racks. A pistol. It looks like an old forty-five. I checked and it is empty. Did that belong to Dad?"

"Yes, Chad, I should have thrown it away years ago, but I didn't want to throw his things away. I loved him very much. He always said that the gun was used for target practice, but I sensed there was more to it. I never wanted to cast any shadows on Johnny and have never told you about his secret life. I think he was involved in criminal things, although he never gave me an inkling of it while he was alive.

He disappeared right after Nick was born, but didn't die of a heart attack, as I told you and Nick before. He never returned and I cried for days. He was a good husband and father. He loved us all.

In, I think it was 1951, I was contacted by the FBI. They had somehow located a mass grave and they thought Johnny had been identified by dental records. Although the science isn't always completely accurate. It appeared that he had been shot several times. The FBI had pieced together the premise that these murders had been related to hijacking in New York City. They were mobsters, according to the agent who called me!"

****

Day 16 – Browning Memorial Hospital

The dimly lit green-and-white-tiled corridor was quiet and a few staff members passed through during the lonely hours of the graveyard shift. This was the time when every hospital worker was isolated to his or her station, daydreaming—or night dreaming, as it were—watching the clock inch forward, and praying for no casualties to roll in and upset the serenity. They all prayed that the Grim Reaper would lay down his bloody scythe until another shift.

The ICU nurse, Judy, in a white dress and traditional Dutch-type nurse's cap, bent over adjusting the station knob on the new RCA Victor mahogany radio. The hospital had sprung $29.95 for this state-of-the-art gem just a few days earlier!

As she moved her slender body to the sound of "All Shook Up," her big tits bounced in unison with the rhythm of the song. That new guy from Memphis had a golden voice, but even he would have choked on his words if he could see Judy now!

Inside room 140, the boy lay still on the bed, his mind seemingly a tabula rasa. Nick's bodily functions were stabilized. His face was sweaty from the humidity, but the mild sweat was contained by the churning blades of the sleek, black steel floor fan.

Day 21 – Browning Memorial Hospital

"I'll take ninety even," said nurse Serina.

"And, I'll take eighty-three," mumbled the other nurse, Sally.

Nurse Judy stepped forward and said, "You're both way off base. We're in the full moon phase and it's at least ninety-four. You'll see I'm right!"

Serina smoothly grabbed the patient charts with the ten forty-five p.m. updates and tabulated the average pulse rate of the thirteen patients occupying the ICU on her Olivetti adding machine.

"What is it?" Judy asked impatiently.

"Yeah, right, it's ninety-five!" said Serina "How the hell did you know?"

Serina and Sally combed through their pocketbooks for cash. A two-dollar bill and two ones were slid across the desk to Judy. As she laughed, her large, round tits jiggled up and down.

The double doors of the ICU swung open and Frances walked in. She was wearing a pretty white and blue sundress with straps hanging over her soft feminine shoulders. At thirty-six she looked great. Her long black hair was perfectly curled in a cute pageboy style. The emotional agony took a backseat to her youthful beauty as she held in that dreadful anxiety.

The nurses said, "Good evening, Mrs. Packard."

Frances forced a smile with great anguish and said, "Hello." Johnny's widow silently walked toward room 140 with dreaded anticipation!

Inside, Nick was sprawled out on his back with his right hand in the air. His fingers were partially clutched. Frances approached the bed and circled little Nick's forefinger with her palm. Suddenly Nick's finger moved, grasping her hand with a squeeze. "Mama," Nick uttered. "Where am I?" He had spoken clearly and logically after twenty-one days of unconsciousness!

Tears flooded her eyes and she burst out crying uncontrollably. Astonished and overwhelmed with joy she hugged his little body, stroked his whiffled head, and kissed his cheeks incessantly. Frances said, "I love you so much, honey!"

Nick murmured, "I love you too, Mom."

Day 23 – Browning Memorial Hospital

First, Danny arrived in the hospital lobby, trailed by Chad, who had stopped to tie his black, ankle-high Keds sneakers. The mood seemed lighter today. Nick had miraculously talked after three weeks of silence! Chad sneezed and wiped his nose with his shirtsleeve. Fall allergies were back!

Danny was wearing pegged pink pants, neatly tapered, and blue suede snap jacks. He had matured that summer and looked like a young Gene Vincent. His wavy brown hair was combed straight back on the sides and parted in the back in the popular "duck's ass" style. His sideburns were cut even with the earlobes.

The boys had started the fall 1957 semester of school at Braintree Junior High. Danny had started the seventh grade and Chad the eighth. As they walked down the long corridor connecting the east wing which housed the ICU, Danny said to Chad, "Boy, did you see Lisa Williams today in school? She looked so fine, and when she walked down the corridor wiggling her ass I got a hard-on. Then she bent over at the water cooler and I could see the panty-line on her skirt. Part of her tits were showing as the blouse parted. This year is going to be cool. Nick, you, and me together later this fall in school. What a blast!"

Chad said, "You know it, buddy!"

The pair laughed and sauntered along to the ICU. As they passed the administration office they heard a loud clicking noise, like castanets. Then they heard a high-pitched "Yah! Ya, ya, ya, yah yah! Yah, ya, ya, ya, yah! Ya, ya, ya, yah, yah… Oh, little darling, little darling, oh, oh, where are you…"

"Cool man, 'Little Darling,'"said Chad. "I think it's number one now in the Top Ten. I heard Arnie Ginsberg say that on the radio last night. The 'velvet voice.' He's awesome. And I love the Diamonds!"

The secretary at the front desk in the administration office was tall and thin with a pixie-type haircut. She had one of those built-in, continuous smiles and was very attractive. Starry-eyed, she stared at the wall in a sort of trance, listening to the song on her radio. On her desk was a vase of fresh red roses and a half-full, twelve-ounce glass bottle of Coke. She appeared to be daydreaming about her lover!

Day 27 – Browning Memorial Hospital

It was Saturday morning and an aroma of freshly brewed coffee permeated the ICU. The Packard family had assembled in room 140 awaiting the arrival of Dr. Rangely. Frances and Chad stood beside Nick's bed. Chad's paternal grandmother sat in the armchair while two close cousins, Tina and Matt, stood in the corner.

Dr. Rangely arrived at 10:35 a.m., dressed in a tan cotton vested suit. His thick gray hair was neatly parted. He carried a leather bag. After family introductions by Frances, he proceeded to examine Nick's eyes and reflexes while listening closely to his now normal speech.

The doctor stood up straight and faced everyone, saying, "You're all very fortunate. Nick has apparently recovered from most neurological effects of the injury. I will, of course, follow through with more EEG testing this fall, but I believe it will show fairly normal results."

"Doctor, when can he go home?" asked Frances.

"Very soon. A few more days," said Dr. Rangely, then he bid farewell to everybody and left the room. Out the window Chad could see him walk across the parking lot and open the door of a brand-new Edsel.

Three days later, Nicholas Packard filled a suitcase and

received emotional hugs, kisses, and farewells from the staff. At 11:10 a.m., he rode in a wheelchair pushed by his mother through the lobby and rolled out the swinging doors, embarking miraculously on another chance at life!

CHAPTER 4

Spring 1967 – Boston, Massachusetts

"Mr. Packard, you must sit in row A, seat twenty-one. It's the first seat in the second section of the graduate seating area over there." The dean of students, Roger Whittier, a heavyset man of forty or so, pointed at the sea of chairs and to a section directly in front of the podium. The first-row seat would put Nick within about fifteen feet and in direct line of sight of the podium. Seat assignments?

Dean Whittier had worked for the Massachusetts Bay University for the last twelve years and had served the students well in coordinating all housing requirements and student functions, in addition to one-on-one student advice and consultations about any problem. His door was open ten hours a day every weekday to students.

Roger had been living with Bart, a black man, for the past seven years, and it was known in most circles that they were gay. One student had reported seeing the couple walking into the Rialto Theater with arms clasped and smiling lovingly at each other one night last year.

Nick had developed into a handsome young man of

twenty-one and had a powerful and muscular physique. His shoulder-length, wavy black hair complemented his "baby blues" and made Nick a very attractive young man. Though his sexual preference was purely heterosexual, he had no disdain for Dean Whittier. He respected their differences and had the highest admiration for this man who devoted much of his life to helping novice students survive this first major life change.

Nick slowly walked across the seating area. The tassel of his graduation cap swung back and forth against his long hair. His black gown was neatly pressed and pleated. The crowd was gathering and the rows of seats were gradually filling up.

Larry Bowdoin, standing on a metal chair, yelled to Nick from four rows back. "All right, Nick! Congratulations! I knew you'd do it." Do what? "I'm having a bash at the Ocean Club after we get out of here. You'd fucking better be there, Nick!"

"I'll get there as soon as possible," Nick responded. He wondered what Larry meant about "doing it"? He proceeded to walk to the front, found seat twenty-one in the first row, and sat patiently as a feeling of excitement arose within him. The weather was perfectly matched for this momentous occasion. It was bright and sunny, the sky an endless blue spotted by puffy white clouds. A cool summer breeze titillated his face. Life is so great. And it's just begun!

The Mass Bay University band began playing "Fleur De Lis" while the faculty and honored guests took their seats. The excitement grew intensely.

After the music stopped, President Gregory B. Altman,

a stately man with more degrees than any other faculty member, rose and stepped forward to the podium. His eyes surveyed the crowd as he began the opening address. There was stone silence from the audience as he said, "It's a distinct pleasure to be here on such a fine and glorious day to address the commencement of the fifty-seventh graduating class of our hallowed university.

In 1910, the founding fathers of…"

About ten minutes into the traditional opening address he changed the mood of the speech and continued with, "These are turbulent times for the United States of America. The war in Vietnam, which has been the longest of wars in American history, beginning in the 1950s, has escalated on a major scale. Many American soldiers' lives have been brutally snuffed out by the ravages of this war. President Johnson, this past week, ordered an increase of troops by a staggering fifty thousand." President Altman hesitated with a wary look then stated, "Many of you may be called to service to defend your country. My prayers go to President Johnson to end this debacle."

The audience made a standing ovation, then, somberly sat down. A buzzing could be heard within. Altman went on. "And now, on a more pleasant note, I would like to present our honorary guests."

After thirty minutes of introductions and speeches, President Altman approached the podium and said, "It is my pleasure at this time to present the coveted student award for this year. Each year in the honor of tradition we present a gold plaque to the outstanding graduating senior of our university. Rather than explain the merits of this award, I will read the inscription on this plaque: 'Presented to the outstanding senior of the graduating class in recognition of academic excellence and enthusiastic participation in community and technical activities.' This year it is my pleasure to call Nicholas A. Packard to the podium to receive this award."

Nick sat stunned for a moment then stood in a state of disbelief which quickly changed to exhilaration. Am I dreaming? Is this real? He walked up the stairs to the podium praying that he wouldn't trip and look foolish. He accepted the award from President Altman and, not having a speech prepared in advance, calmly said, "Distinguished faculty, fellow students, and guests, I am extremely honored to receive this award, which probably belongs to many others in this class as well, and will try to live up to it in my lifetime." The crowd cheered.

Nick received his degree and left the stage. At his seat he glanced at the degree which read: "Bachelor in the Science of Accounting, Highest Honors." The gold-plated Student of the Year award was even more impressive. Nick breathed a sigh of relief. He did it! He captured the grand prize!

After the ceremony, as Nick made his way through the crowd, the proud graduate accepted handshakes and accolades from faculty and friends who wished him good luck in the future.

Nick looked askance and noticed his mother, Frances, and Chad having a conversation with Dean Whittier and President Altman. The president was the focus of attention and was waving his arms as if describing some colossal event, which was true to his style. He walked toward them and Dean Whittier said, "Oh, hello, Nick."

"We were just talking about the grave situation in Vietnam and the tremendous burden being placed on LBJ and the Congress to dispose of it," Altman said.

Nick thought, You mean you were talking about it!

"Enough of that!" said the president. "Today is certainly your day and should be joyous. How do you feel, Nick, about being bestowed with such an honor?"

"I'm overwhelmed with excitement, sir, and sincerely thank you and the faculty for choosing me. I'm sure there were others who equally deserved it!"

"Son," President Altman remarked, "don't under estimate yourself! You have great potential! You earned it. You earned it!" he repeated.

Frances threw her arms around Nick and, choked up with tears, uttered, "I'm so proud of you!"

Nick hugged her and said, "I love you, Mom."

Chad repeatedly shook his hand and bellowed, "Way to do it, dude!" Nick laughed and rubbed his hand through his brother's hair. Chad was so proud of Nick.

The group insisted on photographs of Frances, Nick, and Chad, of President Altman, of Nick and Dean Whittier. Then the whole group. It seemed endless.

Finally, Frances inquired, "Now, Nick, you're coming right back for a celebration at the house, right? We have—"

Nick interrupted and said, "I can't, Mom. My friends are having a party at the Ocean Club and I promised to go. We'll celebrate tomorrow. I promise!"

Frances reluctantly said, "OK! But please come."

"Of course, Mom! Chad, come with me to the party," Nick implored.

"You don't have to twist my arm, Nick, let's go!"

After bidding farewells to all, the two brothers left the group and excitedly rushed to the university parking lot. Nick whipped off his cap and gown and opened the door of his shiny black Corvette Sting Ray, throwing the outfit in the backseat. He jumped in and yelled, "Chad, let's rock and roll!"

They both started shouting the lyrics of "Light My Fire" blaring on the radio. The great sound of 'The Doors' set the mood .

CHAPTER 5

The shiny Sting Ray smoothly wound its way down Surf Side Blvd. As the speedometer ticked off seventy-five miles per hour, Nick's long black hair blew wildly in the wind and Chad hung on to his hat. The surge of the engine and rising tachometer brought sheer exhilaration to both. Shimmering waves reflecting the boulevard lights bounced off the seawall and receded into darkness. It was nine p.m. The two were on a natural high!

Chad and Nick had left after the graduation ceremony late that afternoon. Chad had wanted to go home and change clothes for the party. He went through a changing routine like a woman prepares for a major event. The party will probably be over by the time he is ready to go, Nick thought. Nick waited patiently and retrieved a telephone message from his grandmother who was staying in Braintree on a visit. It was a call from some guy about a job. That was fast! Nick tried repeatedly to reach the telephone number he had left, but it rang incessantly with no answer.

The pair left the house, finally, and realized that they both were starving. They stopped at Hawthorne's By the Sea in Swampscott, where they ordered prime rib which was an Athena's special. It was superb, and the popovers melted in their mouths. Chad insisted on paying the bill. He wanted to impress Nick desperately.

"Danny Levin is coming to the party," Nick said, as he flawlessly negotiated the contours of the road. "You know, Chad, he's visiting here from LA, celebrating his graduation from UCLA last week. I had a long telephone conversation with him last week. He and Larry Bowdoin are good friends and I think Larry and Danny are coming together," Nick went on to say.

Chad had also talked to Danny, but Chad thought that he seemed real cocky, boasting about his LA accomplishments!

The Corvette stopped at a red light and Nick revved the engine. The powerful whir of the engine gave Chad goose bumps. On the left-hand corner two young ladies, scantily clad, waved toward the car. One laughed, but the other, with a miniskirt and gorgeously shaped legs, said, "Hi, guys! We're lonely. Do you two studs want to join us?"

Nick drooped and replied, "We can't. Late for a special appointment."

"Whew!" both brothers uttered with excitement.

"Ciao, baby!" Chad blurted out, as the women chuckled and blew kisses.

Nick slammed the gas pedal and the Sting Ray screeched out; the neon lights of the beach concession stands were quickly left shimmering behind.

The road inclined upward and soon a wide, paved drive veered off into the parking lot of the Ocean Club.

The Ocean Club was a large complex of restaurant/bar/ function facilities located high upon a bluff overlooking the Atlantic Ocean on the North Shore of Boston. The windows on the south side of the complex afforded a panoramic view of the Boston skyline, and on a very clear day, anyone with good vision could see clear down to Provincetown on Cape Cod, the easternmost end of the United States.

Nick's "black beauty" pulled up next to the main entrance of the club, where a few valets were congregating, and a tall youth opened the door for Nick, then for Chad. Nick slipped the valet a ten-dollar bill and said, "Please take good care of my wheels! There will be another Hamilton on the way out." The valet, knowing what he meant, replied, "No problem, man, we'll park right over there." He pointed to a special space ten feet away from the door. As he spoke, the chrome wire hubcaps glistened under the entrance lights.

The Packard brothers entered the club through a huge set of brass doors. They looked handsomely groomed. Nick wore a navy blue linen blazer, red and black-striped tie, white oxford shirt, and tan-colored chinos. However, Chad was dressed quite differently, sporting the new-wave style advanced by the Beatles. He was wearing a dark gray Nehru jacket with black bell-bottom trousers and buckled boots.

Straight ahead they saw French doors leading into a maroon carpeted lounge area with many lamp-lit tables and a mahogany bar at least thirty feet long. Beside the French doors a sign with an arrow pointing to the left read: "MBU CLASS OF 1967."

Chad and Nick walked slowly down the corridor and

entered the Cape Cod room, which had a spectacular view of the lights on the hook of Cape Cod. The room was crowded and smoky. Larry Bowdoin, who was having a conversation with a familiar couple, excused himself and walked toward the Packards.

"I didn't think that you were coming tonight, Nick. What with all the invitations you must have gotten after that award. I thought a recruiter from Harvard University would probably scoop you up today!"

"Larry, I don't think it's that easy to get accepted at Harvard! But I did get a call about a job right off."

"Good work," Larry replied. "You're here with big brother. Let's have some fun!"

"Larry, you've met Chad, haven't you?"

"Sure have. He's the patriarch of the family, isn't he? How are you, Chad?"

"I'm fine, Larry, but I think you're mistaken as to who deserves that title!"

All three laughed and made their way to Larry's table, then seated themselves. "Larry," Chad went on, "this is some room, and look at that ocean! A seafood buffet and open bar, too! Your father must be cranking out some heavy money at his car dealerships. The tab for this shindig is going to be high, I'll bet?"

"Yeah, Dad's doing all right, but he works his ass off around the clock. Not my style, man!"

"Will you be working full time for him now that you've graduated?" Chad questioned.

"Why not? It's a hell of a sure jump start for me. But I'll

eventually have more assistants than Dad when I take over, then retire comfortably to enjoy life."

Larry will probably run it into the ground if he takes over! Nick remained silent. Nick's father had taken the easy route and never came close to retirement!

Music suddenly filled the entire Cape Cod room and was so smooth and clear that it seemed live. A new stereo system had been installed last week. "I feel good…like I knew that I would now…" blared from the many speakers around the room and James Brown set the mood for the rest of the evening. Chad was moved by the song and tapped his fingers to the rhythm against the tablecloth.

Nick relaxed in his chair and loosened his tie. He beckoned a waitress and ordered a round of drinks for the trio. This included a double martini for Chad, which would be the first of many that evening. A toast was proposed by Chad to Nick and Larry. "May the sands of time run evenly and smoothly through the hourglass of your lives until the last grain falls to its resting place."

"Well said!" chanted Nick. "Bravo!"

"Where did you hear that one?" asked Larry.

"I made it up tonight, just now," Chad chimed.

"You made that up?"

"Yeah, I did." Chad was insulted by the subtle remark.

"Don't pay any attention to him, Chad, m' lad. He's just a joker."

The drinks were getting them all pretty buzzed! Chad pretended to laugh and hummed to the tune "Groovin'" which filled the Cape Cod room with the voices of the

Young Rascals. On the dance floor couples embraced and swayed to the tune.

Chad lifted the martini glass to his lips and swigged it. He then hurried to the bar for another, bypassing the waitress. He couldn't get it fast enough waiting for the waitress!

CHAPTER 6

The music had stopped for a while and the trio rejoined for a champagne toast to the "Student of the Year." Nick felt chills run down his spine as Dean Whittier delivered an endearing soliloquy.

"I'd like to make a toast to the handsome and hard-driven young man who rose from the hospital bed after defying death or incapacitation from a serious head injury ten years ago. He became the most honored student of your class based upon his academic achievements and class participation, and will no doubt rise to the chief executive level and boardroom of corporate America in time. It is with great honor I toast Nick Packard, the 1967 MBU outstanding senior of the year."

The crowd lifted their glasses and sipped, then one by one set them down on any flat surface available and made a lengthy hammering applause. Chad stood proudly, although a bit wobbly, beside Nick, clapping frantically to let everyone see that they were together. Buddies as well as brothers. Larry jokingly hissed and booed in his usual clown-like style, his affection for Nick pouring out at the seams.

Nick raised his arm with fists clenched in the style of a champion and with a raised voice modestly cried, "I'm not the only one who deserved it, but thanks. I love you all. Let this evening never end!"

The music began again with "I'm a Believer." Mary Lou Higgins, who Nick had known throughout his college years, shyly asked Nick to dance. Her adorable dimpled smile turned Nick on. "Um, OK," Nick uttered, and they swayed to the dance floor.

"Congratulations, Nick!" she whispered as they made a swath across the wooden floor. "Aw, shucks! 'Twas nothing Mare."

Both laughed heartily and then exchanged jokes, reminiscing about their times at MBU. Suddenly, the couple spontaneously held each other in a warm, emotional embrace. Out of the corner of his eye Nick noticed a well-dressed young man escorting a pretty lady on each arm. Nick recognized Linda Fuller, an MBU classmate. Her curly blonde hair spread over each breast protruding from her low-cut neckline. The other girl was tanned and was wearing hot pants. She didn't look familiar.

Danny Levin was escorting the pair. Danny and Nick exchanged glances and simultaneously stared and scurried toward each other, embracing and hugging, followed by vigorous handshakes. "You old invalid, Nick. Where's your cane?"

"I left it outside the door beside the cage they brought you in. You old desert rattlesnake!"

The immediate crowd roared with laughter. Danny and Nick, together once again. It had been a long time. Danny had moved to Las Vegas with his parents after the eighth grade because his father had taken a job as dealer in a casino under some Jewish guy named Green, or something like that. High school in Vegas was easy for Danny and he sailed through the courses. After high school he was accepted to and attended UCLA.

Danny had studied hard at UCLA and this year had graduated at the top of his class. His major had been marketing and he had learned the important principles of success well. Additionally, he had that rare persuasive personality that enabled him to sell just about anything. The old adage of "selling ice cubes to an Eskimo" fit him perfectly.

"What are you doing now? Where are you living?" The questions spilled out in rapid succession as

Nick and Danny slowly walked toward the table, joining Larry, Chad, and Mary Lou. Danny's two escorts trailed behind and sat beside Mary Lou, who knew Linda from Advanced Psych. The group all were seated at a large round table which only moments ago had seemed so lonely and was now beaming with life. The table's occupants conversed separately in groups and chatted incessantly, laughing a lot. Nick couldn't keep his eyes off Mary Lou. She looked hot!

Nick tapped his glass on the solid oak table in an effort to stimulate group discussion. "So what are your plans, Linda?" Nick inquired.

"I'm headed for DC in August to work as an assistant to Senator Jake Morris. The job will involve secretarial work and the scheduling function at first, but maybe I'll get lucky." She giggled and sipped her half-empty screwdriver.

Nick hailed the waitress for another round. Linda's grades as a political science major placed her in the top ten of students in the whole country. "You couldn't ask for a nicer entry into politics," Nick said.

"And you, Mary Lou?" Nick asked with a deep smile. "You're a math major, and a genius, I hear."

"Well, don't believe everything you hear!" she modestly replied. "I have been accepted to MIT for the master's program. And with scholarships." Her sweet face beamed with radiance. "You're pretty good at math, Nick," she humbly said.

"I hope good enough to succeed in business!" he retorted.

Larry interrupted and said, "Well, I guess I'm pretty lucky. My old man has done all the legwork for me. I'm beginning a sales position next week in Quincy and soon will be floating between dealership locations. After that, I'll become sales manager and then soon own and manage the business. My old man is getting along in years, you know."

Chad laughed, but didn't say a word. Larry glared at him with a scowl. Silence ensued for the next few moments. Then Mary Lou said, "I wish you the best, Larry, I really do." Some of the group raised their glasses and clinked them together in a toast to Larry's success.

"Nick, you didn't finish what you were saying about business?" Mary Lou inquired excitedly.

"Is that the accounting business? Come on, Nicky, tell us. Are you going for the CPA certificate? Your accounting grades were incredible! Tell us," she repeated.

"I guess," Nick replied. "It's my strongest suit. Maybe

the exam, work for one of the Big Eight firms. Eventually, I'd like to get an MBA from Wharton! I don't know yet, but I do know that I want to make some serious money."

The group shook their heads in agreement. Serious money, yes, they all thought!

"Danny, you've been pretty quiet. What's going on these days? Bring us up-to-date!"

"Well, Nick, to change the subject for a moment, if I may, that tie you're wearing doesn't quite make it with that linen jacket. I have a line of pure silk ties from Italy that you will not be able to resist. A bit more expensive, but a bargain for the discriminating young executive. And for you, Nick, a substantial discount."

Nick laughed with glee and said, "Sold. I'll take five of them. Please set aside five for me before they're all sold! You're something else, Danny. I have to admit. If I ever operate a high-profile marketing business I'd call you, for sure!"

The group laughed as the music pumped out the lyrics to "Yellow Submarine."

In the men's room, the joints were passed around merrily as the smoke trailed out the windows. The graduates were ending a treasured time and didn't want it to end. Ever! A few of them tripped out on LSD. They were finding a new and truthful meaning to life. At least that's what Dr. Timothy Leary said would happen!

At the table, Danny continued. "UCLA.1967. I graduated with a marketing major and am selling top-of-the-line clothing at I. Magnin. I'm doing quite well. But let me tell you, guys and dolls, real estate is where it's at. Lynn's father builds and sells buildings in LA and San Fran. The business is booming! He predicts that the boom will sweep America."

Lynn, Danny's girlfriend with the hot pants, spoke." My father is doing quite well and wants Danny to work for him. He's building, ah, condoms, or something like that. He sells each apartment separately."

Nick and Larry laughed and listened with interest, but didn't quite understand what she meant. The term was unfamiliar to all this East Coast group!

Nick again stared at Mary Lou. "Let's dance, Mare," he said, as he swung his chair around. Her eyes opened wide and she smiled as she stood and followed him to the dance floor. They did the Frug, then the Fish, frolicking in fun. In between the songs they grabbed their glasses off an empty table nearby, locking arms and taking sips from their drinks as they murmured passionately to each other.

A slow dance followed, and as they wrapped arms around each other, they kissed and caressed. Moist tongues darted together in ecstasy. They held hands tightly as if to prevent anyone from breaking up this wonderful encounter after four years of friendship.

Dreamily they walked hand in hand to their table. Nick said, "Good-bye, we're leaving and, Chad, you've had enough. Danny, call me before you leave and we'll get together to talk more. And please drive Chad home tonight!"

"Done!" said Danny, and Nick and Mary Lou exited the room.

CHAPTER 7

The newly hooked couple walked down the corridor, arm in arm, toward the main entrance of the Ocean Club. It was one thirty a.m., Sunday, nearing last call for drinks. Mary Lou kissed his neck and then, sensuously, his ear. Titillated, Nick turned and they kissed passionately as he traced her bra strap with his finger. What a night! What a day! Nick thought, as they meandered down the corridor leading out of the club.

Their embrace seemed to be locked for an eternity as they walked through the brass doors. Nick broke away for a moment and handed the parking slip to the valet along with the promised additional ten-dollar tip. Soon his sleek automobile rolled in front of them. The valet smiled and held the door for Mary Lou, guiding her arm as she meandered unsteadily.

As they drove down the boulevard, Mary Lou snuggled up to Nick and said, "Let's go to a hotel, Nicky."

He agreed. "We probably can get a room at the Holiday Inn in Peabody."

"Umm," murmured Mary Lou. "You're such a hunk,

Nick, and strong too!" She hiccupped a few times as they drove down Route 1 toward the hotel.

Nick pulled into the packed lot and parked beside a Studebaker Avanti. What a work of art. Maybe I should trade in for one of those babies!

They walked into the hotel holding hands, approaching the front desk where Nick paid in cash for one night. They checked into the only room available. The desk clerk slipped a key for Room 404 across the counter. The couple walked arm and arm to the elevator. Mary Lou was hanging on to Nick like he was about to fall off a cliff!

Nick could see that the room was located on the fourth floor across from the ice machine. Oh well, no one will be crunching ice, at least before dawn, I hope! Unlocking the door they entered the room and fully embraced. Mary Lou kissed Nick's lips while she freed a hand in order to snake down to his groin area. She rubbed his inner thighs, and then squeezed his hardness. Nick explored her, with his hand up her skirt caressing the inner thighs. Filled with excitement, he used his fingers to rub her softly.

They kissed passionately and she unbuttoned her blouse, revealing perfectly shaped breasts, covered only by a lacy bra. She lifted Nick's hand and placed it on them. Soon her blouse and bra disappeared. His hands massaged her soft, feminine chest as he lowered his head and explored the shapely contours.

They noticed two double beds, neatly made, and the air in the room had an antiseptic smell which seemed to assure cleanliness. The air was cooled from the G.E. window air conditioner, which droned steadily. The color TV was on, showing a Johnny Carson rerun.

Nick whipped off his linen sports jacket and tie and threw them across the room toward a swivel armchair in the corner and, as Mary Lou unbuttoned Nick's shirt, they lay down on one of the double beds. His shirt then flew through the air onto the other bed and the two lovers locked in embrace, bare chest to chest.

Mary Lou's hands grasped Nick's muscular body and pulled him against her. Her skirt had risen in the heat of passion, exposing skimpy black lace panties. She massaged him all over while she pushed herself against him. After this erogenous move, Nick quickly rose and shed his chinos and briefs.

Overwhelmed with passion, Nick rolled her on her back and proceeded to finish undressing her while she assisted. He performed that titillating tongue act and she moaned with extreme pleasure and squirmed. She returned that pleasure to Nick.

In the corner, Ed McMahon cracked a funny joke and the audience roared. Off in the background, Doc. Severnson made one of his usual smart comments, then the band belched out a few notes and the drum rolled.

Nick mounted Mary Lou and they kissed deeply while he held each of her soft hands flat against the pillows. The passion was intense as they whispered physical comments to each other.

She spread her legs wide as he entered her partially for a minute or so. Mary Lou moaned with anticipation and squiggled around. Nick then thrust deep inside her and they, almost hysterically, climaxed together. It was sheer ecstasy.

The aroused couple held each other for what seemed like an eternity. Exhausted, they lay there in a stupor, a semiconscious state before deep sleep. On the television, Johnny Carson was chuckling and finally said, "Good night, folks," followed by the appearance of that familiar station sign-off screen accompanied by the shrill tone.

Nick suddenly snapped to consciousness and realized that the bedspread had become soaked with their bodily fluids. They were soaked. He rose and walked to the bathroom, where he retrieved two bath towels from the shelf and went back to the bed. The alarm clock hands pointed to four o'clock, and the night had faded into early morning grayness.

He wiped off Mary Lou and himself, then nudged her. Nick said, "Honey, the bed's soaked. Let's use the other bed!" He proceeded to pull down the linen on the other bed. There was silence and an audible snore came from his new lover. "Nicky, I'm so tired," she mumbled, as she stumbled out of one bed and dove onto the other. Nick laughed.

He pushed her over a bit and she ended up lying with her back toward him. He lay down, putting his arm around her in a spooning position. A shampoo smell emanated from her long, silky brown hair, which Nick inhaled and savored as he fell into a deep sleep.

They awoke late in the morning, around eleven thirty a.m., with the room still darkened by the closed curtains. They were quite hung over from the alcohol and late-night jaunt, but felt alive. They were hooked on each other! Mary

Lou rose first, wiggling her cute ass while she picked up her clothes, and went to the bathroom to shower and dress.

Nick then sat up on the side of the bed. "Whoa!" he mumbled. "What a night! Now for a good breakfast and coffee. Yes, coffee!"

After a while Mary Lou emerged from the bathroom, her clothes a bit wrinkled, but her face still as beautiful as the night before. The small crease in her lower cheek widened as the dimple appeared, complementing her smile. Nick smiled back as he rose with his clothes in hand and walked to the bathroom, kissing her on the lips as they passed each other.

Twenty minutes later Nick tromped out of the bathroom looking wide-awake and refreshed. His long hair was pulled back and an elastic band held it in a '60s fashionable ponytail. The couple gazed at each other for a moment, then spontaneously hugged tightly and kissed. They really were attracted to each other, far beyond the sex!

They checked out of the Holiday Inn and walked past the Studebaker Avanti while Nick admired it. In the daylight he noticed the license plates were from California and read CAL-CONDO. Nick's thoughts turned to the comment made by Danny's girlfriend, Lynn, and her statement that her father was building "condoms, or something like that"!

As they walked toward the Sting Ray, they heard a cry from off in the distance, "Hey, Nick. Wait up!" It was Danny, walking hand in hand with Lynn. As they met, Danny said, "You two stayed here last night?"

"Danny, Mary Lou and I were so entranced with each

other last night we didn't even ask where you'd be staying for the night. Or early morning, that is."

"Yeah, well, Lynn and I booked in here early yesterday afternoon. We rode to the party with Linda."

Nick said, "I saw the Avanti parked here when we pulled in about two a.m., but had no idea it was your car because we had just left you at the club. This is super. That Avanti is to die for!"

"It's Lynn's father's car. He let her take it for the trip."

"Let's go for breakfast," Nick responded. "My treat, and let's all go in that Studebaker. I'm dying to ride in it!"

The Avanti peeled out of the parking lot. Nick and Mary Lou held hands as Danny maneuvered the five-speed gear shift. They rolled down Route 1 with glass packs popping and pulled into the Big B Diner, where they were seated at a large booth. Everyone scanned menus immediately. They were starved after a long time with no food and ordered the Hungary Man and Big Palooka breakfasts.

"Tell me, Danny," Nick inquired, "where exactly are you living in California?"

"Nick, I live in San Bernardino, but Lynn lives on Malibu Beach. She lives with her parents and you should see the house. Directly on the beach!"

"And you two drove all the way here?" Mary Lou asked.

"We've always wanted a cross-country road trip, and believe me, it was worth it. Especially in Daddy's car!" Lynn responded.

Nick questioned, "How long have you been working for I. Magnum?"

"Oh, about six months, and I love it. I'm a good salesman, Nick!"

"I always knew that, Danny. And Lynn, do you work?" Nick went on. "I'll bet you work for your father."

"That's right, I have been on and off since I was sixteen."

"Tell me more about these housing units that your father sells individually," Nick said, curious.

Danny then chimed in and said, "By the way, they're called condominiums, not condoms. Condoms back home are what you call safes here!"

They all laughed hysterically. Lynn blushed.

"Well, I don't know too much about it, but her father builds an apartment building or a townhouse community and then deeds it over to what they call a condominium. This enables him to sell each unit individually with an undivided interest in the common areas outside the unit walls. Each owner pays a share of the common area expenses based on a percentage of what they paid for the unit to the total project selling price. And the owners pay separate real estate taxes on their units. That's my understanding from discussions with Tom, Lynn's father."

"Wow!" Nick exhaled. "A person can own their apartment or townhouse and build equity during ownership. Nice concept!"

"And what's nice also is that they're generally cheaper than single-family houses, and some people buy more than one at a time. And all the outside maintenance is done by the management company hired by the owners. Just the inside of the house is the sole responsibility of the owner.

They're pretty hot out there and it's predicted the trend will spread around the country eventually. Tom has probably about four developments in progress right now. Maybe five hundred units!"

"That's incredible!" both Nick and Mary Lou said at the same time. Nick's mind couldn't dismiss it during the rest of the breakfast.

"And you two. What are your plans?" Danny asked.

"Well, Mary Lou is going to MIT in the fall to study engineering. She got a full scholarship, by the way."

"Phenomenal!" Danny and Lynn both clapped and congratulated her sincerely. Mary Lou blushed.

Nick went on, "I'm either going for a CPA certificate or might pursue Wharton Business School for postgraduate courses."

"Double wow!" Danny exclaimed.

They moved on to small talk and wolfed down their huge breakfasts. Danny decided that they should leave because they should be on their way back to California. They bid farewells and promised to stay in touch.

The newly cast lovers sat quietly for a while. She then leaned over and held Nick's wrists, rubbing her index finger around his gold chain bracelet. She asked him, "Nicky, did we do the right thing last night? I mean, you know, not even our first date and we—"

Nick interrupted, saying, "Mare, we've known each other for four years. Last night was spontaneous. I'm not sure why it didn't surface a long time ago. I loved it and have very strong feelings for you."

"Me too, Nicky! Me too!" She sighed with relief as she squeezed his hands.

"Nick, your brother drinks a lot! Doesn't he? I mean, he was pounding down martinis last night like he was going to the electric chair in the morning! I really like Chad and am concerned. Should I be?"

"No, you're right, Mare, and I'm concerned also. Ma doesn't know how much he drinks and I won't tell her. It will upset her too much. I don't know how to help him. He has very low self-esteem. He shouldn't have, because he's brilliant with mechanical things and is a handsome kid!" Nick shook his head and said, "I don't know."

Mary Lou somberly replied, "My father died from cirrhosis of the liver, you know?"

"I had no knowledge of that, Mare. At what age?"

"Oh, forty-five!"

Nick was shocked.

"I'll fix him up with my friend Cindy," she replied. "He'll like her and maybe it will pull in his reins."

"Please do. He needs a good romance, or at least a good friend!"

The conversation rolled on for a long time. They were so interested in each other's lives.

Mary Lou then said, "Larry Bowdoin is so sure of himself. I hope he can do what he says."

"Yeah, Mare, he's in line to take over the business and does know it well, but his attitude sucks and I think he'll take a fall. I know his father, and also know that he built that business on hard work and perseverance. Larry will probably take it down!"

She sighed and asked Nick who he thought would make it big.

"You and I, Mare, and I think Danny will succeed fine." Maybe Chad, if he can shed those alcoholic tendencies. Nick pondered this, but said nothing. He grabbed her hand and kissed her knuckles, saying, "Who knows, Mare? Life works in mysterious ways!"

They left the restaurant hand in hand and Nick said, "Where's your car, Mare?"

"I didn't drive last night. I rode with Linda, Danny, and Lynn. You can drive me to Winthrop if you'd like. Land's End Apartments. OK?"

"Anything you want, babe!" he replied.

Nick pulled up in front of the lobby entrance. Mary Lou, quite disheveled after eighteen hours of merriment, kissed Nick softly on the lips and asked, "Are you going to call me, mister?"

"Maybe." Nick chuckled as he laughed and hugged her tightly. "For sure!"

The couple squirmed in a locked embrace, relaxing with the release of muscle tension. The Sting Ray then departed with a roar!

CHAPTER 8

The following week Nick relaxed for a few days and slept late, enjoying his newly acquired freedom even though it was just temporary.

He had returned the telephone call from Saturday and discovered that Mr. Henry P. Littleton III, a senior partner in the distinguished accounting firm of Barker, Tibbs, and Graham, requested an interview. Nick thought this seemed unusual: a senior partner conducting the initial interview and calling him on graduation day. He must have really impressed this firm with his academic performance and Student of the Year designation.

BTG, as it was called, was a top-level accounting firm with many national clients. Nick had read recently in a trade magazine that they had some huge real estate clients. His interview was scheduled for Friday of this week. Nick was excited about this meeting and planned his discussion with Littleton carefully.

He called Mary Lou on Wednesday evening, amorously speaking words of affection to her. They had become quite intimate quickly.

"I called Cindy, Nick. She was interested in meeting Chad. What night is good for you? Saturday night?"

"Let's do it, Mare! I'll call Chad, who I know will do it. I mentioned the possibility a few days ago and he was interested, if she was."

Mary Lou seemed excited about the date and wished him the best of luck with the interview.

On Friday morning, Nick, dressed in a gray cotton vested summer suit and wearing black Cole Hahn wing tips, drove his Corvette down the Southeast Expressway toward Boston. Weaving in and out of the jammed traffic he passed the Boston Gas tanks. He couldn't be a minute late for this interview. As impressed as Mr. Henry Littleton III was, he probably wouldn't tolerate a lack of punctuality!

After a few near misses with the "bird" flying in many directions the Sting Ray slithered through. He pulled into the garage of the State Street Bank building and leaped from the car, leaving it with an attendant, slipping him a ten-dollar bill. He was now ten minutes late and ran down Franklin Street, moving hurriedly through the revolving doors of the granite lobbied building. If Littleton can't allow for Boston traffic, then screw him!

He entered the BTG reception area where he waited for thirty minutes. Finally Mr. Henry P. Littleton appeared. He was apparently perturbed. A tall, salty-haired and middle-aged man with a twitch in his brow, Littleton cordially said, "Henry Littleton, Mr. Packard. How do you do?"

Nick replied, "Fine, sir. My pleasure to meet you."

"A bit late, you are. I called you when you weren't here at nine. Punctuality is important, young man!"

What a prick! "I'm sorry, sir, the traffic was very heavy." Littleton didn't respond. He must have thought that I should have allowed sufficient time for delays, Nick thought.

In Littleton's office, Nick took a seat and noticed the degrees on his wall: BSA from Bentley College, Master in Finance from Wharton University, both with highest honors. His CPA certificate hung in the middle of them. Whoa, Einstein's great-grandson!

Littleton began with, "Mr. Packard, your academic performance is superior, to say the least. But, do you understand that hard work and perseverance are equally important in gaining success?"

"I do, sir, and I'm prepared to work hard ,and I will make you proud of me!"

He appeared to peruse Nick's resume and congratulated his acceptance this past week to Wharton's master's program. Nick could see why he was so interested. They were a carbon copy of each other! With no further questions, he said, "OK, Nick, you can commence with BTG on Monday at fifteen thousand dollars per year as a junior staffer and advance from there. An immediate offer."

Nick chuckled to himself and replied, "Mr. Littleton, I'm worth much more than that and you know it! I had something different in mind. I know that I have to prove myself and will do that. I want twenty thousand dollars."

"You think you're worth that?" Littleton replied. "OK. Nick, because of your superior academics we'll start you at nineteen thousand dollars, but you have six months to prove it, and it won't be easy."

"Wharton will have to wait! You won't regret it, sir. Thank you," Nick replied, as he relaxed in his chair.

"You'll need to be certified within a year!" Littleton advised.

Nick accepted the offer, shook hands and exited Littleton's office. First interview. That was easy. Nineteen thousand is good, for now, but not for long! A gargantuan feeling of excitement arose within him. He stepped the Frug down the hall to the elevator.

On Saturday evening, Mary Lou and Cindy met Chad and Nick at the Twister on Route 1 in Saugus. The club was a popular dance haven and hosted top-of-the-line talent. The couples had missed a performance by Chubby Checker a few weeks ago. Tonight an unknown group called the Peppermints was performing.

The two couples were decked out in tight clothes. The guys wore tight pants and silk shirts, while the girls wore similarly tight skirts and colorful blouses. It was now disco. They were excited about the early sixties music played at the club. Not just twist music but some of the newly introduced disco was spun.

After brief introductions between Chad and Cindy, they took a table at the far end of the crowded club and ordered a round of drinks and relaxed a while, taking in the scenery. Chad and Cindy talked incessantly to each other. They were a hit immediately and had very similar interests. Cindy talked about her life while being certain to ask Chad many questions about himself.

There were some good dancers which inspired Chad to take Cindy by the hand and lead her to the dance floor. Nick and Mary Lou soon followed. A medley of Bee Gees' music was playing. They danced to "I've Gotta Get a Message to You." Chad loved that song and sang it to Cindy while they danced. Cindy's wide smile excited him and he twirled her around at the end. Mary Lou and Nick cuddled while dancing.

After a few dances, the couples went back to the table and Chad and Nick, not seeing any waitresses, walked toward the bar, pushing lightly through the crowd. Sitting at the bar were two bikers from some motorcycle club with an insignia on their jackets. They were gaping at Mary Lou and Cindy and began walking in that direction, lingering a bit.

The brothers returned to the table with the drinks. Suddenly, a thumping sound pervaded the air, followed by the live band's singing "Everybody clap your hands and I wanna do a dance that goes like this pa, pa, pa, peppermint twist." Chad and Cindy broke into a perfect twist.

Suddenly one of the bikers approached Cindy and grabbed her wrist. "It's my turn!" he mumbled, slurring his words. Cindy tried to pull away, saying, "No thanks!" The biker wouldn't back off and proceeded to split the couple up and dance with her. Chad grabbed his shoulder, and as he pulled the biker away the large man jolted and swung around, throwing a quick punch at Chad. Chad blocked the swing and cold-cocked the biker, who fell to the floor with a cut lip. He was drunk and didn't or couldn't retaliate, lying in a stupor.

The other biker was packed solid with muscle and mean-looking. He stepped forward toward Chad while three others appeared from across the room. Nick grabbed his arm and said, "It's not worth it. Your friend is drunk and swung at my brother!" The man seemed to agree and backed off.

Cindy stood silently in awe and thought, What a man! He did that just for me!

Chad hugged Cindy while the two bikers were ushered out by bouncers, but very gingerly. There was much trepidation with this group. Four others left with the pair while winking at Chad and Nick!

Soon thereafter the bouncers politely asked the two couples to leave. They had waited for the bikers to leave in order to prevent any further trouble. On the way out Nick said, "Chad, don't be surprised if we run into them before the night's over!"

"Yeah, Nick. Who the fuck cares! That big dude violated Cindy and then swung at me. Was I supposed to stand there and apologize to him?"

Cindy wrapped her arms around Chad and squeezed him tightly. "Thank you, Chad!"

It seemed the motorcycle gang had left, and Nick started driving down Route 1. Chad rode in front while the girls chatted in the backseat.

Nick noticed wavering headlights in back of him and soon realized that they were motorcycle headlights. As they multiplied, they arced out around Nick's Sting Ray and literally forced Nick over into the far end of Kowloon's parking lot. Nick stopped the car and watched through the window as many men walked toward the car, surrounding it.

When they began rocking the car fast and furious, intent upon tipping it over, the girls screamed loudly. Chad then slammed the passenger door open and jumped out, and Nick did the same on his side. They instinctively knew that they had to act and do something colossal before they all got hurt badly.

Chad took the lead, stood firmly, and loudly but calmly said, "Listen, you motherfuckers, you're not cowards, so be a little fair, back off and let any ten of you step forward." He clenched his fists and rolled his eyes, surveying the crowd while shaking inside. He didn't concentrate on the bluff he had to pull off. "Before you decide which ten would even have a small chance, remember your man started the trouble and I was only protecting that sweet young woman inside this car. You guys don't need the trouble and would be wise to take your friend home to sleep it off." Nick could see guns hanging off the sides of a few!

There was an austere silence among the bikers. Was this guy for real? A guy nicknamed Deuce, a huge, muscular man who could have been the leader, stepped forward and apparently realized that if the group pulverized Chad it would indeed be cowardice. "There's just me!" he yelled as he raised his fists. Chad knew that he had to act quickly!

Chad stepped forward in total trepidation, but with superhuman strength produced by fear, grabbed the leader and wrestled him to the ground. He pinned Deuce down like a wrestler and wouldn't let up. Deuce was immobilized and struggled, but couldn't move. Chad bellowed, "Can we call it quits? I've got you!"

Deuce knew that he was no match of strength for this man, and Chad hadn't hit him! He got up and brushed himself off, then surprisingly shook hands with Chad. Chad wisely said, "We've all been partying tonight, drinking too heavily. I apologize for anything I did wrong. Take your friend who started this whole thing to sober up and let's get on with life." No one said a word as Chad and Nick entered the car and slowly drove away.

The two couples drove northerly on Route 1 and turned at the Route 16 exit. They drove to Kelly's Roast Beef on Revere Beach and ordered fried clams and lobster rolls. Nick said, "What a treat after that! Whew!"

Cindy and Chad sat in the backseat. She was enamored at the way Chad had handled the situation. She slowly rubbed Chad's shoulders and back with one hand while eating a fried clam with the other as they chatted incessantly. Her pretty face beamed with excitement. Chad was in a state of bliss and becoming infatuated.

CHAPTER 9

December 15, 1968

"Hi!" Frances greeted Chad and Cindy at the front door. She wore a full-length apron with a rooster on it. "I'm so glad you could come today. Chad, I know you've been very busy working a lot of overtime. Is that new job too much? Wearing you out? Maybe you should find another one?"

"Ma, not to worry. I'm a tradesman, a carpenter, and a foreman. I don't have to be constantly lifting and carrying things. Laborers do that. Besides, my paycheck is hefty. Don't worry. I am only twenty-five, Mom."

She mumbled something, a typical mother's concern, and then said,

"Dinner will be ready in about an hour. Nick and Mary Lou are already here. Nick will mix some drinks. Sit down and relax before dinner."

Chad went into the living room and greeted his brother and Mary Lou. Cindy followed Chad.

"Hey, how's it going, you two?" Nick queried.

"Excellent, bro! The work just keeps pouring in. I've got ten people working under me now. I heard on the news today that the unemployment rate is three-point-three percent, the lowest in fifteen years! Can you believe it?"

Mary Lou chimed in, "I hope when I graduate from MIT I'll be as strong."

"You certainly don't ever have to worry about getting a good job, Mare. You'll have a master's from MIT, and with your grades they'll all be chasing you!" Nick bellowed.

Cindy was quiet because she was unemployed at the moment, but was seriously trying to get a job. Chad didn't care, he made enough for them both to live well. They had recently moved in together, but hadn't talked about marriage yet, even though they had been going together for over a year. He loved her and gave her everything imaginable. Cindy hoped it would continue and eventually they'd get married. She was enamored with Chad.

The couples relaxed, talking for a long while and having many drinks. No one was drunk but all were feeling pretty good. Nick asked his brother and Cindy how their relationship was working out and they hugged and said it couldn't be any better. They reminisced about that first date at the Twister and laughed about it. Nick was so impressed at how Chad had bluffed a tough motorcycle gang that he had told the story numerous times to friends and praised Chad at parties and other events.

Soon dinner was ready and Frances called them all into the dining room, where each took his or her customary seat. Frances had prepared a scrumptious meal with a spiral ham and a huge turkey. Everyone dug in and thoroughly enjoyed the treat. After they all were filled they leaned back in their chairs. It seemed the tryptophan had kicked in!

Nick spoke up, saying, "What a year 1968 has been! Can you believe the things that happened this year? It will certainly go down in the history books. Besides getting a new president this year, the administration under Johnson has deescalated the war in Vietnam substantially. The halt in bombing last month was major progress. I have hope that Nixon will end the war before too long! I wonder what would have happened if Humphrey had been elected? You know I'm twenty-three. You're, what, twenty-five. We could both be drafted if the law lingers for a while. It doesn't seem like the war has been very successful for the U.S. and the Tet Offensive has really soured Americans against this war. A good thing is the South Vietnamese government's joining in the Paris peace talks."

Mary Lou interjected, "Did you ever think, Nick, that the U.S. shouldn't be in this war? It seems senseless! After hearing about the mass killing of so many woman and children by American soldiers in that My Lai village I'm dead set against that war!"

Nick was very patriotic and didn't agree. They argued a bit. Nick said that he would go if drafted. He could become an officer, given his ROTC training in college.

"Let's talk about lighter things," Cindy said. "How about Jackie's marriage to that wealthy guy, Onassis, the shipping magnate? Do you think that she really loves him? He's so much older than her! She has plenty of money on her own, I think. Doesn't she?"

"Maybe she really loves him, Cindy. He's pretty suave and he has that Greek charm."

"Maybe," Cindy replied.

"On a lighter note, that Arlo Guthrie concert, at the Newport Music Festival this past summer, was incredible! I love music. We have to go to a major concert together sometime!" They all agreed.

Nick chimed in, "We're talking about the major events of this past year and no one has even mentioned the assassination of Martin Luther King last spring by that fucking nut, James Earl Ray!" Nick was getting a little carried away by the port wine he was swigging down. You know, I've been to the Lorraine Hotel in Memphis, and when I saw the TV footage I remember seeing that view of the aqua and blue hotel where King was standing on the balcony giving his speech. And I remember when Chad and I rode down Massachusetts Avenue in Roxbury by mistake last spring, we passed many angry black protesters. What followed, I understand, were many riots in Boston and other cities. Many people were killed. His murder really sparked black emotions because of King's peaceful ideals which were snuffed out by a white fanatic! We were fortunate to have avoided the violence. Huh, Chad?"

"Right on, bro!"

"And do you remember the follow-up by Ralph Abernathy and how he organized the encampment on the mall in Washington, DC? Resurrection City, I think it was called. It too got violent and many were arrested."

Nick continued, "What about Bobby Kennedy? That was the biggest news event of this year. I mean, a presidential contender." He hiccupped and stopped a moment with a laugh, then went on. "Another Kennedy down. What bad fucking luck for them!"

Mary Lou slapped him gently and said, "Nick, your mother is here! Stop swearing!"

"OK, sugar blossom," Nick replied.

"And go easy with that port wine," she responded.

"As I was saying, before I was rudely interrupted," Nick laughed and clasped Mary Lou's hand. She smiled.

"He had won the California primary and was well on his way toward the presidency. Then pow, shot in the head. Dead! Sirhan Sirhan. Sounds as fake as the claim of the press that he hated Kennedy for pro-Israeli speeches made during the campaign. Fuck that, it was a cover-up! He had an ulterior motive which will never be made known. I do have some ideas, though. I think it was Mob-related, as I do about his brother, John Kennedy's, assassination."

Silence followed. "You've been drinking too much, Nick," Chad interjected. "That's macabre. Let's get off the subject."

Nick said, "Yeah, let's."

"What a year!" Frances replied. "These are certainly violent times!"

"What else happened?" Cindy queried.

"How about the USS Pueblo? Those North Koreans captured all those sailors and charged them with sailing within the NK territorial limits and held them captive all year!" Chad remembered.

"They are tough people and have a huge army. I think we'll have problems with them for years to come. They may be one of the worst enemies of the U.S. Communists and very dangerous. They hate Americans!" Frances said.

The group listened closely, but had no response. It was

depressing to them. Nobody ventured a solution for this horror.

Nick blurted out, "On the financial end, what about the ten percent surcharge on our income taxes signed by President Johnson? The war in Vietnam has grown so large that we're having problems staying afloat, Johnson maintains. You know, on my present twenty-two-thousand-dollar salary it's not a lot of money. Maybe it's a few hundred dollars, but project that over the national income and it's absorbing a lot of spendable income from the economy. What's that going to do to the present economic boom? Guns and butter have made it boom, but this will certainly put a damper on spending if it lasts for a long time. When I earn the one-hundred- thousand-dollar annual salary that I'm planning on soon, it will certainly reduce my spending!"

They all agreed. It's a major problem for consumers, which they all were! Chad wasn't concerned because he also planned a huge income down the road. "We'll survive quite well and it probably will be eliminated after a while."

The women went on. Mary Lou first said, "Let's talk about women's liberation. Now I'm for that! Just a few months ago that protest against the Miss America contest in Atlantic City was cool! The following burning of the bras was a profound statement."

"Who are you kidding?" Nick laughed uncontrollably. "If you didn't have such beautiful tits requiring a bra you'd be depressed and would probably want a boob job! Although they would look beautiful without one, you know that you need a bra. I don't care if you don't wear one. It would really turn me on." She couldn't make her point, and didn't need to after Nick said, "Mary Lou, you're more than equal to men in all respects. You're smarter than most men and better-looking also. Whether you wear a bra or not you have nothing to prove. You are liberated."

Mary Lou had nothing more to say.

The conversation went on to sports with the brothers. The women stayed on women's liberation for a while. The year was spectacular in sports, however.

"I liked the Celtics series the best," Chad said. "What's not to like about that? The way Bill Russell led the Celtics to beat the Lakers in the finals was spectacular!"

Nick went on, "Well, Chad, I think we're just going to celebrate the Celtics victory. The Red Sox finished fourth only in the American League and didn't make the Series. And the Boston Patriots didn't fare too well. Fourth in the AFL East."

Chad replied, "You're right, Nick, but in defense of the Patriots, they have some fine players.

Jim Nance and Gino Cappelletti are two of the best in the American League. But you're right, our Celtics stole the show this year. Russell is super!"

"The only thing left I can think of for 1968 is the Apollo missions. Can you believe that the U.S. can now send a rocket to the moon and revolve around it?" Cindy went on. "We can shoot a rocket about two hundred fifty thousand miles to the moon and orbit it! We'll be landing on it next! Do any of you think that there is any form of life up there?"

"No way!" Nick replied. "There aren't any living organisms up there! The moon is just a light at night. Hey,

I'm a poet." The group laughed at Nick's remark. "But we'll see what is up there before too long."

Everybody yawned. "This has been a good conversation," Chad replied, as he looked at his watch and downed a half-full glass of port wine. "It's nine fifteen and I have to be on the job at six tomorrow morning. Time to leave."

They all agreed because most had to be up early. They arose from the table and hugged each other. Frances thanked her sons and the girls for a wonderful time and warned them to drive safely.

Nick felt that Mom needed more company and vowed to visit as much as possible. "We'll spend a lot of time over Christmas," Nick told her. Chad and Nick simultaneously said, "I love you, Mom!" Then they left.

CHAPTER 10

August 15, 1969

Nick's shiny black Sting Ray roared out of Beacon Hill where Nick now lived and entered Storrow Drive, headed for the Massachusetts Turnpike. Mary Lou and he were exhilarated about their trip to Bethel, New York, to a free concert featuring many of the great musicians of the day. Santana, Janis Joplin, the Grateful Dead, Jimi Hendrix, and many more! Nick particularly liked Creedence Clearwater Revival, which he had heard would be there.

"Mare, this trip is confusing. The concert is billed as Woodstock, New York, but we're headed for Bethel?"

"That's what the newspaper printed, Nick. I'm sure that I read it right! It was something to do with it being in Woodstock initially, but was banned by the town because the citizens feared trouble with a huge 'drugged-up crowd of hippies.' That's what they called us. The promoters changed the location to Yasgur's farm in Bethel. I read that a huge crowd, maybe two hundred thousand, was expected." They each became more excited as they talked!

"OK, honey, we're off. I told Chad that we'd meet him

there late this afternoon behind the stage area wherever the tents have been raised. Chad brought all his camping gear and he and Cindy left two days ago. Chad has grown a beard for this concert and hasn't had a haircut for a long time." Nick chuckled. "That hot shit!"

Nick's hair was neat but long, down close to his shoulders, and both he and Mary Lou were dressed for the occasion. Jeans and a vest over a T-shirt for Nick and tight miniskirt and halter top on Mary Lou, with a headband and beads. Her hair was cut straight and very long. She looked great.

The ride to Bethel was long, but the scenery interesting. When they arrived in Bethel the setting was very bucolic and peaceful. But, on the way to their destination they had hit traffic as if they were riding down Fifth Avenue in Manhattan during a heavy commuting hour. They couldn't believe the mass interest in the concert. Nick and Mary Lou inched along the country road and were lucky to get into the farm. They were stopped for periods of time and greeted by many with peace signs, some riding on the trunks of the cars playing instruments and singing. Shortly after they squeezed through, the police began turning vehicles away because of the sheer number of cars headed in.

As they drove in and alighted from the Sting Ray they saw a spectacle never experienced before.

Throngs of youthful singles, couples, and even families, babies! A virtual sea of people.

"I'll bet there are more than two hundred thousand people here," Mary Lou said in awe. Nick was mesmerized.

It was now evening, and they made their way squeezing through groups of long-haired youth down a slope, some dancing to the music of Richie Havens, who was performing on stage. Some were obviously smoking grass and drinking beer and wine. The crowd was orderly, however, at least at that point. Signs of peace and love were everywhere. Everyone was friendly. The mood and excitement of the music to come overtook the distaste of Vietnam! One description Nick had read earlier dubbed the concert Three Days of Peace. He hoped that would be true. What, with such a huge crowd?

Mary Lou and Nick worked their way through the crowd to the back side of the stage area where most of the tents were situated, looking everywhere for Nick's brother and Cindy. It didn't take too long to find them because this area was not as crowded as the other side of the revolving stage area. They met Cindy first and hugged and kissed. She wore a floppy Bollman hat with a wide brim and hip-hugger jeans with a sleeveless top.

"Where's the man, Cindy?" Nick asked.

"Oh, he's over there with our new friends from San Fran, Haight-Ashbury, as a matter of fact." Just as she pointed Chad turned and saw them. He walked unsteadily toward them holding a bottle of vodka in his hand. It was half empty.

Chad was jovial and couldn't hug his brother enough. He was pretty high at that point. It was about seven thirty p.m. and the night was just beginning. He kissed Mary Lou on the lips and held her hand. All around people were hugging and kissing. Many groups in the crowd were sitting on the ground with crossed legs, talking and laughing. Many were singing and chanting. Drugs were used in the open. Mushrooms and LSD, they were told by others. The smell of pot pervaded many areas.

Chad had a lightweight pullover caftan on with loose sleeves and flower prints all over it. He fit right into the crowd with his beard and mustache, now quite full, and his long hair below the shoulders.

"Well, brother," Chad slurred, "over there is a tent already set up for you and Mary Lou, in it is a cooler with beer and wine. If you want hard liquor just come to my ride. It's well stocked. And there's plenty of food in there. "He pointed to a van with psychedelic paintings on each side and the roof. "We have a new supersized grill for cooking. I came prepared." Nick was impressed by his brother's heart of gold.

That night they all sat around the campfire smoking pot and listening to songs by Joan Baez, Sweetwater, and others for a long time. Nick and Chad lay on the grass and at about midnight were feeling high as a kite. Nick with a bottle of wine, and Chad now on beer and a bit less drunk.

"Nick, don't you wish that people could be so loving and friendly all the time?" Chad queried.

"I sure do, Chad. The only time I've experienced this loving feeling was from the crowds on New Year's Eve in Boston, when everyone was friendly and joking. The subway fares were eliminated while people happily walked about and freedom prevailed. It's too bad that people have to get high to achieve that feeling. I think that we all have it, but are constrained by the everyday pressures of life." Chad agreed, and then talked about how lucky they were to live in America.

They drank and talked until about two a.m. They finally hit the sack and didn't get up until eleven the next morning. The festival was coming alive again and the musicians were beginning to practice before their performances began. Even though they had to wait for at least an hour to use the bathrooms or get water, they were happy to be there. As they walked around they saw families with little kids. Some wearing jerseys with flowers printed on them. Everywhere Nick and Mary Lou walked people spoke to them and introduced themselves, shaking hands. They had many offers of food sharing. The concession stands and trucks also were adequate for the occasion and they felt quite comfortable.

Beginning at noon on Saturday the experience went into overdrive. Quill opened the show after noon and the music blared nonstop pretty much through the afternoon and night. Santana belted out "Evil Ways" and had the crowd cheering loudly. And, when John Fogerty of Creedence Clearwater Revival sang "Susie Q," followed by "Bad Moon Rising," the crowd went into frenzy, and so did Nick! Everybody there seemed higher on alcohol and drugs than the day before!

The music continued on all night into Sunday morning, with Janis Joplin singing "Piece of My Heart" along with numerous others. Then there was the Grateful Dead. Mary

Lou liked "Turn On Your Love Light" the best of all their songs.

When Canned Heat sang the great song "Going Up the Country," depicting the rebellious American counterculture which was embodied here on Max Yasgur's farm, couples danced frantically, and Nick noticed couples having sex in places a little bit out of the way but very obvious. Some men and women were openly nude. Nick and Chad had a tough time keeping their eyes off the naked females when walking with their girlfriends, who were having a great time taking it all in.

Chad went into his tent at one point and ate some "magic mushrooms." He was so buzzed on top of the alcohol that he danced around the campfire naked for a while, laughing heartily. Nick roared with laughter at his brother. Chad wanted Nick to eat some too, but Nick wouldn't. He was only drinking beer and wine, and hadn't gotten to the point of total inebriation like his brother. He did, however, have no shirt on and only skimpy shorts. The girls were a little more reserved, but did take off their tops for a while and stripped to their panties. Tits jiggling as they danced, wine bottles in hand.

The Who took the stage late, but the crowd's response to "Pinball Wizard" and "See Me, Feel Me" was no less jubilant. The concert went on and on all night and early morning, up to around nine a.m. Sunday. The Packard brothers and their girlfriends all saw the sunrise together, holding hands. Love was everywhere on Max Yasgur's farm!

Nick and Mary Lou had planned on leaving late Sunday because of their work commitments. "No way are we leaving today!" exclaimed Chad around two Sunday p.m., after they awoke and had some breakfast. "The performance I came for will not be until tonight. I talked with some dudes down at the water spigot. Jimi Hendrix is scheduled for late today or tonight!"

Like all good things, the crowd thinned out as the day moved on. Many had to go back to the real world. Nick and Mary Lou left at five thirty Sunday evening, when the crowd had dwindled by at least 80 percent, leaving trash and mud everywhere. It had rained a few times during the concert and some people were sliding in the mud for fun they noticed as they left.

On the drive home they still felt buzzed and the excitement was high. They had just experienced something extraordinary and wouldn't realize the full extent of it for years to come. It was an indelible memory, with no trouble witnessed anywhere throughout the three days by either. But there were some bad LSD trips which required medical treatment and one death, but not from violence. They would learn at a later time that around five hundred thousand people had attended the event which rebelled against custom. This generation would change the country forever in many ways! Cindy and Chad stayed and listened to Joe Cocker and Jefferson Airplane's "Somebody to Love." And, as the "dudes" at the water spigots had pronounced, Hendrix was the last performer and didn't perform until well after midnight, with his final rendition of "The Star-Spangled Banner" evoking much emotion in the twenty thousand or so people remaining.

CHAPTER 11

Mary Lou Higgins had begun the program at Massachusetts Institute of Technology in the fall of 1967, and yes, she studied hard, but had a profound ability to solve any mathematical problem confronted by her. In the spring of 1969, she graduated at the top of her class from MIT's School of Engineering with a Master of Science degree.

She was sought-after by many emerging high-tech companies along the Route 128 belt in Massachusetts ("Silicon Valley East") making substantial salary offers, but she refused them all.

Mary Lou instead opted to work at MIT as a professorial assistant in mathematics for a mediocre salary. She assisted in student course structuring, curriculum planning, grading papers, and became a major asset to the school. She was so well liked that the faculty and students gave her a bang-up party when she left the hallowed halls in the winter of 1972 for a high-level technical position with NASA. She received many gifts from the faculty, showing great affection for her work.

When she was offered the position with NASA at a

$28,500 annual salary she was overwhelmed, and couldn't work hard enough for this top-level employer. She became completely enmeshed in the space program and created some sophisticated mathematical solutions. NASA was quite impressed.

Nick and Mary Lou started dating after their MBU graduation and continued on for almost six years. They had fallen in love right from the beginning.

Shortly after Nick began working for Barker, Tibbs, and Graham, he rented an apartment located on Walnut Street in one of Beacon Hill's upscale residential neighborhoods. It was small, around 550 square feet of living space, but the monthly rent was only $258. Nick thought that was a real bargain!

Mary Lou had remained living in Winthrop with her mother and her boyfriend, Carlos, who always had a wad of cash and sported expensive cars. Even Mary Lou had no clue what line of work Carlos was in, but didn't want to know! Living there enabled her to save big.

She spent many nights at Nick's Beacon Hill flat. Weeknights she reviewed her work while Nick reviewed his client's work. On Saturdays, quite often they went to the Haymarket near Faneuil Hall for fresh produce, and occasionally downtown to shop at Filene's or Jordan Marsh. At night they would dine at the Charles Restaurant on the Flat of Beacon Hill, or they might go across town to the waterfront and have dinner at Jimmy's Harborside or Anthony's Pier IV.

They were struggling at their jobs, but certainly not at their relationship. The bond between each other seemed so strong.

CHAPTER 12

One night after dining and drinking a lot of wine very late, the brothers and their girlfriends returned home to Nick's apartment. Mary Lou and Nick were feeling a little cocked while they sat on the sofa in the living room. Chad and Cindy were sitting in an armchair across from Nick and Mary Lou; Cindy perched on Chad's lap while he balanced a glass of cognac on the arm of the chair as they kissed.

The group roared with laughter as jokes were subtly exchanged concerning Chad and Cindy's upcoming marriage. It was planned a year ahead for June 1973. The couple had hit it off quite well ever since the night at the Peppermint Lounge and were attached to each other like glue!

Everyone began nodding off to sleep. It was three a.m. and the lights of Beacon Hill were dim. Chad, who was still wide-awake and wanted amusement, said, "OK, everybody, listen up!" A few eyes flinched while he went on. "If I have a seven-quart container and a four-quart container, and can fill or empty them of liquid as I please. How can I scientifically measure out six quarts?"

The test was a classic brainteaser, and there was silence for several minutes until Cindy, who hadn't had much to drink, said, "Fill the four-quart to the brim and empty it into the seven-quart container. Then, fill the four-quart half full and empty it into the seven. You have six quarts."

"That would be fine, except it's not scientifically measured, an estimate only. How about you, Nick, the numbers man?"

"I have no clue," Nick mumbled.

"I'll bet Mare can get it!"

Mary Lou stared for a few minutes and, as if her mind were a maze of computer circuitry, calculated the answer momentarily. "You fill the seven-quart container to the brim, then pour the contents of the seven into the four-quart container and empty the four. Finally, you pour the remaining contents of the seven into the four-quart container. Fill the seven-quart to the brim. Empty it into the four-quart, which already holds three quarts, and will take only one more. The seven-quart container then holds six scientifically measured quarts."

Although the others were half asleep, they were stunned by Mary Lou's brilliance at three thirty a.m. after countless drinks. She was a genius, they concluded. The couples snuggled and fell fast asleep as the young Al Pacino strolled across the TV screen in a scene from The Godfather.

Mary Lou at first kept hinting marriage and Nick listened, but never responded. He was in no position financially and wanted success before even entertaining the idea! It wasn't that he wanted more variety and spice in his life. He could have most any woman he desired; however, he loved Mary Lou, deeply, and that was adequate, but the time had to be right.

She broached the subject often, but Nick would say, "Mare, it will distract us. Let me succeed in business first, then we'll follow suit. You're the only one for me." Mary gradually backed off.

Nick's career had advanced quickly from the start. He was assigned to an audit of a seafood packing and wholesaling company that first week with BTG and thought that the week would never end. The atmosphere was cold and smelly. Reconciling accounts receivable and payable to the general ledger was extremely dull and boring. Nick knew the temporary nature of this level of work. It was the "bowels" of the business, but he persevered and gave great effort to this work.

In the following months he was exposed to audits and reviews only, in some cases, of restaurants, convenience store chains, auto dealerships, retail stores, discount chains, and a myriad of others. Nick performed his job tasks quite well and was pleased, but an inner desire to be on the client side swelled up inside of him. He wanted to manage his own business and create wealth. It's in the cards, he thought.

Over the course of the first year Nick studied relentlessly, nights and weekends, for the CPA exam, and in November 1968 sat for it. He passed all four parts with high scores. Once again he had achieved a lofty goal. He now had the distinguished title of Nicholas Packard, CPA, and was promoted to audit supervisor.

The ensuing years were more difficult as Nick's responsibilities grew. Despite the added weight, he persevered and successfully moved forward. By 1972 he rose to the position of audit manager.

Recently, Nick had acquired a special interest in real estate as a result of the early 1970s boom in apartment construction. The youthful baby boomers were showing their strength in numbers. Apartment demand was swelling as that unprecedented need for housing mushroomed! Single-family developments were on the increase, and a new concept had emerged for working couples who didn't want the headache of property upkeep and maintenance. Condominium ownership of apartment flats and townhouses became popular in Massachusetts and all around the country.

Danny's girlfriend, Lynn, from the West Coast, had unveiled the phenomenon to Nick and the others at the graduation party years earlier in 1967 at the Ocean Club, when she spoke of her father's success in building "condoms, or something like that." The concept had arrived in New England and could develop into a major housing opportunity.

Nick used some influence acquired over the last few years and began specializing in audits of real estate clients, ranging from general contractors, syndicators, developers, and owner/managers of real property. He learned the financial side of the real estate business and became obsessed with it!

CHAPTER 13

December 1973

Inside the Barker, Tibbs, and Graham office located on the fifteenth, sixteenth, and seventeenth floors of the new Boston high-rise building certain staff members and secretaries conversed in small groups. Others moved briskly around desks and through corridors. Partners could be seen raising and moving their hands in certain gestures of discourse, both in the corridors and in their offices in frenzied telephone conversations. Something out of the ordinary was happening!

This week was the scheduled deadline to finish the audit and finalize very complex certified financial statements and cost certifications related to HUD section 8 projects for one of BTG's largest clients, Dawson Homes, a national real estate company based in Boston. A true blessing of a hefty one-million-dollar annual fee!

A lot of raises and bonuses rode on the successful completion of this noble project. Nick was the lead manager of the Dawson account and reported only to Bobby Jameson, a young senior partner who was tough and had been known to fly off the handle on occasion.

BTG occupied sixty thousand square feet of floor space on three floors. The sixteenth floor contained the reception area, with a dividing wall on which sparkled a huge brass BT&G logo in Old English font. Large leather armchairs and sofas were symmetrically arranged around the waiting area and rested on an exquisite red and black oriental carpet with various other colors blended in.

Beyond the reception area was a maze of cubicles with movable partitions. These cubicles averaged about nine feet by seven feet and were occupied by junior and senior staff members, with their support personnel clustered around them on the outside. All services were on the fifteenth floor; i.e., copying, library, mail room, and lunch room.

The seventeenth floor was decorated in a plush manner and housed all the firm's executives in mostly sizable offices around the outside perimeter of the space. Secretarial support stations flanked the middle of the floor, all neatly arranged with rows of IBM Selectric typewriters perched on high-quality oak desks.

Nick's office was on the far wall and was smaller than the partners' offices, but had a nice view of the historic Customs Tower. At night the orange and blue hues of the lit Roman numeral clock glittered spectacularly.

Sitting at his desk, dressed in a red-striped Brooks Brothers shirt with suspenders and a maroon bow tie, Nick tapped a pencil on the top of his large mahogany desk as he gazed out the window. It was a bleak December day with murky gray skies. The forecasted snow appeared imminent.

He thought to himself, This afternoon is the review meeting with Dawson's people, and Jameson and I have to be to the Dawson meeting at two p.m., and tonight I should stay late to be sure the guys make all changes decided at the meeting and finish the final drafts. It was probably good that Mary Lou canceled our dinner engagement this evening. We have three days to prepare the final documents. Typing, final review, reproduction. Three days, then Friday delivery. No problem!

Nick pondered, I wonder what's wrong with Mare? She seems so preoccupied lately when I call her. She doesn't even respond with the usual "I love you" at the end of our telephone conversations! She's under great pressure at NASA and probably wants to give an ultimatum on the marriage discussion. I'm getting close, with a probable promotion looming at BT&G. Pretty soon, Mare. Pretty soon!

Nick and Bobby Jameson met with the Dawson executives promptly at two p.m. and discussed many issues relative to the financial statements. The meeting went well and many Dawson people patted Nick on the back for a job well done. He was on a roll!

Back at the BT&G office around six p.m., Nick made the rounds and found the staff diligently working on the Dawson statement changes. They were scribbling facts and numbers like morning freshness. It was now eight p.m.

Nick went to his office and sprawled in his chair in total relaxation. He rested his feet on his desk and punched Mary Lou's number into his phone. No answer! She's really busting it for NASA! He sat back in his padded chair and scrutinized the revised Dawson consolidated financial statements. They showed fifty million dollars in gross income and fifteen million dollars in net cash flow. What performance! I'm on the wrong end of the real estate spectrum. I should and will move to the client side soon!

Nick enthusiastically played with the numbers, percentages, and other tests. He called Mary Lou at ten p.m.…no answer!

CHAPTER 14

Nick arrived at his office at eight thirty the following morning. He dialed the Dawson main number and spoke to Jerry Dawson, the CFO. They discussed Dawson's pending insurance claims. Two claims totaling fifteen million dollars for major fire damage had been settled and a third for five million dollars was uncertain. Nick made careful notes.

At ten forty-five a.m. he dialed Mary Lou's number at NASA. She answered and indignantly said, "Yeah?"

Nick cringed and said, "Honey, it's me!"

"Oh, Nicky, I'm very busy and frustrated. I'm sorry."

"Can we meet tonight for dinner?" Nick queried nervously.

"We need to, Nick!" Mary Lou replied.

"I'll meet you in the lobby of Anthony's Pier Four at seven," Nick said.

Mary Lou sped across the Northern Avenue Bridge and strolled into Anthony's at eight. Nick had been waiting patiently in the lobby for an hour. He was mesmerized for a while, viewing the photos of Anthony Athanas shaking hands with many famous celebrates. They were very impressive and certainly made their mark on the restaurant.

He got fidgety after a while, but tried to act calm when she walked in and apologized. She had been stuck in traffic on Route 128 for an hour, going slow because of the snowstorm. She had no way to contact Nick.

She looked beautiful yet very businesslike. Under her Fisher coat she wore a navy blue suit with a white blouse. She looked gorgeous in her form-fitting suit, and her long brown hair traced down to her chest. They kissed softly on the lips and the maître d' quickly ushered them to their table, situated with a view toward Boston Harbor. The lights of the ships in the harbor twinkled in a cozy fashion.

After being seated, Nick cupped his hand over hers and leaned forward, kissing her lightly on her cheek. "How's it going at NASA, honey? How many more weeks until you become Mary Lou Higgins, senior engineer?" Nick said playfully.

"Oh, Nick, I've worked so hard. Upper management has even praised me on my work. I want continuing success on this job with a passion and have created some new approaches to improve the space program. I pray that I'll be successful!"

"I do too, Mare. I really do, for your sake."

A waiter in a white shirt and black bow tie then gracefully handed large brown leather and embossed gold leaf menus to the couple. They each chose exotic fish. After they ordered, Mary Lou asked, "Nick, how's the Dawson project going?"

"Quite well," Nick replied. "We wrapped it up today.

They liked our display of professionalism. I'm in for a good bonus this year and I could possibly make a junior partnership soon. That's good for thirty-five thousand dollars."

"Congratulations, Nick!"

"Not yet, Mare. I don't want to jinx it."

The dinners were served and tasted as scrumptious as always. Both ate quietly, but savored the fruits de mer. After dinner there was a lull in their conversation and stone silence ensued for many moments. Nick started to say that he was almost ready to tie the knot and get engaged now.

"Mare, you know that I'm ascending the ladder at BT&G, and—"

Mary Lou quickly interrupted him and said, "Nick, I'm seeing someone else!"

The time bomb exploded, sending shock waves through Nick. Silence followed, then anxiety and despair. Nick lost the color in his face and tried to muster up strength. Finally, he replied, "Is it serious? How long? Why?"

"It's not you Nick. You've been so wrapped up in your work, and I did try to talk about marriage many times. You wouldn't respond. It just happened!"

"Who, Mary Lou?"

"He works at NASA," she replied.

"Who, Mare?" Nick said, starting to become angry.

"His name is Tom."

"Tom who?" Nick retorted with anger and despair.

"Tom Flanders," she uttered.

"Oh, the boss. No wonder he says you're doing excellent!" Nick then hesitated and said, "I'm sorry, Mare. I'm hurt and I didn't mean that. I love you."

"I love you, too," she said, and broke down in tears. "I don't want to hurt you."

"Drop him and let's get married. Right now. I'm ready!"

Silence ensued for what seemed like an eternity to him. Finally, Mary Lou said tearfully, "I can't, Nick. I'll always love you, Nicky."

Nick, feeling beaten, replied, "Your call, Mary Lou. Your call!"

He paid the bill, even though Mary Lou insisted that she pay half. "Don't make me feel worse," Nick angrily replied.

They silently exited the room. Nick retrieved their coats from the check room and gallantly placed Mary Lou's on her shoulders as she slipped her arms through.

They walked into the packed parking lot through the snow and now mist. As they approached her car she turned and grabbed Nick by the waist. She kissed him softly on the lips, then they locked together in what seemed so reminiscent of the embrace at the Ocean Club graduation party years back, when they first realized their emotions.

Nick became very reserved and said, "Mare, think it over. We've had many good years together."

"I will, Nicky. I do love you." The wine had kicked in. She drove off.

Nick drove his newly acquired Jaguar through the now blinding snowstorm to the Charles Street Garage. The snow had continued to fall again after he left Mary Lou at Anthony's. He was shattered and in a state of disbelief as he walked down Charles Street at the bottom of Beacon Hill.

The hurt from within surfaced as he walked and tears rolled down his cheeks. The blinding snow increased his misery.

He vaguely saw the Sevens Pub sign, but managed to get in the door. A seat was empty at the bar and he squeezed in, and proceeded to order Michelobs one after the other. Staring at the bottles he imagined her dimple shining inside. For the moment he was in a state of denial, thinking that it was only temporary, but intuitively knew that a rekindling of lost lover's feelings is usually the exception.

At one a.m. Nick staggered from the Sevens and made his way to another bar where he negotiated the purchase of a six-pack. He hailed a cab and went back to his apartment, where he drank more, killing the pain but not the reality. It hit him like a ton of bricks in the morning.

CHAPTER 15

Spring 1976

"I've got a hundred and thirty-nine yards of concrete in quite a few trucks being delivered to the site beginning at ten this morning to pour the foundations and basement floors in houses on lots nineteen, seven, and three. Rusty, you examine those delivery slips carefully before you sign them. I don't want any screw jobs on yardage!" Chad bellowed.

"OK, boss, OK. I understand," the labor foreman promised him.

Chad watched proudly as Nick's Jaguar wound its way up the lengthy as yet unpaved road to lot 7 where Chad was working. Nick jumped out of the Jag and vigorously shook Chad's hand, then hugged him tightly. Chad's faced reddened with embarrassment. After all, he was the superintendent of a macho construction force who were watching this display of affection closely.

"Ginny sold three more houses in the last four days directly from the trailer. The market is hot! I think we'll all emerge from this project quite well," Nick crowed.

In late 1974 Nick had quit his job at Barker, Tibbs,

and Graham to take a shot at home building and had formed a partnership with his brother, who had been an excellent carpenter since he was a child, and held electrical and plumbing licenses as well. He had also acquired an ABC contractor's license which made him well qualified to supervise the construction operation. Nick momentarily recalled to himself how Chad had won a state championship miniature house building contest at the age of sixteen. He was a mechanical genius and a hard worker. A valuable asset to the business.

Nick, while still at BT&G, a year and a half earlier had been assigned a client who was a successful real estate developer. Carl Johnson, the principal owner and wealthy entrepreneur, had taken a liking to Nick because of his smooth personality and impeccable work ethic.

Carl sold Nick a parcel of land in the upscale suburban town of Norwell, Massachusetts, at a reasonable price, on which they were now building single-amily homes. Carl financed it with a 10 percent interest-only purchase money mortgage subordinated to construction financing. Nick agreed to pay off the loan on a lot release basis as the houses were sold in the thirty-lot subdivision.

Further, Carl helped Nick coordinate with the civil engineers and architects. He also helped get the subdivision plan approved by the local planning board. Royal Estates of Hingham was now a reality. Carl treated Nick like a son and Nick would never forget that!

Now, a year later, ten houses had been sold in the fifty-thousand-dollar price range and foundations for six houses had been poured. Only one was a spec house, unsold as yet. The houses, mainly colonials, were architecturally attractive.

The brothers were excited about their pro-forma projected pretax net profit. A cool three hundred sixty thousand dollars. Nick's share would be 50 percent or about one hundred eighty thousand. Chad was ecstatic to receive 50 percent when Nick had done all the legwork. He deserved a greater share, but Nick loved Chad and wanted him to feel important, an equal. Maybe this will build his confidence and curb his drinking, Nick thought.

Chad was greatly respected by Nick. He did the work of many men combined and never hit the bottle during the workday. As a matter of fact, he was relentlessly attempting to quit drinking and was regularly attending AA meetings. He showed up for work every day and was punctual.

Chad had married Cindy in 1973 in a spectacular June wedding. Cindy's father had paid for the reception at the Ocean Club, but Nick and his mother, Frances, contributed substantially to make it a special event. They loved Chad dearly. He had a "heart of gold."

Cindy and Chad had a baby on the way. Her six-month pregnancy caused a major swelling in her tummy, but she was otherwise in great shape through diet and exercise. She looked adorable, with curly red locks and a youthful, bright smile. She also had a "heart of gold" and was involved in much charity work.

Nick had recently married Jacqueline Hines, Cindy's friend from the South Shore, whom he'd met a year after the split with Mary Lou Higgins. He had been abandoned by Mary Lou, as his good sense after that night at Anthony's had forewarned, and had broken off all communications with her after that night, preserving his dignity but suffered greatly to himself. Mary Lou ultimately married Tom Flanders, causing Nick much grief during those days.

When he met Jacki, at his cousin's wedding, his romantic interest in women was dull. He had been severely hurt by the loss of Mary Lou, and had a major void in his life which had been partially filled by his penchant for business. Surprisingly, Jacki had sparked an interest in Nick. She was a very attractive former model for Vogue magazine. Her long brown hair and twinkling blue eyes mesmerized him, but even more so, she was bubbling with personality. She was considerate and not self-centered. An intense interest once again sparked Nick's life as she quizzed Nick about himself at the wedding reception.

Nick tried to reciprocate and she answered questions about herself with brevity, always responding sincerely with the utmost curiosity toward him.

Nick quickly became fond of her and they danced many dances together. It was so reminiscent of the Ocean Club, Nick thought. But she's not Mary Lou!

He carried the spark for a few weeks thereafter and couldn't resist calling Jacki for a date. She accepted, and they met for a delightful evening at the Charles Street Playhouse on Warrenton Street in Boston, where the play Brown Sugar, a great musical, was in its fifteenth week. Afterward they dined at Jimmy's Restaurant on fresh Maine lobster and carried on more of their compatible conversation. Jacki was very romantic and held Nick's arm firmly throughout the evening. She was very affectionate, which Nick liked a lot. Kissing tenderly at times made Nick feel whole again.

The couple dated for six months and were totally congruous, a perfect match, it seemed. They finally married and moved into an old house in Milton, Massachusetts, which they renovated together, transforming the house into their little castle. Nick was extremely happy and now well settled to move on to new heights. Life was great once again and Nick was poised to commence his long-desired career in real estate development.

"Chad, let's have dinner tomorrow evening at the Black Angus," Nick happily suggested in a telephone conversation one day. "You and I, Cindy, and Jacki. It's on me. I think we should celebrate because we'll soon have a new site to develop. I've located a new site for us. You'll really like this one! It's in Hingham."

"All right, Nick. You're on," Chad replied. "I'd like that."

CHAPTER 16

The next evening the two couples met at the Black Angus at eight p.m. and commenced the evening in the lounge, sitting at a solid oak table in large, heavy oak chairs covered with soft velvet cushions. Nick ordered a round of drinks. Coke for Chad, who didn't seem to care. Nick was proud of him and patted him on the back.

Chad and Nick began discussing the daily events at Royal Oak Estates. Chad had caught an overstated concrete delivery slip that morning just a day after Nick had cautioned him to watch for this sort of thing. Chad, through experience, had known that a typical foundation and basement floor requires thirty-one to fifty yards of concrete, depending on the size. The delivery slip submitted showed sixty-seven yards for the pour on lot 3. When questioned, the driver acted dumb and drew a blank, shrugging his shoulders. Chad terminated that relationship on the spot and called a new supplier. They also discussed Nick's new land parcel for their next housing development.

"Chad, I've made an offer on an extremely well-located

parcel in Hingham," Nick said. "I estimate that it's good for about sixty lots in a nice rural setting. I'll drive you out there tomorrow and show you the site. I think that you'll agree it's prime.""That's your area, brother. You know best! Thanks for including me again," Chad replied.

"Chad, I couldn't do it without your expertise." Chad's face beamed with joy.

The women conversed about Cindy's baby. Her amniocentesis had revealed that a baby boy was on the way. Cindy was overwhelmed with joy, and Jacki felt extremely elated and happy for the parents to be.

"Chad, did you read the article today in the Boston Globe about Larry Bowdoin?" queried Nick.

"No, I didn't. What about him?"

"You haven't heard? Chad, my lad. Do you remember that I called you that at my graduation party back then? When Larry teased you about your wit. Something to do with sand in an hour glass. You were quite insulted!"

"Yeah, that bustard was making derogatory remarks about a toast I'd made to you and him. I had planned it carefully and rehearsed it many times beforehand. I thought it was very appropriate for the occasion."

"Well, I did too," Nick exclaimed. "But listen, Larry has been indicted by a federal grand jury for criminal fraud. It seems that he was involved in a scheme to bill GMC for warranty repairs never done. It's big-time, Chad. I mean millions. There probably was another criminal element involved, but they'll never take the hit. They seldom do.

At least four others in Larry's company have been named in the indictment. Our attorney, Mike, told me this afternoon that, if found guilty, they could serve ten to fifteen years in federal prison!" Nick continued. "Twenty or more for Larry, who was apparently the mastermind."

"It serves the bastard right. I never did like him. Too cocky, an egomaniac," Chad said.

"You know, you're right, Chad. He told me at the graduation party that his father had set him up for life. Hard work was something his father did before him in the auto dealership and that paved the way for easy street, no hard work for him. Only golf and martinis! I knew he'd take a fall sooner or later."

Jacki interrupted, inquiring, "Does Larry have a wife? Children?"

"He has both," Nick answered.

"Well, you have to feel sorry, have compassion for them," Jacki replied in her sincere way. "I do, honey. He has a few young children and a very personable wife. I think that one child is a paraplegic. One evening a few years back I met them at Lock Obers Restaurant in Boston. Nice family, it really sucks."

"Tell me, Chad, what was the hourglass toast? What did you say?" Cindy inquired.

After a half-dozen botched attempts Chad remembered and proudly recited, "May the sands of time run evenly and smoothly through the hourglass of your lives until the last grain falls to its resting place."

"Oh, that's great, honey. That's profound!" Cindy murmured with tears in her eyes. Jacki and Nick clapped their hands in rapid applause while Chad's handsome face beamed with joy. His long, blond curly locks accentuated his good looks. Cindy seemed to be so in love with him.

After a delightful dinner of the highest-quality beef on the South Shore they all hugged and parted.

CHAPTER 17

September 1977

Mike Kensington, the Baystate Builders counsel, asked Nick, "Do you have the P and S deposit check?"

"Have I ever been to a closing without it? Do you have the deed and second mortgage documents?" Nick bellowed to the brothers' attorney. Both men chuckled. This was familiar dialogue between the old friends.

This closing was the twenty-ninth for Royal Oaks Estates. The brothers had agreed to take back a second mortgage on the lot 28 oversized colonial which was being conveyed for an unprecedented price of $79,500. The development was sold out because the thirtieth and final house was firmly committed under contract. It was a great success for the Packard brothers.

Chad and Nick, now doing business as Baystate Builders, had received all required town approvals for their second development in Hingham, Massachusetts, months ago, and had closed the acquisition a month later. The approved sixty-six-lot subdivision was nestled in an extent of sturdy oaks and pines surrounded by rolling meadows. The area neighborhoods consisted of two old farms. A typical scene from Currier and Ives, it was a very desirable setting. Many alternate architectural plans were being produced by Niles Sutphin and Associates, a renowned architectural firm out of Watertown, Massachusetts.

The luxury houses were to be priced in the price range of one hundred five thousand dollars to one hundred forty-five thousand dollars and would be mostly custom built. Some lots would be sold separately, but heavy deed restrictions would be imposed on quality and design. This was necessary to create the upper-middle-class character of the development.

Earlier that spring Chad had commenced building an attractively designed garrison colonial on lot 26, a prime acre lot in Royal Oaks Estates, which he had carefully chosen in the early stages of the development. The site was perfectly contoured with a gradual stepped-up and brick-walled grade. A thick forest of towering pines had been preserved on either side of the four-thousand-square-foot house.

The interior, not quite completed, was exquisitely finished with a marbled foyer, large rooms, mahogany trim, an extensive top-grade appliance package, French doors in the front and rear leading to an Olympic-sized swimming pool with a huge patio area, central HVAC, many skylights, and a spacious two-car garage.

Life was grand! The happy couple had just moved in with their two-year-old son, Dougie. Cindy was elated and was planning a celebration for Columbus Day. She thought she had never experienced such exhilaration in her entire life. Her curly red locks bounced in unison as she shouted finish instructions to the last of the tradesmen. "Can you move that lighting fixture? And please replace that gaudy wallpaper!" It had been ordered erroneously. She was a proud and savvy wife and mother who had married a man proven to be a responsible and providing husband. A better father could not be found anywhere. He made Cindy feel like a real woman. And, he had been sober for over a year!

CHAPTER 18

The Packard brothers left the lot 28 closing at one p.m. and accompanied their attorney, Mike, to lunch at Maison Robert on School Street in Boston. As they walked up State Street, the three happy businessmen exchanged accolades for the successful roles of each in completing Royal Oaks Estates. In turn, they each patted the other on the back and beamed with confidence.

At the famous French restaurant tucked away beside the old City Hall, they were seated and Mike said, "First, a round of drinks is in order, and by the way, it's all on me so live it up." His firm had generated a hefty one-hundred-thousand-dollar fee on Royal Oaks, and although steep, their service was impeccable. Mike's gymnastic legal maneuvering had probably returned half of that in cost savings.

They ordered drinks, and when it came to Chad, he straightforwardly ordered a double martini, on the rocks. Nick immediately responded, "I don't think so, Chad. Not for you. Don't take a chance!" He tried nonchalantly to dissuade Chad.

Chad, filled with anxiety, hesitated and then replied,

"Come on, Nick, one drink won't hurt. It's my celebration too, you know. Only one, I've learned how to deal with it after abstaining for more than a year."

Mike innocently agreed and said to Nick, "Let him have one drink to relax and celebrate the occasion." Nick didn't want to cause a scene, and reluctantly said, "Your call, Chad. Be careful."

The businessmen toasted while Chad nursed his martini and each man eagerly ordered dinner.

Following the drinks, they dined heartily on French cuisine prepared meticulously in a style only Maison Robert was capable of. Their conversation flowed in a graceful, hearty manner.

After a period of discussion on the now completed Royal Oaks Estates it moved on to the forthcoming Hingham development. Mike's law firm, Kensington and Flaherty, had represented Baystate Builders, the brothers' company, on the acquisition and had made a stellar performance assisting Nick in a generous last-minute purchase price renegotiation because of the wetlands flagging substantially exceeding initial estimates, thereby reducing the number of buildable lots from seventy-one to sixty-six. They discussed optimum house pricing and the status of the pending Department of Environmental and Quality Engineering approval for the development.

Then, the conversation drifted to Larry Bowdoin's pathetic situation with the warranty fraud case dragging so long and how he was in serious trouble. Each man expressed sincere compassion for Larry, and more so, for his family who were the real victims.

Nick soon eyed his watch and noticed that it was three p.m. He had urgent calls to make and correspondence to draft before day's end. Nick said, "I hate to cut this conversation short, amigos, but I've got a lot of work to do."

"Me too," Mike replied.

Outside on School Street, the men set down their briefcases and vigorously shook hands. Mike parted and walked away toward his office. Nick turned to Chad and asked, "Are you OK, Chad? Can you handle that drink? I mean, it won't precipitate anything, will it? Like a binge. You know you're not a stranger to that!"

"Of course not, Nick, I'm fine," Chad replied. "Hey, Nick, brother dear, do you have any cash with you? I'm short right now and want to buy Cindy a pair of earrings that she saw at Filene's last week and admired. A sort of celebration, you know." Chad was being sincere about his intentions!

"Why is it I'm brother dear when you want something?" Nick laughed as he pulled a wad of bills tucked in a money clip out of his pocket and peeled off six crisp hundred-dollar bills. "You deserve it, Chad. You're an excellent partner, and brother too. I love you. Is this enough?""Sure, Nick. I'll get it back to you soon, brother. Don't worry. I love you too."

CHAPTER 19

Chad departed and headed down Washington Street to Filene's. He walked straight to the jewelry department and happily inquired about the onyx earrings set in twenty-four-carat gold, but the last pair had just been sold! He sighed with overwhelming disappointment. He desperately wanted them for Cindy. She would be ecstatic. The sales lady said that she could order a pair from the Chestnut Hill store and have them shipped COD to Norwell in about three days. This will have to do, Chad thought. He placed the order and left the store.

Outside he noticed on the famous post-mounted clock with Roman numerals that it was now four fifteen p.m. Too late to go to the office! Besides, he felt a buzz from that long-missed martini and his alcoholic mind began to churn.

He sauntered his way toward the adult strip dubbed the Combat Zone, reiterating in his mind that he was killing time to avoid rush-hour traffic and did not want to venture inside any of the clubs. He queried himself as to why he was doing this because his car was parked in the other direction, near School Street. Go home, he thought to himself. But he didn't!

As Chad walked by Club 66, then the Naked I Lounge, he stopped and hesitated. I've been good for a long time. Just a few beers and I'll go right back to sobriety tomorrow. No problem! He walked further going by a few more clubs to the Harem Club's double doors and uncontrollably entered. It took a few minutes for his eyes to adjust to the austere darkness, but around the corner he noticed a quite attractive blonde dancing on the long, rectangular stage-lit runway. Its length made it look like an airstrip lit up in the dark.

The encore had just begun. The buxom beauty was slithering her curvaceous thighs as she slid down her skimpy G-string. The crowd was roaring with applause. A smile beamed on her adorable face which was accentuated by her wide lips. The stimulation from this caused the alcoholic urge to flood his body.

He found an empty bar stool about midway down the stage and ordered a bottle of Bud. Four dollars, the waitress called for. He pulled out the first hundred-dollar bill that Nick had given him. He felt guilty for a moment remembering that it was for Cindy's present. He loved Cindy and thought that she would get the earrings and Nick would be repaid his cash. A sense of relief ensued as he slid the bill to the waitress.

After five more Buds Chad's half-shot judgment urged him to leave. He was heavily buzzed, but still OK to drive he thought. It was now seven thirty p.m. but his mind resisted the thought to leave. He knew that he must call Cindy. He left for ten minutes to call her at a restaurant a few doors down from the Harem Club. The music in the club would have been a dead giveaway.

No longer inhibited by what he was doing, he called Cindy and guiltily fabricated a story about working late on the Hingham project planning. His speech was close to being slurred, but he managed to pull it off. "I'll be a bit longer," he lied. "I love you," Cindy said as she hung up.

Chad, selfishly thinking that he "had it by the balls," returned to the Harem Club with the alcoholic thought of "just one more." This time he meandered through the crowd, mixed with all races, to the back stage where he took a seat on the second tier of the stepped-up bar counters.

Momentarily, a gorgeous brunette with a skintight, low-cut dress approached Chad and asked him if he wanted to buy a bottle of champagne. He remained silent, but after a few moments, out of character, he accepted the invitation, and in a flash, a champagne bottle was served. The waitress poured the first glass quickly for each. They drank as she nuzzled up to him and whispered erotic words. The bottle had cost Chad a hundred dollars!

Continuing to drink heavily and feeling substantially buzzed, Chad laughed as he poked holes in cardboard Heineken drink coasters, stuffed the holes with twenty-dollar bills and hurled them through the air like flying saucers. The dancers were elated as they retrieved the coasters from the stage floor. Chad and the brunette beauty, Delia, conversed for a long period of time, laughing and drinking as she sipped at a constant pace.

After the first bottle had been drained the waitress approached the couple and asked if he'd buy another. He acquiesced and got drunk as Delia caressed him all over his body, playfully. She rubbed his crotch and proceeded to ask Chad if he wanted to spend the night with her. He didn't answer.

He looked at his watch: 11:50 p.m. He knew that he had to leave now and excused himself to go to the men's room, where he took inventory of his cash. One hundred and twenty-four dollars left. What a waste, he thought, as he maneuvered from the men's room. After approaching Delia and bidding her good-bye, he exited the Harem Club. What a beauty! But I'm not violating Cindy! I love her.

Chad hurriedly walked north down Washington Street toward the garage. He was high on alcohol and passed two hookers as he walked past the Club 66. They snuggled up to him and tried to rub his groin area, asking, "Do you want to go out, honey?" Knowing the old pickpocket scheme he quickly buried his hands in his pockets where he carried his cash. He also concentrated on his watch. The female duet persisted as he tried to pull away. He then raised his voice in a tough macho manner, warning them to back off. The women assumed that he could be trouble and quickly departed.

Chad's thoughts centered on Delia and her beauty as he walked. His erotic nature was extremely aroused by the booze and he was about to turn back toward the Harem, but then thought that it just wasn't worth it. His alcoholic mind pulled in one direction while his deep love for Cindy pulled in the other. He moved on. Thank you, God!

CHAPTER 20

At the parking garage he took the elevator to the fourth floor level and fumbled, searching all pockets for his keys. He finally found them after three tries. The Mustang roared as it screeched down the circular ramps, barely missing the walls. At the cashier's booth he handed the attendant a twenty-dollar bill and smiled as he sped away.

The Mustang maneuvered through the streets of the Financial District and cruised down Kneeland Street, finally entering the Southeast Expressway. Traffic was light and he tromped on the gas pedal, pushing the speedometer up to ninety miles per hour, passing every car on the highway. His long blond curly locks blew in the breeze swishing through the open windows. Chad was relieved and feeling proud that he had resisted the temptation!

As he headed south on the Expressway determined to go home to Norwell, his alcoholic thoughts kicked in, suggesting that old fateful thought of "one more and that's it." The urge was uncontrollable at this point. He had crossed the border of judgment and continued to take the exit at Neponset Street in Quincy, and drove across the Neponset

River bridge reducing his speed, wary of seeing blue lights flashing in his mirror. Moments later he pulled into the parking lot of Sammy Wong's restaurant and bar.

Inside the restaurant, Chad headed for the bar, passing two pretty Chinese waitresses who smiled admiringly at him and said, "Hi, handsome!" He beamed with satisfaction. It was a wonder that he looked so good and could walk a straight line after eight hours of serious indulgence! He took a seat at the bar and watched couples dancing to disco music on the small, crowded dance floor.

As he tapped his fingers on the bar to the rhythm of the music he ordered a Mai Tai, which was mixed with rum, and an order of chicken wings that he quickly devoured. He hadn't eaten for nine hours and was famished. Feeling somewhat satisfied after this he ordered another Mai Tai; he soon got groggy and the room began to spin. Whoa! As he stood up he stumbled and reeled against the bar. Fortunately, the room was packed and most, who were themselves half-lit, didn't notice the embarrassing scene. Except for a few disgusted glances he went unnoticed. His battle with alcoholism could not be understood by social drinkers, which included most of the world's population.

He paid the twenty-five-dollar bill with two twenties and, surprisingly, staggered out the door with no response from anyone. After missing the keyhole six times he finally unlocked the door, staggered and fell into the Mustang, sprawling on the front seat. His head was spinning and he was feeling the need to vomit. Chad lay there for some time.

After a while, devoid of most judgment, he sat up and

fired the ignition. He pulled out of his space and sped away, scraping the Mustang's wheels against the abutment.

The remaining fringes of Chad's judgment clamored, warning him to drive slowly and to stop and call Cindy, but he was too drunk to do that and proceeded on. As he was driving down Quincy Avenue he tried to correct his double vision by shutting one eye, but that didn't help too much!

He was so intoxicated that even without double vision he wavered back and forth over the center line of the road. He suddenly caught a glimpse of a bright flashing blue light in the rearview mirror and froze. Then blackness followed as he passed out, crossing over the Neponset River Bridge.

The Mustang suddenly careened against the low side-guard rail and toppled over it, falling forty feet through the air and landing upside down. Slowly, the car began to sink!

The police cruiser which had been following Chad momentarily called dispatch to send a rescue team. The rescue squad and fire trucks arrived on the scene quickly and frantically tried to rescue Chad.

Within twenty minutes a horrible, gruesome scene unfolded. Chad's lifeless body was raised to the surface by divers and was mangled beyond recognition. He hadn't thought to hook up the seat belt after leaving the bar. While it was late, a few cars had stopped to see what was going on and watched with horror. One woman vomited while the crowd groaned in repugnance. The fatal crash had severed Chad's head completely!

CHAPTER 21

The police cruiser quietly pulled into the driveway at 147 Royal Oaks Drive. The house was dark except for a dim foyer light. Only the front portico light was shining brightly. It was a beacon for Chad's safe entry home from his day's journey.

Cindy was fast asleep when the two Valiums she had taken hours earlier had kicked in, after she had begun to worry about Chad. First, a tap on the front door, then a rap slowly woke her. Maybe Chad's key isn't working? She wobbled down the front stairs and tried to gain her composure as she opened the front door expecting to see him. Her heart pounded frantically and panic ensued when she saw the two policemen and the blue cruiser light flashing.

"Mrs. Packard?"

"Yes?" Cindy answered with trepidation.

"Is Chad Packard your husband?"

"Of course," she replied. "Is he OK? Is my husband OK?" Cindy earnestly inquired as she began to tremble.

Both officers hesitated a moment and then one

pronounced "He was in an automobile accident earlier tonight. I'm sorry, Mrs. Packard, he died!"

All hell then broke loose as Cindy screamed with pain. "No, no, no, not Chad! My husband!" Cindy shrieked with terror and passed out, falling into the officer's arms.

As she came around the policemen spent moments trying to comfort her and finally brought her to the level of rational speech. They managed to prompt her for Nick's name and telephone number, which they called in to dispatch.

Nick was sound asleep, snuggling Jacki, when the phone rang. He took the message in shock while Jacki slowly awoke in horror. The pair fumbled into their clothes and the Jaguar flew out of the garage moments later with Jacki at the wheel, zigzagging down the long driveway. Nick could barely speak!

At 147 Royal Oaks Drive Nick and Jacki entered the foyer. Jacki was stumbling and nearly hit the wall as she caught her balance. Nick noticed. She's half asleep. It's three a.m. The policemen who had waited gave Nick as much information as they had at the moment, then left. He thought about all that cash he had given Chad that afternoon. Had his good sense left him? Chad was a recovering alcoholic and had a drink against Nick's warnings. Yet he let him go because Chad's demure attitude had fooled him. He didn't understand the alcoholic mindset!

Cindy rushed toward Nick and embraced him fully, with tears drenching her face. "I loved him so much!" she cried. "Much of my life has died." She screamed, "I want to be with him now. Please take me, God!"

Nick feigned strength and mumbled, "Cindy, he's in a

better place now. I know it." Then, lost for words, Nick cried and hugged her silently for what seemed like an eternity.

Nick and Jacki silently exited without any idea of how to break the news of the tragedy to his mother, Frances. He'd have to be careful, she was vulnerable to strokes. He drove to Braintree and visited her the following day. Somehow he explained it successfully, after feeding her a few of Cindy's Valium and an hour of small talk before he dropped the bomb!

CHAPTER 22

The funeral that followed three days later was extremely emotional for the entire family and friends. At least two hundred of the Packard family's friends and many business associates of the brothers came to pay their respects. The wake was held at the Weeks Funeral Home and the service at the family's church in Braintree.

The flower baskets at the funeral home were so numerous that they covered three full walls of the receiving room. Chad had been only thirty-four years old, but had amassed a huge number of friends and acquaintances. His construction employees, who had sent a towering floral piece to the funeral home, six feet wide, sat in the third and fourth rows of the church at the service, sincerely shedding tears. They had loved this man who treated them exceptionally well, even though he demanded full productive workdays and sometimes "cracked the whip."

As Reverend Mathers, a Methodist minister, began with a sad but eloquent eulogy that transcended the room, Cindy cried loudly. Nick, visibly in a painful state, hugged Cindy while uttering comforting words. Frances sat on

Nick's opposite side wailing with tremendous grief. Nick then turned and hugged her with both arms, dropping a rose held from his hand.

Then, the room was filled with tears and weeping; Jacki stood up and quietly, but unsteadily, exited the room. She went to the ladies' room and sat with her head buried deeply in her hands, and as the room spun, her anxious thoughts brought her to another world. Her obsession was haunting her, but she had to be cool for just a little longer. She would excuse herself from the church service and the burial and the following visitation at the house. Then she could continue! She would say it was a female problem. They'd believe it!

The scene by the casket was sad, as Cindy rubbed her husband's arm and kissed his cheek while clinging to Nick's hand. The entire Packard family stood around the casket and prayed for a long time. As in most deaths, this was a highly intense moment. The last viewing! Tears gushed from everyone.

After what seemed like an eternity, Jacki was oblivious to the sound of the crowd entering the foyer of the church. She quickly entered the crowded foyer unnoticed. As the family was entering the church, Jacki approached Nick and said, "Honey, I'm sick. My period is bad and I feel nauseous. I have to go home and lie down for a while. I'm sorry. What a time for this, huh?" "Are you OK?" Nick asked.

Jacki answered, "Yes, honey, but I have to leave!"

"Jacki, I love you. Do what you have to do. I'll be OK. Come to the house later if you can, but, if not, I'll call you. Take my car." He handed her the keys and sullenly moved on.

The casket lay beside the cavernous pit. Nick approached and knelt by it. He rested a rose on its top and uttered tearfully, "Chad, I love you, and I'll miss you so much. I will carry on our business, and will protect and care for Cindy and Dougie as long as I live. This I vow!"

The Baystate employees, followed by other mourners, patted Nick's shoulder and touched the hands of Cindy and Frances as they walked away.

The house at 147 Royal Oaks was packed with people conversing and munching on food from a catered buffet. For Cindy and Frances the healing process had just begun!

When Jacki didn't show, Nick called her at home a few times. No answer. She must be sleeping.

CHAPTER 23

At first Nick dragged his feet on the Weiler Farms housing development in Hingham, immersed in grieving thoughts about his lost brother. What worsened the matter was Jacki's seemingly growing indifference toward him. Something was wrong. Exactly what he wasn't sure. Before long he'd have to confront her about it!

Early that summer of 1977 Nick had negotiated a sweetheart financing deal for the acquisition and site improvements of the Weiler Farms Estates in Hingham, Massachusetts. He and Chad had dubbed this name to the development before Chad's untimely death.

The land acquisition price was one million four hundred thousand dollars, and the improvements for roads, sidewalks, utilities, and other soft costs were projected at one million one hundred thousand, which included bringing in-town sewer to the lots. First Shore Bank was willing to lend one million eight hundred thousand to finance the two million five hundred thousand funding requirement and, once again, Carl Johnson who had sold the parcel to Baystate, stepped up to the plate, taking back a four-hundred-thousand-dollar purchase money mortgage at 10 percent interest. Of course, he had to subordinate his mortgage to the bank's position. That was sufficient because initial lot sales after mortgage releases would fund the project also. Once again no equity requirement from Nick.

Carl insisted this time on an additional kicker of 2 percent of the finished house selling price or 4 percent of raw lot sales to be paid at the time of conveyance to individual buyers. Nick had no choice knowing that "the man with the gold makes the rules." He could live with that.

The average house was priced at $139,900. First Shore Bank would offer an attractive end-loan package to the buyers. Baystate Builders as the developer would also act as general contractor. Nick projected a combined lot sales and construction profit of one million two hundred seventy-five thousand dollars on completion. If only Chad could be here to enjoy it, he sadly thought.

On a sunny and crisp autumn day in late October, Nick sat in the sales trailer parked at the front of the Weiler Farms site which he and Chad had moved on site in August. He was alone and had not yet decided how to properly market the development. Nothing had been sold in a few months. He was still preoccupied with his brother's death.

He sat at the desk in a state of oblivion, tapping his fingers on the table. A maze of thoughts ran from Chad to Jacki to the strong profit potential of this project. Then he called a few construction supers from telephone numbers on their resumes and made an interview appointment for the following week with one who sounded good. Leaning back in the swivel chair he stared into space. Chad will be hard to replace! Nick sighed uncontrollably.

Moments elapsed, and then suddenly someone rapped on the trailer door. It took Nick a few moments to snap out of his reverie, and by then the rapping had become a banging. Nick jumped to his feet and quickly opened the door.

A thin young man with curly black hair and thick glasses stared at Nick, inquiring, "Are you open for business? Can we see what you have available?" Nick did a double take. He looked just like Buddy Holly!

"Oh, of course," Nick replied. "I was on the phone. Please excuse me, and come right in."

The man at the door awkwardly stumbled up the trailer stairs and entered, followed by an attractive young woman and two straggling kids. The little girl with adorable blonde locks and a cute dimple was squeezing a Little People doll with both arms. "We've been riding by here for weeks and love this area," the wife went on to say.

After moments of discussion Nick learned that the man's name was Dr. John Golden and he had an extensive cardiology practice in Norwell. He and Adrian, an attorney, lived in Scituate with Mark and Hanna, their two children. They chomped at the bit to see the basic house plans. Nick was charming and made a superb sales presentation, showing them the site plan and eight alternative house plans with numerous elevations. Their excitement rose. Nick was impressed by this cute little family, the prototype upper-middle-class buyers.

Nick went on to explain the sales terms, finish

specifications, and possible delivery dates while the doctor, John, and Adrian listened with intense interest. "Now, which lot do you want?" Nick inquired. The couple zeroed in on a spectacular one-and-a-half-acre site with frontage on Golden Pond, as it was named. The kids paid no attention and fumbled with everything on Nick's desk. They were especially amused by the miniature concrete truck holding Nick's business cards.

They drove to the selected site in Nick's car and walked to the water's edge. The entire family was excited and Nick continued his sales pitch. They fell in love with the towering oaks, the view of the farm on the abutting land, and most of all the glimmering pond view. The day was exceptionally sunny and the water sparkled.

John whipped out his checkbook and asked, "How much of a deposit do you require, Nick?"

"Just give me a thousand dollars now to reserve it. Then we'll sign the P and S agreement next week." John didn't even review the price terms, he was so excited.

"I won't lose it? I mean, to a higher bidder?" John implored.

"No, no, that will secure it," Nick retorted. "It's your new home if you want it!"

The couple beamed with delight. As they drove back to the trailer to execute a reservation agreement, Nick noticed two more expensive cars parked by the trailer with people strolling the area. He had perked up out of his doldrums and was now exhilarated!

Nick went through a similar process with the recently arrived potential buyers and spent hours with them. As it turned out, one family was only window shopping, out for a ride.

However, the other family was comprised of a structural engineer, his wife, and son. He earned a ninety-thousand-dollar salary and was a partner in his firm. The couple was enthused and highly motivated.

They had sold their home in town two months ago and were anxious to replace it soon for income tax purposes. They also loved the setting, and Nick was confident they'd return soon with a deposit.

CHAPTER 24

At four p.m. Nick dragged himself into the trailer. He was fatigued from the hectic activity of the day unwinding on top of the tremendous stress piled on in the past few months. He flopped on the couch and began to doze off, thinking of the events of the afternoon. Something troubled him. Yes, it was his lack of interior design knowledge. Actually it was crude. Not his forte! He knew that he'd need a strong discipline in this field to be successful. The visual aspect is key to the sale. He began to doze, thinking that he needed assistance, but was stymied as to who to call.

Nick suddenly snapped out of it and jumped off the couch, fumbling through the yellow pages. He saw Delightful Designs, Designs of Grandeur, and then Noel Cardigan, Interior Design. "You describe it; we design it and more." The last entry caught his eye. It had an honest ring to it and he dialed the number. The phone was answered formally. "Hello, Noel Cardigan speaking, how may I help you?" Nick introduced himself and talked a bit about his project. "I can come now," Noel replied. Nick agreed and hung up.

Her soft voice and that final choice of words sent a tingling through Nick's groin area.

A half hour later, as Nick was beginning to doze again, the door flew open and Noel Cardigan casually walked in, introducing herself. Nick was stunned and momentarily speechless. She was the most beautiful woman he had ever laid eyes on. She had large brown eyes accentuating a nearly wrinkle-free, soft face with gorgeous features. Dressed in a navy blue suit, her curves protruded in all the right places.

Nick finally regained his composure and tried to act businesslike. Noel did the same and they proceeded to discuss Nick's design requirements in depth. They hit it off well and decided to try out the relationship on the Weiler Farms deal. For an hour afterward they talked about their lives in general and then departed. Nick mused. She's pretty sharp and seems quite creative. I might have lucked out!

CHAPTER 25

May 1978

The BMW slowly meandered into the parking lot as its gleaming red finish shone brightly in the reflection of the neon sign of the Mi Casa Club. The woman alighted from her shining mass of expensive metal and handed the keys to the valet.

"Buenos noches," the valet proclaimed in perfect Spanish. "Will you be staying long, senorita?"

"No, amigo!" she responded.

"I will park it in front, senorita, and watch it closely."

She handed him a twenty-dollar bill while saying, "Gracias, senor." Then shook his hand. Her BMW E23 would be protected like a baby! This was a tough neighborhood. She'd been here before.

The doors swung open as the woman sauntered her way into the club and down the open aisle between the crowded bar and densely occupied tables. She half saluted Hernando, the bartender, who nodded with a grin and pointed toward an empty table, which she walked to quickly. After hanging her Fisher coat on the back of a chair, she crossed her shapely legs, with her short dress rising to mid-thigh level.

The lights were dim and the Latin musical sound of castanets, drums, and percussion pervaded the entire room. In a far corner she noticed a small wooden dance floor where two South American couples were grinding to the beat. One man was slowly moving his leg into his curvy partner's groin area as she swayed back and forth.

After a few moments, Hernando left the bar and approached her table carrying a Kahlua sombrero, which he carefully placed in front of her, smoothing her napkin while the pair exchanged the usual accolades concerning their respective appearances.

Hernando then whispered in her ear as her blue eyes gleamed. She then uttered a few inaudible Spanish words back to him and they both chuckled with laughter. She slowly sipped the Kahlua as Hernando walked away and disappeared in the crowd.

A few moments later she glanced toward the rear of the spacious lounge and noticed Hernando discreetly talking to two men at a back table. As they were talking one of the men glanced over at her and smiled. She smiled back briefly, then turned her view toward the dance floor.

Suddenly the music blared, a strong beat pounded, and the lights dimmed further as a set of strobe lights flashed through the crowd. Many couples rushed to the dance floor swaying their hips. The excitement level rose throughout the darkened room.

A hand grabbed the woman's arm and began to ease her from her seat. She looked up at the tall, dark-skinned man who was wearing a Panama hat and shiny silk shirt. He was drunk, and when she said, "No thanks!" he continued to urge her on."You and I can make good moves, muchacha."

"No!" she firmly insisted.

The man who had smiled at her earlier stepped out of the crowd and placed a hand on the shoulder of the drunken Latino, who quickly turned, ready for action. When he saw who it was, the Latino grinned sheepishly. "No problem, Juan Carlos, just having some fun. The muchacha is playing hard to get."

"I don't think so, amigo. Get your fucking manos off her and go back to the bar or I'll cut them off right here and use them for swizzle sticks!"

Juan Carlos was an extremely feared man in the Latino community and was known to carry out his threats. The tall man immediately apologized to Juan Carlos and the woman. He hurriedly walked toward the exit, leaving the club.

Juan Carlos pulled out the chair across from the woman and sat down. "That man is a snake. You would shudder if you knew of his business. I am surprised that he is still alive," he said. The woman didn't want to know and began to tremble, but suppressed it. She desperately wanted to leave this vile place, but couldn't yet. She needed it!"You look very beautiful this evening. I am glad to see you again. That coat is exquisite, senora. Your husband, he does very well, no?" She tensed, wishing she had never worn it to this place. Where was her mind this evening? It was obviously hazed.

"He does OK, but this coat came from my dead aunt's

estate," she lied."Well, she had good taste," Juan Carlos replied. "What can I do for you tonight senora, hermosa?"

"I need more, Juan. Tonight! May I call you Juan? Is that OK?"

"Si, call me anything you'd like. We are amigos."

Right! Sure! Jacki didn't like him much. It was only business!"How much can you spend?" Juan Carlos inquired.

"Same as last time, five hundred dollars," she replied.He nodded and excused himself, heading for the men's room.

Another drink was served momentarily compliments of Juan Carlos. She sipped it as she waited eagerly while watching the dance scene. Then waited for his return which seemed like an eternity. She needed a fix right now!

Juan Carlos slowly walked back across the room, exchanging greetings and embraces with many people before he sat down facing the woman. "In a few minutes I will slip you a pouch under the table. You will place the cash inside and hand it back to me. I will then replace the cash with a package and slip it back to you. Put it in your purse and please return the pouch."

The transaction was carried off with extreme precision, except that Juan Carlos rubbed her leg and inner thigh below the table after handing her the pouch. She wanted to spit in his face, but refrained. She needed the pills badly! The bag of four-milligram Dilaudid and one-milligram Xanax pills was placed by Jacki neatly in her purse.

"Thank you, my dear," Juan Carlos uttered with a smile. "I hope to see you again soon."

Jacki forced a smile as they departed. Oh, how she loathed that man.

Outside the club, the valet retrieved her car, saying, "Buenos noches, senorita." Jacki nodded and murmured obscenities as she slipped behind the wheel and sped away toward home. She had a "monkey on her back" and was disgusted with herself, but couldn't stop!

CHAPTER 26

Nick was away in New York meeting with potential investors for some new projects. Jacki was safe for now, but the addiction was mushrooming.

For hours Nick had met with wealthy businessmen to discuss investing in his projects. He knew that there was a huge market for housing in New England, both in single-family home subdivisions and in condominium developments. His dream was to build a company similar to Kaufman and Broad or U.S. Homes. These behemoths built thousands of homes each year.

Being a little early in the process, Nick had built a bit less than one hundred single-family houses, but had three hundred more at various stages in the approval process. They humored him on Sixth Avenue in Manhattan and really weren't interested in this neophyte. Although two of the partners sensed a strong business acumen in Nick and a brilliant knowledge of the business, the group as a whole turned him down. They had financed the likes of Kaufman and Broad to the tune of millions of dollars, but this man, Nick Packard, was unproved. Many builders had achieved his level and some much higher! They didn't know his capabilities. He was smart, but was he savvy enough? They liked his style, but weren't willing to commit at this time.

"Come back after you've successfully built and sold, say, a thousand houses, and we'll talk again," one member said. Nick casually arose and thanked them for taking their time to meet with him and proudly exited the conference room.

That night he stayed over at the Helmsley Palace and, after receiving two Michelobs in a chrome ice bucket adorned with a rose from room service, proceeded to map out his strategy. He had another meeting in the morning at Chase Manhattan Bank with Nita Kensington, Mike's cousin.

Probably no deal with her either, but exposure and possibly future business! Nick thought as he drained the two beers and then went to bed. He planned on staying in New York for four days and had five more meetings scheduled.

CHAPTER 27

Jacki went straight home to Milton from the Mi Casa Club and downed two four-milligram Dilaudid pills and a Xanax immediately. Her addiction was so strong that not even a herd of bulls could have prevented her from taking these pills. She slowly began feeling high for hours. Everything was so good and so right! Even Carlos was a good guy! Every guy wants to cop a little feel now, and then and he does supply her with precisely what she craves, Jacki assured herself. She soon fell asleep for a long period of time, but kept awakening then nodding off because of the opiates.

When she awoke seven hours later she was losing that grandiose sense of feeling good as the opiates wore off. She took more and lay in bed in her splendor for another day, downing two Dilaudid and two one-milligram Xanax at intervals. She was heightening the addiction but didn't realize how much. Her mind deceivingly convinced her that things were so good. She had financial security, a great husband, and she now felt better than ever. What more could she ask for? She decided that she'd cut down on the pills and would live happily with Nick. Her addiction would be controlled!

On the final day before Nick was due home she realized that she had taken a huge portion of the pills, and in addition had dropped many in the toilet by mistake in her drug-induced state and began taking them sparingly. She needed another supply and that would take care of it for a long time, but she had to get them today before Nick arrived home. She became paranoid as she worried that maybe she couldn't reach Juan Carlos today and she'd run out. The opiates were wearing off and she was going into withdrawal. She started shaking and quickly got dressed for the first time in days. Jacki unsteadily walked the stairs to the garage and fell into the BMW. She proceeded to drive to a public telephone booth down the street where she dialed the Mi Casa Club. A voice on the other end said, "Hola, Casa."

"Please, I have to speak with Juan Carlos! Now! Is he there?" Jacki desperately asked. "Hold on, honey," the man bellowed.

Juan quickly answered the phone. "What can I do for you, muchacha?"

"Juan, this is Jacki. I need some right away," she stated in desperation. "Where can I deliver it?" Juan queried. "You can't come here. It's too hot!"

She was unstable and gave Juan her address in Milton. Jacki was smart and never under any other circumstances would have given him the address, but she couldn't overcome the addiction and had to have the drugs!

"I'll be there sometime today," he said teasingly, knowing that she'd be chomping at the bit to get his wonder drugs and be quite vulnerable.

CHAPTER 28

Six hours later, Juan Carlos approached the Milton house in a baby blue Cadillac and rapped on Jacki's door. She woke from a stupor upon hearing the noise and put on her robe. Unsteadily she made her way to the front door and opened it. With no salutation, she beckoned Juan to come into the foyer. His coal-black hair was in a ponytail and he grinned as he entered.

"Muchacha, I didn't know exactly what you wanted," he lied. "I've brought you amphetamines. That's what you wanted? Si?"

Jacki's heart sank like a rock in the ocean. "Amphetamines! You know what I've bought from you before. Cut the shit, you asshole, I mean, really, Juan. Where are the Dilaudid? Xanax? Why did you come here, Juan? Why?"

"I don't have much anymore. The DEA is pressuring our supply," he lied. "I wanted to tell you in person, not over the phone. We're being watched. A few amigos have been busted," he lied again.

"Juan, I need some now! I'll pay anything for them! I

have the money, you fucker." Her craving had enraged her and caused her to talk out of character.

"But, muchacha, it's not me. Money can't buy what I don't have."

"You have some. You must!" Jacki cried."Well, maybe a little, but it's now too expensive."

"How much, Juan?"

"Five thousand dollars for a hundred pills. I'm sorry, but I can do nothing about it. Ah, if only I could," Juan uttered in his manipulating style, as the snake slithered through the grass. Juan knew that he'd lose his customer in the future, but so what? Her body drove him crazy.

Jacki wanted it so bad that she went for it, even though she didn't have that amount of money readily available. She opened her robe partially and exposed her sizable breasts. It was just what Juan was longing for. She had never done this before, but her addiction drove her on. She loathed this man, but he was in control.

Juan Carlos was paranoid about rape, and when Jacki walked to the kitchen for a drink of water to moisten her dry throat, he flipped the record button on a tape recorder resting in his shoulder bag.

Jacki returned from the kitchen with her bathrobe opened wider, exposing more of her naked body to Juan. "You're turning me on," she lied, in an attempt to get the drugs for a reasonable price, not the five-thousand-dollar thievery price, which she didn't have. Oh, how she hated this man, but she was so addicted that she would do anything to get them.

He played it out. "But muchacha, I need cash, it's my

business."Jacki was persistent and thought otherwise as she stepped forward and massaged Juan's groin area. Unzipping his pants, she unleashed him and softly stroked a few times, teasing him greatly. Then she stopped abruptly and said, "This is wrong, Juan. I can't do it!"

Juan was excited at this point and softened up. He would go a long ways to have this woman and knew that the time was up for gamesmanship. He said, "OK, senorita," and pulled a plastic bag from his shoulder bag. It was stuffed with pills that she was quite sure were Dilaudid and Xanax.

"You can have these for two thousand dollars and will get them later on, after we go upstairs."

"No, Juan, the usual five hundred is more than enough, considering what we're about to do."

Juan changed his tough stance and said, "OK, OK!" while Jacki sighed with extreme relief under her breath. She only had $510 in the house. She beamed with excitement and, uncharacteristically, stooped down and took him completely. She knew she had to complete the transaction to get the drugs.

He moaned as she went on, then stood her up and rubbed her beneath her robe with his finger. Jacki unexpectedly got wet and said, "Oh, do it, Juan, do it!" He led her by the hand upstairs, where he rightly assumed the bedroom would be and, after carefully setting his bag right beside the bed, lay her down, spreading her legs and rubbing more for a moment. She was on the birth control pill and knew his kind would not tolerate a condom. She'd have to run the risk of disease and her obsessed mind justified it. The drugs were totally in control!

Juan soon lay on top of her and thrust deeply inside. She pretended to like it and moaned softly, praying for it to end. And finally it did, after seeming like an eternity to Jacki. It was over for the moment, and Juan lifted his shoulder bag from beside the bed and put the bag of pills on the night table.

He wasn't finished and kissed her on the lips. She felt so disgustingly dirty and guilty but could do nothing about it. Juan was still in ecstasy and wanted it again. Frustrated, Jacki complied and he climaxed again. She lied once again, saying, "That was hot, Juan!" He lay beside her totally spent, then got up, dressed, and handed the bag of pills to her as she retrieved the money stashed under her pillow and slipped it to him.

Juan left with both "heads" satisfied, and Jacki started by downing two Dilaudid with the Xanax. Both had achieved their goals in a sense, or so it seemed. Her pretty, youthful face soon beamed with drug-induced euphoria. She knew that she had to wind down and sleep for a while before too long because Nick would be home tomorrow.

CHAPTER 29

August 1978

Months had elapsed since that horrendous evening with Juan Carlos. It had slipped by unnoticed on Nick's part. No evidence of what had transpired ever emerged and Nick was completely clueless. Jacki restrained herself and kept her visits to the Mi Casa Club on an infrequent and totally business basis, rejecting Juan's continuing attempts to seduce her. She struggled to restrict herself to usage during the workdays until three p.m. with some success, but it was very difficult to deal with the withdrawal at night. She did appear to be normal, though, by eight p.m., Nick's usual time of arrival home. She longed for the times when Nick would travel away on business and would stay high all the time. She could do that because she didn't work and the couple's now sizable income allowed her freedom to spend and not be noticed.

The effect on their social life was significant, but Nick just blew it off. He was so busy and naively assumed that the decrease in their sex life was natural over time.

Lately a strange feeling was overtaking her and her

stomach had been bulging for a while. She became paranoid! Am I pregnant? she thought. It's not by Nick! He didn't want children until he could devote quality time to them which would eventually come with a maturing business. He didn't trust the pill and used condoms to be safe. Having children was sacrosanct to him.

The realization of fear ran through her innermost awareness. Had that animal, Juan, impregnated her? Her stinging fears were realized first by a home test and then confirmed by her doctor. She was pregnant! My luck, and I was on the pill! she thought. She finally realized that her drug addiction caused her to forget many things. She probably had slipped and missed taking it during that hazy drug-induced period when Nick was away in New York.

On a Thursday evening in late August, Nick came home after an arduous and extremely stressful day at work. After dinner, he pushed his chair back on two legs and said, "Jacki, why are you getting such a bloated stomach? You've always been concerned about your weight. You're not pregnant, are you? Or, is it that you've become so complacent with our marriage? I really don't mind. You're still beautiful to me!"

Suddenly, Jacki burst out in tears, flooding her face, and she couldn't stop crying. Nick meandered around the table and tried to console her. "I am pregnant, Nick!" She proceeded to tell the truth, partially changing the story.

Nick seriously listened and was in complete shock. Two distinct problems arose. One was her addiction to drugs, which he could deal with, but the other, her allegedly being raped by Juan Carlos, was abominable! He demanded that she tell him where the Mi Casa Club was located and became blinded with fury. Silently, he walked out of the room and took ten thousand dollars from his office wall safe on the way to the garage.

CHAPTER 30

At 9:57 p.m. the garage doors rolled up and Nick's Mercedes W 123 screeched out and down the long winding driveway while the expensive mass of metal laid rubber around the corner, headed along Route 138 toward Boston. He was so distraught that he felt like he should go to the Mi Casa Club alone and kill this animal, but that would be like walking into a pit of snakes and wasn't rational for his own good.

He decided to go first to that place in Boston where he had gone with his old friend, Richard, years earlier. Richard had a problem to "resolve" over a debt owed to him! When he and Nick were out having a few beers one night they stopped there. Richard had introduced Nick to a few characters and had disappeared into the back room while Nick waited exchanging small-talk, nervously, to these men.

Later Richard had explained very little to Nick, except that he was making arrangements to collect a debt and this was where people can go to assure collection or buy other services! Nick was desperately in need of these services now and slowly pulled up to the curb, entering that same building from years ago, but only after identifying himself as Richard H.'s friend. Inside a group of men talking in Italian were sitting around a few tables and drinking. They pointed to a rear door which Nick knocked on, then entered after hearing "Yeah?" from the inner room.

Inside, a man sitting at a desk was yelling obscenities loudly at two other hulking men, one with slick black hair and the other with long hair and a mustache. Both were wearing packed shoulder holsters. The atmosphere was tense, but Nick managed to state what happened quite smoothly.

"What the fuck do you want from us?" bellowed the apparent boss sitting at the desk."I need your protection when I confront this character who raped my wife," Nick humbly requested.

"It'll cost you, man. How much cash will you pay?"

Nick offered five hundred dollars for each man sent. They all laughed heartily! "Don't waste our time. There's the fucking door!" the boss responded.

"Now, wait a minute. How much. then?" Nick inquired.

"You give us a thousand dollars per man on the crew. We'll send, ah, four men. If they have to get involved, you'll owe another five thousand dollars, or maybe more. And you'll give us nine thousand dollars now. Come back later to get the five thousand refunded if it goes smoothly. You'll go inside the club and two men will stay with you inside his office. The others will remain close, outside at the bar. I wouldn't expect too much trouble. They know who we are!" he bragged. "He'll be roughed up, but no physical action on your part. Capisci?" Nick agreed.

Nick, after thirty minutes or so, slowly pulled alongside

of the Latino club with a car following him. He noticed that the doors of the club were open due to the unusually warm fall weather. It was alive with people. As he cruised he saw a half-empty lot and pulled in to park. He wished at that moment that he had a gun. He would blow away this excuse of a man without a second thought. This Latino pig will pay. I would go down fighting him, but have to restrain myself if possible. Who the hell does he think he is? Raping my wife! He was in great emotional pain!

Nick, blinded by rage, not knowing what he would do inside, thought that he might have to leave in a flash and backed out of the space. He drove down the street, parking a distance away instead. He was so blinded by fury that he didn't even care that his expensive car stood out under the illumination of the street lights. He didn't give a fuck. It's only a car!

As he walked to the club he passed a few hookers and, then, some unsavory-looking characters. He just looked them in the eye and walked on, intent upon confrontation. His usually good judgment was mired by anger. He knew that he shouldn't be here but couldn't stop himself.

Two of the Italian crew, the toughest-looking members, got out of the car and talked to the bouncers at the door. The Latinos shook their heads as if understanding something. The warning was enough for them. The crew at the door accompanied Nick inside while the third stood outside the building on the sidewalk. The fourth man sat in the driver's seat of their car holding a sawed-off shotgun!

As they walked through the doors of the club they moved between two Latino hombres who fingered their side belt holsters under their coats for effect. They seemed to expect trouble from these angry-looking gringos. Nick became nervous but realized that he couldn't back down now.

Nick cautiously walked to the long bar and asked for Juan Carlos. After many moments of waiting he was told by the bartender that Juan would see him now and to go through the door in the rear of the club. The three Italian crew members momentarily waited at the bar and attracted much attention. The area cleared out around them! Nick's anxiety became more heightened as he walked toward the back followed by his protection. His mind spun while musing on how to handle it!

Juan Carlos knew big trouble was at hand and had summoned three of his soldiers, each carrying weapons, virtual cannons. He took no chances, not knowing what these ballsy gringos would do.

As Nick and the crew entered the room behind the door of the club's office, Juan diplomatically greeted them and said, "Sit down, amigos. How may I assist you?"

This man is exceptionally smooth, Nick thought. He will try to con me!

"So you raped and impregnated my wife, you pig!" Nick bellowed.

"Is that a question or a statement?" Juan asked, showing no fear or remorse as his soldiers placed hands on their obviously hidden pieces.

"Don't get frisky, fellas. These are my friends," and he swept his hand in front of the Italians. "You wouldn't want to fuck with them. They'll eat you alive and you know it!" Nick bellowed.

"You're, as they say, 'barking up the wrong tree.' Yes, I had her, but at her request, and she said that she was on the pill," Juan retorted.

Nick suddenly became violent and swept the top of a nearby table in the office clear of its contents, including liquor bottles, glasses, and ashtrays. Glass flew in all directions as he screamed, "You fucking animal!" Juan's henchmen drew their guns and cocked the hammers. They would have killed him in a heartbeat, but hesitated because they knew they'd be slaughtered. The crew pulled their guns and quickly overtook them and slapped them around. Juan quickly made a hand gesture to stop. He didn't know for sure if his gang could recuperate, but couldn't afford any trouble. Besides, the office was full of dope. He couldn't afford any police raid. There was silence for moments as both groups stared at each other. Now the Italians did the cocking against Latino heads.

Juan exited while the Latinos apologized and tried to calm Nick. Outside, a few other Latinos watched the back office door and the front door upon Juan's orders. They were no match for the Mafia! And, this man wouldn't be here faking Mafia support with a group of his buddies! Would he? The fourth Italian crew member had come inside to the bar and glared at Juan Carlos as he walked by. He had the sawed-off under a long coat. He was ready to barge in the back if Nick and his crew didn't return after a few more minutes. He followed Juan Carlos back to support the three others in the office.

Juan Carlos returned to the back office with a tape cassette recorder in his hand while guns were aimed at him. He stood beside Nick and said, "You calm down and listen to this." He flipped the play button on the recorder and what Nick heard next sickened him to the depths of his being. Nick recognized her voice. It was Jacki's voice unmistakably. No urgency for drugs showed in it!

It started with sounds of a zipper being pulled down followed by sounds of Juan groaning with pleasure. And it went on, with Jacki saying, "Oh, do it, Juan!" and then her moans softly echoed. Finally, Nick heard, "That was hot, Juan." Much dubbing had been done to the tape and it painted the intended picture. It sent disillusionment through his minds ear.

Nick stopped struggling and lay back in despair. He had heard enough. It was Jacki's voice throughout, unequivocally. Anger ensued. "Fuck her!" he uttered. "Well spoken," said Juan. "Let me go. I'm out of here!" Nick bellowed, and the Italians relaxed their grips upon Juan's advice to his gang to give it up. One wrong move could have caused them to be shot right there in the club and taken out to Boston Harbor to be disposed of. They were no match against the Italians! Nick held fast.

"Leave, amigo, with this knowledge, and never return again. Comprende?" Juan said.

"Yo comprendo, you fucking slime!" Nick screamed in anger. Juan Carlos winced but smartly let Nick walk away. The Mafia crew warned them all to stay away from Jacki and never to let her in the club again. If it ever happened again they'd all be buried not far away, with Juan Carlo impaled on a pole over their graves! Juan Carlos agreed, bobbing his head at Nick and the crew. He had had his enjoyment and won anyway! Nick could achieve no more!

Nick sensed that he was now safe, and fearlessly toppled every beer bottle and glass in his path as he exited, releasing his anxiety. Patrons screamed as liquid poured in all directions and Nick threw them the bird. He strolled outside the front club door followed by the entire crew and thanked them. Taking their time, they left after a while. The Latino men outside held back cautiously.

Nick hopped in his Mercedes down the street and knew that he had no case, but only against Jacki. He drove the streets for hours tearfully wishing it weren't true, but needed no more proof.

CHAPTER 31

The Mercedes slowly wound up the S-shaped driveway in Milton. It was like a warship entering the harbor limping after defeat in battle. Nick alighted from his vehicle, then kicked the trash cans inside the garage three times. He stomped inside the house. Jacki was waiting for him at the head of the stairs. She was white-faced with fear and anticipation. It was now 1:37 a.m."How could you do this to me? Worse than the guns aimed at me tonight, I had to hear your voice asking the scum of the earth to fuck you! You are pitiful! And I feel sorry for you."

"Oh, Nick, it's not how you think!" She had been a victim of a very serious drug habit, but couldn't express the total loss of control caused by it. "What are you saying, Nick?"

"Cut the shit, Jacki, I heard you calmly asking that animal to 'do you,' and telling him how hot it was and much more. Your voice, Jacki, your voice!"

Jacki was hesitant for a moment, realizing that Juan Carlos had probably taped it all, erasing all but the sex parts. Then she came clean with the truth and the events of the horror unraveled. What she tried to explain, but couldn't explain well enough, was the power of the addiction, to the point of doing what disgusted her and to further act it out in order to get the drugs.

Jacki knew that Nick could never understand the power of the addiction and she didn't blame him. She had gone too far to get the drugs. She needed help and would try to get it professionally, but sadly, it was over with Nick.

Nick listened to her side intently, but couldn't believe that she would do what she did if she really loved him. All attempts on her part to explain were considered feeble by Nick after hearing Jacki on the recorder. The damage was irreparable.

In the morning, reticent to Jacki's pleadings, Nick packed his clothes and left the Milton house. She was pregnant, yes, but not by him! He couldn't deal with it and moved into a partially finished spec house at Weiler Farms Estates and took residence temporarily. Nick decided not to go back for the five-thousand-dollar refund and vowed never to use the Mafia's services again. He might owe them indefinitely if he did!

Jacki, with a baby in her womb, stayed at the Milton house, which eventually Nick deeded to her, furniture and all. He also put a flat sum of money in trust to help her start over. The stipulation attached was that no money would be released until she was drug free for at least a year. Jacki was honorable and gave birth to a baby girl named Nicole. The child might not be Nick's, but it was hers. She did seek help for the addiction.

CHAPTER 32

Spring 1980

The door of the Mercedes-Benz slammed shut and sped away from the sidewalk on Newbury Street in the Back Bay section of Boston, where Nick stood admiring the brick building facades, many with huge full-length bay windows. What ambiance. Maybe Boston should be my future focus! Tommy Fletcher has it by the balls! My old college buddy. It's been fourteen years!

Nick had read about Tommy's success in the Boston Globe and called him to say hi and set up a meeting. His secretary had arranged it. He walked down the stairs of Tommy's office townhouse which housed his real estate operation, Fletcher Realty. The stairs were steep going down and Nick almost tripped.

He approached the receptionist, who said, "May I help you, sir?" The attractive red-haired lady had such a nice personality. Nick liked her immediately. "Nick Packard. Here to meet Tommy Fletcher."

"Oh yes, Mr. Packard, he's been waiting for you."

Nick remembered that Tommy was a great charmer!

Liz led him down a narrow corridor and ushered him to an armchair facing Tommy, who was in the middle of a telephone conversation. Nick waited fifteen minutes for Tommy to wrap up the call. After all, Tommy was anxiously waiting for him to arrive!

Nick looked around the room as he waited for Tommy and noticed a beautiful chandeliered ceiling adorned with corniced moldings. The floors were a handsome polished oak. Tommy's desk was made of mahogany and on it rested a huge brass lamp with a green glass shade. Even the interior displayed antiquity.

Tommy swiveled in his large oak chair. He was a large man with thick blonde hair and his stomach shook and rolled as he hung the receiver and laughed heartily. "Nick, old buddy, it's been eons. How the hell are you?" The pair stood and hugged each other in a masculine embrace.

"I'm fine, Tommy. You?" "Oh, I'm feeling well. Things are good!" "You married Anna way back then. How is she? And, how many babies?" Nick asked.

"Two, Nick. Seven-year-old boy and an eighteen-year-old daughter. The lights of my life. You, Nick?"

"I'm dating now, but am legally separated from my wife. No children. I'll tell you more later. You won't believe it!"

"Did you find a space, Nick?" "No, my super, Shaun, drove me here and he's cruising around."

"I heard through the grapevine that we're in the same business?" Tommy inquired.

"That we are, Tommy. My company has been building houses in suburbia," Nick replied. "We've built about a hundred and seventy-five houses since I left Public Accounting in '74. But that's nothing like you've accomplished I hear, Tommy."

"You've acquired many in-town apartment buildings, I understand."

"A few, Nick," Tommy responded modestly. "What do you have to talk about?"

"Tommy, let's get to the point. I put a hundred-unit apartment complex in Stoneham under P and S last week. Great location close to Route 128. I need a partner with cash and good credit for a condo conversion. I have a few options in place now, but would like to rekindle old times with you if we can come to terms. What do you think, Tommy?"

Tommy squirmed a bit. It was now all business. "Tell me more, buddy. Why should I get involved?"

"Tommy, a hundred units under agreement for twenty-five thousand dollars per unit, with a rehab cost of about twelve thousand per unit for improvements and soft costs. We can sell the units for fifty to fifty-five thousand dollars per unit. That's a minimum of five million dollars sellout, and after six percent commissions of three hundred thousand, we can net a cool million dollars."

"How do we split, Nick?" "Fifty-fifty, of course," Nick replied. "But my cash, Nick, and my credit!" Tommy said, with a trace of indignation. "But my finish construction experience and financial expertise, and my cash also," Nick retorted. "Take it or leave it, friend. You're not the only source, you know."

"And I get the six percent brokerage commissions. Right, Nick?"

"Of course, Tommy. Who else?"

"Let's visit the site sometime this week, Nick."

"Give me a date, partner," Nick responded.

"You know, Nick, I always liked you. You're smart. I remember those reports you wrote in college . They were very impressive and creative. Miss Tolman liked them too. She used to fix her eyes all over you when you stood before the class reading them." The two men laughed and Tommy raised his eyebrows few times.

Nick then told the story of how he met Noel at the sales trailer and how Jacki had unintentionally gotten impregnated by the drug dealer. Then the horrible night at the Mi Casa Club. Tommy was shocked by the story. "All that behind you now?" Tommy inquired somewhat skeptically."No problem, Tommy, a few years have passed. Everything put to bed!" Nick answered.

He went on to tell Tommy that he and Noel had been dating for a year and were deeply in love. Nick believed that he had finally found a lifetime match and felt very secure. They planned to marry soon and have children.

Tommy patted Nick on the back. "I like you Nick. You're a survivor, like me."

The next day Nick drove Tommy to the Stoneham apartment complex where they walked through the building and were able to talk the super into showing them a few units. The property location, apartment sizes (780 to 910 square feet) and amenity package impressed Tommy. He lingered with Nick after a prolonged walk of the site. They talked by the pool for an hour engaging in much reminiscing of their youth together.

Both men were on a high. The deal might be a major score! One million dollars was a bonanza for either man. "Let's do it. I'm in!" bellowed Tommy. The two old buddies from MBU were off to a start.

In the following weeks Tommy and Nick negotiated a three-million-one-hundred-thousand-dollar acquisition and improvement loan and a three-hundred-thousand-dollar purchase money second mortgage with the seller. Tommy and Nick contributed seventy-five thousand each in cash and they closed the purchase, and soon thereafter began the improvements. The financing required personal signatures and Tommy gave a second mortgage on his Commonwealth Avenue property as side collateral.

The project then took its course with every nuance imaginable, from whining customers and kids to wrinkled sheets in the model condo units. And the wrinkles weren't from inadequate ironing! There were, however, many excited buyers and the project became a great success.

The deal proved to be the right move, propelling the partners to new levels. The condo concept had arrived just as Danny's girlfriend, Lynn, had profoundly alluded to in 1967 at the Ocean Club when she referred to her father's West Coast success with "condoms or something like that"!

CHAPTER 33

After 60 percent unit sales had been achieved in Stoneham the new partners both had the idea to build new condo units in townhouse clusters in the one hundred twenty-five thousand to one hundred sixty thousand dollars price range.

One afternoon in late September 1981, Tommy got a call from a broker in Salem, Massachusetts, who had a fifteen-acre parcel of vacant land in Beverly, Massachusetts, under an exclusive listing. According to the broker an informal discussion had taken place between the seller and a few planning board members, wherein the board members gave a nod to a maximum of ninety units which could be built "by right" with no variances required, but as usual a special permit had to be obtained. The asking price was one million one hundred thousand dollars.

Tommy's face lit up (this sounds great…ninety units at one hundred fifty thousand dollars…a thirteen million five hundred thousand dollar sellout! Can I handle it?). His calculator was on fire!

The big guy knew that a townhouse-zoned land parcel

close to Route 128 with informal planning board approval for twelve thousand dollars per unit was a great find. The land had just been listed on the market and he knew it would go fast. The greater Boston residential real estate market was becoming hot as a pistol despite the high prevailing interest rates.

They excitedly agreed to meet at the site the next day and Alan, the broker, gave Tommy detailed directions. Tommy hung up the receiver and quickly donned his new sport coat. He patted his fat belly as he smiled with delight. He wasn't waiting until tomorrow to see this gem.

Tommy's assistant called the Newbury Street Garage with an order to "bring down Mr. Fletcher's BMW."

Tommy hurried out the front door and walked briskly down the street to the garage. As the silver gray BMW screeched out of the garage Tommy could think of nothing but the deal. Dusk was near, but he couldn't wait until tomorrow.

Dusk was upon him as he drove up to the site. As he walked it he could see that the gently rolling site consisted mainly of grassy fields, which was basically upland with no ledge outcroppings. Ahead of him was a thick group of trees. It was now dark and he hesitated as he heard branches snap in the thicket. Suddenly, a dark mass moved at the tree line!

Tommy backed up a ways and pulled his Wilson baseball bat from the backseat of his car, shuddering with anticipation. The big guy then walked slowly toward the shadow and implored, "Who's there?" No answer. He yelled louder, "Who's there?" Still no answer!

The black mass edged its way up toward Tommy, dangling a large object. Tommy stood ready to swing the bat, but in a flash the black mass was facing him closely and the object strewn upon him. It tangled him up as he frantically tried to free himself.

Then a hearty laugh filled the air as Nick pulled the blanket off Tommy and cried, "Tommy, you snake! Trying to do the deal without me, huh?"

"Et tu, Brutus, or should I say Nickus?" Tommy joked with relief. The two old friends roared with laughter until tears filled their eyes.

"My car is parked over there. You didn't see it when you drove up?" said Nick."No, I was too engrossed in the deal," Tommy laughed. Again the old friends roared with laughter.

They soon got serious and walked the open areas of the site. The bright moonlight provided the basic outline of the site and they knew it was a winner! Nick said, "Tommy, I guess you got a call from Alan too. The site is ours. Don't you agree?" They both stared at the steady stream of headlights on Route 128 a short distance away and accessible from an entrance to the highway nearby.

"Great access!" Tommy bellowed, but said no more.

They walked on, with unintended identical sport coats and striped ties, looking like the Bobbsey Twins.

CHAPTER 34

The following week Nick and Tommy made a joint offer of eight hundred thousand dollars for the Beverly parcel, which was refused outright. The sellers countered at one million fifty thousand and they finally settled on nine hundred seventy-five thousand, with financing and special permit contingencies. The partners assumed an approximate one hundred fifty thousand dollar down payment would be required at P and S execution. Tommy and Nick would each ante up seventy-five thousand once again.

In the following weeks they met with the same bank officer who had financed the Stoneham deal. They had established credibility and were offered eight hundred seventy-five thousand dollars financing for the land acquisition. However, they did have to pledge their remaining interests in the Stoneham condo project, now dubbed Kingsley Estates, to the bank. Again, they had to sign personally and Tommy was required to pledge his interest in, now, two of his Commonwealth Avenue apartment buildings. Tommy was quite unhappy about the additional burden on him, and not Nick, who shared equal ownership!

Nick engaged engineering studies for soils bearing and wetlands studies which proved acceptable. He hired the civil engineering/architectural firm of Rodman & Associates to lay out the buildings on the site that maximized at eighty-three units. A bit short of the original plan, but it would do. Both Tommy and Nick agreed.

They hired a general contractor to perform construction management and price out construction of the eighty-three wood-frame townhouse units with a two- and three-bedroom mix. The six million six hundred sixty-three thousand dollar construction estimate was in line and included site work.

Fletcher Realty's lead broker, Nelson Thatcher, undertook a rigid marketing study and priced the two-bedrooms at an average of one hundred thirty-four thousand dollars, and the threes at one hundred forty-two thousand five hundred dollars. The total project costs, including soft costs, were estimated at nine million one hundred ninety-one thousand dollars.

The projected total sellout came out at eleven million three hundred fifty-four thousand dollars, and after 4 percent commissions of four hundred fifty-four thousand dollars to Fletcher Realty, the project would net approximately one million seven hundred and nine thousand dollars to Nick and Tommy. The two old friends, now partners, were in awe!

The profits would not be received soon enough. This was a minimum two-year project from start to finish. The partners eked out their now fifty-thousand-dollar down payments and closed the Beverly land acquisition, but they knew that they needed more cash flow to operate and expand.

Kingsley Estates was well under way and the Beverly site secured. They now needed smaller deals with relatively quick cash flow. Headed into 1982 they were confident this was possible.

A major real estate boom was under way. In Boston, brownstones were doubling in value within a year and condo conversions were surging to new heights in terms of square foot selling prices. Commercial real estate prices were following suit. In suburbia, a like trend was in force! Single-family houses were relentlessly sought and new developments sprang up everywhere.

The old friends were on a roll!

CHAPTER 35

The old college buddies and new business partners opened a real estate development office in the spring of 1982 after the purchase of the Beverly land parcel. They proceeded to set up a sub-chapter S corporation in the name of Boomer Development Associates. After all, it was the baby boom that had fueled the explosion in real estate.

The office occupied the entire second floor of Tommy's Newbury Street buildings. It was located directly over the brokerage and management offices and was connected to the first floor by a private stairway to facilitate the flow of outside professionals serving the now involved development operation.

There were architects and structural engineers, civil engineers, environmental and mechanical engineers, all visiting Boomer at times. Then there were the general contractors with their subs on occasion in addition to bankers, attorneys, insurance agents, and others. The stream of people providing indispensable development services was endless.

Nick and, occasionally, Tommy coordinated them very

well. They met often huddling over schematic drawings for the many planned projects and construction drawings for the jobs in progress. Many days and nights computer printouts of every type of financial analysis related to the various projects were strewn everywhere.

Every discipline was "let out" to outside contract professionals or contractors. This was the easiest way to begin the development business and required only a receptionist, secretary, construction assistant, and accountant/bookkeeper. In the beginning, with the use of a second-generation PC, all bookkeeping and accounting could be done by one full-time assistant, even though the software was very crude.

Kingsley Estates in Stoneham was 91 percent sold out by the spring of 1982. The two brick-on-frame buildings built on slabs contained fifty apartments each which posed the traditional challenge with a condo conversion: maximization of rental income during the conversion; i.e., maintaining the apartments on a rent paying basis up to two months prior to sale closing, at which point the cosmetic improvements would be done; i.e., new carpet and vinyl flooring, repainting, all new appliances, new bathroom fixtures and vanity, and lighting fixtures and vanity. Of course, in reality, only about half of this rent would materialize.

The common areas were entirely refurbished. On the interiors the hallways were repainted and carpeted with a medium-grade covering. New lighting sconces were hung on the walls and chandeliers were installed in the high ceiling lobbies. New laundry room equipment was purchased. On the exterior a ten-foot awning was placed over each main entrance and the parking lots repaved and striped. A seven-foot stockade fence was installed around the perimeter of the parking lots. The fourth side in the rear was naturally treed and left open on Kingsley Estates property.

This first venture of Nick and Tommy's really played out quite smoothly. Although beginner's luck maybe was in play the success stemmed in part from Tommy's uncanny marketing and design expertise. Also, Nick's construction and financial ability and business strategy was equally helpful. Tommy was quite happy with Noel Cardigan's interior design input. She had been hired after the project commenced.

Only a few problems arose at Kingsley Estates, which set the partners back about fifty thousand dollars.

Nick had convinced Tommy to let him contract for a newly installed twenty-foot-by-forty-foot swimming pool. None was existing. It would have appeal to potential buyers. One sunny spring day the pool contractor who held the contract called Nick and apprised him of the existence of peat beginning at five feet below the surface.

"What's the extent of the problem?" Nick queried. "I don't know for sure, Mr. Packard. Won't know until I keep digging," Curly Mattson replied.

"Fuck that, Curly, I paid for the test pits to avoid this. Good hard pan the report concluded!"

"Not below five feet though. And I had nothing to do with the tests," Curly stated angrily.

"Well, don't stop, Curly. Stoke up that backhoe and

finish the job. Bring in as much fill as required. I'll be there tomorrow morning at seven AM. sharp!"

In the next few days the damages were set at thirteen thousand dollars. Nick chuckled when he received the change order. Their engineer missed the problem. Their problem, not ours, he thought. He quickly drafted a letter of dispute to the pool company rejecting the change order for the peat removal.

At the 75 percent sellout level with sale closings spinning at many banks and attorney's offices, sales slowed down to a snail's pace. The ground level units were sticking.

The natural light was dim because of the small windows and the lack of outdoor space gave occupants a boxed-in feeling. All the upper floor units had ample balcony space outside.

Enter Tommy Fletcher, the Guru of Marketing. As the two partners stood in front of the buildings and stared for a while, Nick spoke first. "We have twenty ground units. That's significant. Let's slash the prices. Cut ten thousand dollars off!"

Tommy growled, "On the contrary, amigo. I'm not taking a pay cut for the past year's work. You can slash with your profits if you want,"Tommy went on. "No, I'm going to cut glass sliders into the existing living room windows and brick the outside areas as patios. Then install a six-foot fence around the patio which will afford privacy. Then, guess what, hot shot? I'm going to raise the prices and they'll sell!"

And so it was. Tommy was "on the money" and the twenty units were modified and sold out by the end of 1982.

Boomer Development netted eight hundred seventy eight thousand dollars pretax profit on Kingsley Estates. Not the originally estimated one million dollars, but a pretty good take! Nick mused.

With the profits from the flip of a Beacon Hill building and a Back Bay brownstone purchased six months earlier, Boomer netted one million one hundred ninety-five thousand dollars after deducting one hundred ninety-one thousand dollars in administrative overhead for its first partial year of business. And the beat played on!

Tommy ecstatically sheltered the pass-through income for tax purposes with excess depreciation from his Boston apartment buildings. He had paid no income tax in the past due to this "artificial loss "windfall. Nick, however, had no depreciation because he had no business real estate holdings, only cash. He had only built and sold houses and Kingsley estates revenue was taxable ordinary income. He wrote a big check to Uncle Sam for 1981.He realized that he needed real estate for equity build-up and tax losses, but it would have to wait for now.

The P and S agreement had been executed on the Beverly land purchase in the fall of 1981 and closed in November when the work began. All hell broke loose when Mitchell Environmental discovered PCBs and arsenic in the soils of an area covering about an acre of land. This was at the far end of the field where Nick spooked Tommy. Was this an omen? A considerable level of these contaminants were discovered. It had apparently been dumped on at some time in the past and covered up!

Nick read the engineer's report in shock, moaning, "What's the extent of these chemicals?" What the fuck? What about the soils tests Tommy ordered?

He called Tommy on his new Motorola cellular car phone installed in the console of his Mercedes. "Tommy, what did the pre-acquisition environmental tests show for the site?"

"What tests?" replied his esteemed partner. "Oh, the venereal disease tests! What the hell do you think? The soils, Tommy, the soils tests that you said were OK!" "We didn't need soils tests on this site. It's a natural site with trees and fields, never polluted. What's the problem, professor?"

"Well, it's polluted with shit!" Nick moaned.

"Do you mean that sewage is running into our property?" Tommy replied. "No, Tommy. Worse. PCBs and arsenic in an acre area where a cluster of townhouses is designed. There apparently has been dumping on the site previously. I can't believe you skipped the study!" Tommy was silent for a minute and then Nick hung up.

The first major screwup for the two partners was in play. Starting right off the contaminants had to be carefully excavated and hauled to a dump in Maine. The price tag for this first fuck-up was four hundred thousand dollars. A lawsuit under the Massachusetts Hazardous Waste law was filed for one million dollars by Nick's old buddy, attorney Mike Kensington, and was against the sellers. This lawsuit would certainly be dragged out for a long time.

After the hazardous waste debacle the Beverly site was

thoroughly cleaned up. However, the negative publicity affected pre-sales for a while, but engineering certifications with references in publications minimized the problem over time.

The Burgess Design Group had designed a scheme of cedar-shingled clapboard and brick sided townhouses with individual architectural features predominant in various surrounding North Shore towns. The Salem House was Nick's favorite. The historical accounts of the Salem witchcraft trials of the seventeenth century had always fascinated him.

The townhouse interiors at Beverly Gardens as it was now named were designed unsparingly with good quality materials and workmanship. There were lofts in some models, cathedral ceilings with brass fans, large fireplaces, ample-sized marble foyers, top-of-the-line appliances, and attached garages in many units. The rooms were spacious, with walk-in closets in the master bedrooms. Private twenty-five-feet-by-twenty-feet decks overlooked picturesque tree-lines. The deck on unit 49 directly viewed the tree where Nick stood the night he scared the shit out of Tommy.! This unit was to be retained by the partners for investment.

Nick had hired Noel Cardigan once again, whom he met in the sales trailer during the Weiler Farms development and had used for design of his model homes. Then again for Kingsley Estates. Noel and he had started dating after his divorce from Jacki three years back and were very serious. Nick had hired her to design the interiors of the Beverly

Gardens models, not because they had fallen in love, but because he truly admired her design work. She was a genius at her work.

Tommy's brokers prepared a spectacular sales brochure and, under Noel's supervision, a sales office and three models were elaborately decorated.

One afternoon Nick met with Nelson Thatcher in the sales office. When Nelson arrived Nick was perched in an armchair with his feet resting on a hassock and his tie loosened. He continued to scratch penciled changes and notes on a copy of the price-list. After a few moments of silence Nelson spoke, inquiring, "What do you think of the sales brochure, Nick?"

"Nelson, you created an excellent presentation. The narrative…the photos…renderings. Floor plans and optional upgrades listing. Superb, my friend! Only one thing, the prices are way too steep."

"Tommy set them, you know? He feels the booming market will bring them in," replied Nelson. "Look, Nelson, I believe that these prices may be attainable at some point in the sales effort, but not yet. We've had some negative publicity in connection with the contaminated soils problem and, also, there's a large condominium inventory on the market now which is expanding. No, cut the average price of one hundred sixty-two thousand dollars to one hundred thirty-nine thousand nine hundred dollars to start, and then let demand guide it. You know that our original pro-forma was based on an average price of one hundred thirty-eight thousand dollars."

Nelson lamented, "Tommy's not going to like it. You tell him. He'll castrate me if I suggest any changes."

Nick's anger emerged. "What the hell is he, the king? Does he intimidate you that much? Where are your balls, Nelson? In Tommy's pocket? I'll handle him, and don't give that price list to anyone! Capisci?

"OK, OK, Nick!" Nelson cried.

That evening the Boomer Development office was lit up like a circus until late at night as Nick and Tommy reviewed all existing comparable sales data for recent North Shore townhouse sales. Tommy was stubborn and held fast. There were comparables at the one hundred fifty thousand dollar level.

Nick preferred a quick and conservative sellout and, after Tommy's idle threats to dissolve the partnership and his persistent bellowing, suggested a settlement of the argument by a draw of the cards. Tommy shuffled and Nick cut, then, Tommy dealt one card each face down while the two men stared, stone-faced at each other. They slowly turned the cards over. Tommy drew a seven and Nick a nine!

There was complete silence for many moments. Then Tommy said, "Fuck you. What if I refuse to lower the prices anyway?"

"C'mon, Tommy. You lost and I won, fair and square. Don't be a fucking cheat!"

"Yeah, right," Tommy angrily replied. The big man pushed the table over, and plans and reports flew everywhere. Nick got nervous looking at Tommy's fists, the size of bear paws, curled and aimed at him. Tommy stepped toward Nick poking him on the chest and screaming obscenities.

However, Tommy soon calmed down somewhat and stomped out the door as Nick murmured a sigh of relief!

The grand opening occurred the following week and the price list offered prices averaging one hundred forty-nine thousand dollars, a fair compromise between the partners. Three hundred visitors came through that first week and nineteen sales reservation deposits were taken, at 5 percent discounts off the list price. Following the grand opening, reservations were taken at four per week, with prices slowly edging up. It appeared that Beverly Gardens would be successful, but come in under the pretax profit budget because of the early sales lag and the hazardous waste problems.

CHAPTER 36

June 1983

The Boeing 747 floated through the clouds like a soaring eagle cruising on extended wings. Outside the skies were aqua blue and joyfully, there had been no turbulence along the way. They were already an hour into Delta flight 357 headed toward Santo Domingo in the Dominican Republic.

Noel and Nick were visiting the remote island to "tie the knot." After over three years of dating they were very committed to each other. Both were still legally married but had obtained consents to remarry in the Dominican republic from their previous spouses and agreements to enter into uncontested divorces after the settlement. The U.S. recognized these Dominican marriages, at least that's what Attorney Lipschitz had advised them when he collected his hefty fee up front. The attorney arranged for a travel package consisting of a three-night stay at the Hotel El Conquistador and a justice of the peace to perform the ceremony. The couple had thought this trip necessary because Noel was pregnant and wanted to be married before giving birth to their baby.

Noel lay back in her seat and read an issue of Time magazine, comfortably, while Nick sat back, clasping her hand on the armrest. He drifted in thought and mentally focused on the tremendous success of Boomer Development, beginning with Kingsley Estates and the good progress of Beverly Gardens. Fifty-seven units sold as of yesterday, with forty-nine already closed.

He hoped they weren't biting off more than they could chew, however, with the recent purchase and sale agreement executions of the Shipley & Sons two-hundred-thousand-square-foot former piano factory in Boston's South End soon to be rehabilitated and the twelve-building Commonwealth Avenue package unloaded by Josh Dawson, his old client back at Barker, Tibbs whom he had met in his public accounting days. Boomer could create 296 residential units in total according to preliminary architectural drawings.

Of the aggregate fourteen million one hundred thousand dollars purchase price for all the buildings Tommy and Nick were required to put up equity of one million two hundred thousand dollars in cash, which put a major strain on the partners considering their numerous other cash commitments. The cash was necessary to commit because limited junior financing would be allowed under their primary mortgage commitment.

This strain caused Nick concern in addition to the fact that Tommy and he were at odds on many things. We'll be OK, Nick tried to convince himself. "What's the matter, honey? Are you OK?" Noel inquired of Nick after he made a deep sigh.

"Yes, Noel, just the stress caused by thoughts of overwhelming business issues!"

"Well, forget about it now, Mr. worry wart. We're getting married tomorrow and that's cause for peace and joy," Noel purred.

"I'd love a little piece right now," Nick uttered, and they both chuckled."You'll have to wait a little while for that, at least until we land," Noel teased.

They eased back in their seats while Noel resumed reading People magazine. This month's issue featured Donald Trump, the rising Manhattan real estate mogul who had developed the Grand Hyatt Hotel at Grand Central Station on 42nd Street with the Priztker family and other Manhattan buildings. This handsome young tycoon was Nick's age and had developed a mega luxury condominium tower on Park Avenue and East 56th Street: Trump Towers!

Well, Nick is better looking, she thought, even though he hasn't yet appeared in any magazines. Someday he'll build "Packard Place," a larger tower than Trump's. She was so impressed with Nick!

Nick's thoughts then floated off into oblivion as he thought about Jacki and that horrendous series of events years back when she became pregnant by that slimy hoodlum. Where most men would have hated their wives for such contemptible behavior, and abandoned them flatly, Nick had compassion for her and felt pity. Jacki had been a victim caught up in a deadly addiction to Dilaudid and Xanax. He believed that evil, selfish animal had used the drug as bait. He now believed Jacki's story, but would never understand how she could have thrown it all away for the drug!

He felt extreme sorrow pondering her fate. He would not regret the cash settlement of three hundred thousand dollars that he had set up in a trust fund which Jacki could not draw from until she was drug free for at least a year as certified by periodic tests, which she had already achieved. That slime bag drug dealer would never give her a cent, Nick mused, and it is his daughter!

Jacki had tried desperately to rekindle the flame with Nick in the last few years, but it was in vain. Nick had fallen deeply in love with Noel. Jacki and Nick's dream had been washed away forever. Nick prayed for her and silently decided to visit her and her daughter, Nicole, when he returned from this trip. He was prepared to help them all he could.

Blocking all further stressful thoughts he returned to the present, the joyous occasion at hand. He felt relieved now. He was so fortunate to have Noel.

The couple was seated in first class and were pampered by attendants all the way to their tropical destination. Mixed drinks were served followed by a rather fine-tasting champagne, which the two lovers sipped to each other, locking arms and kissing softly. A while later a dinner of steak au pouivre was served, which was superb by airline standards. Then, while watching Magnum Force, the couple dozed.

CHAPTER 37

As the pilot announced the aircraft's descent into the Santo Domingo area the "No Smoking" sign lit up. The happy couple kissed softly. They had arrived and were thrilled by the occasion.

It took a while to push through Customs, but the Dominican officials were very cordial and retrieving their bags was a surprisingly easy process. Each knew that Customs would be much tougher on the return trip at Logan Airport in Boston.

They hailed a cab outside the main building and Nick, remembering his high school Spanish fairly well, managed to give their destination to the driver who sped out heading toward the EL Conquistador. Along the way a scene of sheer poverty unfolded. One room, tar-papered shacks were scattered everywhere and naked children were bathed in mud, playing while apparent mothers and daughters lazily sat in front of their humble abodes. The men around seemed to be doing some sort of imperceptible labor. A striking contrast was made between this scene of poverty on one side of the road and the sandy white beaches with sparkling blue green water and towering palms on the other side.

Nick thought if only there was some significant government housing assistance here he could really help these people while making money at the same time. This is reality, Nick thought as the cab rolled along. This was a poor country which abutted Haiti, one of the poorest in the world. It was an oxymoron that Christopher Columbus, the founder of the USA, the greatest country in the world, was buried here in Santo Domingo!

The El Conquistador was a good hotel by American standards. It was surrounded by healthy palm trees and was set on a tropical white, sandy beach with palm-thatched huts serving exotic drinks and melodious steel bands providing that soothing Caribbean relaxation. The interior was well furnished and relaxing, except that signs inside the room stated "no bebe la agua" (don't drink the water)!

Nick and Noel got settled in their room and pulled down the cleanly made bedcovers. It smelled sweet and the traditional chocolates wrapped in foil rested on starched clean pillows. They were allured to this invitation and rolled in while their clothes flew in every direction, Noel's panties landing on the bedpost. The newlyweds "to be" passionately made love in every position for hours until they were completely spent and fell asleep with Nick's arm wrapped fully around her soft breasts.

When they awoke refreshed, Nick ordered room service and called the justice of the peace, who informed him that the ceremony would take place the following morning at eleven. Nick clasped Noel's soft hand and kissed her gently while smiling with happiness. He embraced her softly and lifted her in a twirl. Life is so good again. I'll never let her go!

The food arrived and the two lovers dined on the balcony, watching the sunset slowly wane over the exotic Caribbean Ocean. They ate heartily and chatted incessantly about their future plans.

CHAPTER 38

After an exhilarating day with Noel, Nick decided he would try his hand at the blackjack tables in the El Conquistador Casino. It was early evening and they both dressed formally. Nick pulled a thousand dollars from a hidden compartment in his luggage, and although he could afford to lose a lot more than that, he decided to be frugal. He drew the limit.

Downstairs in the casino there were many Spaniards and a few American couples who were most likely tourists. The couple both felt more at ease with the American presence who seemed to be enjoying themselves immensely.

Nick sat at a blackjack table with Noel standing behind him, watching. First, a fifty-dollar bet was placed by him, and within seconds it was swept away by the dealer, his two kings squashed by the dealer's ace and queen. He then bet another fifty dollars and watched it, too, slide away. One more try, Nick thought, then I'll back off for a while. He doubled down on a nine and a two and was dealt a queen. His hundred-dollar loss was quickly erased! Boring, he thought, but that's how the game goes quite often.

Nick turned and saw that Noel had disappeared. He

quickly glanced around the room and noticed her sitting at a small cocktail table in a far corner conversing cheerfully with an apparent American couple.

The room was crowded, and as Nick weaved through the crowd of gamblers he bumped into a few Latinos. They smiled as Nick humbly apologized and they eloquently responded, "Excuse me, senor, por favor."

He approached the table and was introduced by Noel to Mario Cavallaro and his wife, Gina. They were a very suave couple indeed. Both were full-blooded Italians and lived in Reading, Massachusetts, a town abutting Wakefield where the Packards had just purchased a home on the lake. The couple was very personable and quite extraordinarily good-looking.

"I can't believe that we'd meet here in this remote paradise so far from home and we're practically next-door neighbors! Of course, Noel has probably filled you in on our mission?"

"She has," Mario replied. "And it's an honorable quest for you and your lovely wife, I mean, with a baby on the way. Cheers to you both. Salute a cent'anno!" Mario proclaimed, as he clinked his wine glass with Noel and Nick while Gina joined in. Nick knew that meant "may you have good health for a hundred years." He had heard it before from Italian subcontractors.

"What is your mission?" Nick asked the Cavalleros nonchalantly.

Gina chimed in, saying, "Oh, my husband is here on business and I'm taking the opportunity to relax for a week."

Noel smiled and said, "Oh, how nice. You're a very lucky woman, Gina. Many men seize the opportunity of a business trip to get away by themselves for whatever reasons. You seem to have a solid relationship."

Mario put his arm around Gina's shoulders and playfully squeezed her. "I do love you, Gina," he replied. "You know, friends, where I come from a wife and mother are highly respected, put on a pedestal." Everyone nodded in agreement.

They chatted on for a long time about Gina's daughter, their houses and basic interests. Their friends and relatives and a myriad of subjects. They hit it off quite well and seemed like close friends already. New paisanos, as Mario mentioned.

Mario ordered another round of drinks, now the third shared with this couple, and the genders split to talk separately. "Noel mentioned earlier that you have been quite successful in real estate, Nick. What, in brokerage of properties?" He knew differently after Noel had spoken openly, but vaguely, about Nick's development feats while Nick was at the blackjack table.

"Not quite Mario. I'm a developer. Mainly housing. Singles, condos. Some commercial."

"Have you done a lot of this?" Mario inquired.

Nick went on to herald his success at Royal Oaks Estates, Weiler Farms, and Kingsley Estates. Further, he described how well Beverly Gardens was progressing. Then his ego swelled, pumped by the alcohol, as he further continued on about his latest acquisitions and plans to develop 296 units in Boston. Mario listened quietly with great interest.

The drinks were taking their toll and Nick was revealing far too much. He didn't know these people from a "hole in the wall." Nothing was known about this suave man while Nick's ego was spewing out his business accomplishments.

"Tell me, Mario, what's your business?" Nick probed with interest.

"I'm in finance, Nick. I help people."

"In what way? Do you own a finance company? Lend on mortgages? Automobiles? Appliances? Are you a venture capitalist?" Nick further probed. "What do you do exactly?"

"My friend, I lend money on all of the above and more. My terms are very reasonable and I have many satisfied customers," Mario replied.

"Are you closing a deal in Santo Domingo?" Nick went on.

"Yes, a good business arrangement. Strong principals." Mario was very evasive, unlike Nick had been!

"Well, good luck, Mario. I hope that you do well. The best to you." Nick clinked wine glasses with him. Nick was perplexed, but he dismissed it.

"Now, shall we try our luck at the gaming table? I feel lucky," Mario said, as he patted Nick on the shoulder.

"Let's give it a shot, Mario."

The men excused themselves as the women chatted on incessantly. The men took seats at a blackjack table in front of a huge window wall which displayed a pounding surf two stories below highlighted by strong floodlights. Four others were playing at this table. One short of a full cast.

Nick placed a fifty-dollar bet while Mario put down

two crisp hundred-dollar bills, acquiring more chips, and smiled while nodding at the dealer, who remained almost straight-faced. They seemed to know each other, but didn't speak. Mario was dealt two kings and Nick received a jack and a nine, then the dealer flipped a queen with his seven. Both men smiled as they doubled their money while the excitement intensified.

As the clock ticked away the lucky pair won 80 percent of their hands. At one a.m. Nick was up by two thousand dollars and Mario's winnings totaled eight thousand five hundred dollars. Nick was in awe. He thought this luck on their wedding eve had to be a good omen. But Mario was no ordinary man. Eight thousand five hundred dollars with ease, Nick mused.

After vigorous handshakes by the men and much laughter, Mario nodded once again at the dealer, saying nothing. The two men returned to the round, marble-topped table and found the women still deep in conversation.

On the way out of the club, Noel became exhilarated over Nick's good fortune and hugged him tightly. Gina said, "Oh, Mario does this often. He's lucky!" The couples shook hands and talked about getting together for dinner before the end of their stay. They, then, departed sauntering to their rooms. Twenty minutes later Nick was snoring, while Noel quietly slept like a baby.

CHAPTER 39

The wake-up call came precisely at nine thirty a.m. The happy couple woke up and fumbled in the bathroom with their morning hygiene. They hugged between tooth brushing and smiled longingly at each other as the warm Caribbean sun beamed through the glass sliders open to the balcony. They both thought this to be the greatest day of their lives.

Nick dialed room service for a pot of coffee and croissants because no time could be wasted over breakfast. They'd eat later on. Nick dressed in a Louis's tan cotton suit with a medium brown silk tie and soft leather Ferragamo loafers imported from Italy. He gazed in the mirror noticing that he needed a tan, but that, too, would have to wait until later.

Noel squiggled into a beautiful off-white silk dress and filled a stunning Judith Lieber purse with all those things women need for survival. She looked like a goddess with her soft, long brown hair. Nick was extremely proud of her and realized how fortunate he was.

They walked through the lobby at ten thirty a.m., holding hands and, outside the hotel, stepped into the hired limousine which, by Dominican standards, was a

1976 Buick. It was shiny and clean and would suffice. Only their marriage was of importance, not the fancy trappings desired by most newlyweds.

As the limo cruised along the streets of Santo Domingo they noticed sidewalks lined with drab and scrubby palms. Dirty and lackluster. National police, soldiers, stood erectly on many street corners with rifles poised on their chests. Youth gangs walked the streets and hovered in doorways. Old and worn pick-up trucks were parked alongside American and foreign cars decades old. A gully of grayish water running on the side of a back street caught Nick's attention.

The poverty was horrendous. Nick solemnly uttered, "If this is the better of the two island countries, I can't imagine the condition of Haiti! Noel, let's remember this scene always and not forget how blessed we are!"

The couple squeezed each other's hands tightly and Noel lay her head on Nick's shoulder. "We're blessed because we have love," she replied.

Inside City Hall the crowd buzzed. They were mainly locals speaking a Caribbean Spanish dialect it seemed. A few oblivious European and American couples meandered about. Apparent local city officials passed by the couple. Some with short ties hanging on protruding bellies. A thin, brown-skinned, and bony-faced attendant greeted them in the front hall and ushered them to room cuarante, where they met the justice of the peace. He was a smooth-faced, jovial man.

The ensuing ceremony was uneventful and lasted for only seventeen minutes. Much of it was in Spanish, including the

Dominican marriage certificate handed to them following the ceremony. All that mattered to the happy couple was that they were legally married. At least they hoped that they were!

They kissed and whispered their own meaningful vows to each other, then left City Hall exhilarated and went to Casa Grande in the resort section of Santo Domingo for a delightful lunch. The rest of the afternoon was spent on the beach at the El Conquistador Hotel where they casually stretched out on chaise lounges provided by the hotel. The steel drums twanged as they relaxed beside the palm-thatched, open beach-bar hut set on pure white sand. Noel lounged lazily in a perfectly contoured bikini while Nick read a recent issue of Fortune magazine.

"Hello, my friends," a voice chanted.Both looked up quickly as Mario Cavallaro gazed down on them with intense black eyes. He was wearing a navy blue polo shirt and perfectly pleated khaki shorts. His docksiders were new. Mario looked like the proverbial jet-setter."What a beautiful day. Congratulations on your marriage. Everything went well, I presume?" Mario inquired."Well, it was hurried and very informal, not even a best man or bridesmaids. But we're married. She looked gorgeous."

"So I can see!" Mario replied, staring first at the wedding ring and then at Noel with wide eyes. "Let me buy both of you a drink. May I?" Noel declined, but Nick assented and the two men treaded over sand to the beach-bar hut.

They conversed for over an hour while Noel dozed on the lounge. They talked about the isolated beach paradise, the island poverty, the few fine restaurants and then inevitably to business. "Nick, your business is very interesting and your track record very impressive. I can help you. Provide financing, if you're interested?"

Somewhat wary of this man, Nick replied, "I'm all set for now, but maybe on future deals. Can you give me a business card. I'll call you." Mario had run out of cards and promised to send one to Nick in Wakefield, but didn't ask for an address. He then quickly changed the subject.

"Let's have dinner tonight. My treat," Mario went on.

"Well, Noel and I were planning a quiet night in our room. Dinner on the terrace."

"I understand, and would be inclined to do so myself on such a precious day. Congratulations once again, Nick. Perhaps tomorrow night, our last night here. At the Dungeon?" Mario replied.

"That's fine, Mario, let's do it!"

The following day Nick and Noel spent casually. They shopped for duty-free items and bought many gifts for their friends. Nick purchased clothes and toys for Nicole, Jacki's daughter. He had decided on the flight down to visit them the following week. Noel had thought that was noble and admirable.

The Dungeon Restaurant was quite unique. The couples descended a winding stone staircase into a literal huge stone cave below sea level. They dined on a very delectable multi-course meal of exotic seafood. They conversed at their table for hours and lingered for a long time seeming to get along quite well, especially the women. The restaurant was only about half full which afforded much room to stretch and they could talk freely.

A cart bearing raspberry and peach tarts, chocolate truffles and cakes, mousse, cheesecake, and many other fine delights was periodically rolled back and forth. Each person at the table ultimately indulged. Gina's raspberry tart was, by far, the best ever tasted by Noel, who took a sliver from Gina. No mention of business took place the entire evening! Just friendly conversation.

Right before leaving the restaurant Mario excused himself to go to the men's room. Nick took the moment to get up and stretch and walked around a bit. Out of the corner of his eye he saw Mario in a far corner talking incessantly with two large men, one dark-skinned with black hair slicked back and wearing gold chains around his neck. They seemed to be having a serious discussion. Nick walked back to the table and said nothing.

The next morning Nick and Noel checked out with a baggage boy close behind them. They hailed a cab and left the miniscule island paradise behind. As Delta flight 967 lifted off the ground they hugged and kissed. They were married. At last!

CHAPTER 40

Through the windows of the thirty-fifth story a scene of beauty and sheer magnificence unfolded. The visage of a powerful lady. New England's mother city: a world-class city so new, yet so old. A glimmering mass of towering high rise buildings with varying architectural designs. A scattering of skeletal steel frames at various levels of completion heralded the new Boston's vibrant commercial atmosphere.

The old wharfs on the waterfront, many rehabilitated recently into luxury condominiums, and the antiquity of the Customs Tower and older rehabilitated structures in the microcosms of such areas as Post Office Square provided the exciting contrast. The transformation of the Quincy Market buildings complemented the grandeur. On the horizon could be viewed Bunker Hill in Charlestown and in the harbor the gallant USS Constitution.

The founding fathers of our country lived and fought here to ensure the country's sovereignty, the names of Paul Revere, John Adams, Alexander Hamilton, and others were indelibly inscribed on this soil. Boston is certainly the premier historical city in the country. Had the British not been defeated here, perhaps Americans today would still be subjects of the Crown!

Boston's innate value is evinced by its world leadership in medicine and education. The revered institutions of Massachusetts General Hospital and its sister hospital, Mass Eye and Ear Infirmary, Beth Israel, Brigham and Women's Hospital, Children's Hospital, and many others are eagerly sought out worldwide by people with serious medical issues.

The educational institutions of Harvard University, Massachusetts Institute of Technology, and Vassar College are ranked on top in the nation. Others such as Boston College and Babson Institute are renowned. These ideas flashed through Nick's mind and reassured him that development here was sound.

"Can I pour you more coffee, Mr. Packard?" Donna, an attractive young assistant, inquired.

Nick broke his hypnotic gaze of this overpowering scene outside the windows and replied, "Oh, no thanks. I've had my quota for the day." Donna smiled.

Nick's glance turned toward the P&S agreement and his checklist notes and began to study them for a few moments. Mike Kensington, who had been hired once again to protect the Boomer interests, diligently shuffled papers with the seller's attorney and lending bank's attorneys as they took pot shots at legal issues. Mike smiled at Nick while addressing his client's concerns and preferences as was customary. Nick smiled back and was pleased once again with his attorney's creativity.

Tommy was seated beside Nick at the head of the huge

conference table. Mike had arranged the seating position, which he customarily did to render importance to his clients. Always head of the table!

The two Boomer partners were hunched over, musing at the updated piano factory pro-forma net profit projections cranked out by Nick earlier that morning. This was their last chance before closing the acquisition. The projections looked sweet:

Condominium unit sales (200,000. gross sq. ft. x 90%= 180,000 net sq. ft. @ $`130. per sq. ft.)		$23,400,000
Less: Commissions, tax stamps & recording @ 5.4%		1,264,000
Net Sales		$22,136,000
Costs:		
Acquisition	$3,520,000	
Architectural + Engineering	867,000	
Construction ($55.per sq. ft.)	11,000,000	
Insurance, Taxes & Administration	300,000	
Financing - ($14,000,000 - 1 Pt.)		
(Interest rate -10 ¼%)	2,292,000	17,979,000
Projected Net Pretax Profit		$4,157,000

"Tommy!" Nick bellowed. Tommy had projected one hundred thirty dollars per square foot, or one hundred thirty thousand dollars on average for a one-thousand-square-foot unit in the South End. "It seems like we're grasping! I wasn't sure when I put this analysis together, but now I'm doubtful.

South End is not this," Nick said, as he swept his arm toward the scene outside of the windows.

Tommy replied caustically, "In the next thirty-six months? Are you shitting me? Easy, Nick, relax!"

"Well, the preliminary construction budget was prepared by our construction manager and is probably quite solid and the other soft costs are based mainly upon financing. But, the sales are uncertain and if there is a drag it could substantially increase carrying costs!"

"Nick, don't worry. Four-point-two million dollars is a lot of money. It's an eighteen percent pretax profit! If we only got half of that it's still a lot of money," Tommy quickly replied. "Anyway, the factory buildings are structurally sound and well located. The market in Back Bay is booming and it's spreading out. And Boston real estate is hot. Needless to say, we'll come out ahead of these prices over the next thirty-six months. I feel confident."

"OK, Tommy. I'm comfortable. Just had to play devil's advocate, let's sign!"

The two partners went forward signing mortgages, personal guarantees, disclosures, indemnities, and a host of the customary documents. The partners were ecstatic when, finally, all parties shook hands, and many accolades and good wishes were offered by all.

All participants were invited to dinner at the Seasons Restaurant in the nearby Bostonian Hotel. The dinner was on Boomer Development. It was 6:17 p.m. Upon exiting the thirty-fifth floor, Mike pulled Nick aside, shaking his hand. "I need to talk with you regarding legal issues on the Commonwealth Avenue building closings. Also, you need to know that your partner, Tommy, is not very happy about once again pledging his side collateral in order to obtain nearly one hundred percent financing on the acquisition!" Mike stated, "Did he tell you that? He never said anything to me," said Nick. The two decided to meet the following week.

That same evening Nick's Mercedes rolled into the circular driveway at their home in Wakefield. It was only six days after the relaxing Dominican trip, but Nick was dead tired. Preparation for the piano factory closing and its final consummation had been grueling. He dragged himself onto the porch, his heels scoffing.

Noel met him at the door and gave him a peck on the cheek as he entered, then he went into their living room and sprawled on the couch. "How was your day, honey? Nick mumbled.

"I went shopping, and wait till you see what I bought you at Neiman's. The most beautiful leather briefcase, I hope you like it! Oh, and you got a call earlier this evening from Mario Cavallaro. He wants you to call him this evening whenever you can."

"What does he want, Noel?" Nick groaned.

"I don't know, but he was very friendly and complimentary. A real charmer! Nick, be friendly to him, but I feel that you should stay clear of any business arrangements. Don't you?"

"I certainly do. He obviously had something going on down in the Dominican. He knew too many people, and not just on an acquaintance level, it seemed. There were things that I noticed. I think that he might have some connection to something sinister down there."

Nick slept heavily for an hour and then fumbled with the telephone, dialing the Boston number Mario had left with Noel. "Sonny's," a deep voice answered. Loud background music could be heard and the man on the other end was barely audible.

"Mario Cavallaro, please," Nick nonchalantly said.

"Who's calling?"

"Nick Packard."

"Hold on!" the voice replied somewhat disgusted, as if he'd been distracted away from something of interest. Nick was apprehensive and wondered why Mario was there and not at home with his family at eleven thirty p.m.

Suddenly, Mario spoke. "Hey, Nick, my friend, how are you? How was your flight home? Good, I hope." Without waiting for an answer, he continued, "I've been thinking about the two hundred and ninety six units in Boston. We could help you with your equity needs." Now it was "we" not just "he". "How much do you need? One…two-million?" Mario queried.

"I'm all set," Nick warily replied.

Mario seemed oblivious to his answer and went on. "We can deliver it tomorrow, my friend, no Ivy League closing! Sign once and we shake hands. Done deal. Only for my friends would I arrange this."

We're friends? I've only known him for nine or ten days. This is bullshit, Nick thought. Any doubts previously held were dispelled. This man was from somewhere on the dark side!

"Hey, buddy," Nick responded, trying a new tack. "Seriously, my company has arranged for one hundred percent financing on these acquisitions. Lucky for us we're all set, as I mentioned earlier in the discussion. I feel honored that you have so much faith in me. That you believe in me is so uplifting, thank you, friend. I will call you on any future supplementary financing needs. And, please send me that business card!" He gave Mario the Boomer address in Boston. Nick and Tommy were squeezing to come up with the remaining one-million-dollar equity requirement for the Dawson building closing, but Nick would never reveal that! They had barely been able to produce the two hundred thousand dollars needed for the piano factory.

Mario had no reply; Nick had prevailed. "Sure, my friend, I'll talk to you next time around. Give my best to Noel, please."

Nick hung up and said to Noel, "It's done. He accepted my decline to his financing offer. Can you believe that he said 'they' would lend one million to two million dollars with no formal closing, only signatures on one document! I wouldn't dare to ask him the interest rate! And, what if the projects went bust and they lost their money?!" Noel sighed with relief.

Four weeks later Boomer Development Company closed on the Dawson Company Commonwealth Avenue multi-building acquisition for ten million five hundred eighty thousand dollars. To get the one-million-dollar cash down payment required by the lender for this deal, the partners had sold a block of eleven units in Beverly Gardens to Barry Cotter, a wealthy Beacon Hill businessman who was also a competitor of Tommy's in real estate brokerage. The eleven units were sold for nine hundred ninety thousand dollars— ninety thousand dollars each, in cash. Boomer had done it by the skin of their teeth!

They were now hog-tied and seriously strapped for cash. The new acquisitions would support the company and could substantially increase their cash flow in the future, but for now they were cash poor.

CHAPTER 41

March 1985

The room was dimly lit. Overhead on the mezzanine level, the orchestra played a rhapsody from the past featuring a violin solo. The setting was very romantic. Outside the view of the Customs Tower was spectacular. The Bay Tower Room had, probably, the best view in Boston.

Nick and Noel sat on one side of the table, their backs facing a four-foot-high mahogany partition accentuated by a gleaming brass railing. Nick's hand stroked Noel's lightly as she rested it on the linen-covered table top. Her skin felt so soft and pure to Nick.

Tommy and his wife sat opposite the couple and he was whispering something in Anna's ear as she smiled demurely. It seemed quite intimate. Noel chuckled.

The couples were dressed for the occasion. The men wore black tie and the women silk dresses. Nick's tuxedo was a very expensive fine wool from Louis and was designed by Ermenegildo Zegna of Italy, as were most of Louis selections. Nick looked very handsome and wore the clothes well. If Zegna could have seen him then he would implore him to model his designs. Noel wore a lavish Bob Mackey dress which had been purchased at a handsome sum from Yolanda's. She looked so elegant and refined.

Tommy sported a green tuxedo with a green bow tie and, appropriately so, it was St. Patrick's Day, a highly popular holiday in Boston. His brothers and sisters were all celebrating their solid national heritage on their mother's side at pubs in South Boston following the annual holiday parade. Anna wore a fine silk dress which complemented her long, straight red hair and beautiful face.

Nick seized the opportunity to toast and clink the glasses of everyone. "I would like to toast my friends and partners and to give thanks to God for our many blessings. We're thirty-something, the first of the baby boomers, and sitting on a gold mine in Boston. We hope! Cheers to all this!" Clink, clink. The glasses met.

As they sipped their drinks they gazed out of the huge floor-to-ceiling windows across the entire window wall and were temporarily mesmerized by the lights of the Custom Tower clock, Quincy Market and of a few boats in the harbor. The scene was intoxicating and got better with each sip of wine.

A waiter in black tails approached the table and cordially introduced himself as Jacque, "your waiter for the evening," as he individually fanned colorful menus with a watercolor etching of this spectacular view facing them. The friends studied them and struggled with their choices.

After a few moments they decided to split an appetizer of caviar Beluga Malossol glace and an imported goose liver pate. As an entree Anna chose a baked lobster filled with crab meat and Tommy, a grilled Norwegian salmon with Viking butter. Nick and Noel ordered a rack of lamb for two with assorted vegetables.

Tommy hailed the wine steward and after much thought decided upon the house recommendation, a fine cabernet. Before the wine was served, the steward, according to tradition, poured a sample of wine into Tommy's glass for his approval. Suddenly, Tommy spit the wine from his mouth on the exquisite carpet and wiped his lips with a napkin. He yelled, "This wine isn't fit for swine, let alone my friends. Bring me something good. Now!"

The others were startled and Anna was embarrassed as the flush-faced steward left the scene. Many heads quizzically turned toward Tommy. He laughed heartily while waving his arms. The many drinks of Crown Royal earlier had kicked in. Tommy bellowed, so that everyone close would hear, "For these prices I expect the best. Waiter, a round of drinks for everyone around us! "He swept his arm around in a circle.

Nick and Noel silently held their composure while Anna slouched a bit and appeared to want to slip under the table and disappear.

Momentarily, the steward came back with a bottle of Dom Perignon, compliments of the house, which he assumed no one would resist. He apologized, unwillingly, to Tommy, then left. Shortly thereafter their dinners were served and looked so good that the wine incident faded a bit.

CHAPTER 42

"Query, Tommy," Nick said, after the superb dinner had been consumed. "Do you think we underpriced the townhouses at Beverly Gardens? We netted ten percent of sales pretax, unlike Kingsley Estates' seventeen percent. And, Beverly sold out damn well after a slow start."

"Don't complain to me, partner, you slashed my original prices! Do you remember that you were concerned about the possibility of an initial overpricing stigma."

"Well, I guess I probably was right after a bit more thought. We did net one-point-two million dollars, and our initial projection was one-point-seven million. Then we sold the units to Cotter to raise cash and took a deep discount of five hundred thousand. I guess that we weren't far off our original budget."

"Nick, your conservatism probably lost five hundred thousand in pretax net profit, easy! The market soared then."

"Well, it's history now, Tommy. I'm happy with my half of the pretax net. Six hundred thousand dollars. Higher prices probably would have resulted in an extended sales drag with increased carrying costs."

"Yeah, right, Nicko," Tommy replied, a bit intoxicated. "You think that you know everything. You don't give me enough credit for marketing intuition! I know what I'm doing."

"Si, you do quite well, El Tomasino" Nick was also half in the bag. "Tommy, based on your profound wisdom I agree that we should change the asking prices for the South End and Commonwealth Avenue projects. I mean a five-thousand to ten-thousand-dollar bump in prices on the remaining hundred and four units would be a hell of a bottom line increase!" Tommy cracked a smile.

The women, although blessed with 1980's materialism because of this business, became bored and separately began their own conversation. They talked about Noel's interior design consulting business and, further, about Anna's university professorship now in her fifth year. Their conversation soon switched to Noel's child, Alexis. She was now one and a half years old and learning quite well. Noel asked how Anna's children were doing. They were doing fine with her son a sports enthusiast and her daughter, Sarah, pursuing a degree in business management.

Tommy went on, "So Nick, let me set the prices on our new beach tower development. A price of one hundred and eighty dollars per square foot to start is in line."

"I think you're smoking dope, Tommy. C'mon, four towers, four hundred and thirty-nine units. We should start the first one-hundred-ten-unit tower much lower and go from there. It's a previously undeveloped area. We're pioneering! I can't believe we're even taking on a project in this area with an ultimate seventy-one-million-plus projected sellout! Are we nuts?"

"Nick, you're losing it again. Listen to me!"

"OK, Tommy, but a bird in the hand is worth two in the bush, as it were," said Nick.

"Forget the birds, Nick. Fuck the birds and ram the bushes!"

Noel and Anna overheard Tommy's remark and burst out laughing. Nick's face became flushed from embarrassment, but he remained silent.

The women continued with their conversation about their children, their friend's children and everybody else's children. Then they switched the conversation to fashion. How certain of their friends dressed. Further, to who they both knew were having affairs with who? Sue, Ginny... wow!

Noel described her recent wardrobe purchases at Neiman Marcus while Anna pointed to the diamond-studded gold Rolex resting on her wrist. "Tommy gave me this for my birthday last week. Do you like it, Noel?"

"It's gorgeous, Anna. You're very lucky. Not just because of material things, you have a wonderful family. We both are and I will never take it for granted."

"What did you get for St. Patrick's Day, Noel?"

"Ah, nothing yet, but Nick promised me a gift tonight when we get home," Noel replied.

"Typical male ego!" Anna roared with laughter. "They all think that what's in their pants is worth even more than fine jewelry. Delusions of grandeur, they're nuts!"

"I don't think Nick had that in mind. I don't know," Noel murmured.

The two partners huddled in serious conversation. "Nick, we've developed in the last six years, or are in the process of developing, over five hundred residential units. The beach towers will increase that to almost a thousand units. You're a genius with acquisitions and the numbers. I honor that. You're the best in the business. But, please let me handle the marketing. Don't second guess me. We did leave five hundred thousand dollars on the table at Beverly Gardens because of you, unequivocally!"

Nick listened in silence.

"On all Boomer projects except Beverly Gardens I set the prices and we are averaging better than sixteen percent net pretax profit. And, don't forget that my real estate brokerage sold all the small projects that we did in Boston since our inception in 1980 to generate quick cash flow." Tommy continued on. "You know, I'll bet if you add up the profits from the Back Bay and Beacon Hill buildings that we flipped, the small condo conversions in Waltham and Dedham and the land sales to commercial developers we easily netted more than twenty percent pretax profit from them."

Nick, while sipping wine, listed the small projects on a napkin and mentally recalled selling prices and approximate acquisition costs. After about fifteen minutes of calculations, during which Tommy chugged another glass of wine, Nick estimated that an approximate three million dollars profit had been netted on about sixteen million dollars in sales. Tommy was a bit off, but close. It was about 18–19 percent.

Nick loudly heralded Tommy's marketing ability and dubbed him "The Guru of Sales." "Don't forget, however, who negotiated the acquisition of most of those properties," Nick continued. "My hammering it out with sellers to minimize acquisition prices substantially added to the bottom line."

"Why do you play the one-upmanship game with me, Nick?" Tommy inquired.

"Because I want you to remember that we're equal partners. It's constructive!" Nick bellowed.

"Construct this!" Tommy replied.

Both men then agreed to sop discussing business for the night. They were almost drunk!

Moments of silence elapsed before the women chimed in. "Let's order more wine. The last two bottles and the Dom were fine," Noel chimed with a slight slur. She had crossed her limit on the wine.

"I'm sure the rejected bottle was fine too!" Anna bellowed. She also was feeling no pain. "Should we bow now to his Highness Lord Tommy?" The group burst out in sheer laughter while Tommy frowned.

Nick whispered something in Noel's ear while a full smile illuminated her gorgeous face. Her wide brown eyes became wider as she listened. Her antique platinum and diamond earrings accentuated her beauty. She, then, discreetly slid her hand under the tablecloth and rested it in Nick's lap. Her hand circled Nick's penis which had become hard as a rock and discreetly slid her hand slowly up and down massaging it. Nick uttered a muffled groan and Noel's panties became moist.

Their table was in a secluded corner of the room and the

other diners could not discern what was happening. That was clear to Tommy and Anna. They gaped with excitement as they recognized their friends' frolic. Anna became aroused and said, "Let me do it too, Tommy!"

He was more than agreeable, and murmured, "We have to do this more often." Anna unzipped Tommy's fly slowly while staring straight ahead out the windows. She whispered in his ear, "Do you want me to kiss it?" Tommy laughed, but wished that were possible. Suddenly, as Anna continued the waiter appeared, saying, "Will we be having dessert this evening?" In the blink of an eye Anna whipped Tommy's linen napkin over his lap as if that would help. The napkin resembled a pitched tent! Tommy tried to block the view of the rise by holding the napkin with his fingertips by its sides like a Matador. El Tomasino the great bull (shitter). Nick chuckled to himself.

The waiter revealed a smirk at the corner of his mouth and never made a comment. He was well disciplined and had seen a lot in his career.

The women ordered truffles and a raspberry tart to share with coffee. The men passed on the dessert but instead ordered glasses of 1957 Fonseca port wine. Nick thought this Portuguese wine was the best port wine he'd ever tasted. There had to be something unique about it at thirty dollars a glass.

Nick's Patek Philippe watch glittered from the illumination of the overhead lights as he extended his arm to toast this fine wine, bidding a fantastic future for all!

After a while Tommy insisted on paying the bill. Another power play, Nick thought. But somehow I'll end up paying for it! Nick didn't argue, and both he and Noel thanked Tommy graciously.

The two couples walked hand in hand to the elevator and smiled dreamily at each other. They took the elevator down the long descent to the parking garage below. The cars were parked on the same level and they alighted from the elevator together. Anna said, "It's been great fun tonight. Don't you think, Noel? Nick?"

Noel replied, "Let's get together again soon."

"Yes, let's. Why don't you two come to our Rockport house next weekend and stay over?" Anna invited.

"We'd love to. Is it OK with you, Nick?"

"It's fine with me, as long as you have a TV to watch the Celtics game," Nick joked.

"How about a thirty-six-inch Sony? And bring plenty of green, Nick, because your Celtics are going to lose to the Lakers and I lay claim to that bet right now."

"You're on, Tommy!"

The couples exchanged "good nights" and Nick beamed. "I'll see you in the morning partner," he said. Tommy and Anna both said, "It's been great fun."

Nick and Noel retrieved their vehicle and as they started to drive up the garage ramp in Nick's shiny new azure blue Mercedes 380L, the couple noticed that Tommy's Mercedes hadn't moved from its space. Only Tommy was visible and had his head stretched way back against the headrest staring at the roof. Nick roared with laughter. Noel had a quizzical look for a few moments, then awareness dawned and she snickered too. They sped away from the garage and headed home, where Noel would find her St. Patrick's gift in the master bedroom.

Under her pillow she found an exquisite Rolex diamond-studded watch similar to Anna's. Retail price at Neiman Marcus: twelve thousand nine hundred dollars. Noel kissed Nick passionately for a long moment and began to undress. As she walked around the bedroom in panties only her ample breasts swayed. She looked in the mirror this way and that many times and then at Nick, who was becoming more and more excited.

Nick was filled with joy seeing her reaction to the gift, and then with ecstasy as she slipped down his briefs and crouched down.

CHAPTER 43

The week following the Bay Tower dinner was hectic as the Boomer Development staff prepared for design review of the plans and general specifications to be reviewed preliminarily by the North Beach Development Council at the Thursday night hearing.

Boomer had optioned the land in North Beach a few months earlier at a very reasonable price for multi-family zoned waterfront property of ten thousand dollars per unit and just named the project North Beach Towers. The development required extensive review and approval of all city department heads and committees before a special permit would be issued by the city council.

The board consisted of heads of the fire department, police department, conservation commission, building department, planning board, and the mayor himself and his assistant. Boomer had to impress them all. Rightfully so, the four towers consisted of 439 units and was a monolith for these small city professionals. They certainly would strive to show their authority both partners thought.

Tommy, who loved the show, coordinated the

presentation. While he knew that a few unsavory characters sat on the council because of information from an inside source. Nick had amassed impeccable site data and the project was zoned and planned properly. Tommy and Nick both thought that Boomer would ultimately receive city site plan approval and be issued a special permit.

Meetings with Baush and Ferber's lead architect lasted late into the previous night. Their plans were well conceived and the building and site renderings were magnificent. The civil engineers created a site plan with good drainage, ample parking, and sufficient grass and shrubs in spite of the relatively small total developable acreage in the parcel. The first 110-unit, twelve-story tower should be a shoo-in for approval in this underdeveloped area. The city's tax base would be pumped up substantially.

On Thursday evening the development team marched into the council chambers in a regimented fashion. Tommy valiantly led the procession and was followed by Nelson Thatcher, Tommy's chief broker; Mark Raymond, civil engineer; Bobby Ferber, senior architect; and Nick.

The room was laid out in the style of a courtroom with the town officials sitting at a heavy oak table raised on a platform above and facing rows of benches. This allowed the officials the usual advantage of petitioner intimidation! The development team was seated in the entire second row of a section to the right and the hall was packed and crowded beyond capacity. The crowd consisted of newspaper reporters and local residents, many dressed in jeans and informal shirts.

The assistant mayor banged the gavel and called

the meeting to order. The council began with handling unfinished business and hammered through the design review on a few smaller projects. They then approved a twenty-four-unit building plan. The building would be set off the beach, but with nice views. Nick had been offered the site previously, but turned it down because of its size.

Finally, the North Beach Towers project was called and Tommy, impeccably dressed in a three-piece suit, stood and cordially addressed Mayor Burns and the other board members.

Tommy then delivered a flawless soliloquy outlining the proposed development which primarily summarized the benefits to the city and the community. It stressed the major facelift that would occur on that end of the beach. Tommy spoke as eloquently as possible, giving a good "dog and pony show," while trying at the same time to appeal the address to the level of each of the disciplines on the council and to the attending residents. He finished in twenty minutes and directed the site and building design presentations over to Bobby and Mark.

He sat down and both partners inconspicuously eyed the members' faces. Only the fire chief was smiling. Out of the corner of his eye, Tommy noticed the chief building inspector and the head of the planning board whispering back and forth briefly. Then they both stared at Tommy for a few minutes and looked away.

The meeting went well and the Boomer team seemed to answer most questions satisfactorily. Even most of the residents were silent and the anticipated jeers and complaints from the local hotshots were few.

Mayor Burns concluded the hearing and said, "Everyone present should be aware that the proposed development is in accordance with the zoning by-laws of North Beach and is permitted by right. But make no mistake, the development must strictly conform to all city regulations as administered by every member of this board. This will be thoroughly reviewed and satisfactory to all members before the issuance of the special permit required." Bang went the gavel!

As the room emptied the development team stood in a few groups discussing the outcome of the hearing and handling of certain plan revisions required by the board as stated this evening.

Bobby Ferber slipped off to the men's room.

Outside of City Hall the Boomer team conversed a while on the sidewalk and Nick could see Tommy huddled in conversation with Bobby Ferber. They seemed to be having a serious low-key conversation.

After a while the team members shook hands and parted while Tommy and Nick walked slowly toward the parking lot. "What was that all about?" Nick inquired, curious.

"Not here, Nick. Let's drive to the site and talk."

"By the way, Tommy, you did a fine job in there. I might have added a few points, but enough was said."

Tommy beamed with a smile. "Thanks, buddy," he replied.

The two Mercedes rolled onto the grassy dirt drive of the vacant portion of the site. A few hundred yards away the neon lights of the Paradise Club glimmered inviting men from all walks of life.

The partners emerged from their cars and began talking

about building set-backs and view orientations. The outdoor lights from the neighboring buildings lit the area sufficiently enough to see site details. After a while Nick said, "Talk to me, Tommy!"

"They want money, a lot of money!" Tommy chuckled nervously.

"Who wants money, the mayor…the entire council? Who?" Nick asked in an agonized tone.

"I'm not sure who. Bobby Ferber was approached by some unknown person in the men's room. Apparently, a development panel member or members wants one hundred fifty thousand dollars in cash or the deal will head south! Bobby was told to deliver an answer within a week. He was given a telephone number to leave a message, yea or nay. Further instructions would follow."

"Fuck them!" Nick screamed. They were on the back side of the parcel and, fortunately, could be heard by nobody. "Do you know what would happen to us if that surfaced? The FBI thrives on that sort of thing. Public corruption is on the top of their list of priorities. I've heard a lot lately from some friends. I'm not jeopardizing my career or family for this mound of dirt." Nick kicked a clump of grass with his shoe.

"I know." Tommy sighed. "We'll work it out somehow! Don't be a wimp."

Tommy calmed down a bit and said, "Hey, Nick, let's have a beer next door at that club."

Tommy peeled off a ten-dollar bill for their admission to the club. It was loud inside and a heavyset man with gold chains hanging on an exposed hairy chest pointed to what was apparently the only empty table. Nick and Tommy sat down and looked around and noticed two stages.

On one stage was a girl no more than eighteen years old, on the other a beautiful young woman with long blonde hair and a superb figure who was dancing in the nude with a muscular guy. It was very intimate and Nick wondered if that was legal. It was North Beach, though, which seemed to be immune to the law!

Tommy lit up a cigarette and both men sat back in the plastic chairs to relax and before they could order a drink a middle-aged waitress set down a tray on their table with four Budweisers in bottles. "These are from the two gentlemen at the stage-side table," the waitress said, and pointed in the direction of the stage-side tables.

The chief building inspector, Tony Valachi, sat with a scantily clad stripper in his lap. His friend the planning board chief, Joe Cataldo, sat at the opposite side of the table and tipped his middle and forefinger against his forehead. The partners smiled back. Nick suddenly got the feeling that maybe the mystery of the bribe was unraveling?

CHAPTER 44

Weeks later Nick arose at five a.m. on Wednesday and showered. While dressing he gazed at Noel whose arm was clasped around little Ali. Both were fast asleep. Their love was his ultimate prize possession that even his newly acquired millions couldn't come close to matching. Billionaire status couldn't even compete with their importance!

"I love you deeply," Nick whispered, and he kissed their foreheads. Noel, in a stupor, responded by mumbling, "Me too." He reluctantly left the room, wishing he could linger in this loving scene.

He drove Route 1 due to the heavy road repairs under way on Route 93 through Woburn and Stoneham, and apparently everyone else got the same idea because Route 1 was jammed and the Mystic River Bridge was backed up for three miles from the tollbooths. Nick used the time to call a few general contractors and a dry-wall sub on his cellular car phone.

The first stop was at the Music Maker, the old piano factory rehabilitation in the South End. Pre-sales had begun in the fall of 1983 in the first building and moved slowly at first. The area was a new frontier for middle-class residential development, but the prices were a lower-cost opportunity for yuppies to live in Boston and soon sales became brisk. The asking price for a typical nine-hundred-fifty-square-foot two-bedroom unit was one hundred forty-one thousand dollars, or $148 per square foot, a good value when compared to Beacon Hill or Back Bay. Tommy had been on the money!

Nick walked through the three huge adjoining buildings which housed 166 units and noticed paint stains in the common areas on various stair railings, wood doors, and even on hallway carpeting. It was so pervasive that even a dog lying beside a flower bed outside had paint on his tail and snout! Infuriated, he called the painting subcontractor directly rather than calling Arch Rival, the GC who had contracted with CJ Painting. Ironically, the name was derived from "clean job"!

"Larry Parker, please." Nick spoke in an angry voice. "Larry? Nick Packard."

"Nick, how are you, pal?" Larry inquired.

"Not so good, Larry! How the hell could your guys leave such a sloppy mess? I'm at the Music Maker and there's nothing musical about what I'm looking at right now! Paint stains everywhere. Even on the fucking dogs. Literally."

"I don't know what you're talking about, Nick. Cataldo, our super, moved on to another job after reporting a finish on your job," Larry retorted.

"Well, fire him and hire a super who knows and cares about finishing a job," Nick demanded. "And, this better be corrected by next week because we've got move-ins scheduled at the end of the week."

"Do you know who his father is? A high-ranking politician who I understand is well connected!"

Nick was surprised. He hoped that Cataldo wasn't the son of the could-be extortionist who sent Tommy and him beers last night!

"Larry, just get it resolved!" Nick bellowed.

At nine fifteen a.m. Larry fired Bruce Cataldo, who was hungover from the previous night's partying. Cataldo denied that it was his fault, and even blamed the dog for the mess, but Larry knew better and knew, also, that Boomer would be a major source of business in the future. However, he did make it perfectly clear to everybody, including Cataldo, that the firing was at Nick's order.

In his car, Nick needed to unwind a bit and called Noel, who answered in a dreamy voice. "Hello."

"Noel, what a horrendous start this morning. The painters screwed up at Music Maker and left stains everywhere!"

"Did you take care of it, honey?" Noel questioned.

"I think so. I blasted the sub and he agreed to clean up. Further, he is going to fire the useless super. How could he walk away from such a mess?" Nick replied.

He wouldn't tell Noel about the bribe or the possible, coincidental relationship between the super and the North Sore politician of the same name! He didn't want to frighten her.

"Nick, I love you so much. Can you come home for a while? I'm still in bed. Come hold me."

"Don't tempt me, Noel, or I'll just turn the car north

and push this clunker out to the one hundred sixty miles per hour on the speedometer and be there in nine minutes. I love you too. That much," Nick uttered.

"Anna called a half hour ago and invited you, Ali and me to Rockport on the Fourth of July. I told her that would be fine but I'd check with you. Is that OK?" she asked.

"Yeah, I guess we'll go very late on Friday night because the Glenside office building sale is at three thirty that afternoon and, further, the traffic will be terrible through mid-evening. Ali and you can sleep on the way. The cash from that sale is sorely needed right now," said Nick.

"Good-bye Sleeping Beauty." "Umm...good-bye, love."

Nick hooked a right off Exeter Street onto Commonwealth Avenue and as he drove his thoughts turned to the one-hundred-fifty-thousand-dollar bribe. What if we ignore them? Will we really get turned down by the board and lose the deal?...It could be a bluff! Is it? I'm not taking any part in it. Too much to lose. Way too much! This development will put Boomer Development in a different class and produce mega profits if handled properly! If it is Cataldo's son, how seriously does that mess things up? I'll speak with Tommy again.

As he drove Commonwealth Avenue he inspected the exteriors of four of the buildings Boomer had purchased from Dawson. They had been substantially rehabilitated as residential condos and sold out around $195 per square foot. He then moved on and stopped at two adjoining buildings also in the Dawson package that were under construction by Boomer's construction crew. The Boomer crew had been used to construct the smaller projects while the large projects were always let out to major GC s. Tommy and the Boomer super, Marty, were watching the Beckwith Elevator workers install the rails for a new hydraulic elevator.

Tommy and Marty were staying cautiously clear of the elevator pit. A year earlier they had lost a carpenter who tripped on a board and fell fifty feet to a violent death. The partners had gone to great lengths to comfort his grieving widow and three children. They set up a college trust fund for the kids and contributed generously to the widow.

Nick pulled Tommy aside and said, "This North Beach situation is a hell of a dilemma. If we don't pay we lose our flagship project and if we do we'll jeopardize our careers."

"Nick, calm down we're not paying anybody. I have a friend at Tri-Star Bank who knows the mayor well, socially. You know Phil. He is going to try to influence him to push our deal through."

Nick breathed a sigh of relief. He was pleased. "Good play, Tommy!" He never mentioned the firing of Cataldo.

"Yeah, that's why I am CEO of Boomer. I'm the strategist," Tommy boasted.

Nick went home that evening and had an early Schezuan dinner with Noel and Ali on the terrace of their Wakefield house overlooking the lake. Later in the evening he and Noel kissed and fondled each other on the couch while watching, but not seeing, television. They were still like newlyweds. Life was good despite the intervening problems.

CHAPTER 45

July 4, 1985

The North Shore outing at Rockport was ultimately delayed for several weeks after the dinner at the Bay Tower Room due to the strenuous workload of both Tommy and Nick.

Anna and Noel constantly bugged the men to stop and "smell the roses." After, all both men were pushing forty years old now. Tommy would turn it on July 17 and Nick four months later. They needed more relaxation from their enormous stress.

On Saturday morning Anna's son, Sammy, organized a softball game with them and two of their friends against the adults. The game was played on the back lawn behind Tommy's twelve-room colonial house which was built on a ten-acre parcel of land stretching back from the house to a bluff overlooking the broad Atlantic Ocean. At the edge of the bluff wooden stairs with handrails led down to Tommy's private beach.

Sammy was short, but broad and very muscular. At twelve years of age he was very athletic and made the adults look foolish. Anna hit a few home runs and Tommy pitched a good game, but there was no match of athletic skills between the generations. At one point Noel slid on damp grass and did a somersault in midair, landing on her back. It was a blessing that she landed right and was OK!

After the dreadful loss at the hands of the youth, the adults took a ride in Tommy's jeep and rode through Rockport, passing the quaint shops. As the jeep inched through the typical summer traffic heading into Rockport , one of seven villages in the Gloucester area, Nick and Noel noticed attractive old, but impeccably maintained buildings in a quaint North Shore motif. The small shops raised their curiosity and they took a walk through the shops, browsing everything from antiques to zucchinis, and had lunch at a small local restaurant on the oceanfront terrace, dining on fabulous seafood.

Later the couples drove around town while they all gawked at the huge, magnificent houses out on the beachfront. Many were second homes whose price tags soared into the millions. It was a picture-perfect day with few bright white clouds and a salt smell from the ocean permeated the air. This was certainly a unique place.

On Saturday evening at sunset Tommy's part-time maid, cook, and waitress, Jessica, served a delicious lobster dinner to the entire family on the large terrace. For dessert the cannolis and cakes were superb and the coffee the best. What a lovely ending to a soothing, peaceful day, thought Nick. But what came next eradicated most of that!

After dinner the women retired to the living room while Tommy and Nick stayed outside.

""Tommy, do you have any cigarettes lying around

anywhere by chance? I could go for a smoke with this cognac."

"I might, I'll check." He returned moments later with a half-empty pack of Marlboros which were a month old, but would have to do.

After a sip of cognac and a puff on the cigarette, Nick said, "What a great life we have. We're both extremely blessed. Business success, wonderful wives, great kids. And, look at this piece of Paradise you have here!"

"I've worked hard for what I have, Nick. I sure hope you appreciate what I've done for you. If it weren't for my banking relationships and willingness to pledge my properties as side collateral we never would have gotten this business off the ground. How much are you worth, Nick? Approximately?" Tommy ranted on. "Five or six mil," Nick replied. "Why?" "Well, I'm worth at least twice that. I have a lot more to lose on my personal signature for our debts. You know what I mean, Nick?"

Nick finally realized that Tommy was setting him up for a squeeze play. He wanted more, a larger percentage of the profits. He held his cool and queried, "What are you getting at, Tommy?"

"Nick! Who is setting the ball in motion to resolve the North Beach bribe situation? You know your insistence on CJ Painters firing Bruce Cataldo almost blew that situation apart. What the fuck were you thinking of? Cataldo on the planning board wanted a thumbs down on our deal, but my finesse saved that situation. He and others want to castrate you for that. Bruce claims that you have some kind of vendetta against him. That he left the Music Maker in acceptable condition!"

Someone had told Tommy the botched paint job story, Nick mused. "He's deluded, Tommy. Probably brain-dead on drugs and alcohol."

It was confirmed that fate had struck a sharp blow. Cataldo's son. Whoa! thought Nick.

"What are you getting at, Tommy?" Nick repeated the question. He wanted to hear it straightforward.

Tommy replied, "You know there's inequality in our respective input into our projects. We need to rethink the profit sharing structure!" "Tommy, I am very grateful for your side collateral pledges of the past and your introduction to important financial sources. However, you know that there are offsets. I work double the hours than you do on Boomer projects and have brought some valuable negotiating and financial expertise to this company which has generated a lot of profit. Not to diminish your expert marketing skills. Tommy, I don't know why this is an issue. This weekend has been fun. Why spoil it? We'll talk next week about any inequalities on either side and resolve any differences next week. But I'll never be more than an equal partner!"

Tommy grunted, "Well, it is an issue, but we'll drop it for now."

That night the group went to a fireworks display which rendered everyone in awe, except Nick, who couldn't concentrate on this spectacular scene or anything else!

The next day Nick and Noel parted and warmly thanked the couple for their gracious hospitality. Nick was quiet most of the way home pondering Tommy's anal assault. He didn't mention a word to Noel about it!

On Tuesday of the following week, Alan, the broker responsible for the Beverly Gardens land sale called Nick heralding a rare estate site newly on the market in Waltham, Massachusetts."Nick, this deal has your name on it Alan diplomatically stated. A signature property with Route 128 exposure and no wetlands. That is if you can handle a commercial development? The site consists of five acres fronting on Silicon Drive and Route 128. What would you build?""Maybe a three-bedroom house with a small pasture for cows and goats." Nick chuckled. "Definitely a pig pen included!"

"Nick, you're a hot shit. And, you really know the principles of land use," Alan roared.

"I am really good. I even built horse stables in a prime Beacon Hill building I acquired," Nick retorted comically. His mind churned, and he finally said, "Of course I can handle it, Alan. Without knowing the site conditions, I could probably comfortably build a fifty-thousand-square-foot office building, maybe a bit larger. I'd like to see the property," he responded with enthusiasm. "What's the asking price, Alan?""One million seven hundred thousand dollars, but they'll take less, I think."

On Wednesday Alan and Nick met on Silicon Drive and walked the site together. There were no wetlands and, although core borings would have to be performed, there were no ledge outcroppings.

This is a signature location. Twenty dollars per square foot rent is probably realistic. It won't be available long. Cabot, Cabot and Forbes or American Development Company will jump on it! Although it's probably too small for them. I hope.

"I'm going to make an offer, Alan. Subject to satisfactory soils tests and special permit approvals. The offer will stipulate that a minimum of fifty thousand square feet must be buildable with all municipal and state approvals," Nick stated."What about Tommy? Do you need his approval?" Alan queried."Fuck him, Alan! If he wants to do it as equal partners, fine. If not, I'll do it myself. You know I can pull it off. I've got the track record and financial strength now."

Alan seemed confused, but sensed a struggle between his clients. He diplomatically didn't pursue the issue and went on. "I know that you can, Nick, but I also know Tommy the Bull!"

"You mean Tommy the bull-shitter." Nick thought briefly of the night at the Bay Tower Room where Tommy held the napkin up looking like a bullfighter. He chuckled as he walked away.

CHAPTER 46

Nick drove to his office on Newbury Street contemplating the Waltham property. As he walked the stairs and entered Boomer's modest reception area he was greeted by Liz, The slim red-haired receptionist stood and bent over her desk to retrieve Nick's messages. She showed enough of her soft breasts to catch Nick's attention, then fluttered her eyelashes. Liz laughed. She loved to play with him and he knew it.

"Thanks, Lizzie," Nick replied, as he winked and picked up his messages.

Nick thumbed through the stack. Ronnie of Blaire Construction, Kenny from Blandis Builders, Saginsky of Tri-Star Bank…must call him right away about the 9/15 North Beach hearing! Danny Levin. Danny Levin? Danny from Braintree High School? My childhood buddy! Really? An LA area code, 310-731-2790.

He promptly dialed the LA number.

"Nick Packard calling. Is Danny there?" Nick inquired."Just a moment," a female voice responded."Levin speaking!" a voice sounded.

"Danny, you old rattlesnake. How's life in the desert?"

"Nick, you Zombie! You know that's what I thought you would become after that bicycle accident. What, twenty-eight or twenty-nine years ago? Any repercussions over the years?"

"Yeah," Nick wailed. "I get horny too often!" The old friends laughed heartily.

"That's serious Nick! Ha…ha."

"What are you doing these days, Danny?" Nick queried."I'm leasing office space in LA. Downtown and up to the Hills. Got some fantastic exclusive listings and earning a six-figure income."

"Who's the lady that answered, Danny?"

"My girlfriend, Susie. We're living together."

"Where do you live, Danny?" said Nick.

"Laguna Beach. I'm sitting on the deck here right now."

"Whoa!" Nick groaned. "I'm so envious. Off your deck right now what do you see?"

"Nick, I see a few surf boarders riding the crest of a wave. And over there, a blonde chick on roller blades floating on the boardwalk."

Nick could hear "What's Love Got to Do With It" playing in the background.

"Well, Danny, I'm looking outside my window ad all I can see is a bunch of clouds. It's raining, but not just water, money also. We're having an unprecedented real estate boom here in Massachusetts. Boston is hotter than a pistol! I've made a lot of money in recent years developing real estate. Mainly residential. Condos, or should I say condoms, like Lynn did at the graduation party?

The new West Coast concept Lynn spoke of back in 1967 at the Ocean Club has swept the country. Whatever became of Lynn? Do you ever see her?"

"You didn't know? I guess you wouldn't. We haven't talked for years. Lynn is dead! She got stoned one night at a tub party in the Hills about eight years ago. Left alone to go home. I wasn't there or would never have let her leave alone. Never! Danny's voice cracked. Must have met up with a freak in the Malibu area. Some of her clothes, outer wear, were found by the police in a thicket of bushes off the beach, but she was never found!"

"That's horrendous!" Nick responded. "And I comically tell about the "condom" statement to so many people. I'm shocked!"

"Nick, I'm coming to Braintree the first of October to visit my family for five days. Let's get together for dinner."

"I wouldn't miss it for the world," Nick replied. "Call me when you get here. OK?"

Danny agreed to call when he arrived and they hung up after warm good-byes.

A while later Tommy walked into Nick's office speaking anxiously and was about to tell Nick about the city council hearing scheduled 9/16 for the North Beach Towers special permit decision. He prided himself in being the first person to know everything.

Nick, sensing this, said, "Tommy, North Beach final hearing is scheduled for September sixteenth. Mark it in your appointment book."

"How did you know? Huh?" Tommy quizzed.

"Oh, Mark Raymond called me this morning. He was up at City Hall getting some topographical engineering data on the site and was informed by the Town Engineer."

"Hmm…good," Tommy mumbled.

Then the partners spent the rest of the day on sales issues relative to the rehabbed Commonwealth Avenue buildings from the Dawson package. The Dawsons may have generated substantial cash flow when they were rentals, but Boomer Development was doing even better selling them off as condos!

CHAPTER 47

September 16, 1985

The night was balmy, summer still lingered in Greater Boston with an average of ninety degrees and humidity hovering over. The Kansas City Royals were the front runner in the league for the World Series to begin in October and were playing the Seattle Seahawks this evening. The game would be televised and Nick really wanted to see it. The teams were well matched, in Nick's opinion, and probably would provide some fine entertainment.

He and Noel had a five-hundred-dollar bet between them on the winner of this game. Nick had picked the Royals and Noel, Seattle. He was delighted to bet with Noel on home view events because they would traditionally cheer their teams on hysterically, argue over plays and pretend to fight physically. Then she would pretend to fend him off as he pinned her down and kissed her. Finally, they'd get very serious about the remainder of the game. Maybe there would be time to watch the end this evening with Noel?

The hearing was at eight p.m. and the game began at eight thirty. Maybe I can catch the last few innings with

Noel. Nick was in deep thought as his new 560 SEL purred veering off Route 1 and smoothly negotiated the contour at the Revere Beach exit. The speedometer reluctantly wound down from eighty miles per hour. Oh, one stop for a clam roll, a rare treat, at Kelly's Roast Beef!

At Kelly's on Revere Beach Nick waited in the usual line of patrons for twenty minutes during which time he scanned the building line to the north and then to the south. The construction flood lights which had just turned on produced a view of new structures in both directions some of them mid-rise condo buildings. Both steel frames and others, further along in the construction process with pre-cast concrete or brick and dry-vit sidings.

This place is hot! All these condos with some well along on sales and only one or two completed. If North Beach can attain half this success we'll be flying high! What unspoken business did Tommy have to tend to before the meeting that will make him a slight bit late? I hope that Tommy's contact at Tri-Star was successful in convincing the mayor?

The remnants of his fries and Coke were tossed into the trash barrel beside the seawall. A slight mist of ocean spray brushed his face as he approached his car and leaped into it. He couldn't be late for this one! It was 7:50 p.m..

As the Mercedes whined down Revere Beach Blvd. Nick sailed past a Pontiac Firebird and accelerated. His engine whined like a Lockheed Tristar jet. Just then, the youthful passengers in the Firebird angrily flipped him the bird as he laughed and waved. He had the power edge.

The Firebird went into pursuit, chasing Nick. The Mercedes slowed down as Nick saw an MDC police cruiser parked in the shadows of the ramp of the bridge over water to Lynn. The Firebird concentrating only on its prey sped by Nick as a long-haired youth hung out the window screaming "You fucking…" Nick didn't quite catch the last high-pitched word used.

Nick slowed even more and watched as the cruiser pulled out with its flashing blues lights, chasing the Firebird over the bridge. A few minutes later Nick rode by the Firebird as the driver was handing his license to the cop. The obviously intoxicated occupants of the vehicle glared at Nick as he slowly passed by! It's a good deed that I have just accidentally done! Nick chuckled out loud as he drove along the 10 mile stretch toward North Beach.

The 560 SEL was pushed to the limit along Route 1A headed north. Fortunately, traffic was light and Nick would be to the hearing on time, but with no time to spare. As he meandered down Surf Side Blvd. at North Beach, driving parallel to the spray washed seawall, he passed the now well-known Paradise Club which glowed like the Strip in Las Vegas. The parking lot was full as it was the night he and Tommy stopped in. The old saying "the grass is always greener" rings so true. I'm certainly glad it's as green as possible at my home!

Something caught Nick's eyes as he passed the club. He stared, then gawked! Parked close to the building was a silver Mercedes similar to Tommy's. Nick swerved into the parking lot running over the curb and hastily snaked around to the silver car. He screeched to a halt and studied the plate "Deals – BB." Deals – Back Bay. It was unmistakably Tommy's vehicle! He was confused for a moment. He's not a problem drinker? Then the light dawned on him. But maybe Cataldo and his cohorts are!

Nick began trembling. He thought he knew what Tommy was up to! He revved the engine and screeched out of the lot headed toward the high school which had been chosen for the hearing due to the anticipated overflow of the crowd. This was the first monolith of its kind on North Beach!

Inside the auditorium the crowd buzzed with excitement. The 439-unit development was the largest ever and attracted a lot of residents. The effect on the tax base of the city would be substantial. However, if it was subject to a vote by the residents it probably wouldn't pass because of the usual public opposition to such change.

Fortunately, no zoning changes or variances were required, but that still didn't assure Nick that other issues wouldn't arise to thwart the special permit which needed unanimous council approval. Was Tommy fixing this himself. Nick shuddered to think of it!

It was now 8:37 p.m. and the minor business had just been disposed of. The mayor rose and began to speak, and suddenly the hall doors swung open and in walked Tommy, smiling from ear to ear. He took the reserved seat beside Nick and patted Nick's leg as the crowd buzzed.

Moments later as the mayor began to speak again Cataldo walked in, apologizing for his late arrival, and took his seat near the council panel. The chief councilor looked at him and nodded, then went on. "We are assembled this evening to vote on a request for a special permit by Boomer Development Company of Boston. The permit will be to allow the petitioner to build four hundred thirty-nine condominium units on tax parcels 4795 and 4796 fronting on Surf Side Blvd. in this city. The parcel consists of ten acres of land owned by the Tillis family.

You should be aware that the development parcel is in accordance with the zoning by-laws of North Beach and can be done by-right if the project complies with all North Beach regulations and restrictions to the satisfaction of each member of this council as approved by all North Beach boards. The permit, if approved, will be issued directly on order by this council to the planning board."

Of which Cataldo is head of! Nick stared at the floor while Tommy smiled at the panel straight ahead.

Chief council member Hicks, continuing on, said, "I will now ask the council to discuss any further issues." The fire chief has inquired about fire access and the police chief has asked a question about outside lighting in the rear and below the building at garage level. These were quickly disposed of satisfactorily by Mark and Bobby. Finally, the long pending issue of signage required in the garage below warning of the possibility of a wave pounding over the seawall and flooding the garage in the hundred-year flood was resolved by Mark agreeing to appropriate signage.

Joe Cataldo, in concert with Tony Valachi, the Building Inspector, sitting off to the side began hammering away with fruitless questions and concerns. Tommy had the right answers each time, and finally the pair backed off, saying, "No more questions." Tommy seemed relieved. Then Hicks called for a final vote. As the motion passed each council member some voted thumbs-up. The remainder in a quandary. Cataldo interjected after moments and said to the council, "It's mammoth for the beach…but yes, my board is in favor." All boards were now in favor of the project and the city council all gave thumbs up to issue the special permit.

The Boomer team stood in complete relief and clapped a major applause. Tommy and Nick approached the council platform and shook hands gratefully thanking every member. The audience joined in the applause even. North Beach was ready for a facelift!

As the Boomer cast of characters all shook hands and beamed with joy, Nick extended an invitation for dinner at the Continental Restaurant to all development team members. As the crowd dispersed Tommy and Nick shook hands and hugged each other. Nick knew the line had been crossed. He prayed that there would be no repercussions!

CHAPTER 48

The room was dimly lit and crowded, A festive atmosphere pervaded the entire Continental Restaurant. It was Monday evening and everyone was fresh after a relaxing weekend. The Boomer party occupied a table for eight in the rear of the room. None of the North Beach council members could be invited because of conflict of interest concerns. This seemed farcical to Nick, but he knew that most of them were clean.

Bobby Ferber beckoned for the waitress and ordered a round of drinks. A toast was made by Nelson Thatcher, Tommy's marketing chief. "To the great success of North Beach Towers. May the driving of those mighty piles plant the seed for the rebirth of North Beach." The beach had long ago been graced with a beautiful and classy seaside hotel secluded from the world in an ocean paradise, but the old site was now a vacant weed-infested lot. Nelson's research had determined this fact.

The applause from Nelson's toast hammered with a few whistles from the group. Tommy said, "Nelson, I never knew that you had such a profound way with words." The grouped clapped again and continued imbibing. Tommy asked Mark when his wife was due. "When the Good Lord sees fit. Right now it's on target for December." Nick was impressed by his reference to God and put a manly hug on Mark. "You're a good man, Mark, and a very talented engineer. Without your input we couldn't have pulled this off tonight. Thanks, buddy."

The conversation then turned to the forthcoming real estate development. Bobby cried out, "I'd like to thank you, Nick, for hiring my firm to work on this monumental project! Uh, you too, Tommy."

Tommy winced with displeasure, but said nothing. I made it a reality, not Nick!

"What is the score of the game?" asked Bonny, Nelson's assistant.

"I just went to the bar to check," Tommy announced. "Five to one, Seattle. Final score. Hopefully they're on their way to the Series." A few of the group cheered, halfheartedly, but if the Red Sox were not in it no one cared who wins. Tommy, however, was ecstatic, because he had bet five thousand dollars on the Seahawks and had won!

The meal was then served beginning with a tasty Arugula salad. The traditional popovers were served along with mounds of butter and the main courses of prime rib, a house specialty, salmon, veal, and chicken Marsala kept everyone silent for some time. After dinner the revelry began. Many more toasts were presented by some of the group as they drained three bottles of Dom Perignon which Tommy had so graciously ordered. Bobby spewed lofty accolades to Tommy to minimize his earlier thoughtless remark. Tommy seemed pleased and was in his glory.

Nick, then addressed the group and attention from everyone at the table focused ardently on him, with the exception of Tommy who was carrying on a soliloquy with the occupants of the table adjacent to the group. He was busy waving his arms describing some colossal event he had been involved in. The people at that table just sat mutely.

"Tonight we've reached a milestone in our pursuit of the rebirth of North Beach, as Nelson so profoundly described it." All eyes turned toward Nelson with smiles and chuckles. "Even though I've virtually lost five hundred dollars on the Series game this evening to my lovely wife, Noel, I have gained access to a major new challenge. We all have! If we succeed on the Beach project most of our lives and our bank accounts will be headed north like the Towers." A rapid applause ensued.

"I am pleased to announce that with tonight's approval our financing commitment is firmly in place with Tri-Star Bank. We will close the loan next week and immediately begin driving piles. Deep Earth Foundations will be on site next week." A rapid sound of applause filled the room. Nick's zealous announcement had apparently been heard by others in the room. Nick had gotten carried away and was a bit too loud. The Boomer team roared and shouted catcalls.

He hadn't mentioned that he had agreed to give Tri-Star all existing checking accounts on Boomer projects, and further, to purchase a one million two hundred thousand dollar certificate of deposit to be pledged as side collateral on the deal. It wasn't necessary to reveal any of the financial details to most of the group.

"And, what the hell, the five hundred dollars to Noel

at least is still in the family!" Nick bellowed. The crowd roared with laughter and more toasts ensued. And a lot more drinking! It was a joyous occasion.

The Boomer crowd was buzzed conversing in pairs and threesomes. Tommy left his seat and meandered around through the crowd to Nick's chair. "Let's leave and wind down the night at the Golden Sparrow. A few more drinks to celebrate. Besides, you and I should talk," Tommy solemnly whispered in Nick's ear. "Let's pay the bill first, though," Nick answered.

"It's already paid. We'll settle it later," Tommy replied.

Nick agreed, and after many handshakes and hugs from the crowd, thronged with emotion, the partners departed from the festivities.

Outside the leather-covered double doors the weather had changed dramatically. They encountered wind-driven sheets of rain threatening to drench through to their soles. A lightning bolt lit up the sky like a fireworks display followed by an eerie crash. They stepped back inside where the maître' D offered an umbrella for the walk to their cars. Nick accepted and the two men huddled together like lovers prancing out into the parking lot. The embrace seemed endearing, but, it was to be their last!

Nick held the umbrella over Tommy's head while he squeezed into his Mercedes then moved on to his. Nick drove up to the leather doors and passed the umbrella through his passenger side window. The maître' D said, "Be careful driving. It's treacherous out there!"

CHAPTER 49

The wind howled and the 560 SEL shook as Nick slowly inched his way down Route 1 toward the Golden Sparrow. The visibility was so murky that he almost missed the entrance at the sign which heralded the Gentlemen's Golden Sparrow. In the middle of the lot he noticed Tommy's "Deals – BB" license plate and managed to find a space three cars away.

Inside the club it was packed and the music blared. Gorgeous ladies in tight fitting dresses mingled with the patrons in what seemed somewhat like a night in Monte Carlo. A few ladies were shooting pool with customers in the rear of the sparkling, chandeliered room. The partners clad in impeccably tailored, expensive suits got many female stares as they individually walked in. Both still looked very youthful and their good looks hadn't been diminished by age.

When Nick entered he scanned the room in search of Tommy and finally noticed him seated at a table secluded in the rear of the club. This struck him as being unusual. Tommy liked to sit at stage side and talk briefly to the strippers while they danced. Nick worked his way through the excited crowd who were clapping and shouting catcalls at a gorgeous young dancer with a well-shaped ass bent over and cupping both ass cheeks.

As Nick squeezed through the crowd to the less congested area in the rear he first went to the pay phone and called Noel to tell her the good news. Then he walked to Tommy's table and pulled out the chair across from him. Shaking Tommy's icy-cold hand Nick exclaimed. "Good pull tonight, Tommy!"

"Yeah, really good. I called the right shots," Tommy bellowed.

Just then Edy, the MC, introduced the next dancer, a long-legged lady from Texas with Auburn colored hair. The catcalls resumed.

"You called good shots on this deal, Tommy. Your input was spectacular." Nick was trying to diffuse what he knew was coming."

Then the bomb. "That's why we've got to discuss our relationship, Nick!" Tommy got very serious. Nick's muscles tensed with anticipation. It was a continuance of the discussion started in Rockport. Tommy cannot screw me, I won't tolerate it. He's trying harder now after the hundred and fifty thousand-dollar bribe payoff. He wants to recoup that and much more! Maybe the price went up after the firing of Cataldo's son? I've got no idea.

Tommy proceeded to say "I pledged the side collateral required, my buildings, to secure Kingsley, Beverly Gardens,the Music Maker, the Commonwealth Avenue properties and maybe, yes there were more.

You couldn't have done "squat "without me! Also, my banking relationships made it happen. Can't you understand? It's time I get paid back!" Tommy ranted on.

"I understand all that you've done and I'm appreciative. But, where is your appreciation for my contributions? No matter how you slice the pie they were at least equal to your input! I got the development operation off the ground and brought the Stoneham P and S agreement and the concept. And, that was just the beginning. I located and negotiated all our major land deals, then working twelve hours on some days, I coordinated the work of architects, engineers and general contractors. What the fuck, Tommy! You don't remember all that? You spent no more than four hours a day on all that you did. Where is the inequality, I ask?"

"My input was so much greater than that, Nick. You're blind, you weasel. I had so much more to lose than you!"

"Tommy, you're smoking dope. I'm, unequivocally, no weasel and an equal partner and will remain that until we split!"

"No, two-thirds and one-third on North Beach is what's fair, pal," Tommy demanded.

Then, to Nick's surprise Tommy grabbed his collar from across the table and shook him violently. Nick furiously pulled back and said with extreme anger, "Get your hands off me, you fat prick!" Tommy finally let go, but was full of rage.

Nick stood up and said, "I'm out of here, you madman."

Tommy yelled, "We're not finished!"

As Nick walked toward the door Tommy nudged him

forward and Nick stopped abruptly while Tommy continued pushing him forward. Tommy was drunk and his mean streak had emerged.

Outside in the parking lot Tommy continued to push Nick forward. Then Nick turned around and screamed. "You paid off those whores. Didn't you Tommy. How much? You sold out and jeopardized both of us. We don't need that project to survive. Not for that risk! Well, I'm not going to let my career go down the drain. I'd testify against you if it ever came to that!"

Tommy got blindly ferocious after that remark and yelled, "None of your fucking business!"

"None of my business? It certainly is!" Nick yelled.

Tommy suddenly threw a right punch, hitting Nick's shoulder and knocking him on his back into a puddle of water. He was stunned, and rose, saying, "You're an animal! The truth hurts, doesn't it? What fucking guilt!" Nick swung back at Tommy and hit his multilayered stomach while Tommy slipped back.

Nick walked to his car and proceeded to open the door. Tommy rushed him from behind, swung him around and hit him squarely in the forehead with brute force. Nick slid down the door on the driver's side in excruciating pain, then lost consciousness as he fell.

The rain soaked Nick's bloody face while the blood poured profusely from his mouth! He wiggled and shook spasmodically as if in a seizure. He then lay motionless on the rain-washed pavement.

Drunk and panicked, Tommy ran to his car, jumped in and backed up smashing cars in the next row back across the aisle. Petrified, he screeched out and sped away sideswiping a few more vehicles as he fled the scene!

"Pretty serious. I don't know if he'll make it. Maybe a DOA!" the EMT cried into the ambulance microphone moments later.

Momentarily, the crowd gathered outside the club, mostly under the extended awning, and watched the gruesome scene in shock as the rain poured down heavily. A lightning bolt flashed followed by an eerie boom!

Nick's open wallet lay on the ground beside him displaying a photograph of Noel and Ali. It contained five hundred dollars in cash also. The EMT picked it up and tucked it in his pocket!

CHAPTER 50

The emergency room was hectic at 12:09 a.m. with arms and legs draped over every available chair. Some were in severe pain, but some were in the wraps of psychosomatic illness. The medical profession thrived on such malady. Nurses and resident doctors bandied about trying to quell emotions.

When the outside ER doors swung open and the gurney carrying Nick's bloody and seemingly lifeless body was wheeled in, a great silence pervaded the whole area. This man was in serious condition thought many people who watched the scene. A somber mood prevailed everywhere.

After a quick exam by the resident doctor many tests were administered . EKG, CAT-SCAN and others. Nick was alive but seemingly hanging on to the bare threads of existence.

Noel rushed in. She had been informed a half hour earlier by the police and was still hysterical. She furiously hugged him while he lay stone cold on the stretcher. I love him so much! Who could ever do this to him? Why? Even a robber would probably not be so violent! Noel queried the doctors, but they couldn't answer these questions.

As the early morning hours lingered on with no explanations, Noel harbored intense frustration. Her husband lay there in complete silence. She sat by his bedside in the ICU and realized that this was the second time in Nick's life that such a brutal head injury occurred. Tears flooded her eyes while she pondered: why Nick? She didn't understand because he was a good man?

Nick's gaze stared upward fixed on the ceiling. He lay there in the ICU hopelessly unconscious it seemed. Noel sat, her mind in deep thought. Tears trickled down her cheeks as she softly rubbed his forehead. He'll regain consciousness. I know he will! I pray he will. I hope he will?

After a short while she stood and as she exited the room she noticed the number 40 on the door. Tears flooded her eyes as she recalled their marriage in room cuarenta (forty) in Santo Domingo, that paradoxical paradise. She hurried to the lobby to use the telephone.

After eight rings a voice answered, "Um…hello."

"Anna!" Noel cried. "Is Tommy home?"

"Why wouldn't he be? Noel? Uh, it's four o'clock in the morning!"

"Anna, I'm at Unity Hospital. Nick's been beaten severely! He's unconscious and might not pull through! He was with Tommy last night after the North Beach hearing. That was, last I heard from him."

"Oh my God!" Anna screamed in shock. Noel could hear in the background "Tommy, Nick's in the hospital. Unconscious. Here, take the phone."

Tommy took the phone and said in a low tone, "What happened, Noel?"

Odd, he seems so calm? She quickly dismissed the thought. She had awoken them from a sound sleep. "When? Where? Why?" Tommy queried. "I know nothing!" Noel cried. "Someone found him lying in the parking lot of the Golden Sparrow. You were with him earlier. He told me when I talked to him around nine thirty. He was on a pay phone at the club unwinding with you." "I left him there about ten thirty and told him to go home and be careful driving. He was drinking heavily and wanted one more drink before he left. I left then." Tommy's voice cracked and he cleared his throat. His nervousness almost became apparent! "I left before him because I had an early morning appointment today." He had been rehearsing this lie ever since he left the scene. His only hope was that the blunt trauma would erase the memory of the night. That is, if Nick even lived. Maybe he'll die! Tommy was so paranoid that he had mixed emotions about this. "Tommy, why did you leave him in a drunk condition? Why didn't you take him home?" Noel screamed into the telephone. "Noel, he's a big boy and quite smart. He made his decision to stay. He wasn't staggering drunk and he talked fine."

"Well, he wasn't fine and was apparently drunk enough to get attacked and rolled."

"Rolled?" Tommy replied quizzically.

"Yes, his wallet was missing and hasn't been found!"

"We'll be there as soon as possible," Tommy replied.

Tommy placed the receiver on the phone and inwardly sighed with temporary relief. She has no clue of what happened. Thank God for the missing wallet? I pray Nick comes out of it with a memory lapse. I remember his story about the bicycle accident when he was a kid. He said that twenty-six or twenty-seven years or so later he still can't remember the accident! It appears to everyone to be a mugging. Whew!"

Tommy was battered with guilt. The irony was that he had been drunker than Nick. He knew he shouldn't have drunk so much because of his violent anger problem caused by alcohol. He was now frightfully scared!

Noel returned to the ICU, obliviously bumping into passersby. She was in a serious state of shock. As she entered room 40, a doctor was checking Nick's vital signs, which were almost back to normal. Blood pressure 139/95. Heart rate ninety-five beats per minute.

"How bad is he, Doctor?" Noel pleaded.

"Well, the tests show no permanent brain damage. But, the concussion is severe. We think that he'll regain consciousness soon."

"Who's we?" Noel inquired with concern.

"That's the opinion of Dr. Gibbons, Chief of Neurology, myself and other doctors here now," the doctor stated. Noel drew some relief from this!

At six a.m. Tommy and Anna walked into the room. Anna was laden with tears and tried to console Noel with a hug and reassurance as she held Noel's hand. Tommy's face was whiter than snow. He was apprehensive about being caught in his lie. He wanted to confess but didn't dare.

"What do the doctors say?" Anna asked.

"A severe concussion. He'll most likely come out of it and regain consciousness soon. And, thank God, no brain damage showed on the Cat Scan. I pray all this is accurate."

Noel then burst into a steady stream of tears. "He'll be OK! He will. He will!" said Tommy and Anna in unison while caressing Noel's shoulders.

At six thirty a.m. two burly men entered room 40 and stared at Nick a moment. One of them, a long-blond-haired, youthful man displayed a badge. "Detective Biff O'Hara, and this is Detective Julio Martinez. Peabody Police. How's he doing?" O'Hara queried.

"He's still unconscious, but he only had a concussion and, although quite serious, the doctors think that he'll come out of it soon and he'll be OK," Noel explained. Both detectives showed sincere relief and tried to comfort her.

"Ma'am, what do you know about this?" Julio went on in typical police style.

"Nothing, Mr. Martinez. I would hope that you could tell me something," Noel replied, somewhat frustrated.

"We know little, Mrs. Packard. With one exception. A witness noticed a man dressed quite well standing beside another man but, didn't get a good look at either of them because of the pelting rain. This was around eleven p.m. and was right where the beating took place. Beside Mr. Packard's vehicle. That's all we have. Was he with anyone that you know of, Mrs. Packard?" Martinez inquired.

"Yes, he was with his partner, Tommy Fletcher." She turned to Tommy and said, "You tell them, Tommy!" "I was with him after a city council hearing until ten thirty p.m. and then left to go home," stated Tommy. Then, the detectives asked a barrage of questions concerning the entire evening. Tommy had prepared for this over and over in his mind and answered all questions innocently, displaying no guilt. He then leaned back in his chair against the wall and began to sweat profusely. His heart beat rapidly and paranoia set in. He imagined that all eyes were on him, but they weren't, with the exception of Noel who felt, suspect fully, that there was more to the story.

"We'll speak with Mr. Packard soon then." Hopefully! Martinez concluded with. The two lawmen left the room bidding good luck to all.

Tommy slowly regained his composure. He was ecstatic that they had left. Do they suspect me? O'Hara's glance was very unnerving!

Tommy and the women then left for coffee in the hospital cafeteria.

Later on that afternoon a white-haired nurse entered room 40. She had a stethoscope hanging off her neck and wore a crisp, neatly-pressed blue uniform. Surprisingly, she noticed Nick raised up in bed looking quizzically around the room.

"And how are we this morning, Mr. Packard?" she inquired.

"I don't feel very bad, but why am I here?"

"You suffered a very serious concussion to your head and you're in Union Hospital, Mr. Packard." That's all she felt she should say when Nick spewed many questions and she said, "You rest, and the doctor will be in soon."

After a few moments of his confusion, Noel entered the room from a walk through the hospital to stretch. She let out a cry of relief seeing Nick sitting up and looking around.

"Honey, are you OK?" Noel kissed him again and again while he kissed back.

"I'm pretty good, but please tell me what happened," Nick said impatiently.

Noel went on to tell the entire story to Nick about the attack by someone at the Golden Sparrow and the serious concussion resulting from it. How he and Tommy went there for whatever reason? "I don't care that you were there. You did call me and told me where you two were. I know that you are and always will be a good husband." She repeated Tommy's explanation of the events that night and about the missing wallet presumably stolen by a mugger. Then she hesitated and said, "Nick, I don't think Tommy's being totally straight about the story. He doesn't look me in the eye when he talks about it. There's something missing, I can sense it? Please, let's review the events of the evening. Do you remember anything Nick?"

They began with the hearing which he remembered. He remembered the hearing quite well. The project had been approved. The dinner at the Continental was very hazy and the following jaunt to the Sparrow vaguely remembered, but no memory of anything that occurred there. Beyond that was very hazy. Noel tried very hard to get him to remember the events at the Golden Sparrow, but Nick's memory was too sketchy.

The neurologist stopped in an hour later and was very pleased with Nick's progress. He decided to have Nick stay at least one more night then possibly be discharged after a final visit by the doctor around noon.

The detectives, Martinez and O'Hara, entered the room

later in the day. They were surprised to see Nick sitting up in bed and talking with Noel. Both men repeated their introduction for Nick's benefit. Martinez was more gruff and determined than the previous day. Only their last names were stated.

"What happened at the Golden Sparrow?" O'Hara asked, after all the pleasantries were disposed of.

"Where?" Nick asked, responding as if in total confusion.

"You have no recollection of what happened last night? Is that right?" Biff asked.

"A little earlier in the evening, but nothing later on. I remember that my company and I had a hearing earlier in the evening and then I think a victory dinner. Beyond that I don't remember!"

"Do you remember being with Mr. Fletcher at any time last night?" Martinez inquired.

"Of course! We're partners, and both of us attended the hearing, then I vaguely remember talking to him at a restaurant."

"You still don't remember the Golden Sparrow?" "No, sir, I don't. And my head is pounding now. If you'll excuse me, I have to sleep."

The pair stopped questioning Nick and wished him well as they left the room. They had questioned Tommy earlier that afternoon and got the story about how he and Nick had gone to the Golden Sparrow to unwind with a few drinks. Further, he told them that he left around ten thirty p.m. because of an early morning meeting scheduled the next day. Anna could corroborate the facts Tommy said to them.

He was very convincing and gave the detectives nothing to "chew on" . It was a dead end street and they would close it out for now as an unsolved mugging. Nick's wallet was missing!

The following day Nick was discharged and sent home, with doctor's orders for at least a four-day bed rest. This head injury was déjà vu. A repeat after twenty-eight years. Nick prayed that it was the end of it all!

CHAPTER 51

Nick casually lay in bed at home while Noel helped tend to his needs. She served many meals in bed for the first few days and brought him everything he needed outside their home such as his mail and new magazines and books. She also gave him much attention and affection which really turned him on. I'm so fortunate to have this relationship with Noel! She is the light of my life and I would die for her.

After a few days Nick began to feel much better physically and mentally. His memory was improving and the events of the night of the debacle beginning to register in his mind. On the evening of the third day, Noel began questioning him about the night again, starting with the drive to the hearing which he remembered. The stop at Kelly's, the hearing and who was present and the outcome of it all was crystal clear to Nick. He also remembered the bribe that evening, but said nothing to Noel about that. Some things should never be discussed outside the business!"You know, Noel, I remember what occurred after the hearing much better now. The dinner at the Continental was a happy occasion. I had Salmon I remember. Then, Tommy wanted to go to the Golden Sparrow to wind things down. I liked the celebration and any club would have been fine with me," Nick stated. "I know, honey, I trust you completely, but that's not the issue in this situation. Please go on," Noel purred."I remember Tommy going directly to a somewhat isolated table in the rear of the club. Tommy started arguing that he should get a larger interest in North Beach because of the fact that all his contributions to our deals far exceed mine. He had some idea of a new percentage split on North Beach that I can't quite remember. I think that I argued a bit and denied any inequality and refused to discuss any changes. He apparently was drunk and flew off the handle pushing me around. That I remember quite well. As I left I think that he pushed me out the door. Outside he continued to push me and knocked me over." Nick was silent for many moments. "I just remember Tommy yelling at me, but I draw a blank after that."

"Wow," Noel said. "I knew there was more to Tommy's story, but not to these extremes! Nick, do you think he hit you? Why was your wallet missing? Did he hit you, then panic and take your wallet to make it look like a mugging?"

"I have no idea, honey! Maybe the wallet fell out and someone picked it up later? I don't know. But the chances that Tommy dealt the final blow are quite high giving the intense situation between us! What other explanation?! I know he has a problem with anger and especially when drinking alcohol, but, the fact that he'd hit me like that and then leave the scene is hard to believe!" Nick said as he began to tremble. Noel hugged and tried to console him.

I'm through with him…fuck him…dissolve the partnership! He'll settle under my terms!

As his thoughts cleared, his mind shifted to future business while he recuperated. His thoughts focused on the Waltham land deal which he had put under P and S agreement earlier in July at a price of one million two hundred fifty thousand dollars. I'm going to close on the land as soon as possible…must call Lenny at Tri-Star to button down the financing commitment…And, Danny. Maybe he's my marketing chief? Fuck Tommy. He and I are history. I'm nervous about even being around him now!

Nick, then, dialed the Tri-Star number.

"Hello, Tri-Star Bank. How may I direct your call?" a soft voice answered."Lenny Saginsky, please. Nick Packard."

"Nick, how are you, buddy?" Lenny replied after he picked up the receiver."Oh, I'm fine, Lenny," Nick exaggerated. "I'm calling about the five acres in Waltham under agreement that I ran by you a month or so ago. I am planning a fifty-thousand-square-foot office building for the site, with ground level parking below and outside, which, by the way, I plan to move my office to. We'll take about three thousand square feet."

"Why don't you and Tommy drop by here later this week?""Lenny, it's just me on this one. Tommy's sticking to residential only. I'll need an acquisition/construction loan of about five and a half million dollars. There's an NOI of about six hundred seventy-six thousand dollars using a nineteen dollars per square foot rental rate with five percent vacancies. It's supported. Nineteen dollars is conservative in that location."

Lenny banged away on his calculator for a few minutes. "Nick, using a one-point-two coverage ratio at a ten percent constant on the five hundred sixty-three thousand dollars, it sounds like it'll be covered by the takeout. You will need some pre-leasing, maybe forty percent, which we'll talk about after I run it up the ladder. Send me a letter of request, including the financial projections, and list any pending leasing interest."Nick didn't have any at this point, but just replied, "OK, Lenny."

Lenny went on, "You probably will need some side collateral, Nick, because of the North Beach project and the tight coverage with a ten percent constant. Maybe one million dollars. That's maximum. Maybe less."

"No problem with the collateral, Lenny." Ironically, Tommy will be the source of side collateral on this one too. He fucked me so bad! We'll settle on my terms! Yes. "I'll send the projections within a few days," Nick promised."Fine," Lenny replied. "I'll talk to you soon, pal."

Nick, relieved after the positive response, reclined and called 310-731-2790.Danny Levin answered abruptly. "Hello, Levin speaking,"

"Danny, you sound so serious. It's Nick!"

"Oh, I'm sorry, Nick. I had an extremely difficult day and Susie, my girlfriend, and I are in the middle of a major argument." "Susie, will you pipe down. I'm trying to talk to Nick, my old childhood buddy." A few more muffled comments echoed in the background. Then complete silence ensued for minutes.

"Nick, again, excuse me! Susie's at that time of month. What a bitch. Does Noel react that way too?"

Nick roared with laughter. "What woman doesn't? They bleed and we suffer as much as them. But what would we do without them? We're lucky to have them!"

"True," Danny replied.

"Danny, are you still coming to Boston on the first of October?"

"Yeah, sure. I'm flying into Logan around eleven a.m."

"Good, Danny. Can you meet me for dinner at L'Espalier on Exeter Street? Do you know the restaurant?" Nick inquired.

"I've been there once before. It's a fine restaurant. I'll be there. What time?"

"I'll meet you at eight p.m., and it's on me. Good-bye, my friend." Nick had unconsciously picked up Mario Cavallaro's cliché. He despised that!

On October 1 the childhood friends met once again after seventeen years and emotionally exchanged hugs and handshakes below the sparkling chandelier in the exquisitely adorned lobby of the L'Espalier Restaurant.

After being seated by the maître d', Nick ordered a round of drinks and inquired, "How was your trip, Danny?"

"Fine until we flew over the Great Lakes and hit some pretty heavy turbulence. It was a bit unnerving, to say the least. Then, all of a sudden the plane seemed to hit a concrete wall and veered off while glasses and trays flew into the air. Then the pilot descended rapidly until it smoothed out. For a moment I thought we were going down. Horrible feeling! The pilot never announced a word over the speaker!"

"You know, Danny, a similar thing occurred when I was on a flight between Boston and New York City. A pilot riding as a passenger told me that it was wind shear. I know the feeling. It's pretty scary! But, you're here in one piece," Nick said, as he clinked his glass against Danny's."Well, enough for that. How's your business going, Nick?""It's going quite well. We've made a fair amount in residential real estate development. We now have close to one thousand units in various stages of planning and development."

"Wow!" Danny replied. "That's incredible. But, who's we?"Nick didn't respond to the question at first. He wouldn't mention the serious problem between he and Tommy.

"Danny, I'm going to do a lot more commercial development in the future. I'm switching gears to commercial. Much easier to deal with if the projects are well located. It's a solid market "We, includes my partner Tommy Fletcher who I'm splitting with. He wants to develop residential only. Condos and apartments."

Danny became excited. "Do you have a good marketing team. I mean are you all set to move forward?"

Nick continued . "Well, Danny, I have excellent brokerage relationships with Coldwell Banker and other smaller firms, but no in-house marketing professionals yet." He led Danny into it well. He knew Danny was a good salesman years ago at the graduation party and had further checked into his LA dealings and found him to be a top notch commercial broker. He had leased over five hundred thousand square feet of California retail and office space to some prestigious companies in recent years.

"Nick, I'm thinking of making a move back to the

Boston area and would seriously like to get into development here. Could you give me a shot at it on some level?""Well, Danny, I don't think so. You're way too expensive for me. West Coast and all. You probably earn more than I do right now," Nick teased."Oh, cut the shit, Nick. That's a joke. I would be willing to take a reasonable base salary and a small commission percentage on leases."

"What, a hundred-fifty-thousand-dollar annual salary and ten percent of the annual base rent?" Nick chuckled. "That's not far off from what the brokerage firms get."

"No, no. I'd be willing to take a seventy-five-thousand-dollar salary and five percent of base rent if I lease the space, and one percent if an outside broker leases it, for openers!"

Nick hesitated, then, extended a hand shake to Danny. "Welcome aboard. Can you start by November tenth? And what about Susie? Will you bring her?"

Danny gave an uncertain response. "Don't know yet! Let's see how it goes before Susie comes, and November tenth is fine."

"By the way, Danny, our first project will be the development of a fifty-thousand-square-foot office building in Waltham, Massachusetts. The land acquisition will close on the fifth of November. So November tenth will be a perfect start date for you and as of now no leasing efforts have yet been made on this building."

CHAPTER 52

November 1985

On November 8, Danny moved into a one-bedroom apartment at Kingsley Estates in Stoneham which Nick had retained as an investment. Nick offered him three months free rent to allow Danny enough time to scope the job out. After that, he would pay a token amount of four hundred dollars per month for rent. An amount unheard of since the 1970s!

Danny exhibited professionalism from the start. He took command of the marketing effort for Ford Plaza, the new Waltham office building, immediately. He made cold calls, gave open listings and advertised all over the East Coast in the New England Real Estate Journal and other publications for this new first-class office building.

Financing had been committed and Nick's closing on the Waltham land was delayed until November 15. The date had finally been set. He needed an additional five hundred thousand dollars in cash to satisfy the Tri-Star Bank one million dollars cash collateral requirement. He had four hundred thousand dollars in personal money market funds available. He tried to pledge the Fletcher note for the remaining side collateral but couldn't get that approved. He did, however, get it reduced to four hundred thousand dollars, which he could just about handle.

Nick was sitting in his temporary office space in Wakefield that he had leased for fifteen months pending the completion of Ford Plaza. He had not been back to Boston since that fateful night when Tommy had betrayed him.

His secretary, Beth, chimed over the speaker. "Mr. Packard, Mr. Fletcher on line three."

Nick shuddered with relief. He had been waiting for this call for some time. He could never have called Tommy first. It would have been a complete sign of weakness!"Hi, Nick! How are you? Are you feeling better?" Tommy inquired after two months of silence except for a few brief calls after the hospital to check on Nick's condition each time speaking with Noel."Not good at all, Tommy, I've been experiencing excruciating headaches. At least every other day!" Nick slowly wove his fabrication.

"I'm having a series of CAT scans next week. I can't sleep most nights. "Umph". I'm having shooting pains right now! Thank God for Percocet!"

Complete silence ensued and held for a moment as a sick feeling permeated Tommy!"Tommy, are you still there? Hello?""Yes, I am. I'm sorry to hear this Nick. Have the Peabody police found any more evidence to help solve the case? I mean anything? New witnesses?" Tommy uttered.

Nick noticed his main interest was the possibility of him getting caught. "Zilch, Tommy! Nothing." Nick moaned for effect. Then more silence.

"What are we going to do about North Beach?" Tommy inquired. "It's been at least two months since the council approval and nothing has been done? You never followed thru on the pile driving contract? What's up, buddy?"

The opportunity was sprung! "Who's to blame for that? Do you think I'm out in space or, even more so, a mental retard? The case was solved that night when your giant paw thrust in my face! Nick was certain enough now about what happened to make the accusation. You're guilty Tommy. I do remember what happened. No permanent memory loss like I suffered way back in 1957. That was more than a concussion then. Sorry!"

Tommy was struck dumb. He stuttered a few words and then regained his composure. He mumbled something about Nick being on a fishing expedition or maybe even hallucinating. He stated, "Nick, I think you belong back in the hospital!"

Nick became furious and couldn't believe how this man, a friend from childhood, could strive to keep the lie intact. But, he held his cool.

"Tommy, needless to say, after what you've done we can't continue as partners. I want you to buy me out. I'll take twelve million dollars—a ten-million note and two million in cash. A bargain for you!"

Tommy got belligerent and replied, "Yeah, do you want my house and kids' bikes too? You buy me out. I'll gladly sell if the properties are worth that much now!"

"Tommy, you called the shot when you attacked me and almost put me six feet under." Nick knew he was justified in doing this at this point. "I'm not buying you out. I'm going commercial and don't have time to take the unfinished projects on. That's your cup of tea, Tommy. You're geared up for that."

Tommy sat back in his antique desk chair and thought. Nick could bring charges for assault and battery. Not for attempted murder. I hope? That bastard is holding this over me to settle! Extortion? Maybe. But he's crafty. Not once did he threaten charges as leverage to settle!

Tommy stared at the wall white-faced as he became fear stricken. He was claustrophobic and thoughts of jail sent chills of horror through his body. Paddy wagons…holding cells…heavy metal doors with tiny glass windows…and potential prison rape! It was too much to bear. As tough as he was he couldn't take that.

Twelve million dollars. He's crazy. Maybe I should have him killed? Ten thousand, maybe fifty thousand for him. I'd be free, and there were no other witnesses. Even if he told Noel, she was not a witness.

Tommy took Nick off hold and said, "I'll call you back." He hung up.

The next day after the telephone conversation Tommy sat and contemplated his thoughts about what could be the easy way out. He knew a lot of people and knew who to call. He called a discreet telephone number and made arrangements to meet the following day to discuss possibilities to solve a money problem with his business partner. He, unwittingly, said too much. He wasn't experienced in this sort of dealing! "Say, no more!" The phone went silent.

Tommy sat there at his desk while his thoughts ran rampant. His chest tightened like a vise with anxiety. This was a first, but he was more afraid of Nick than dealing with these people.

How much is his real interest in Boomer Development worth? He thought. Tommy grabbed a legal pad and current sets of financial statements from his credenza, then scribbled:

So. Boston Condos - 72 unsold units @ $135 K =		$9,720 K
Less: Mortgage balance and other related debt,net		6,358
Net value		3,362
50% Packard	$ 1,681K	
Comm. Ave. - 49 unsold units @ $180 K =		8,820
Less: Mortgage balance and other related debt,net		5,133
Net value		3,687
50% Packard	$1,844 K	
Net Value of Packard		
Real Estate interests	$ 3,525 K	
Money Market instruments, net of admin. Debt		2,976K
50% Packard		$1,488K

North Beach land- $ 15,000. per unit x 439 units= $6,585K value, net of $ 4,390 K Purchase Price committed = $2,195 K - 33 1/3 %

Packard	$ 732K
Total Value of Packard interest	$5,745K

So, he wants over double what he is rightfully entitled to! That little prick. Maybe I'll offer him two million dollars in cash from the money market investments and the North

Beach land which I can value at twenty thousand dollars per unit with the approvals in place. That will bring him up over six million dollars in his mind and I'll still have all the Boston real estate! That will suit me fine. I'll be way ahead of him down the road.

He thought about the settlement all afternoon and the next day. He was a God-fearing man and thought of what his fate might be if he took the route he had contemplated yesterday. He had to quickly squash this nightmare. He couldn't bear the internal conflict which had arisen!

At 5:37 in the afternoon he reached a mental decision and dialed Nick's office number. When Nick came on the line after a few minutes he then spoke softly and Tommy,at the same time, remained composed. "Ni-ick," Tommy said, as if they were still good friends, "despite your lack of understanding about what happened that night, I think you're right. We should split. Too much damage done already! But how can I give you twelve million dollars? That's more than both our shares together."

"My numbers are quite different and that's what I want," Nick replied.

"I've done an analysis of value and have come to a fair opinion of values. I am offering you your requested two million dollars in cash and one hundred percent of the North Beach property, which has to be worth at least twenty thousand dollars per unit now," Tommy exaggerated, "with the four hundred-thirty-nine-unit special permit issued. That's a market value of eight million seven hundred eighty thousand dollars, Nick! That would give you a net equity value of four million three hundred ninety thousand dollars." The total settlement will, therefore, be six million three hundred ninety thousand dollars. Take it, Nick, it's a good deal!"

"Tommy, don't waste my time. You must think I'm a neophyte. You want to take the best located properties in New England. Boston is almost a sure thing. Then you want to give me the lion's share of my equity in Boomer Development projects in an undeveloped parcel of land in a honky-tonk area where the project is pioneering! If another recession strikes during this development, which it will, the project will go out with the North Beach tide if building and sales are occurring at the time!"

"Please, my head is aching," Nick moaned. "This discussion is over!" He hung up.

Tommy called back in five minutes. "We need to meet and discuss this further," he meekly suggested.

"I wouldn't meet with you unless I was escorted by a squad of Green Berets and I don't know any. So forget it! Look, I don't care about settling as much as I do about healing. If that ever happens? Our settlement will come to a head before long."

"Hold on, Nick. Be reasonable. What do you want realistically? Huh?" Tommy then broke down and sobbed. "Nick, you're relentless and I can't take much more! We have to get on with our lives."

"You're right we must settle," Nick mused. Tommy, a man of great strength, a tough negotiator. And, now he's sobbing? His guilt is pouring out!

"Tommy, I just want what's fair. Half the equity in all our interests."

"What Nick? How much?" Tommy pleaded. He never said a word about his excessive input and about changing the profit split! Nick knew he had him good and rightfully so. He proceeded to revise Tommy's calculations as rattled off and arrived at a high Boomer total equity value of twenty million dollars. Then he said, "Tommy, I want at least half, ten million dollars. A million and a half in cash and a promissory note of eight and a half million secured by mortgages in whatever position available on everything you own except your house and, uh, kids' bikes. Are you with me on this?"

"Nick, you're brutal! You and I both know that your interests are not worth more than six million dollars to you. Please, be reasonable?"

He never used the word please since I've known him! It's time to finalize this, now!

"Tommy, I'll give you the benefit of the doubt. I'll take the million and a half in cash and reduce the note to seven million dollars, secured by all properties, and I approve all your future property sales and re-financings. You'll need mortgage releases from me anyway. This is final, and if we can't settle on it we'll say good-bye and let it work its way out!"

Tommy was paranoid and knew when to stop. "I assume that I get a complete release of liability of any and all nature from you? And, a letter absolving me from any criminal matters to date whatsoever?"

"Tommy, can you say you're sorry for what happened?" A long silence ensued. He could be setting me up for the admission of guilt! Is he recording the conversation?

Finally. "Nick, I'm sorry our relationship turned out like this!"

Nick knew that was all he was going to get! "We have a deal, Tommy. I'll get Mike Kensington to prepare the documents when he has the time."

Tommy replied,

"It must be done within two days. I'm going to Ireland for vacation with Anna after that."

Nick agreed and hung up.

Tommy wiped his brow, then craved for a drink. But, first Tommy had to take care of unfinished business. He nervously dialed the obscure telephone number and postponed the clandestine meeting until further notice. Everything was now on hold, but had to be left open! Nick could change his mind and press harder.

As the hours passed Tommy watched the clock more and more closely. He arrived at his final decision. No way was he going to let this deal and opportunity for peace of mind go by the boards, no matter what the price!

Two Days Later

At four thirty in the afternoon Tommy entered Mike Kensington's office and after a period of verbally accosting Mike, reluctantly signed all necessary documents. He didn't dare piss Nick off and took it out on Mike whom was used to such verbal assaults. The mortgages given as security for the note were spread over every inch of Mike's huge conference table. Tommy signed the agreement and all other related documents. Then he signed the mortgages without any review and made no changes! Nick had really screwed him through his perception.

Mike collected a bank treasurer's check for one and a half million dollars, payable to Nicholas A. Packard.

The signed note also was handed to Mike. The interest rate was 9 percent per annum.

Nick proceeded to reach into his brief case and retrieve the golden nuggets for Tommy, a mutual complete release of liability and a letter absolving Tommy from any criminal violations signed by Nick to serve as a release from all criminal acts to date. Mike's assistant then notarized both signatures on all recordable documents. It was completed!

Suddenly, in a burst of uncontrolled anger Tommy grabbed the conference room tablecloth on the table's end and pulled hard. The documents flew in every direction while he proceeded to tip the large table over on its side. Mike backed up and stared in horror as Tommy glared in his direction. It was quite well known that Mike was Nick's ally. The relationship had been forged way back in Nick's house-building days.

Tommy soon regained his composure, but angrily said, "Fuck you, Mike, we're history! There is a conflict of interest here!" Tommy wailed as he exited the room.

Mike knew better. He had only prepared documents reflecting a mutual agreement between his two clients and had structured them fairly from a legal standpoint. He felt truly sorry for Tommy's blunder. The uncontrollable anger had flared again and would someday be his downfall!

Mike and Nick sat for a while after the closing. "Here's your check for a million and a half, and a copy of the executed note. I'll keep the original in the safe," Mike said. "Quite a coup!"

"Yeah, yeah. But Mike, am I guilty of extortion?"

"I doubt it, Nick, under the circumstances. You suffered serious damage from him. Besides, if I understand you right, you never threatened criminal charges if he didn't settle. Right?"

"Mike, I never did. The furthest I went was to say If we can't agree I would walk away from the table and it would "come to a head" eventually. That wasn't a threat for criminal charges. It could have meant many things."

"Such as?" Mike inquired.

"Such as if I didn't cooperate and agree with future condo selling prices I could block sales closings and we'd have to settle sooner or later, for example."

"Very good. And, Nick, before you leave I need a check for twenty-one thousand dollars. Overdue legal bills. Finally, since you struck gold today, you can take me to dinner."

Nick said, "You whore," and they both laughed.

CHAPTER 53

Sitting back reclining in his office chair with his feet on the desk, Nick contemplated his future. He now had one million seven hundred fifty thousand dollars in cash, a seven-million-dollar note receivable fully secured, and another two million dollars in real assets, with no debts. That's almost eleven million dollars of net worth. His interest income on the note was fifty-two thousand five hundred dollars per month. What a nice start on my own!

His thoughts turned to the house in Hamilton, Massachusetts, that Noel had dreamed of. He was at a point where he could build the house with his own cash and even retire. I could retire with a nice income and Noel, Ali and I travel around the world. Europe...Caribbean...anywhere else. But, that's not in the cards now! I love my work, and besides, Tommy's empire could fall apart. There are no guarantees in life. His note to me could become worthless and I'm not about to lose it all, if I can help it!

Without further thought he called a few brokers in the Hamilton area and discussed a few listings and made an appointment for the following weekend to view them with Noel.

That night as Nick slid under the warm blankets of his canopied bed, he wrapped his arm around his wife's soft-skinned body and cupped her ample breasts. He soon fell into a peaceful slumber.

Suddenly, the phone rang. And rang. He looked at the bedside clock. The illuminated face showed 11:37 p.m. Nick was startled and concerned by the ring. He wanted to ignore it. But, after many rings he decided that it might be important. He lifted the receiver.

"Hello," Nick murmured. "Is this Nick?" a voice asked. "Yes, this is Nick. Who's this?"

"Well, hello, Nick. Mario Cavallaro here. You sound half asleep so I won't keep you long. It's been a while since we last spoke, my friend."

Sure, Mario, I'm your best friend!

Mario continued. "Ni-ick, just calling to see how you're doing." The sound of Phil Collins's "In the Air Tonight" blared in the background. "How's business?" Before Nick could answer, Mario said, "And by the way, did you settle with your partner? What's his name? Oh, Mr. Fletcher!"

Nick broke out in a sweat. How could he know about the settlement? Is Tommy connected? If he is then why did he settle with me today. I'm confused!

"Mario, I told you that I'd call you when the need arises."

"I thought you might need me know. Maybe you do!" Mario knew the "contract" discussion alluded to in Tommy's call to that clandestine telephone number was now on hold and hung up after saying, "Good night, my friend." Everything going through that clandestine number filtered up to Mario!

Noel awoke and yawned. "Who was that, Nick?" She had been half asleep during the entire conversation.

"Oh, Mario Cavallaro. What a pest. Will he never get it?" Nick moaned.

The next day Tommy decided to call that number and canceled the clandestine meeting for good. It was settled and Tommy could relax now. Nothing else needed to be done.

The cancellation filtered up to Mario who took notice. He had wanted to squash the contract himself to do a huge favor for Nick, the Golden Boy. He might even have had Tommy disposed of, but now the opportunity had slipped by! Tommy was luckier than he knew even though he paid dearly for his violation to Nick.

CHAPTER 54

Summer 1986

"I did it!" Danny exclaimed, waving a document in the air as he paraded into Nick's office. "Did what?" Nick queried. "Successfully typed a letter with your right forefinger?" He chuckled.

"A little better than that. I got ISCM Corp. to execute the lease. And, guess what? The ten thousand square feet Johnson was initially interested in was bumped to twenty thousand. They've decided to consolidate and move their corporate offices from New Jersey to Massachusetts. They committed to the space for November first for a five-year term with two renewal options at market rates. Sixteen dollars per square foot rent with tax and operating escalations."

"Excellent job, Danny," the handsome CEO commended as he slid a bottle of Crown Royal from his credenza pouring an ounce or so into each glass. They clinked glasses together joyously. "Cheers, Danny!" Nick toasted.

The new company formed by Nick, Prime Commercial Inc., had closed on the Waltham land under a nominee trust owned by a limited partnership, of which he was the limited partner and Prime was the general partner. This occurred in late November 1985 with Nick providing the funds for the reduced four-hundred-thousand-dollar certificate of deposit which was pledged to Tri-Star Bank as side collateral. Construction had commenced 3/27/86 after the achievement of the revised 25 percent pre-leasing requirement, which occurred fast with Danny's expertise. Tri-Star had gone easy with the pre-lease requirement. The steel was being hoisted and set in place on the finished foundation. Nick's good fortune was back.

"Why the hell didn't you get a ten-year term, Danny?" Nick jested. But Danny came right back, saying, "Because I think that the market will be much stronger in five years. Don't be so conservative, boss!" Nick was pleased and only teasing.

"Boss, I feel confident that Larouche and Baxter will take at least ten thousand square feet. Their accounting business is booming, by their own claims, and they love the prestigious location. Also, there are at least six other firms in the two-thousand to three-thousand-square-foot range showing interest at this point. Route 128 West is a real hotbed and we're right in the middle of it!" They were virtually leased."Thank you, Danny," Nick replied. He was very pleased. Danny was doing a superb job. Danny had not only signed Johnson up, but had drawn them in at the beginning from his intensive search for tenants and had signed up other tenants for fifteen thousand square feet in March 1986. Prime Commercial would save a considerable amount with Danny's $26,250 commissions for the first thirty-five thousand square feet. Outside brokers would have charged a minimum of ninety-five thousand dollars. Danny was in line for a substantial bonus at year end.

Danny left the office and Nick sat back in his chair immersed in thought about Tommy's debacle last year. I hope he's doing OK. I do forgive him and wish him the best. I pray that he tames that anger. It's deadly!

He then dialed his home number.

"Hello. Noel speaking."

"Honey, it's Nick. How's it going today?""Well, everything is OK, Nick. You?""Well, I'm fine today. We just leased up to sixty-six percent at Ford Plaza, including our own office space, and can see pretty clearly toward at least ninety percent."

"Oh, Nick, I'm so happy."

"We'll discuss it tonight. Hartwell House for dinner. OK?""Fine, but I'll have to get Janie to babysit Ali. That shouldn't be a problem, though," Noel replied.

"And, honey," Nick went on, "I think that we should buy the Heffernan land in Hamilton. Are you sure that's the location that you want? I mean we've looked at so many comparable parcels in surrounding towns. They were all nice in our price range, but Hamilton is superb and there just aren't many land parcels available.""Sweetheart. Yes! Yes! Let's do it."

The following day Nick made an offer through the Heffernan's broker of five hundred sixty thousand dollars on the four-acre parcel, which was swiftly rejected. He countered with six hundred thirty-six thousand, which was accepted after hours of haggling back and forth with the sellers. Nick had made a good deal for prestigious and sought-after land in Hamilton, Massachusetts, close to the domicile of the world-renowned Myopia Hunt Club which was attended by famous equestrians.

In the following months the happy couple designed a house of magnificent splendor in conjunction with Niles Sutphin & Associates, an architectural firm Nick had commissioned years ago to design the Weiler Farms housing subdivision in the '70s. Niles the major principal was an unsurpassed residential architect.

Most of Niles's ideas relative to exterior pillars, structural components, gables, roof pitches, third floor configurations, sidings, lot positioning, tennis court, pool/cabana layouts, fence settings, garden locations and driveway plans were implemented into the design. Noel added other refinements such as a three horse stable and corral. It would be a grandiose visage.

Construction began in the spring. Their new eight-thousand-square-foot house carried a price tag of one million seven hundred thousand dollars, including the land. It was mortgaged for one million two hundred thousand dollars with Coastal Bank at an 8 percent interest rate under a standard direct-reduction mortgage, and Nick invested five hundred thousand of his own cash.

He would like to have reduced the mortgage balance significantly, but was down to eight hundred fifty thousand dollars in personal cash savings after the Hamilton house down payment and the purchase of the four-hundred-thousand-dollar certificate of deposit pledged to Tri-Star on Ford Plaza, which would be released as soon as 85 percent of the space was under lease. That would be soon, he hoped.

His interest payments from Tommy Fletcher kept coming in on a timely basis at fifty-two thousand five hundred dollars every month and were loaned to Prime Commercial to fund operations. The development fee from the Waltham project added valuable cash flow, but Prime had to manage very efficiently to conserve cash. As of now all payments of every nature were current.

Prime needed new business and decided to blitz the retail development market which he perceived as a lucrative business. He had been pursuing land deals for retail development since late 1985. The economy was strong and money was being spent for goods and services. Retail space had not kept pace with demand. Rental rates were rising at a quick pace.

Prime Commercial, slimly-staffed, scurried to acquire sites directed by Nick. By late 1986 two more sites were under agreement. One site—a fourteen-acre parcel on Route 38 in Wilmington, Massachusetts—was promising. One hundred fifty thousand square feet of retail could be built out by right with a special permit.

The other site, in Arlington, Massachusetts, consisted of twenty acres and could take two hundred ten thousand square feet, but required a few variances along with a special permit. Both sites were high and dry and would require no wetlands approvals. Prime went to work on obtaining the required approvals immediately.

Danny, knowing that time was of the essence, gave an exclusive listing to a prominent Boston real estate firm specializing in retail brokerage on both sites, but retained owner's right to lease and work began immediately contacting every retailer he could find. Between them the brokers diligently showed the site to every top notch retailer in the east. First to potential lead tenants such as Stop & Shop, Shaw's Supermarkets, Curtis Farms, De'Moulas Bros, CVS, Osco Drug, and others. Then on to smaller stores involved in everything from clothing to photography to restaurants to general merchandisers.

Many were very interested and both projects started to become successful.

CHAPTER 55

Spring 1987

In February, Prime Commercial closed the permanent mortgage in the final amount of five million two hundred fifty-one thousand dollars on Ford Plaza and soon moved into its new headquarters.

Danny's new office at the plush headquarters in Waltham was furnished with a computer terminal, large oak desk, credenza with a lamp and a designer couch facing the desk across the room. His office had the look of success. He was second in command The office staff had grown to eight employees and would expand if Nick's plans materialized.

As Danny perused the Boston Globe he noticed an article concerning arrests made by the FBI charging political bribery schemes. Five Massachusetts real estate developers had been charged with bribery of political officials and two arrested at their homes after extensive investigations. Last evening FBI agents had arrested Emilio Santana and Thomas Fletcher in addition to pursuing three others undisclosed at this time who could not be located. The charge against Santana and Fletcher was for bribing local officials for various permits required in the development process. A North Beach, Massachusetts, town official, Mr. Joseph Cataldo, was also arrested. He is the chief of the planning board for the city.

Danny rushed into Nick's office full of excitement and waving the newspaper. "Look at this! You won't believe it!"

"Won't believe what? Did I win my Celtics bet? Oh, I hope so. I bet five hundred dollars on them," Nick chuckled.

"Be serious, Nick! Tommy Fletcher was just arrested for bribery!"

Nick was stunned and absent of speech for moments. Tommy? "Who did he bribe?"

"Come on, Nick. You have no idea?"

"Nothing that involves me, my friend," he rejoined.

He silently reeled with anxiety. Am I guilty too? What do they call that?…obstruction of justice. I knew what happened but didn't report it to authorities. But I didn't witness it nor was I informed by anyone that it took place! Tommy might try to implicate me, but he never admitted it to me. I am clean. I hope? I would probably be more credible in the courtroom!

"Danny, the man fucked up royally. Not only did he pay off—I mean, allegedly—but he retained one hundred percent ownership in the project. That was damaging to him. At any rate, Danny, it's not our problem. You know, he did want me to take the North Beach project in our settlement, but I refused it because I wanted cash. God was with me!"

"I hope they don't try to involve you, Nick? You had nothing to do with it?"

"Nothing, Danny, I swear. I knew of the request and sensed it was carried out, but never condoned it. I actually warned him against it."

Danny sighed with relief and said, "Thank God, because we have a great thing going here."

A week later Agent Scott from the FBI visited Nick in the Waltham office and quizzed him for hours. Nick's recollections were honest, but he never at any point accused Tommy. He told of Cataldo's alleged request through intermediaries, but how Tommy stated that his contacts knew the mayor and the mayor would be requested to use his influence to get the project approved. "The mayor was a major advocate for the development project! Then, we got approved. That's all I know." Agent Scott left with no further questions. Tommy never involved Nick. Perhaps because of Nick's legitimate non-involvement in the bribe. But Tommy's nature was to pass the blame, Nick mused.

Tommy was ultimately found guilty and received a sentence of five years with a possibility of parole in eighteen months. His daughter, Sarah, took full control in her father's absence. Reluctantly, she called Nick and assured him that his note payments would continue. The family's empire was wobbly at this point. She didn't show the animosity bubbling inside her, but Nick could sense it!

CHAPTER 56

Fall 1987

Prime Commercial was moving and shaking by the fall. Ford Plaza was 98 percent leased and occupied. The remaining one thousand square feet would not be a problem to lease. A few start-up firms showed strong interest including Alan Bollard, Nick's long time broker contact and friend who was breaking out on his own as a developer.

Ford Plaza was generating approximately one hundred fifty-six thousand dollars annualized operating cash flow at 98 percent occupancy carrying a permanent mortgage of five million two hundred fifty-one thousand dollars at a 9.5 percent constant which had closed in February of this year. Nick personally received a release of his four-hundred-thousand-dollar certificate of deposit pledged to Tri-Star Bank. He was now back to holding approximately one million two hundred fifty thousand dollars in personal cash savings and decided to contribute five hundred thousand of it to Prime to increase working capital.

The Wilmington retail site had been acquired in February 1987 and was now under construction. It was 70 percent leased to a supermarket as the lead tenant and had significant leasing interest pending. The Arlington site was in the approval process with the Town but had substantial leasing interest. It appeared that obtaining the approvals would be a slam-dunk! Nick sat back in his office very pleased with the progress of his company. Is there no end to our luck? Trump… That's where Prime will be some day, although that's a pretty tall order! He left early that day and met Noel for lunch after which they drove to Hamilton to view the progress of the new house.

The shiny black Mercedes 560 SEL cruised through the rod iron gates at Equestrian Drive which for some reason had been left open. It contoured its way along the private, winding subdivision road leading to the Packard driveway which linked to a five-hundred-foot brick section leading up to the stately new eight-thousand-square-foot house. A red van bearing the name of May Contractors, Inc. was being loaded by Dan May. It was the end of the work day. Nick rolled down his window and inquired, "Dan, how's it going, pal?"

"The house is almost finished. Another week to achieve perfection and completion as you ordered! By the way, Nick, two men were here today earlier asking a lot of questions."

"Did you get their names, Dan?"

"No, they wouldn't say when I asked them. Just friends they replied. A few more punch-list items and we're done. You're a fortunate couple, to say the least. Can I live here? As a servant I mean?" Dan joked."If you only knew the pressures of maintaining this lifestyle! How about you live here and I'll be your servant?" Nick laughed. Everybody roared with laughter as the workmen entered the van and swiftly departed.

The happy couple entered the house after viewing the yard which was in a state of messiness at that point. Noel curled up to Nick and murmured, "Honey, can we christen the house?" Tickling Nick's thighs, she implored, "Do me on the kitchen counter." Noel had designed the counter of mosaic tile and thought it looked superb. Nick got excited and firmly agreed, then embraced her.

They entered their new home through the stately pillars outside the elaborate double French front doors into paradise. As they walked across the imported Italian marble floor their excitement grew. They walked through each room and viewed many changes since their last visit two weeks ago. They were like the kids in Willy Wonka's chocolate factory.

When they meandered out the back to the rear patio they were in awe over the sight of the large pool and cabana which had recently been completed. The surrounding sodded yard encased by rod iron fences accentuated the area immensely. A brick walk wound through the grassed area and led to the stables set far to the rear in a bucolic setting. Natural fields and old wooden fences made the area so rustic. The jubilant couple had arrived. This would be their home now and forever. The devoted couple prayed to God together for a few minutes and walked back through the patio doors, then through the mudroom and into the kitchen.

Nick wrapped his arms around his beloved wife from behind and felt her silk blouse and cotton slacks as he kissed her neck while she turned her head and flicked her tongue back. He turned her around and lifted her onto the mosaic tile counter. He then undid and rolled her slacks down exposing her well contoured legs. Both needed no foreplay because of the anxiety response brought on by this beautiful new life about to explode. And, soon, they each exploded together for countless minutes.

After hugging and caressing for what seemed like an eternity, the couple left. They never heard the newly installed wall phone ringing incessantly and never received Mario Cavallaro's call!

The next week they moved into 911 Equestrian Drive beginning a new segment of their lives.

CHAPTER 57

December 1987

Nick walked through the steel doors of Danbury State Prison and waited for the second door to unlatch. He was encased between the insurmountable walls and didn't like it at all. His claustrophobia kicked in momentarily, but soon the second steel door screeched open. What a relief! Thank God that he wasn't incarcerated.

Walking by a sparsely toothed correctional guard, Nick uttered, "How are you, pal?"

The guard replied, "Which asshole are you here to visit?"

Nick swiftly replied, "If I wanted to see an asshole I wouldn't have to walk any further. No, I want to visit a friend, not an asshole!"

The guard chuckled loudly. "Only assholes in this place. I certainly am one for working this job!"

"Tommy Fletcher," Nick replied."Third cubicle on the left." The officer then started talking to the next visitor. He sat down in the third cubicle on a hard bench and faced the wire mesh looking directly at Tommy. "You shouldn't be here, Tommy!" he cried out.

"Yeah, but you should be here if I have to be!"

"Why, Tommy? I didn't make the bribe." Nick raised his voice.

"It was your project too, and you condoned it, buddy!"

"I don't want a shooting match, Tommy! The F.B.I cleared me because they believe the truth. I never acquiesced to any payoff. We didn't need the North Beach project to survive. Now, I'm not here to discuss that anymore. I'm here because of concern for you. Nick never mentioned the story of how Mario knew about their settlement or even who he is. He, also inquired, vaguely to Tommy about mentioning the settlement to others. According to Tommy he had entrusted the facts to Anna only who swore not to discuss it with anybody. No new light dawned on Nick! "What's it like in here, Tommy? Anything of a positive nature?"

"No, Nick, and you've fucked me good! Most of what you left me is dissipating. I can't make it successful from in here!"

Nick didn't respond to Tommy's accusations, but replied, "You precipitated the whole mess! First the greed, then the unwise bribe. What goes around comes around. You should know that by now. But, I forgive you, Tommy, and promise that I'll never foreclose on anything you own and have pledged to me. I'm doing fine on my own deals and don't need your sweat and blood to survive. You almost deep sixed me, but I'm willing to forgive it!"

Tommy beamed a smile and said, "Thank you." But, in his resentful mind he thought that he should have had taken

Nick out when he had the chance. Unbeknownst to either of them Tommy was alive because he hadn't pursued it! Mario's excuse had been blown away with Tommy's cancellation!

Tommy in his debilitating anger still thought that maybe he'd have another chance. He had no inkling of the danger that could unfold for him. The Mob wanted Nick alive and healthy. He was their ace in the hole. Their golden goose! Tommy's contract call was opportune for them to help Nick and put him under leash, but had been thwarted.

After much small talk Nick wished Tommy farewell and promised to visit him again soon. The two shook hands, Tommy very meekly. He meandered back to his cell under guard supervision. Tears welled in Nick's eyes as he felt the utmost compassion for his old friend's ordeal.

He walked away in deep sorrow and departed from the steel fortress. Outside an ominous cloud hovered over the prison. As he walked to the outside a torrential rain fell and soaked him thoroughly. He was forlorn on the drive home.

CHAPTER 58

May 1988

The shopping center in Wilmington, located directly on Route 38, was 92 percent leased, with a major supermarket as the anchor tenant for a hundred thousand square feet. A drugstore occupied another ten thousand square feet. The strip was named Prime Plaza, given its prime location on Route 38 and close to Route 128. Construction was virtually complete and the satellite stores had begun to fall in place following the occupancy of the behemoths. Other smaller tenants were, also, very interested. It looked like 100 percent occupancy would be attainable soon.

Danny Levin stood outside facing the conglomeration of stores, his long red hair blowing in the warm breeze. I am on my way to becoming a millionaire because of Nick's deals and his willingness to share some equities. I can now bring Suzie here from LA, and maybe get married soon. I am a very lucky man and I owe it mainly to Nick. We are both going places! God bless him!

It was six p.m. and still bright outside. The clocks hadn't been set back yet. After checking on the sporadic air flow problem and deciding that he should call Air Systems for an adjustment, Danny sat back on a bench outside the stores with a pro-forma income projection in one hand, balancing a calculator in his lap and a slice of pizza in the other. A cool breeze brushed his face as his thoughts mesmerized him entirely.

Nick bought this fourteen-acre parcel for $3.8 million. And spent ten million to build this gem staring me in the face. He mortgaged it for almost 100 percent on the construction loan, I think, and it is yielding an NOI of $1.8 million when completed, which is predictable at this point. His $1.38 million of debt service, assuming a fourteen-million-dollar permanent mortgage, leaves him approximately four hundred twenty thousand of cash flow if 95 percent occupied on average, with no outside partners to split with. Incredible! And I get a 10 percent ownership interest!

Danny brushed his mustache with his right forefinger. He had a good grasp of numbers and, also, enough wisdom to realize that the man who builds the organization after endless personal risks gets the lion's share. He was happy for Nick and ecstatic about his nest egg that was building up.

His work day wasn't over and he opted to visit the Arlington Heights construction site before going home. Two weeks ago he had negotiated a deal with Monumental for sixty-two thousand five hundred square feet and one hundred thousand square feet with Home Supply, large Southern retailers forging a path into the Northeast. He wanted to monitor the construction progress of these behemoths. Their leases called for October 1 and 30, 1988, space delivery dates. Time was of the essence and he was very sensitive to the issue.

As his BMW weaved into the mall's entrance, he downshifted and the 635 CS I engine squealed as he spun into the undercoated parking lot at the center's east side. The foundation was completed and the steel erected. It was on target.

He noticed a black Lincoln Continental parked fifty feet away from him. As he alighted from his vehicle two men stepped out of the Lincoln. One had a black wool sport coat with a black tie and was heavy set. The other man had a brilliant silk, long-sleeved shirt and pleated wool slacks. He was quite handsome and slim.

Danny walked toward them and inquired, "Can I help you?"

After a moment, the slim man replied, "I'm Mario Cavallaro and this is Carmine. Nick Packard and I are good friends. Our kids are classmates." Danny introduced himself, then Mario asked, "Have you leased this place yet?"

Danny was somewhat apprehensive. But, typical of management ego, he expounded his knowledge to prove his position. "Oh yes, this section has been leased by Monumental. And, this other section is leased by Home Supply. They both will occupy by October. And, I have strong interest from others for another thirty-seven thousand square feet on that end." He ecstatically pointed toward the west end. "Many others have shown interest, but are in the shopping stage. It's progressing extremely well. This is a desirable location," Danny proudly proclaimed.

"Very interesting," Mario went on as he smiled at his

cohort. "Just out of curiosity, how much revenue does a place like this generate?"

Danny should have stopped there and ended the conversation. He didn't know these men from a hole in the wall!

"I can't give more information. It's private."

"My friend, Nick and I have been close for years," Mario lied. "Our kids go to school together. We've even vacationed together. Call him if you'd like. I've been invited to invest in one by another developer and am trying to get some independent information."

Danny relaxed a bit and said, "Well, I can tell you, Mr. Cavallaro, the total revenue is close to three million dollars."

"Whew!" Mario responded. "Well, I assume you couldn't net more than, say, two hundred thousand, tops. Could you?"

Danny then made one last mistake. He couldn't restrain his need to expound his knowledge. Where he should have answered that he didn't know, he said, "I can't say, but it's higher."

Mario said, "Maybe this investment being offered to me by my friend is a good deal. Thanks, Danny!"

The trio shook hands and Danny wished Mario good luck. As the Lincoln departed Mario said to Carmine, "Packard is wealthy. I soon will do him a favor concerning that partner of his. I'll call it in, in time!" Carmine knew Mario quite well and that he delivers on every threat he makes. He was merciless and was feared even by the higher bosses!

The next day when Danny was meeting with Nick he mentioned the conversation with the two men, Mario and Carmine.

"What did they say, Danny?"

"They asked me about the leasing progress. Then the rental revenue. Then about cash flow!"

Nick looked at Danny nervously and asked further what Danny had told them.

"I told them about Monumental and the others."

"What else?" Nick asked.

"That the gross rental income was close to three million dollars. Mario said that he was considering a similar investment and that he was a good friend of yours. That your kids go to school together."

Nick suddenly screamed for the first time Danny had ever heard. "You've got to be fucking kidding, Danny! These men are mobsters! Mario has been calling me late at night from some mysterious places with music blaring in the background asking if he can lend me quick money for the business, no formal closings! What the fuck were you thinking of!" "Nick, I legitimately thought that he was your friend. He said that you vacationed together?"

"Danny, I can't believe this! Noel and I only met the man and his wife once on our wedding weekend in a casino. It turned out that our daughters go to the same school, but they hardly even know each other! He's been trying to get his hooks into me for years, but I've never bitten on that dreadfully poisoned hook!"

Danny was shocked and realized that he had made a

grave error. He hadn't even told Nick about the answer to the cash flow inquiry. He didn't dare.

"Danny, you've no right to divulge company information. I can't have this sort of thing!"

Nick then stomped out the door and drove off. Danny sat in his office with his head on the desk regretting his stupidity. He considered quitting and going back to LA.

That evening Nick called him and had calmed down. "What you have done is a grave mistake, Danny. But, upon reflection I realize that we all make them at times. I thought back to my meeting this guy, Mario, in a Casino in Santo Domingo. Noel and I were celebrating and I was drinking a lot. I made the mistake of bragging about my real estate projects and that started the whole thing. I learned from that and now you have to learn from this!

You must never divulge any company financial information or major leasing coups to any outsiders in the future. Danny, I'll decide what to discuss with whom in that regard. OK? It's a valuable lesson many people should learn: 'loose lips sink ships'! Remember that. And, never carry on any conversation with him again."

"I'm sorry, boss," Danny replied. "I understand what you're saying, and I'll never make that mistake again!"

"You're doing a great job, Danny."

CHAPTER 59

Nick sat back in his swivel office chair and thought about his new house in Hamilton which he and Noel and been living in for four months now. It was everything that they had dreamed of. It was spacious and even afforded Noel room for her office to operate her interior design business which was very successful.

His thoughts turned to Ali's fifth birthday party which was only a few weeks away. They were planning a very special event and would hire a clown and a magician. Also, a few story tellers were lined up. Horseback rides and hay wagon jaunts were planned and, of course, there would be sliding and swimming in the pool for everybody.

A terrific barbecue was planned with hot dogs and hamburgers for the kids and steaks and chicken or meat shish-kebobs for the adults with all imaginable side dishes. It would be a time for Ali to remember forever.

Diane, Nicks administrative assistant, entered his office and Nick quickly snapped out of his revelry. She handed him his mail which he slowly perused until he noticed an envelope addressed form Leanna Fletcher in the left hand corner. He opened it and found a monthly interest check for forty-five thousand dollars signed by Leanna. It was in order because she had paid Nick one million dollars against the principal after refinancing three of Tommy's Commonwealth Avenue properties a month earlier.

This focused his attention on Tommy once again and he decided to visit him again. Nick had gleaned from Leanna earlier during telephone conversations that Tommy was directing the business from prison. Nick was happy for Tommy. He will be out of prison soon and I hope his anger management classes have helped. Nick mused.

At Danbury Prison, Tommy had worked hard in his off time to run his empire, but, his effectiveness could not match the former day to day direct contacts and the business began to suffer. Sarah was helpful, but, could not exercise the power Tommy once wielded! Tommy was forlorn. He had tried for parole last month and was turned down by the board on a technicality. He had been in a few fights which were uncontrollably unavoidable for him. He didn't pay much attention in the anger management classes!

Tommy became angrier with each day and finally snapped. Packard's living a life of grandeur with interest on stolen money from me. That settlement was fucking extortion! And, then he is lily white and has no idea or connection with the payoff. What bullshit! Why shouldn't he suffer too!

Tommy thought hard and long. He decided to call that clandestine number from the prison and revive the contract. He was in the right. Such injustice to him! He nervously made the call knowing that there was now no turning back. He didn't have to say much. He couldn't say much on the prison telephone. The man on the other end knew what he wanted! Tommy would have Nelson Thatcher deliver the money under a false pretense!

On June 11, when Tommy was pushing a laundry cart into the laundry room in a remote section of the prison's East Wing, he was confronted by two muscular, young, white inmates. One shouted, "You've signed your own death warrant, motherfucker!" The other growled, "You offended the wrong person, asshole!"

What quickly ran through Tommy's confused mind was that he might have rubbed someone in the prison the wrong way? Or, maybe it had to do with Packard?! Without further thought he grabbed an iron off the counter of the laundry room and violently smacked one of the assailants squarely in the face who became dazed and fell to the floor bleeding profusely. He, then, spun around but just wasn't quick enough to duck the blasting impact of the second man's fist and lost consciousness. The inmate, a lifer, continued to pound Tommy's face relentlessly. Blood squirted everywhere from his nose and mouth. He, then, kicked Tommy's head incessantly and connected with his temple.

Tommy went into convulsions as three guards belatedly ran into the room and subdued the man kicking Tommy. "Hey, this asshole attacked us and hit Clemente with an iron and then came after me. I defended myself against this crazy bastard." No other witnesses were present and the guards took their time getting Tommy to the hospital. It was too late. Tommy was DOA!

Sarah and Anna along with Sammy grieved for months afterward. Tommy may have been a bull in business, but was a good father and husband always providing for his family. Nick was shocked beyond belief and offered sincere condolences and financial assistance to help Tommy's family. He had no clue as to what had caused this and promised to defer interest payments indefinitely until the family pulled it together. He knew he could always minimize the interest substantially if the Fletcher wealth fell apart!

Mario sat back in his office at the club and smiled. The favor had now been done. He had saved Nick's life! He knew of all orders for hits and had vast power of veto, which he exercised for Nick. Tommy didn't have to die and could have been warned, but for Mario it would make a statement to Nick!

CHAPTER 60

July 15, 1988

As Mario took the winding turns of the long driveway meandering toward the Packard house, he and Gina noticed scores of balloons streaming from the branches of the meticulously groomed pin oaks spaced ten feet apart all along the drive.

"They're going way out for this party! How nice, Mario. Let's give Jan a party like this on her next birthday. Would you like that, honey? Has Ali talked about the party in school?" Gina asked. Jan nodded from the backseat and joyously answered, "Oh yes, Mom, she has. Can we please have one?"

"Certainly, dear," Gina responded, as Mario shook his head approvingly. I'll be rolling in money then, when Packard pays up! And, that motherfucker will pay his debt to me!

The Lincoln Continental pulled into a protracted circular driveway in front of the house and the Cavallaros were escorted out by a valet, one of three. The valet pulled Mario's Cadillac beside a Rolls-Royce Cornice and parked

293

it. Mario and his family were greeted by Danny Levin who winced when he saw Mario, but, remained cordial as instructed by Nick. The Cavallaros were there because Ali had invited Jan one day a few weeks ago in school.

Danny shook hands with Mario and Gina and, as rehearsed, told Mario that is was nice to see him again. He told them to make themselves at home and that Nick was out in the fields somewhere teamstering a hay wagon ride for some of the kids. The Cavallaros then mixed into the merriment of the crowd and disappeared.

Inside the house the crowd was buzzing. Clowns cracked jokes and performed magic acts everywhere as the children watched in awe. It was a circus-like spectacle. One clown turned a rope into a bouquet of beautiful roses, then cried what looked like real tears as they wilted. The children that gathered around him were mesmerized. "Wow!" a small girl yelled. "My dad could never do that!"

The tables were set with a royal feast for the adults and children. Outside Ellen, the Prime receptionist and Rob, the chief financial manager, were flipping burgers and roasting Italian sausage on two large gas-fired grills. Hot dogs were rolling constantly. An adjoining quartet of twelve-foot picnic tables were adorned with platters of potato salad and chips, cold slaw, corn on the cob, and pasta salad. Nothing was spared and every condiment imaginable was spread across each table. A large Coca-Cola chest was filled with sodas in dripping ice.

Ellen and Rob were mastering this task quite well although they became tired after a while. They loved Nick and would work until they dropped if necessary. Nick treated them as family.

Inside a large catered feast had been prepared for the adults and all the older children. The buzzing of domestic staff hired for the occasion permeated the house. Many waitresses served the guests from platters of tenderloin, prime rib, shrimp, and lobster meat. A huge raw bar and crepe station was set up to enhance the dining experience.

Two bartenders served behind the crowded twenty-foot bar of imported marble, brass rails and exquisite mahogany. Any mixed drink imaginable was available. Danny meandered about keeping his sharp eyes on everyone to be sure no one was overdoing the liquor. His handsome youthful face and long red hair attracted many of the ladies, especially those who had a few drinks. A few held his hand and hugged him for moments. The decorum had to be maintained. After all it was a birthday party for children.

In the corner of the spacious family room Mickey and the Mice, a three-piece band hammered out a medley of tunes sung by, who else, Mickey. The music alternated between kids songs which were sung by many of the kids and country western with occasional rock and roll. It was really quite good and had the crowd tapping to the beat! Some were clapping while others danced.

Nick walked slowly away from the barn after his eighth hay wagon jaunt. His weary arm was clasped around Ali's shoulder and his gaze reflected deep love for his precious little daughter. The pair looked really quite comical with straws of hay hanging from their hair and pockets and covering Nick's ten gallon hat. The two were so happy and life was grand.

"Ali, strong confidence is very important for success. Do you understand me?"

"Do you mean not being upset if you make a boo-boo, Dad?" she asked Nick.

"Exactly, honey. Now go in there and do it!" Nick replied, hugging her tightly. "I love you, Ali."

"Me too," Ali said with confidence.

Nick laughed. They sauntered toward the house as the sun shone brightly and reflected off Nick's shiny western belt buckle. Hand in hand they smiled proudly at each other, unwary of Mario's gaze.

Inside the huge family room Ali walked unabashedly up to Mickey and retrieved the microphone as she whispered in Mickey's ear. Mickey smiled graciously and handed it to her. But, before she spoke, Nick grabbed the microphone and said, "Friends, I hope you're all having a good time. To further your pleasure I would like to present a new talent to the stage for your listening entertainment." Nick was really hamming it up! "A voice to soothe your ears, thrill your souls and bring pure joy. Without further ado, I bring you Ali!" He clapped loudly.

Ali blushed momentarily and then started snapping her fingers as the band played a rendition of "Crazy," the Patsy Cline original. Her golden voice spewed the lyrics throughout the speakers in every corner of the room. Everyone was mesmerized by the perfected voice of this small child. The crowd swayed while some sang along.

Her melodious songs moved on to kids' songs with all

the kids singing and clapping. Then, as a grand finale she attempted "Jumpin' Jack Flash," the Rolling Stones song adored by Noel.

She needed a bit more polish, but she was only six years old. In spite of a little roughness around the edges she nearly equaled the sound of Michael Jackson at that young age and had the charisma! After requests for "one more!" Ali finished her performance with "Blue Moon" and the crowd clapped loudly. She exited the stage with a smile as she wound down "without a love of my own."

Nick was proud and elated with the performance and as he looked around the room he caught the gaze of Mario. The cold, hard stare from him ushered Nick toward the man. A foot apart from each other they stared momentarily. Mario then said, "Nick, my friend, can we talk alone in your study or office, or someplace private?"

"Sure, Mario," Nick replied.

The two men walked upstairs from the living room silently and entered Nick's office. The room was walled with mahogany and as Nick took a seat behind his large desk he pointed to a leather arm chair beckoning Mario to sit down. Nick retrieved a bottle of Crown Royal from his credenza behind the desk and poured two small glasses half full passing one to Mario and holding his glass for a toast. They clank in unison. Nick was trying hard to be nonchalant, but was very nervous.

Mario began, "Nick, your daughter has a golden voice. A lovely sound. She means a lot to you doesn't she? Your wife, your daughter, your lifestyle must all be very precious to you. We both have these things very dear to us, but, unfortunately they are not ours forever!"

Nick became very wary of this man. "What's your point, Mario?" He recognized the implied threat!

"Oh, just conversation, but there is another point which must be made very clear to you. You have a debt to settle!"

"What debt is that?" Nick inquired.

"We saved your life, my friend. Your partner Fletcher ordered a contract for your life twice. I called it off both times!" Mario failed to mention that it was Tommy's decision to abort the order the first time.

"I'm not sure that you fucking understood that. Did you?" Mario got angry! "I squelched it, personally!"

"No, Mario, I had no knowledge of that," Nick replied. He was dumbfounded, shocked beyond belief!

"We want to be recognized for that!"

"Did you arrange Tommy's death?" Nick asked, trembling.

A moment of silence was followed by, "I didn't say that." He lied! "I said that I saved you. How much is your life worth, Nick? You owe us. Capisci?"

It was quite clear to Nick now that Mario had Tommy killed in the prison!

Nick stood and said, "I can't even concentrate right this minute!"

"Get back to me soon, my friend. Soon!" Mario demanded.

Nick ushered Mario from the room. He understood the message and was shocked that it had gone this far. He knew that serious problems lay ahead. He felt like throwing up.

CHAPTER 61

The sun shone brightly and momentarily blinded Nick as the new charcoal black 560 SEL wound its way along Silicon Drive. He swiftly lowered the overhead visor to block the sun's rays. Turning into the parking lot of Ford Plaza, the name dubbed for the Waltham office development, he maneuvered into his reserved space and killed the ignition switch.

Walking through the parking lot he met Ellen and Rob. After saying good morning, Nick said to Rob, "I need that pro-forma cash flow statement on Arlington Square before ten this morning. The meeting with HLW Pension Fund is still on for two this afternoon. Isn't it?"

"Yes, Nick, and let's push on it today. Rates are on the upswing," Rob answered. Ellen excused herself and walked inside.

"How much can we maximize the loan for, Rob?" If I can pull some extra cash out of this deal I might get it to Mario somehow. I don't know because once I start paying these guys they'll get their hooks into me forever! I haven't heard from him for a few month? Wonder why?"Well, Nick, using a nine-point-five percent constant and a one-point-two-five coverage ratio, about twenty million dollars. Our construction loan is nineteen million, and we have one million of our own cash into the deal. We can mortgage out the one million," Rob anxiously calculated.

"No, we don't need it." Fuck Mario! "Cap it at nineteen million dollars to pay off the construction loan only. We need a conservative debt structure," Nick stated.

Rob flinched, but agreed. What a sweet deal, they both agreed. Nick told Rob that this project had leased faster than any other project he'd ever developed!

Unbeknownst to either man they were being watched by a pair of cold black eyes perched low inside a nondescript gray sedan parked across the lot. Carlo Puglisi was watching their golden goose. Mario was waiting patiently knowing that Nick's operation was growing and so was his debt to them over time. Mario was waiting for just the right moment to spring on him! His soldiers watched every move Nick made!

Nick walked into the reception area of Prime's office past the huge brass company logo on the wall, a large P in old English lettering. He winked at Ellen as he sauntered past her desk. She looked as sexy as ever. He forced his gaze off her and asked about his telephone messages.

As he walked past the large oak furnished conference room he noticed Rob in a huddle with Chuck, the nerdy looking, but brilliant controller. They were reviewing the projections on the Arlington site for the two o'clock meeting with HLW.

"How does it look?" Nick asked the two of

them."Excellent," Rob pronounced. "We're ninety-five percent leased in Arlington with occupancy in place or close. And we have enough letters of intent to bring us up to ninety-seven percent occupancy. All our projections are being realized."

"What's the projected net operating income? Will we survive?" he asked jokingly.

"Two million three hundred seventy-five thousand dollars. It will support a twenty-million to twenty-point-eight-million-dollar mortgage at a nine and a half percent constant rate using a one-point-two-zero to one-point-two-five coverage ratio, but the downward revised cash flow is around four hundred thousand dollars at the maximum loan amount annually," Rob retorted.

Nick's mathematical mind churned for a minute. "Good, then a nineteen-million-dollar mortgage loan will support an additional one hundred seventy-one thousand dollars in cash flow, reducing it from twenty-point-eight million to nineteen million. That's the number! Don't forget, HLW wants an equity kicker also. You negotiate it!"

Nick strolled into his office and hung his suit coat on the mahogany coat tree. He sat in a soft chair beside his desk and dialed Danny's intercom."Levin," a voice chimed."Can you come to my office. I have some new business.""Sure, boss."

Danny strolled in, in his typical fashion,and curled up in an armchair across from Nick. His long red hair was disheveled and his mustache had a single crumb on it.

"You look drained, Danny. What, did you have a hot one

last night?" Nick joked, because he knew Danny's girlfriend, Suzie, came from LA last month to live with him.

"Yeah, with Les Mannix. What an asshole. You'd think that Venus Video was negotiating a prime tenancy in the World Trade Center! I had to wine him and dine him all evening for a three-thousand-square-foot lease. I mean, he chased concession after concession. He even implied that a high-class hooker could seal the deal!"

"Screw him, Danny. We don't need him. Tell him we leased the space to another store with less concessions."

"No, Nick, I finally closed the deal at seventeen dollars a foot. Let's stay with it and move on. The hooker will be over tonight!" They both roared with laughter at the joke. "Nick, I heard from Mitch Goldwin, a developer on the South Shore, that Venus is a good tenant. Organized and pays like clockwork. Let's put Prime Plaza behind us. With the Venus lease we'll have only three thousand square feet for which I have no interest at present, but that will go fast. The project is virtually a done deal."

"Your call, Danny. Do it!" Nick replied happily. "Look, Danny, I have found a new site which interests me. Forty-six acres in Framingham, Massachusetts, owned by Carl Johnson, an old business contact and friend who sold land to me years ago for home building. It's not on the market now and probably would be scooped up in a day's time if it were. Fifteen hundred feet of frontage on Route 9 and near the Massachusetts Turnpike. I bought a ninety-day option for twenty thousand dollars. Unheard of, huh? He liked me because I treated him fairly back in those days. I never squeezed him and closed on a timely basis. He's old and retired. He sincerely wants to help me, I believe!"

Danny was elated. "How many square feet could we build on this site, Nick?"

"Well, according to the topo and wetland maps it's approximately ninety-five percent high and dry and buildable. We need much more research, but I think it's good for six hundred thousand square feet, or maybe more. A rough estimate. Guess what? It's zoned retail in its entirety and is located in the heart of the Golden mile. An easy special permit if done properly. Maybe two adjoining strip malls. Too small for a regional." Nick talked on incessantly. This would be his largest undertaking yet! He thought about the use of the word undertaking and hoped that wasn't an omen!

"Rents are pushing thirteen dollars to twenty dollars per foot, triple net, out there. That's seven-point-eight million to twelve million dollars gross annually. Of course, vacancies would reduce that somewhat. It's a big one, Danny, and that would put us on the map."

Danny was mesmerized.

"Oh, and also included in the option are two other existing shopping centers in Natick. About one hundred and seventy-five thousand square feet. It's a package deal. Carl wants to liquidate a lot of his properties and I'm getting first crack! Fourteen million dollars for the land and twenty-six million for the two centers. Total acquisition price of forty million dollars for the package!"

"Can we handle all that, Nick?" Danny questioned.

"Not by ourselves, Danny. We will need partners. I'll

deal with that with Rob's assistance. You have to research the market out there and firm up the rental rates. I'd like for you and me to visit the sites after our two o'clock meeting with HLW. What's your schedule like this afternoon?"

"Right after the meeting, boss, is OK with me," Danny said, with visions of huge personal gain dancing in his head.

The two o'clock meeting went well. Ken Walker of HLW was impressed with the numbers and leasing progress on Arlington Heights Plaza. The leasing progress clinched the deal and he offered $20.5 million at 9.375 percent interest and a 30 percent equity kicker as a percentage of appreciation. When Nick reduced it to $19 million Ken was happy. Ken finally agreed on a 15 percent kicker without any squabble. He was fostering goodwill for future Prime projects. Ken stated that the board already approved a $20.5 million loan and that the $19 million mortgage loan requested would be well taken and could be closed quickly.

Danny's leasing presentation was meticulously superb. Rob handled the financial presentation like a solid professional. The project manager, Charlie Watkins, answered every technical construction inquiry with relative ease. Nick was extremely proud of his team. Even Ellen impressed everyone when she entered the conference room and pointed out to Danny that the "expense stops" provisions were incorrectly stated in a lease she was preparing for the Arlington project.

Shortly after the meeting Nick, Danny and Charlie departed the building and cruised out of the lot in Danny's 635 CSI BMW. They were unaware that the gray sedan pulled out and followed them many car intervals behind. As they stopped first at the forty-six-acre parcel and talked for a while on site, then at the two Natick strip malls, the black-eyed man parked nearby taking many notes and photos crouching down in the seat. A .45 automatic was strapped to the belt of Carlo Puglisi, aka "The Grim Reaper"!

CHAPTER 62

The following week Nick, Danny and Rob met with Carl Johnson on two occasions for hours. The Prime Commercial team pointed out all the drawbacks of the site they could conjure up! Soils conditions, zoning restrictions, wetlands, curb cut permits required for the new development. And, new roofs and parking lot expansions and required modernization changes for the Natick strip malls. They really laid it on as they pawed over survey after survey.

Carl was no dummy and knew the value of his properties. He countered every negative argument with variations of the cliché "location, location, location." Each property had Route 9 frontage and was located in a superior location. But, he did finally concede to reduce the asking price from forty million dollars to thirty-five million—thirteen million for the vacant land and twenty-two million for the one-hundred-seventy-five-thousand-square-foot existing shopping centers. He justified the reduction by increasing the Cap Rate on the centers from 8.5 percent to 10 percent and the land by an arbitrary one million dollars because it was a package deal and would shed much burden off him. Perhaps he knew more than they did? He had survived all his life by being conservative yet shrewd! The Prime team thought this was a real bargain!

The men all shook hands at eleven on Wednesday night and then toasted each other with shots of tequila to seal the thirty-five-million-dollar deal. Then they recited humorous anecdotes until early in the morning. Carl had an extensive bar and all parties mellowed out with relief. Carl was tough and they respected his knowledge considerably. He further stipulated a closing in sixty days after the P&S was signed which put much pressure on Rob and Nick. The only glitch now was how to obtain financing and close within that time frame. Carl was firm on this!

The next day Nick, Danny and Rob met promptly at eight a.m. They first reviewed the cash situation. Prime had one million one hundred thirty-seven thousand dollars in money market investments and Nick said that he could invest one million dollars in personal funds if necessary. They were told by Lenny at Tri-Star Bank that they would need at least 10 percent down at the construction loan closing, three and a half million dollars, and that the financing window could close before too long. The real estate market had taken a steep down slide as all were aware! They needed partners right away. For now, the required million-dollar deposit to Carl Johnson had to be made at the P&S signing.

They were not about to give up easily and proceeded with the analysis. The meeting began with the financial feasibility presentation by Rob for the Framingham land development. He handed out a report to the others.

Summary of Financial Feasibility
Projections
46 acre Retail Land Development
Framingham, Massachusetts

Assumptions:

- 400,000 sq. ft. retail - 28 acres
- 200,000 sq. ft. office-18 acres-3 buildings-5 stories
- Parking- retail -2000 spaces; office- 800 spaces
- Land Acquisition- $13 Mil.
- Construction - retail- $50. per sq. ft., office $65.
- Financing -10% construction loan, 2 Points. 48 months phased.
- Marketing- Avg. 25% of annual base rent.
- Permanent Mortgage - 9% interest-1.25 coverage-30 yr. Amortization -15 year term

Project Costs:

Land Acquisition	$13 Mil.
Construction	33
Financing and Marketing	8
Other	3
Total Project Costs	$57 Mil.

PROJECTED INCOME AND
MORTGAGE SUPPORTED:

	Retail	Office	Total
Rental Rates (per sq. ft.)	$14. NNN	$17.	Gross
Projected Gross Rental Income	$5.6 Mil.	$3.4 Mil.	$9Mil.
Less: Vacancies	.3	. 2	
Other Expenses	.1	1 .3	
Replacement Reserve	.2	.1	
Net Operating Income	5.0	1.8	$6.8Mil.
Permanent Mortgage loans supported	42.1	15.2	$57.3mil.
Equity Required (mathematically)	0	0	
Projected Debt Service	4.0	1.4	5.4Mil.
Projected Operating Cash Flow	1.0	.4	1.4Mil.
Projected Project Value at completion (9 ½% Cap. Rate)			$71.6Mil.
Equity value created at completion			$14.3Mil.

As Rob reviewed the assumptions and then the financial results, the three baby-boomers beamed with overwhelming joy! This gem would cost approximately fifty-seven million dollars to acquire and develop. The net operating income from the project at completion could carry a permanent mortgage amount roughly equal to the fifty-seven-million-dollar cost plus one-point-four-million-dollar cash flow would be generated annually for distribution. But on the other hand, the cash flow might be increased, because there will certainly be an initial equity requirement of at least 20 percent, or, say, eleven million dollars for the deal, with the three and a half million at acquisition and another seven and a half million or so at the beginning of construction. They certainly needed heavy weight partners for this one! They all looked at the numbers again.

"Listen, guys, if you help make this one fly there's a five percent equity interest in it for each of you," Nick said.

"Wow! Projected value at completion seventy-two million dollars, fourteen million immediate equity!" Danny exhaled strongly. I might make almost a million dollars if this works, in addition to some hefty commissions!

Rob was thinking along the same lines.

"Fucking nice!" Danny wailed. "We knew it was a winner!"

"I'll second the fucking nice," Nick replied. "But listen up, guys. The fifteen million potential equity is only a painting on the canvas right now. We've got our work cut out for us! And, as you both know the banks are tightening up substantially. Taking fewer deals. Nonperforming loans are on the increase and unemployment on the rise. We've been lucky to date but can't overlook the cyclical nature of the economy. No matter how good any deal seems!

This deal must be approached conservatively and methodically. We've got a meeting at ten this morning with Mike Kensington to draft the P and S agreement. I'm using him as project counsel. Hell, my buddy Mike is counsel for just about everything!

Kearney and an assistant architect will be here at three

this afternoon to confirm our space assumptions and begin preliminary drawings. Rob I'd like you and as much of your staff as is necessary to review and thoroughly analyze the existing Natick strip malls in the package. Comb the rent rolls. Review existing leases, terminations and new leases. Analyze expenses. Run the numbers thoroughly! Rob, you're the best in the land at this so give it hell! I need data quickly. I might be able to finance at least the existing malls temporarily through Tri-Star bank," Nick ordered.

"And, Danny you should meet with Mike and I at ten. Also, brief Ronnie Fontaine for the two o'clock meeting. He's good and is the project manager that I will want on this one if it flies. Don't you agree?" Danny was squarely the number two man in the organization now.

"Si, senor," Danny replied, and smiled at Nick as he scurried to begin his part in this gargantuan development process.

Nick strolled back to his office and leaned back in his large padded leather chair. He stared out the window at the heavy traffic on Route 128. Am I doing the right thing taking this deal on now?

My personal guarantee is still required on most loans. I'm not in the Trump category yet. And the slumping economy is bothersome! Well, we're not developing residential and we can hold on the office development indefinitely. And, retail is strong and hopefully will never be a problem! Nick mused with worry! How do I know that?

The young leader's thoughts turned to his former partner, Tommy, and his violent death. He cringed at the thought of Mario Cavallaro's involvement and his extortion attempt.

Nick strived to suppress it from his consciousness. He didn't know why the time lag, but, he was quite certain that it wasn't over. He felt nauseous thinking about it and the fact that Noel and Ali knew nothing about Mario's demands. Nick cringed at the thought that Cavallaro had mentioned the two of them in the same breath as his extortion demand! Intimidation. But, who knows what he's capable of!"

A buzzing noise sounded sharply. Suddenly Nick snapped from oblivion and realized that the intercom was ringing. "Nick, do you want me to start calling my contacts at the commercial bank level and the permanent lenders to put out feelers?"

"That's right, Rob, but concentrate on land and construction loans for the development. A take-out or a stand-by commitment will be easy to obtain later on as the property leases up. But, do try to find a permanent lender for the Natick strip malls after you're comfortable with the numbers."

"By the way, Nick, Mr. Jameson of Barker, Tibbs, and Graham had a package delivered this morning. Ten copies of your Personal Net Worth statement. Looks pretty impressive. I'll send one in," Rob said.

Ten minutes later, Rob entered through Nick's open door and placed the statement in front of Nick. "Sit down, Rob," Nick implored, as he picked up the CPA firm's statement. He leaned back in his chair and began to peruse the report.

Nicholas A. Packard and Noel M. Packard
Statement of Personal Net Worth
June 30, 1988

ASSETS

Cash in banks and on hand	$ 237,000
Short-term investments – Certificates of Deposit / Repurchase Agreements (1)	2,662,000
Notes Receivable, Due 11/15/91 (2)	6,000,000.
Real Estate Owned, at fair market value (3)	70,850,000
Investment in Prime Commercial Realty, Inc., at cost(4)	3,588,000
Total Assets	$83,337,000

LIABILITIES AND NET WORTH

Accounts Payable-household	$ 24,000
Mortgages Payable (5)	42,300,000
Total Liabilities	$42,324,000
Net Worth	$41,013,000

"This is a decent-looking statement, Rob! Is it real? Am I really worth forty-one million dollars?"

"Well, the cash and short-term investments are exact. The note receivable reflects the exact amount due to you from Tommy Fletcher's estate. The executors might try to discount it at some point but you are in control and have many times that amount in side collateral on his sizable real estate holdings. The real estate values are based on nine percent capitalization rates on established NOI. Pretty conservative!

Yes, Nick, I'd say it's quite real at this time, but remember, we have not considered income taxes due on unrealized profits. They're not of concern right now, and you'll probably do some tax-free exchanges on future sales," Rob expounded.

"Well, Rob, my goal is to increase that net worth at least forty times or more. Do you know why? It's not greed, it's the challenge.

Sure, we're hitting choppy water now, but we'll sail through. Recessions are a fact of life and we're positioned well.

I'm going to provide many wealth opportunities to you and Danny along the way. Already you're both millionaires from your interests in these deals! Has that been considered in this statement?"

"Sure, Nick, this is your true net worth and doesn't include minority interests. And once again, thank you."

"No, thank you, Rob. And by the way, you'll earn another million, maybe more, on Framingham if, not when, it flies!"

****

August 10, 1992

Nick slipped from reverie inside the trash container and became aware of his predicament once again. His mind had been racing for hours with memories of the past.

His business had catapulted him to great heights. Forty-one million dollars net worth. It was real and he thought back then that he could increase it many times. Become a billionaire! It was being accomplished by men like Warren Buffett and Bill Gates. They did it on a much larger scale, but not in real estate.

Trump did it and so did the Reichmans, but they're teetering now too, I've read ! I wonder if the Mafia ever attempted extortion on any of the billionaires or are they too insulated and protected by virtual armies?

And sweet Noel, a ravishing beauty in all respects. Will I ever get back to her? And, precious Ali. The hayrides. A song from the past. He sighed audibly. A few minutes later he heard the voices of at least three men talking outside, near the dumpster. He lifted his ear up to hear better as the opposite ear sunk into the remnants of a TV dinner dish. It was repugnant! He shook the drippings off his ear. They were checking every inch of the basement and when the noises got close to the dumpster Nick wrapped his hand around the butt of the Magnum and slipped it out facing upward ready to use it if he had to.

Santini walked up to the dumpster and opened the lid, but laughed when he saw it filled to the brim. Underneath, Nick's eyes were filled with horror. Santini slammed the lid down. After fifteen minutes the noise faded. They seemed to be giving up in the basement for now!

Nick was so relieved that he forgot about the rats and his claustrophobia. He just might make it. It was now after six p.m. he surmised. He'd have to wait a few more hours until dark which he would determine by slightly opening the dumpster lid and clearing the trash in his face.

Once again, he slipped back into memory.

CHAPTERB 63

October 1988

It was a bright and crisp fall morning. Outside the leaves had turned and peaked creating a splendid scene everywhere. Yellow and red leaves were spotty, but still could be seen.

Nick gazed through his office window admiring the beauty as the sun shone radiantly through his windows. The scene was filled with pulchritude.

His intercom buzzed incessantly. Retrieving the phone he heard music, then Kensington's voice. Ellen had put him through, cognizant of Nick's urgent desire to speak with him.

"The P and S was executed by Carl Johnson as soon as he received it. Thirty-five million dollars was the final price. Do you want to execute now, Nick, or wait a while? You know that you have more time under the original offer. Are you ready to put down the required one-million-dollar deposit with the P and S?" Mike queried.

Nick was ready and excitedly invited Mike to dinner that evening at The Dandelion Green in Burlington.

He sat back and contemplated the deal. Price is right.

Thirteen million dollars for the land produces a 100 percent financing deal. Well, at least on the permanent mortgage. And twenty-two million for the strip centers yields about two and a half million dollars gross rent, supporting a mortgage of twenty-one million! But how the hell are we going to put the remaining two and a half million bank required cash down at the construction loan closing? I will have to cash much of my money market investments and kick it in along, with additional money of Prime Commercial surplus cash. This is scary! It cuts the cash down to bare bones! Then to get started on the project we'll need partners with eleven-plus million dollars to get our cash back. Whew! Well, we can hold on the land development until the business horizon gets brighter and operate the strip centers for a good cash flow. We'll just have to conserve on cash for a while. I'll sign the P&S agreement this week with a million dollars of Prime Development Co. cash to start.

Nick sat back in his chair and dialed Dave Kearney. "Dave, Nick Packard. Can we build what we discussed earlier on the Framingham site?"

"Nick, after preliminary calculations, you can build the four hundred thousand square feet of retail, but the office space must be limited to one hundred seventy-five thousand square feet because of parking requirements and wetlands restrictions. I don't think a parking garage should be considered. It's too expensive."

"Are you sure?" said Nick.

"Well, at the preliminary stage, but we'll run it again," Dave responded.

"Yes, do run it again. I need at least two hundred fifty

thousand square feet of office space." Nick was pushing it to get at least the two hundred thousand square feet. "Think hard, Dave!" Nick thanked him and hung up.

At one fifteen p.m. the intercom buzzed. "Two visitors here to see you," Ellen pronounced.

"Who?" Nick asked.

"Ah, Angelo and Carlo. Are you available?" She was nervous and wanted to slide under her desk.

He had no idea who these men were, but said to Ellen, "Please show them in."

Nick exhibited a surprised look when the two men followed Ellen through the door. The man wearing a grey silk shirt with no tie was of medium height and had long wavy black hair. His thick black mustache gave him a hard, slick look. Behind him a younger man no more than twenty-two flanked the rear. He was huge and wore a tight black T-shirt which exposed massive arms with bulging muscles. Angelo looked like he could, literally, stop a truck! Both men had distinct Italian features.

They were not bankers here to offer a financing deal! That was obvious to Nick and Ellen too. Maybe they were sub-contractors looking for a payment? Nick was very wary. Ellen left quickly.

Without a smile or introduction, Carlo inquired, "You Nick Packard?""Yes, I am," Nick replied.

"Mr. Cavallaro wants to talk to you outside." Nick became very nervous realizing that he hadn't yet responded to Mario. It's been at least three months! He thought. "Let's go," Nick replied, and he stood up and followed them out.

He smiled at Ellen as he left. "Hold any calls. I'll be back in a few minutes." He snickered trying to hide the fear!

The trio walked through the glass doors in the lobby as Nick pulled away from Angelo's grasp on his arm. "That's not necessary," he said in anger. He was going out voluntarily.

Outside he noticed a white Cadillac limo parked in a remote corner of the lot. Nick assumed that he was about to see a power play and the limo and these escorts increased the intimidation! Angelo opened the rear door and ushered Nick inside facing Mario. Carlo opened the passenger side front door and took a seat beside the driver.

Angelo nudged him inside further with a driving push sending a sharp pain through Nick's shoulder. Mario, with a grimace on his face, said, "Nick, I never heard back from you, my friend! Do I take that as a fuck you, Mario? Is that what it is?"

"No, Mario, I've been waiting for an opportunity to return the favor you did for me and for that I am very grateful. I don't owe you any money," Nick said diplomatically. "How can I return it?" Nick knew that this would never go away and if he ignored it there could be grave danger!

"Wrong, Nick, you owe me for your life. How much is that worth? Probably a lot more than the three million dollars that you're going to pay me! But, I know that is a lot of cash to produce and I'm a reasonable man, so I'll take three hundred thousand now and three hundred thousand per month for the next nine months."

Nick replied with a lie. "I don't have any cash! It's all tied up in real estate!"

Mario tapped the window separating the driver,

then,within seconds Angelo who had been standing outside the rear door opened it and grabbed Nick's arm and began to thrust him out of the limo. He slapped Nick's face and said, "Well then, get the fuck out of here, you moron." Immediately the driver started the engine.

"Wait!" Nick implored. He turned to Mario and said, "I'll give you an interest in my latest deal which is sizable and will probably be a home run. It might be worth over a million to you at completion." He didn't know what else to do! Ignoring Mario could be fatal for him and his family!"Is that the Framingham land deal?" Mario asked.

How the hell does he know about that deal?!

"It is, Mario. A five percent interest could yield at least that much money!"

"Nick, offer me that in writing and I'll…" He hesitated and pulled out a cigarette lighter, then, flicked the flame. I'll burn it up as starters. You're fucking me around, Packard! Get out!"

Angelo grabbed Nick's collar and threw him out onto the pavement. He landed on his back tearing his shirt.

"Think long and hard about how you're going to improve that offer, motherfucker! And show me how we get a lot of cash out of this within six months. I'll call you in a few days and be prepared to make us happy! If you don't you won't like the consequences!" Mario bellowed. He slammed the door as the limo moved slowly away and departed.

As he walked back inside the Prime office Ellen gasped when she saw his condition. She cried, then became paranoid. Nick had to console her for hours and explain that it was a case of a contractor debt which was mistaken. She came to the brink of quitting, but he calmed her down after a while stating that it was resolved and convinced her to stay. He couldn't afford this kind of thing happening in his office. He had to resolve this quickly, somehow?!

Nick knew that showing fear and paying any money for threats made by the Mafia was just the beginning of possibly a life-long bondage! But, he had to offer something because he had too much to lose, especially his family and business. Mario was evil and capable of who knows what?! A call to the FBI would totally fuck up his business! His life!

CHAPTER 64

The 560 Mercedes rolled into the dimly-lit parking lot in the North End of Boston. Two spaces were available. Mario had called Nick three days after the horrid encounter at his office and demanded a meeting in another four days. Mario was busy and could only meet him briefly in the Gino Stella restaurant and bar at ten p.m. Mario was in control now!

He locked his car and walked to the rear of the restaurant amongst the old North End tenements. While he felt confident that he could resolve the matter for now, he knew that he could be entering into a lifelong fiasco. The welfare of his family was most important and he had the cash. Fear affected his rationality! The Framingham deal might never get off the ground. Then what? No, he'd do whatever it took. What else could he do?

He entered the rear door of the Gino Stella bar. His eyes roaming he noticed a table with three men sitting in a remote rear corner of the room. The remainder of the bar area was empty of people. They were alone. Nick became fearful. Why was the bar area empty at ten p.m. They wouldn't kill him in here would they? He knew better because they needed him to get anything?

He pulled out the last remaining chair at the table and casually sat down facing Mario. The room was cast in dispersions of silence and Mario stared at Nick for a long time before saying a word to Nick. His hard, black-eyed gaze sent chills down Nick's spine, but he managed to remain calm.

"Nick, my friend, what have you brought us tonight? Some cash maybe?"

"I told you Mario that there is no cash available!"

Suddenly, Angelo Bono who was standing behind Nick wrapped a garrotte around Nick's neck and started twisting. Mario ordered him to stop which he did, but Angelo pushed Nick's chair over to intimidate him. He fell to the floor and winced in pain as he rubbed the burn on his neck!"Wait a minute!" Nick moaned as he got up off the floor rubbing his neck. "I told you Mario that I'd give you a piece of the Framingham deal which we will agree upon now. And, if it becomes "dead in the water" I'll give you an equal interest in my Wilmington or Arlington projects which are already leased up and profitable. Why did I say "dead in the water"? This is all insanity, but what happens if I don't cooperate?

Carlo Puglisi then spoke up. "You must think that we're dumb, Packard. Who knows what will happen to that Framingham deal. Don't you read the papers. We know that economic conditions suck, you asshole! The one million in that deal is pie in the sky! Five percent interest. Fuck you!" It could be a lot more than that you moron over time!

Mario then chimed in with a remark that paralyzed

Nick's rational mind. "Nick, would you bet your daughter's life that we'll be paid at least one million dollars within six months?"

Nick froze with trepidation. The mere mention of harm to his family sent horrendous chills through his entire being! They were really fucking with him painfully. His daughter! He almost burst into tears, but held himself together.

Nick was ready to concede on anything to protect his family. "I don't have any cash, Mario. It's all committed to my deals." He was taking a chance. "Well, give us two hundred thousand dollars now, in cash, and one hundred percent of your Arlington deal!" They didn't want to remain partners with him in any deal. "How's that? OK?" Mario replied.

Then, feeling beaten and wary, but protective of his family, after a long silence Nick said, "I'll give you a hundred percent of the Arlington deal, but I have no cash." He also would not consider remaining partners with them in the Arlington deal. Mario bit for it. He had liked the Arlington Square Plaza that day that he visited it. Carlo had run some numbers and they were coming up with at least five million dollars in equity value today.

"Done, Nick. But if it gets fucked up somehow, you and others might get fucked up too! Capisci?"

"Capisci!" Nick said, praying to himself.

They knew all Nick's business deals, but had no idea that he now had nearly three million dollars in personal cash!

"Mario," Nick said, "this transfer is predicated upon

a final settlement of your, ah, favor. You will release me forever. Agreed?"

"Agreed," Mario stated.

Where that would go was anyone's guess. But what else could he do?

Nick went on "I assume that there will be a handshake? I have to stay on the permanent mortgage. I'll have to close the permanent mortgage immediately! The lender has restricted a conveyance without its approval." "No, Nick. We'll give you further instructions, but we can deal with the HLW Pension fund." They know everything! An arm's length sale by you to our straw with a first mortgage assumption. We'll give you a second mortgage note in an amount to be determined to make it a sale at fair market value. You'll never receive any payment for that second mortgage note and give a full payment release to the straw up-front. You deal with the IRS and be creative. I know you will because you'll be deeply involved! No repercussions! Capisci?!"

Nick realized that these men were coached by a financial wizard like Meyer Lansky, portrayed in the old movies?

Nick agreed to close the deal within one month, then shook hands with all but Angelo, who didn't give a rat's ass. Nick never showed the fear that had welled up inside him.

"Salute a cent'anno," Mario chanted as he lifted his wine glass. He offered wine to Nick, who declined. The others lifted their glasses and toasted in unison. This man is smart thought Mario and conceded what must be only a small fraction of his fortune . Mario mused.

"We have a deal?" Mario repeated."Yes, let's end it," Nick replied.

They shook hands.

Nick stood and slowly walked to the rear door of the bar while his eyes scanned in all directions, apprehensively. Then he drove slowly away, trying to show no fear!

As Nick drove down Hanover Street in the North End of Boston he glanced in the rear view mirror noticing a wet rear windshield. It had begun to rain heavily. No cars seemed to be on his tail. Why would they follow him he reasoned. He had made his deal, A whopper at that! Worth at least four million dollars in equity value today or more and he pays the capital gains tax and receives nothing for the sale! How did he ever get into this mess? He mused.

Forget it, he thought. There's plenty more. What's more important is my family first, then my hard personal money market investments of $2.7 million in the Tri-Star Bank account and about two hundred thousand in my checking account. They hopefully will never locate it, but their knowledge is derived through long tentacles which uncover uncanny amounts of information. If they ever find it I'm history. I'm certainly not investing it into the Johnson acquisition at this point. We'll have to use a million dollars in Prime cash on the Framingham/Natick acquisitions, which we'll get when we bump the Arlington permanent to the twenty and a half million initially suggested by Ken Walker. Then I can probably get Carl Johnson to take back a second mortgage for a while. I think I might be able to persuade him to do that. And, I'll need the consent of Tri-Star Bank which I, also, probably can get.

Nick's thoughts rambled on. I'll sign the P&S agreement on Framingham within a few days and use Prime Commercial cash for the deposit of one million dollars. We'll try to push the Arlington Permanent loan closing for next week and close on the Framingham acquisition by January. There is a lot to do, but I'll do it with help from the staff.

His thoughts then turned to the need to hide his $2.9 million personal cash which included personal checking account amounts. He could deliver it to Zurich, Switzerland and set up a numbered account. Is that the best place. Or, are the Cayman Islands better? Who the hell knows? He thought. He'd never done this before! Oh, how that implied threat to Ali frightened him. How could this man who, also, has a daughter allude to that? Intimidation? Who knows what he might do! Nick thought he was using scare tactics only! He hoped so!

Nick could feel his world crashing in as his heart raced. I've got to cool it or I'll never get through it! They're not going to kill anybody. At least not now! Nick rationalized. He relaxed somewhat pondering this thought.

The rain splashed on the windshield as he drove along Route 128 to his office at Ford Plaza where he retrieved every copy of his personal net worth statement and frantically ran them through the shredding machine.

The Prime Commercial Team was briefed on the schedule of closings early the next day. However, no mention was ever made of the big problem looming. Fortunately, Danny and Rob had no interest in Arlington Square Plaza such as they had in the Wilmington Prime Plaza and Ford Plaza. They didn't have to be briefed. Nick told everybody that he was selling Arlington Square to an old friend and was helping finance it with a purchase money second mortgage. He didn't tell them that the debt would be forgiven and worthless! He didn't have to at this time. He didn't even know who the straw was yet and only used a false name for his friend.

The schedule was set:

- Nick needed a certified company check today for one million dollars payable to Carl Johnson for the P&S agreement execution the next day. He would borrow it until the HLW mortgage closed.

- Nick had already called Ken Walker of HLW Pension Fund and had cleared the twenty million five hundred thousand dollar revised permanent mortgage amount. Rob must line the closing up for a few weeks from now. He would use this additional cash for the loan covering the Framingham deposit.

- Nick would call Carl Johnson today and arrange for a two million five hundred thousand dollar purchase money second mortgage from Carl to be secured by all three properties. This would have to substitute for the additional cash equity requirement which would be needed at the construction loan closing.

- Rob must clear the two million five hundred thousand dollar second mortgage to be given to Johnson with Tri-Star Bank, who had called for three million five hundred thousand dollars of cash equity by construction loan. And, arrange an acquisition closing sometime in January 1989.

I want all of this done before I close the Arlington Square conveyance. None of my staff will ever see any related documents nor will they ever be told of the extortion! Ellen seems somewhat skeptical of what's going on. But, she doesn't know for sure and never will!

Within the next two weeks that led up to mid-November, the HLW mortgage was closed and the Framingham/Natick P&S executed with a one-million-dollar deposit issued to Carl Johnson. Carl had agreed after two days of negotiation to take back a two-and-a-half-million-dollar second mortgage at a 12 percent interest rate and a five-year term bullet. Even though the loan requests were now down to eleven million seven hundred thousand dollars on the land and nineteen million eight hundred thousand on the strip centers, the first mortgage loans were very difficult to work out. Saginsky at Tri-Star, Nicks long-term banking contact, hemmed and hawed about any kind of new development financing at this juncture. Most lending had stopped for the time being until the outcome of the recession building up steam was known. Nick was barely able to convince him to finance the acquisition. Finally, considering the location of the properties and the quality of the occupancy status relative to the Natick strip malls he agreed to issue the loan commitments at a 10 percent interest rate under a five-year term bullet loan for the land and strip mall acquisitions.

However, Nick was clearly told not to plan on construction financing for the Framingham land anytime soon. Nick had no problem with that and felt lucky to get that! He realized what a blessing it was that Mario didn't bite for that interest and become involved as a partner!

CHAPTER 65

January 21, 1989

"We're damn fortunate that Carl Johnson thinks of Nick like a son. We were coming up short on the financing for the deal and Carl came through with a two million five hundred thousand dollar second mortgage," Rob gleefully exhorted. Diane, the Prime office manager, had inquired how they were able to swing this deal as Mike Kensington slid the documents across the table one by one for signatures.

The Prime team had assembled on the nineteenth floor of 60 State Street at the prestigious law firm of Kensington & Taylor to assist with acquisition closings of the Framingham land and the Natick strip malls. Carl Johnson stopped by for a while and spoke briefly with his attorney and Nick. He was using a cane and seemed old, but was still sharp as a tack. He took a copy of his mortgage, yet to be recorded, and left after shaking all hands vigorously.

The closing went smoothly, but Lenny Saginsky of Tri-Star Bank repeated his prior statement about financing and this time he said that the window is now closed even to the giant heavyweights. Nick didn't quite believe that though.

Nick was happy now that most of the excess Prime cash was drained off. The excess five hundred thousand dollars from the HLW loan was much needed, and after getting current on paying bills left two hundred eleven thousand in the till. He still had his personal $2.9 million cash to stash away and would have to deal with that issue soon. The cash flow from Prime Plaza and Ford Place would almost carry Prime Commercial overhead at current levels, but he still had the interest payments from Leanna which he could use to fund the company, now at forty-five thousand per month. They would get by just fine. Just fine, despite the growing recession! He hoped.

Lenny, while sitting at the closing table beside Nick, had told him that a Mr. Cardi had called him a week or so ago inquiring about him. A credit check from a personal lender, he had said.

"What did you say, Lenny?" Nick asked, quizzically and quite nervously.

"Nick, of course I said that our bank policy does not allow giving any information without the client's approval unless it's a court order!"

They're hot on my trail. I've got to end this!"Let's toast to our accomplishments in the last few weeks culminating in today's acquisition," Danny boasted. Rob, then, poured the contents of two bottles of Dom Perignon as everyone in the room said cheers and clinked their glasses together. The party moved to the Seasons Restaurant.

"Danny," Nick retorted, "do you remember 1957, when I was laid out comatose in the Browning Memorial Hospital? Did you ever think that we'd be sitting here together thirty-two years later and would have experienced what we have? Well, I didn't. I guess I couldn't even think at all back then. A complete tabula rasa. Remember how you thought I had gone crazy?" Nick related with a laugh, and rehashed the story to the others.

The group roared with laughter as they sat around a large table covered with a linen tablecloth in the Seasons Restaurant on the top floor of the Bostonian Hotel. Nick had seated the ladies to afford them the picturesque view of Quincy Market."Nick, congratulations on your sale of Arlington Square. I propose a toast to your successful project. Now, we can order anything we want? Right?" Diane joked.

No one, except Danny who had been told this morning, knew about the extortion scheme. Danny was sworn to secrecy. This was no frivolous matter. "Omerta applies to us Danny as much as it does to these mobsters," Nick had said. Silence on this will always be our code too. Nick had not revealed the nightmare even to Mike, his closest business friend and attorney. Mike was sitting across from Nick smiling. He was happy for his friend's accomplishment today!"Diane," Nick responded, "there will be many more deals in the future. I intend to take this company to great heights—with your help, of course." He waved his arm with a gesture to include Diane and everybody at the table.

The business discussion continued and the group decided to order. The Venison entree was highly recommended by the waiter in addition to the Bear meat steak. Everybody ordered the lobster bisque for openers, It too was a house recommendation and was splendid according to the waiter.

"Danny, when's Suzie's and your baby due?" Ellen inquired. "Soon?"

"Oh, around mid-May. I can't wait. It's our first child, you know?"

"What are you hoping for, Danny?" Ellen went on.

"A boy, like most fathers, but either way it doesn't matter!"

"Not so, Danny boy," Nick chimed in. "Not every father wants a boy. I'll take a girl any day of the week." Suddenly, within moments, something seemed to hit Nick like a ton of bricks. His face became pale and he began to sweat profusely. Would you bet your daughter's life that we'll receive one million dollars within six months? How far will they go if they find out that I have cash or if Arlington Square goes negative? This economy! Who knows!

"Are you all right, Nick?" Danny asked with concern of a heart attack!Nick took a deep breath and was still for a minute until the faintness passed! "Yes, Danny, I'm OK now. It must be the air circulation," he lied.

Danny knew better, though.

Nick covered by saying, "You're right, Danny. It really doesn't matter. Boy or girl. They are equally precious."

Ellen and Diane listened intently with motherly instincts, although, neither had given birth to children yet. Ellen was so young and Diane wasn't even married yet at thirty years of age. She was a highly intelligent and organized lady. And, was, also, a gorgeous specimen. Her hair was cut neatly with bangs and her teeth were the whitest Nick had ever seen.

She had ultrahigh standards and might never marry. What a waste Nick thought as he hugged her tightly. They were all feeling the drinks quite well at this point.

As Nick hugged Diane tightly, she blushed as she nestled into his arms warmly. She had a crush on Nick right from their introduction, but she knew it could never go any further. He was totally committed to Noel. The group smiled at Diane. They had all become good friends as well as business associates over the past few years.

"I'm so happy for you, Danny!" Nick exclaimed. "Suzie will look just like Noel did when she gets further along. That is plump and gorgeous. I'm ecstatic that you decided to join my company back in the old days."

"Yeah, the old days. Three years ago!" Danny burst out in laughter. "Way back then. Weren't we driving covered wagons to the office back then?" Danny cajoled.

"I love you all," Nick chanted, feeling in good spirits now. "You've all done a superb job and I'm extremely grateful to every one of you!" Nick said in a voice of intonation. Diane and Rob patted Nick affectionately on the back.

"Yeah, he just committed himself for footing the tab tonight! He's so grateful. Get what you can from him tonight everybody!" The group roared in assent as Danny went on. "There is someone who should pay for their own dinner tonight." They listened intently. "Rob, you blew it big-time on this financing—ten to twelve percent interest rates. C'mon, didn't you do any negotiating?" The women looked surprised and shocked while Nick hung his head low. Then, he chuckled as Danny shook Rob's hand. Ten percent on a thirty-one-and-a-half-million-dollar loan, then 12 percent on two and a half million subordinated to that! It's a wonder that we even got any financing in these times. And, then no side collateral to secure the loan? Why, GMC pays 6–7 percent on its commercial paper. Ellen and Diane were relieved as they realized the compliment just made to Rob! Nick applauded him even though he orchestrated many of the financing arrangements. Rob's work was well cut out for him. He had to line up partners for the approximate remaining eight and a half million dollar of equity which would be required on Framingham to commence construction and get the Prime one million dollars deposit back.

The women got up and hugged Rob while he kissed each one on the lips while they both lingered a while. He was their friend!

The following week, Nick drove to Lynn.

There had was no sign on the door he noticed as he entered and walked up a flight of rickety stairs. A light beamed in one room at the end of the hall. The other rooms were empty He walked in and saw a man seated at a table with a folder opened displaying legal documents. The room was dimly lit and cramped for space and a worn desk plate had the name Att. Cardi displayed on it. Nick didn't connect it for a minute, then realized that he was the anonymous caller to Tri-Star.

"Are you Attorney Cardi?" Nick inquired as he looked around the room. They were alone, at least as far as he could see.

"Yes. Nick Packard?" "We're you expecting anyone else?" Nick chuckled with nervous energy.

"Maybe a brinks guard shouldering a money sack!" Cardi replied. Nick got paranoid. Had they gone back to a cash demand? He feared.

Nick calmly said, "Have you got the documents?" "Maybe," Cardi replied. Right off he didn't like Nick. His attitude! As if they were the good guys!

Cardi pulled a deed from the file and said, "Sign this!" "May I see all the documents first? Isn't that fair?" Without saying a word, Cardi slid the contents of the folder to Nick, who began to scrutinize them. "I don't have all evening, Mr. Packard. Please sign these."

Nick got so angry at this treatment that he felt like punching him! But, he held his composure. It was the wise thing to do!

Nick read enough as he went through the deed to Oceanic Trust, no individual names, and other documents. The selling price was shown as twenty-five million five hundred thousand dollars to be paid by an assumption of a twenty million five hundred thousand dollar mortgage loan from HLW Pension Fund. The assumption document was already approved and signed by HLW. The only other documents consisted of a second mortgage and accompanying note for five million dollars from Oceanic Trust and signed by a straw trustee to be recorded. Also, there was a mortgage release to be signed by Nick now and held by them for future recording!

He signed the deed, second mortgage release and added

payment acknowledgment without any questions. He had seen enough! To regurgitate over!

Nausea set in when he was asked for his check to cover tax stamps and recording in the amount of thirty-six thousand dollars, which he wrote his personal check for. Then, the final blow, a document stating Nick's obligation to manage and lease the property and guarantee a distribution of one hundred eighty-two thousand dollars per month to cover the HLW mortgage and profit to the Oceanic Trust was slipped by Cardi to Nick. That means I get about one hundred ninety-eight thousand dollars NOI per month if the 95 percent occupancy projections hold up? And end up with sixteen thousand per month for management and leasing! Whew! Not much room for economic surprises! Ruthless! He signed reluctantly.

He was given no copies and would have to get the recorded document copies at the County Registry of Deeds. He said good-bye unwillingly, then left, not receiving a response. He loathed these people!

CHAPTER 66

Spring 1989

In the months that followed the Prime Commercial team worked frantically to induce construction financing interest for the Framingham development, but the shit hit the fan in all directions. The savings and loans banks shut off the spigots entirely and the commercial banks wouldn't budge on construction financing without a takeout loan which was hard to find.

The Tax Reform Act of 1986 had driven real estate investors out of the market. The passive tax loss limitation was driving away new tax shelter investors. Although the well located and profitable commercial real estate projects were spinning off operational cash flow, investors in all sectors were getting wary from the elimination of artificial tax loss pass-throughs generated mainly by depreciation. They were a major element of return to the investor.

A severe recession had set in as the massive excesses of the 1980s took their toll. The economy was extremely overextended in its housing expenditures and lifestyle in general. All havoc was springing loose.

Nick decided that it was wise to begin the approval process for the Framingham land development and got everybody in the company working on the presentation to the planning board which was the first step in obtaining the variances and special permit required. Ultimately the city council would vote on final approval. Commencement of construction was probably a year or more in the future, but the approvals were good for two years.

In late spring the team approached the planning board.

A spotlight shined on the architect's easel as version after version of the architectural renderings and preliminary drawings were displayed and explained in great detail by the brilliant architect. David Kearney.

Danny, who was coordinating the presentation, announced in a typical salesman's speech that the response for tenancy in the center was overwhelming. Although Prime Commercial did not have any users ready to sign now, Prime was close to signing a deal with a tenant for 100 percent of building 4. For the retail there were only two retailers showing any interest at the present, but, according to Danny the phone was ringing off the hook with serious inquiries and Prime was showing the vacant lot to many! A "dog and pony show" relative to the marketing of the property was necessary to hype-up the planning board.

The board's response was typical for many public meetings. The members were enjoying the ego inflation produced by their authority acquired through law. They often frowned, shook their heads in disgust and raised their voices to exercise this authority.

Fortunately, Nick pondered, there is no price for approvals in this city. The city's purity was well known. Most municipalities were the same, but there were a few like North Beach where a certain member or members of a public board would demand payoffs through intermediary channels. They knew the Tommy Fletchers of the world would come bearing briefcases, sometimes suitcases, of cash!

And, too, there was the stringent legal municipal demands which seemed unfair such as cleaning or re-lining utility lines off the site of the project or donations of segments of land or municipal buildings and equipment donations suggested by public officials! Legal bribes?

The open discussion was give and take for the most part and the board members were very professional. They understood the site and design issues quite well. Their concentration was mostly on civil engineering issues; i.e., wetlands extent and compliance with Massachusetts statues and DEQE regulations, ingress and egress widths and locations, parking as related to minimum parking space compliance and compact/handicap spaces and the open or green area requirement. Every board member seemed pleased with the building design except for one, an architect! Dave Kearney dealt successfully with his comments and he finally shut up.

The hearing wound down after an hour devoted to the Prime project. As was expected the board decided to delay approval while they thought about it and deliberated. It wasn't the largest they'd voted on in that area, but it was big and could not be approved hastily.

Nick stood and he and Danny both thanked the board for their courteous consideration, then casually exited the hearing room followed by the rest of the Prime team members.

Outside, Nick privately spoke out of the corner of his mouth to Danny and Rob. "We're essentially approved, but, how in hell are we going to build it at any time soon with no financing or serious user interest? The permits might lapse before the economic environment will warrant this project? Well, at any rate, a good property will have been land-banked and be ready to roll later on!"

CHAPTER 67

Fall 1989

The mood around the office became somber over the spring and summer of 1989. Danny and Nick had been working frantically to find tenants for both Prime Plaza and Arlington Heights. Forty-five thousand square feet of space had been put back on the market with the closing down of three stores and some of the others were delinquent in rent payments. The worst case was Arlington Heights!Both men were still trying to obtain interest in Framingham, but that was futile! Office overhead was being cut back and Nick prayed that he didn't have to lay off anyone else in the office, but Ellen may have to go and Diane take her place. Construction was at a stand still and he had already let both project managers go.

Nick sat in his office on a cold, cloudy winter day reading a Wall Street Journal article depicting the gloomy outlook on the economy and even worse for the real estate industry. There was a staunch prediction of many real estate foreclosures for the foreseeable future. The effects on the banking system were disastrous and real estate lending was shut down completely by most lending institutions.

Nick's intercom rang. "A Mr. Puglisi is on line three for you. Do you want it?" Ellen inquired.

"Yes! I do."

"Hello, Mr. Packard," the voice on the other end said. "Carlo P. here. Mr. Cavallaro wants to speak with you. Hold on."

"Ni-ick, what's going on?""What do you mean, Mario?""Don't test my fucking patience! You know what I'm referring to. The cash transferred to our holding trust this month was one hundred sixty-three thousand dollars, only a thousand dollars over the mortgage payment. Our agreement calls for one hundred eighty-two thousand a month.""Mario, you know that we lost some major tenants in Arlington. We, also, lost many in the other projects. You know how tough times are, but we're making a supreme effort to lease Arlington and have been trying to direct interest from all prospective tenants there!""I don't think you are. You're directing them to buildings that you own. To your advantage. Mario was making a guess into a fact! You'll find the cash if you have to and "have to" is what you must do. You could always sell that piece of shit castle in Hamilton. Fucking waste of money! Mario had been extremely resentful of the house right from the start.

"If that cash transfer is less than a hundred and eighty-two thousand dollars for a few more months, then your return favor is considered an insult! Further, any amounts below the one hundred eighty-two thousand monthly will be due before year's end, with interest. Capisci?"Click. Mario had hung up!

Nick sighed. They killed Tommy and they've been receiving twenty thousand dollars cash flow per month over and above the mortgage payment and now own a valuable mall. Just because the monthly cash flow to them drops to a thousand dollars over the mortgage payment in such rotten times, it's now an insult?! I wonder if Tommy really did put a contract on my life? I'll never know? God, do I loathe that slime bag Mario! Chills ran through his body.

Moments later the intercom buzzed again. Nick tried to dismiss the grief and slowly answered Ellen.

"Mr. Saginsky is returning your call. Shall I send it through?"

"Yes." Nick sighed again. "I'll take him."

"Hi, Nick. Lenny Saginsky. How are you, buddy?"

"I'm fine," Nick lied. "As of last night our Framingham project was received favorably by the city council. I called you to discuss the possibility of a construction loan arrangement for the first phase of the Framingham project. One hundred thousand square feet of retail space and ninety-seven thousand square feet of office.""What level of pre-leasing are you at?" Lenny inquired.

"About thirty thousand square feet on the retail and fifteen thousand on the office. But we haven't really pushed it yet," he answered.

"Nick, we couldn't fund it unless you were at least seventy-five percent pre-leased to AAA tenants on both. I mean leases signed. It's not me, Nick, business is at a virtual standstill here now. Over fifteen percent of our commercial loans are non-performing now and there have been a lot of FDIC people around here lately. The word is that some banks are about to be shut down. You know that Capital Bank is closing its doors and New England Merchants Bank is being taken over. Many others will follow. On the S and L level, are you aware that First American Savings Bank is close to being torpedoed? The RTC will end up with their loans. The consensus is a lot more shit will hit the fan before it improves. I'll keep you informed. Especially if it comes to the point of withdrawing your cash. You're exposed. The FDIC insures up to one hundred thousand dollars only, not two million. I forget the exact amount of your balance. But, that's right, we do hold money market instruments for you. You should be OK, I think."

Nick became very wary of Lenny's uncertainty! "Lenny, I have approximately two-point-seven million dollars in money market instruments, which I hope you're right about. Somewhat less than a few hundred thousand in cash, checking account funds."

"Nick, back to financing, you should go to a top-tier bank like Fleet or Shawmut."

"Lenny, you know those banks won't touch my level with a ten-foot pole at this point."

"I don't know for sure. And you could go to Manhattan. The lenders are more aggressive there." Lenny was legitimately trying to help, but it was futile! "Yeah, thanks, Lenny. I'm appreciative of your help in the past." Nick hung up knowing that was his best chance of any bank. He'd fold for now and delay the Framingham construction.

CHAPTER 68

February 1990

Nick sat in his office with his hands on his head in deep distressful thought. His attitude was somber. The ease of the '70s and '80s had faded away. What had been a piece of cake then was now eaten and gone, just crumbs left. Where did all the office and retail companies go that were chasing "Gung ho" for space? A serious recession had set in and was sinking many real estate developers among other business people!

He was now thinking about who would have to be laid off and deliberated for hours over it. No one was put first in his mind. He loved them all and was sad. Should I just close Prime Commercial down and operate from home? "No," he said aloud after a while, and snapped out of it. With a grim facade he called the intercom numbers of Ellen and Chuck. They marched in one at a time and were laid off by Nick. As Ellen cried, tears welled up in Nick's eyes. Chuck shrugged his shoulders and walked out of Nick's office.

Nick then called in Rob, Danny and Diane. They were asked to stay with Prime, Diane handling Ellen's job and

Rob doing the accounting for chuck in addition to their other duties, but take substantial salary cuts. They were depressed, but agreed with the promise of a big reward down the road when Prime returned to prosperity. I should have used the word if!

A few days later, on February 7, Mario called Nick at nine p.m. on Nick's personal telephone line at the Prime office. "Hello, Nick Packard."

"Mario C. here. Do you have our check for January?" The original soft-spoken, suave at times Mario, who referred to Nick as "my friend," had disappeared. His tone had changed completely. Nick hated this side of Mario even more and a shock of fear ran through him! What was going to happen?! The Lord only knows what he's capable of carrying out? How did he get my personal number. It's not listed?

"It's due on the first and today's the sixth. Why?" Mario demanded.

"My accounting is behind. I've laid off half my office staff including the accountant. Times are horrendously bad! You want accurate accounting. Don't you?"

Mario didn't reply and remained silent for what seemed like an eternity. The intimidation was overbearing to Nick, and finally he queried, "You still there, Mario?""Yeah, I'm here. How much is our cash transfer?"

Nick hesitated. This was extremely painful. What the hell does he want? No investment on their part, and with the terrible economic conditions a break-even should be welcomed, and that's what it is this month. Practically! Not quite!

"Well, Mario, it's a bit lower this month with the new

vacancies. One hundred thirty-nine thousand dollars," Nick stated calmly.

Again there was silence, then the dial tone. He was gone.

"Bastard, he hung up on me." The fear really set in then.

Nick left shortly thereafter, filled with anxiety, and drove to Hamilton. He didn't reveal anything to Noel and he was so nervous that he even turned down Noel's sexual advances that night despite the highly sensual thing that she did!

Noel knew nothing about the extortion committed by Mario. Nick didn't want her to panic. He'd tell her when and if he had to. Not right then. It wasn't necessary. Not yet, anyway. He hoped!

The next day, while Nick was studying the progress drawings for the retail section of the Framingham development in the conference room, he thought to himself, again, that he would put the project on hold after this update of the drawings and shelve it. Diane stuck her head through the door and told Nick that Carlo P. is on the telephone.

"Who's he?" Diane questioned.

"Oh, he's one of the owners of Arlington Heights. You can put him through to this telephone." He pointed to the extension resting on the large mahogany conference room table. "Oh, and this was in the mail this morning." She set down a delinquency notice from their office building mortgage lender. Two months overdue on the Ford Plaza mortgage payments! Nick felt sick.

Nick sat down and lifted the receiver. "Hello, this is Nick."

A voice replied, "Packard, Mario C. told me to call you. He wants to meet with you tomorrow night." He hesitated, as if waiting for an answer."I think I'm free. OK, yes," Nick coolly asserted. Carlo mumbled something about being free, but his voice was very muffled. Nick thought he said that he'd better be free!

"Eight o'clock tomorrow night at the Paradise Club. Do you know where that is?" Carlo asked.

"Yes, it's on North Beach, isn't it?" "That's it. And, Mr. C. says for you to make the cash transfer today, before you come. Also, bring a buy-out proposal for Arlington Heights. Don't bother to come without both being done!" He, then, hung up.

The Paradise Club. They probably own it. What a coincidence! Tommy's burial site. Joe Cataldo…he might as well have killed Tommy himself that night with the bribe payment! This time the stakes are much higher. Millions, or maybe his life. I pray that it's not more than that. Noel and Ali are my life. No, only my money and my life are most likely at stake. They have scruples about woman and children. I pray!

Out of character for Nick, he became paranoid. What was about to transpire? Mario and anyone else involved weren't going to wait much longer. His payoff to them was way too generous to begin with, but now even that wasn't enough! The Golden Boy they thought they had found was not so golden anymore and what was left of the gold was melting away.He thought.

A fucking buy-out plan. I gave them a valuable mall which will be fine after the recession. Incredible! They won't stop until they have hard cash and I'm truly broke! Well, I have the money market instruments,but their not getting those. That money is for are for future survival of my family!

Nick mused .This might be a good time to disappear, but, not unless his family including his mother, Frances, were sent to an undisclosed location. Then, all hell would break loose and they'd probably find him someday and he'd suffer greatly. As if he wasn't in agony now! No, he'd stay here and work this thing out somehow. He hoped!

CHAPTER 69

On February 9 at seven fifteen p.m. Nick nervously left Ford Plaza driving Diane's 1986 Chevy Impala. They had traded cars for the night. There would be no more show of affluence Nick thought as he maneuvered down Route 128 to the Route 1 exit. He proceeded down Route 1 until he reached the exit for Danvers which led toward North Beach.

Cruising down North Beach Blvd. The Impala weaved in and out of traffic. A sick feeling ran through his body. He was vulnerable and hated being in this position. A total loss of control. They could change their minds on just about anything and force it down his throat! He would listen to their condescension and threats, but say little. He wouldn't promise anything he couldn't deliver with certainty. He knew that he was conning himself. He was in deep trouble. The safety of his family would be the most important consideration in any decision!

A few hundred yards ahead he noticed the bright exterior lights flickering at the club. Darkness had set in. It was now seven forty-five p.m. The navy blue Impala slowly wound into the parking lot at the Paradise. Déjà vu. They should rename this Club Extortion!

He stepped out of the vehicle and as he walked around back of it he noticed Diane's license plate: Prime 4. Although they knew of his past wealth it would show a cut-back in extravagance due to the bad economic times.

Filled with dread Nick entered through the doors of the club. The lights were so dim that it took a few minutes for his eyes to adjust. "I don't care anymore" blared from the stereo system spilling out Phil's magical voice.

A long-haired, heavy set man about forty sitting on a stool inside the entrance and wearing a black T-shirt with a Harley Davidson patch on it held out his hand. "Five dollars, please," he muttered.

"I'm here to see Mario Cavallaro. "Nick stated. "What's your name, dude?" Nick was dressed down in chinos and a denim jacket. His hair was tussled. "Nick Packard," he replied.

"Hold on a minute." He went inside and soon returned, saying, "Go ahead in and take a seat at the far end of the bar."

On the stage an attractive young lady wearing a pretty sundress strolled around the stage discoursing with the stage-side patrons. She had a nice smile and an apparently pleasant personality. Her cute layered hair-style swished and bounced as she moved her head from side to side. Nick wondered why she was in this place? But, when she raised the sundress in an effort to tease the audience he could see why! He turned and looked away. This was no time to admire a pretty lady!

He sat at the bar as directed and waited for a long time and soon began to languish. After about forty minutes had elapsed a bartender approached him and said, "Mr. C. will see you now."

The bartender led him through a rear hallway and buzzed open the door at the end. He ushered Nick in and quickly exited the room. It was a plush office.

"Ni-ick, my friend! Good to see you," Mario was sitting in a high-backed leather chair behind a large desk. Why the sudden friendly switch back? Nick was perplexed until he noticed a man of about seventy years of age seated in another leather-backed chair across from Franco. He had gray hair and a heavily lined face. He wore a European-cut suit with a handsome silk tie and matching handkerchief. His shoes were of high quality leather with a buffed shine. "Nick, meet Sonny from New York," Mario chimed.

"How do you do?" Nick responded calmly, with a handshake. Sonny said nothing.

Mario went on "And, of course, you know Carlo." He was seated at a small round table off to the side of the room. He nodded at Nick and said, "Hello, Nick. How are you?" The New York character must be the Boss. I've never seen them so polite!

Mario began the conversation. "Nick we're meeting this evening because we have a problem. We have been deceived!"

"How?" Nick inquired casually. He had taken a one-milligram Xanax pill before the meeting to suppress his trepidation. But, hadn't anticipated this level of meeting. He still tried to be cool.

"You gave us a shopping center and assigned a twenty-point-five-million-dollar mortgage along with it. This was for your debt to us. However, we believe that you knew it was headed down the tubes. You fucked us!" Mario bellowed.

Sonny calmly said, "You don't do that to us! The property is worth less than the mortgage balance on it. Do you think that we're fools?"

Nick trying to assuage them, unknowingly, played into their hands and said, "Wait a minute. We recently leased up some of the vacant space and the net operating income is one million nine hundred forty-four thousand dollars annualized as of today. At a nine percent cap rate the value is twenty-one million six hundred thousand dollars. There is still about one million one hundred thousand dollars of equity value in the project. That should increase substantially in the future when the economy improves."

"Fine," Sonny replied. "Then you'll buy it back for one million one hundred thousand and take back the Pension Fund twenty-million-five-hundred-thousand-dollar mortgage? Is that what I hear?"

"No, that isn't what I said," Nick retorted. "The economy sucks. But given the location, it will rebound later on. I know that."

"Settled, then. You'll buy it back for twenty-two million, giving us a million and a half in cash and taking back the HLW mortgage loan. We can arrange that, OK? This meeting is over. It's in your best interest to take care of this right away. Do you understand? Mario, he stays right here until he promises and tells us how he is going to do this! Oh, Nick, by the way, are you related to Johnny Packard?"

"Yes, he was my father. Did you know him?"

"I did. I worked with him way back. He died, didn't he?""Yes, he was murdered," Nick answered.

"Oh, too bad. A nice guy," Sonny lied. That son of a bitch fucked some of the New York bosses big-time. The weasel deserved what he got. Bonati was the trigger man, I recall.

Sonny and Mario left the room.

Outside, beyond Nick's range of audibility, Sonny instructed Mario to fuck him up if he doesn't follow thru. "This has gone on for way too long. And, you have further issues beyond dealing with him. Capisci? On that other matter, those troublemakers in Lynn…you have full sanction to take them out! But, only those two. Keep the heat down."

Nick sat back in the chair at the small round table and stared at the yellow legal pad Carlos had set in front of him when the others left the room. It had,obviously, been left for Nick to write down the possibilities for raising cash. They would confiscate this in the end to glean any additional information possible. He had the cash, but, certainly wasn't about to reveal it!

A telephone set had been left on the small table for him to make whatever calls necessary. It has to be at least nine thirty. How can I make business calls now. Oh God, they are keeping me here all night! I won't use it anyway. It must be bugged. If I produce the cash now I'll be paying forever! They'd play me forever. They don't like me. I should never have given them Arlington Heights. But, who knows what would have happened then?! The old guy is probably Mario's boss and high up the ladder. It apparently is a big hit for them. How the fuck did I ever get into this situation? A New York boss. Whew!

He tried to open the door and found that he was locked in, then sat back in the chair as his claustrophobia unleashed. It worsened as he looked around the room and noticed only a single window with bars on the outside. The tension mounted as the uncertainty of the situation precipitated tremendous terror which he struggled to suppress. He had to somehow work this out?

He began to scribble notes on the yellow pad left by Carlo figuring that he had to make a show of cooperation. After a while, though, he threw the pencil on the table and stood up trying the door again. Still locked! The sound of music in muffled tones and male shouts of approbation could be heard way in the background.

The fear looming in Nick's mind caused him to rattle the door knob and bang the door. A few minutes later he heard a deep gruff voice say "Are you ready to talk to Mr. C. yet?"

"No, I was just trying to walk around and stretch," he lied.

Nick sat back down at the table and continued to write bullshit notes such as second mortgages on Ford Plaza and Prime Place. He then listed five of the top banks in Boston. He knew that would be next to impossible given the huge decline in commercial real estate values. But, he felt that he had to write something. He made no mention of Tri-Star Bank, where his approximate two million seven hundred thousand cash resided in money market instruments, and maybe one hundred thousand dollars or more was in his personal checking account. They knew that he had a relationship with Tri-Star. Thanks to Lenny, however, none of his personal business had been divulged. But the relationship should remain low keyed!

Wasteful hours passed as he tried to figure out what to do. He couldn't think straight given the situation. Soon he began to doze. Outside the door an ear listened closely!

When he awoke, he glanced at his watch: 2:57, presumably a.m. He had slept for at least three hours and fortunately was not a snorer. He was now awake and fresher. He knew that in order to leave he had to acknowledge the debt and have a definite planned source of cash with a definite timetable for payment. This would buy him some time, although, it probably was the last extension of time he'd ever get!

His plan was to offer the second mortgage scheme which he knew that he couldn't produce, then, as an alternative which might be viable, he would offer to discount his note from Tommy for payment in full. That was his only chance of survival! Would Tommy's estate be able to do it? A deep discount would be necessary. The note was due 11/15/91 and was ripe for discount now.

That's it, fuck it! That's it. The best I can do to get out of here now. He rose from the chair and banged on the door incessantly. This time no voice from the other side. He waited…and waited…and waited. No response!

Mandatory closing time in North Beach was one a.m.

Isn't someone staying to get my response? Probably not. Intimidation.

Outside the office door there was total darkness everywhere. The doors were locked as tight as a drum. Two rats scurried across the stage and down the steps to retrieve a pretzel off the floor's carpet. They chomped at each other as they tried to claim it.

Out in the parking lot two men entered a Lincoln Continental and sped away.

CHAPTER 70

Nick first heard the footsteps faintly. Then as they became louder he fully awoke from a light sleep lifting his head off the table. His watch showed 4:39. He assumed that was a.m. The footsteps seemed to approach the door, then stop. A drawn out silence ensued while Nick tiptoed behind where the door would open. If the intruder was a hit-man he might have a remote chance to overpower him if hiding behind the door. Outside the door the floor creaked. Nick waited in suspense while his heart pounded like a drum!

A key could be heard entering the lock and then a click as the latch opened. Nick raised his arms in readiness to defend himself as the door moved slowly toward him. In the blink of an eye a figure spun around the door and before Nick could move a muscle he felt the cold steel barrel of a large gun against his forehead. He closed his eyes and prayed to God as he waited to die!

"What the fuck are you doing, man?" Angelo Bono yelled, and then proceeded to slide the nine-millimeter Browning automatic back and forth across Nick's forehead.

"I had no idea who was out there. It's five a.m.!" Nick choked out.

"You got the answers for Mr. C.? Ready to talk?" Angelo asked.

He pressed the barrel forcefully into Nick's forehead. Nick winced at the intense pain.

"I'm ready. Where is he?"

"Right here," Mario stated, as he walked through the door. "You're a thorough thinker or a con artist. It's taken you eight hours to think out something which you should have done before our meeting last night." Nick didn't even bother to argue with Mario. He just wanted to get this over and leave.

"OK, then, Nick…talk!" Mario demanded.

"I will pay you the million and a half in cash and have two different possibilities. I will attempt to place a second mortgage on either or both, if necessary, of my office building in Waltham or the mall in Wilmington. I will pursue applications for the mortgage or mortgages with five major banks." He then showed Franco his pad which listed the big bullshit banks. "Or," Nick went on, "I might be able to discount my note from the estate of my old partner, Tommy Fletcher." He cringed at saying the name. "It's due November ninth, 1991, and with a deep discount I think the estate would jump for it. His family is weary from disbanding his empire. They want it behind them."

"How much is that note?" Mario eagerly inquired.

"Oh, the balance is three million and some-odd dollars at this point," Nick lied. "The Executors might give me a million and a half for it. They probably will."

Mario seemed to bite for that. "We want proof of your source and a payout within thirty days. Capisci?"

"Please, Mario, be reasonable. I need at least thirty days to button down a deal and thirty days to close," Nick pleaded.

"How's your mother doing these days? Is she still living at twenty-one Pine Street in Braintree?" Mario inquired, and then glared at the nine millimeter that Angelo had set on the table.

"Fuck you, Mario. I'll do what I can, but you leave her out of it. Any of that stuff and you'll never get your money!"

"You'll do better than that. Sonny gets impatient easily. You don't want to test that, I can assure you. You'll wish that you were never born!"

At 6:03 a.m. Nick was released from the horrible scene and set free. For now anyway. He let out his pent-up tension as he walked outside the club and took a deep breath of salt air. He laughed nervously as he entered Diane's car and drove home. Noel must be hysterical. I haven't called her for twelve hours. She must think that I'm dead somewhere.

A half hour later the Chevy Impala passed the Myopia Hunt Club on Route 1A and soon meandered the contours of his long and winding driveway. As he alighted from the vehicle he heard the chirping of birds. A Cardinal resting on a branch in a mound of birch trees caught his eye. As the morning sun glistened through the trees it reflected absolute beauty in all directions. This was truly Nick's sanctuary. But, for how long? He wondered.

Nick trudged up the steps of the portico, past the huge

columns and entered the double French doors. Passing through the marbled foyer he looked in all directions. No one seemed to be around. Of course Ali would be in school. But, Noel? In the kitchen, Nick raised his voice "Noel, you here?"

Moments elapsed before any response. "I'm in here. What do you want?" she replied in a disgusted tone of voice. She was in the breakfast nook beyond the kitchen. He entered the nook he pulled out a chair and sat down facing her.

"Where have you been? You bastard. Not even a call!" Noel shrieked. Nick noticed her moist red eyes. She had been crying a lot. Should I tell her the whole story now? No, she'll only freak out and then what? I've got the money and will work it out. I feel so guilty not telling her. I will if I can't come up with anything! They don't hurt women and children?"Honey, I'm sorry. What was anticipated as a drink with Mike Kensington after our meeting last evening turned out to be many drinks. At the point I realized I should call you, I was too shattered to call, let alone try to drive home. I don't even remember taking a cab with Mike to his in-town condominium in Harbor Towers where he says I flopped on the couch and passed out. I fucked up. I'm so sorry." He was disgusted with himself for telling these lies!"Nick, you're a good husband and father most of the time. How the hell could you have been so irresponsible?" She stood up and walked away. He could hear her footsteps as she trudged up the stairs.

CHAPTER 71

March 31, 1990

Over a month had passed since that horrible night in the Paradise Club. Two meetings with Tri-Star Bank and a meeting with Sarah Fletcher had come up empty. Nick had anticipated bank resistance but had thought that he might have a shot at getting the cash with a deep discount to Tommy's estate. Sarah had told Nick that Tommy's estate had no cash and further that the interest payments which were three months in arrears would have to be deferred indefinitely!

He had been reticent to call Mario and he knew it was long overdue. Mario, who had enough sense to work with Nick a bit had given him an extension to hand over the cash by March 30. He called it the "drop dead" date in a brief telephone conversation. He had received instructions from New York that the deal was "dead" after that date. Mario was wise using standard business terms to get a violent point across.

Nick decided to try again and dialed Lenny's direct number. "Lenny, it's Nick Packard. Hey, I'm your perfect borrower, aren't I? I have never once failed to meet all terms and conditions of your loans. Have I? If you can't lend to me, who can you lend to? Your bank doesn't have giant corporate clients because of its size. I'm your best bet for business. Just lend me a million and a half, secured by second mortgages on my Waltham office building, Wilmington retail mall, and even on my house! How the hell can you go wrong there? More equity than ever committed before!"

"Nick, you've been one of our best customers, for sure. I will attempt to push the loan through. But understand, it won't be easy in this economic environment. Our lending window has been closed for a while now. The FDIC is up our ass even worse than last month when we talked. I'll do everything I can to get board approval, but don't count on it."

He then dialed Sarah's number and got her answering machine. "Hi, this is Sarah Fletcher. I'm out of the country and will return on April first. Leave a message. Ciao!"

What terrible luck!

He then dialed Noel to discuss dinner plans for the evening.

Outside his office the telephone rang in.

"Hello, Prime Commercial," Diane answered.

"Nick Packard there?"

Knowing that Nick was on the phone with Noel, she responded, "Yes, but he's on the phone. Who's calling?"

"This is Mario Cavallaro. Who's this?"

"I'm Diane, Mr. Cavallaro."

"Ah, yes, my dear. And how are you today?"

"I'm fine, Mr. Cavallaro, and you?"

"Fine."

"I'll tell him you called."

"Thank you, my dear."

And, for the first time ever he left a telephone number for Nick to call.

Diane scribbled the message on the message pad, tore it off and placed it on the corner of her desk. Then, another call rang in. She quickly answered, "Good afternoon, Prime Commercial." As she swished her hand the message from Franco slid off and fell into the wastebasket, unnoticed. She inadvertently forgot about it.

Two days later as Nick was about to pack it in for the day he received a call from Sarah. "Hi, Nick. Sarah. I'm sorry that I couldn't return your call. I'm in Dublin and have had a difficult time getting good telephone reception. What can I do for you? Oh, and I'm sorry about the late interest payments. I'm not trying to screw you." It was midnight in Dublin and Sarah had been drinking.

"Sarah, I was calling in a last-ditch effort to raise some cash for debt payments coming up. Tommy, God rest his soul, must have left a mound of cash. His holdings were vast. I am willing to take a substantial discount on the six-million-dollar note balance if you pay it off now. I'll take three million dollars. And as you know, the note is due in only nine months. I don't have to tell you what a coup that would be for you!"

"Would that I could, Nick." That sounds so Shakespearean.

"But no, I can't do it. My father's properties have been selling for below their mortgage balances in many cases.

We just closed a package of buildings in the Back Bay for eighty-six and a half million dollars. The mortgages totaled a hundred and two million. And with all the other catastrophes lately we are flat broke! I think we're going to file chapter seven for Dad's estate." Sarah choked.

"Sarah, I love you," Nick replied. "Have a safe trip home, honey."

A few weeks later, on Tuesday, the evening drive home was arduous. He couldn't focus on anything. It was seventeen days beyond the payment due date to Mario and he had no idea how he'd get it! Nick was tired and completely drained of all energy. He had exhausted all sources but one, his cash! And, he didn't intend to part with that. He was in a quandary.

The sun was setting as the 560 SEL maneuvered around the corner off Route 1A in Hamilton. As he drove along the winding driveway he contemplated his fate. This real estate crash is getting worse and on top of that I'm being extorted. I'm not going to reveal it yet, though, to Noel, and never does Ali have to know about it!

As he approached the house he noticed Noel standing beside the house hopelessly staring white-faced at the ground. Ali was at her side crying profusely. Some horror had seized her face. It was obvious from her gaze at the ground. Then the closer he drove the clearer the scene unfolded. Ali's dog, Prancer, was lying on the ground devoid of any movement.

What the hell is going on he thought as his heart pounded. He alighted from the car and ran to the scene. His worst nightmare erupted as he saw Prancer lying on the ground with his eyes wide open. There was a fixed gaze with no movement! His mouth was frothing and blood seeped from from his tongue. He was apparently dead!"Mom, I love Prancer!" Ali cried."I love him too, honey," Noel replied, then sobbed uncontrollably. It was a gruesome scene.

"What happened, Noel?" Nick bellowed. Ali was speechless and was stroking Prancer's head.

"We just found him lying here on the ground. Like this! Maybe he ate something poisonous. I don't know? I think he's dead!" Noel said still sobbing as tears glistened her eyes and then cried "Oh, Nick," while hugging him.

Nick was quite sure that he knew what happened. He wouldn't say anything to Noel and Ali. But he was confused, because he had until March 30 to pay. It was only April 14! They are serious! Ni-ick, I want you to meet Sonny from New York. Maybe just a warning to ensure payment.

Nick loved Prancer, too, and cried silently. He was dancing on the edge and failing at every attempt to resolve the situation!

The following day Nick walked forlornly into the Prime office and said very little to anyone. He was shattered by the brutal slaying of his dog and the traumatic effect on his little daughter. She had to miss school for today and maybe indefinitely. She sat in her room for many hours flooding with tears. Nick felt extreme sadness for her. That sweet little girl had to suffer for the harsh intimidation tactics of those violent criminals.

He was very worried that it would escalate from here unless something was resolved. He decided late last night to make a contemplated payment of five hundred thousand dollars to Mario now to keep things on hold. The rest would go to Switzerland to a numbered account!

In early afternoon he rang Danny's extension and invited him into his office. After a while Danny strolled in. He had been dealing with a sub-contractor regarding the subs screw up on the Prime Place air conditioning system. "What's up, boss?"

After a few silent moments, Nick uttered, "My dog was killed last night. I think by those henchmen who took Arlington Square from us." Nick had not uttered a word about the extortion to anyone else!"You're shitting me, Nick! Why?"

"Because they want cash. The mall didn't work out as planned, as you well know. They want a million and a half dollars in cash and I've been stringing them out for obvious cash flow reasons. I'm not giving them the lion's share of my personal cash. My family needs that for survival in the future. I'm seriously concerned about what they might do next. Oh, and Tommy Fletcher's note to me has become worthless, blown away by the real estate depression!

I won't jeopardize anything else. I'm going to call Tri-Star Bank and draw out five hundred thousand of my current personal cash money market investments and give it to them to put a hold on things for now. I'll figure out how to get the rest to them later. Also, two hundred thousand as an emergency fund for you and I. Then, I'm sending the now remaining two million dollars to Zurich. That's Switzerland, you know.""Right, Nick," Danny responded.

Danny offered to take the cash to Zurich for Nick. "No, Danny. Too dangerous!"

"Why? They wouldn't expect anybody but you to take that trip. Would they?"

"Danny if they caught you, you'd be history."

"Nick, if anything, all eyes are upon you," Danny replied. "I'll take it. It'll be safe I know it!"

Nick then called Lenny Saginsky at Tri-Star Bank and instructed him to liquidate the money market instruments and to transfer seven hundred thousand dollars cash to Coastal North Bank to the account of Daniel Levin. Also, to cut a check to Daniel Levin for two million. Danny would pick up the check in two hours. That was a slight bit less than his balance, but virtually cleaned house. His personally held cash was down to nothing. Nick felt he could trust Danny with his life!"Lenny said that it doesn't look very good for the million-and-a-half-dollar second mortgage." So what else is new?

CHAPTER 72

April 17, 1990

Danny left his office in Ford Plaza at six a.m. dressed like a laborer and took a yellow cab to Logan Airport. As the cab headed down Route 128 to the Route 1 exit a gray sedan followed unnoticed by Danny. The cab meandered down Route 1 to the Route 62 exit in Revere and took the turn toward Logan Airport. The gray sedan did the same at a distance.

Carlo sat back smoking a Camel cigarette and instructed the driver, Angelo, where to turn. Carlo was the most feared and loyal soldier in the family. He followed his capo's instructions without any questions or second guesses. Mario was the capo of his crew, but the hierarchy ran up to New York. His word was followed without any dissension!

"If it were my call, I'd mangle the motherfuckers." He laughed capriciously. "But," Mario ordered, until we have the cash, just taunt them! No physical violence! . They're not cooperating. I would torture them if it were up to me. The whole family! They'd produce. Watch that fucking cab, Angelo. We don't want to lose it."

The Yellow cab veered off the Traffic Circle and sped down Route 1A to the airport entrance. Carlo watched as Danny alighted from the cab at the International Terminal. He pulled his travel bag from the cab, slipped the driver three twenty-dollar bills, and uttered, "Keep the change." Eyes were upon him as he walked to the Swissair counter and extracted his confirmation, placing it on the counter. The cute attendant slid his ticket to him as he whispered something into her ear. Her face lit up with a bright smile.

Moments later, Carlo walked up to the counter and asked the attendant, "What flight is that last passenger booked on?"

"Sir, I'm not at liberty to give out such information."

"Yes, you are." He proceeded to flip out an FBI ID badge, an authentic looking copy with his photo on it. His group's means were unfathomable. She perked up and nervously assisted him. "He's booked on the nine oh-six flight, number sixty-six, to London and on to Zurich."

"Thank you," Carlo replied.

"He's flying to Zurich I think and I have the flight number. He's most likely delivering cash and probably a lot of it to be taking this trip!" Carlo mumbled to Angelo standing beside him.

The flight stretched over a seemingly boundless expanse of ocean. Turbulence raised its mighty attack all along the way and got so bad at times it caused great fear to many passengers. At a smooth point Danny relaxed and began a conversation with a gray-bearded man on the right seat beside him.

"Looks pretty grim out there," Danny said. It had started raining, with drops tapping on the windows.

"Ah, yes, comrade, but nothing compared to the grim feelings in Soviet Union where I live for sixty years. But, at last Berlin wall has been torn down and Iron curtain has fallen. I defected months ago from clutches of Communism. My sister and brother not so lucky. They have very little. Still there and still rely upon State for most needs. State provide little. How do you say in America?… Sucks! But, maybe new freedom from fall of Berlin wall last year will change things?"

Danny lay his head back on the seat. "Yeah, that must really suck, but, my mission from America sucks also. He went way too far and said that it had to do with criminal activities that he was avoiding."

"Oh, in what way?" the Russian inquired.

Danny knew he was talking too much and said, "Oh, it's a long story comrade. Just that certain criminal types are trying to get what doesn't belong to them!" He would not elaborate anymore. "They are tame compared to Soviets. In Soviet Union their types are capable of anything. They have no belief in God and will stop at nothing to get money. Nothing is sacred! As I understand in America the people you refer to are more constrained by religion. That is to say . They respect people outside of business. I left Soviet Union because I am Christian and can't tolerate their kind. Such power now and they kill anyone for anything!"

This gave Danny some relief. But, what was embarked upon was business and it involved the Mafia!

After many hours the "no smoking" light flashed and

the pilot announced the descent into Heathrow in London. Danny remained on the plane which eventually landed in the Zurich area.

He was nervous. He'd pulled a lot of stunts in his past, but never anything like this. Departing, he shook hands with Dimitri and said, "It's been nice talking, comrade."

The pair exchanged business cards and Dimitri said, "Pleasure to me, friend. May God be with you!"

Danny alighted from the aircraft tucking Dimitri's business card in his pocket. He walked from the plane into a different world. One of diversity. As he made made his way down the concourse he heard what seemed like many different languages being spoken. This was truly a convocation of nationalities. Danny became mesmerized and was excited.

He hailed a cab outside the main doors. It was ten p.m. in Zurich. The cab meandered down a boulevard to the Intercontinental Hotel. He flipped the driver a U.S. twenty-dollar bill who beamed with joy. The ride was so brief it probably should have cost less than five dollars.

He checked in to the Intercontinental Hotel and after receiving his room key he went directly there. Lying down on the bed he turned on the TV and conked out in five minutes. He was tired. When he awoke the next morning bursts of sunlight shone through the partially drawn curtains.

It was a magnificently bright day in Zurich, a sight to behold. Outside his window he could see throngs of people strolling down the Avenue. Some in groups, couples walking with hands embraced and children meandering in merriment. It was eleven thirty a.m. Danny pictured himself in that scene with Suzie pushing a baby carriage. He became so immersed in it and felt a pain of being home sick. He was so happy with Suzie!

Then he snapped out of it. He knew he had to hurry to Bundesbank to set up the numbered account and make the two-million-dollar deposit. He became nervous about what he was embarked upon but he had to hurry. His flight home was at 4:19 p.m.

Outside he deeply inhaled the fresh, clean air. I'm so lucky to be alive. Suzie and Decky will be there when I get back. Thank you, God! And, I do love the intrigue. I'll do whatever possible to help Nick. I love him like my brother. I hope this mission doesn't come back to bite me, though!

At 1:27 p.m. Danny hurried into Bundesbank and was fortunate to get an immediate meeting with the manager. Danny, the lovable red-haired and mustached Jewish boy was treated very cordially. The amount of his deposit ranked him as a good customer. By far not the largest received by Hans, but, nevertheless sizable. Hans liked Danny and the two became good friends right from the start. Hans performed the necessary procedure and handed Danny a numbered slip M75906J after Danny had endorsed and slid the check over. Nick's money was now safely deposited!

Hans wanted to take Danny to a late lunch, but he had to fly, literally, and refused. He shook Hans's hand and replied, "Next time around. I've got a four o'clock flight and must rush. Thanks, buddy." He proudly left Bundesbank at 2:33 p.m. Peering out of the cab's window he noticed, once again, the relaxed atmosphere. Oh, how he longed to be with Suzie and his new son. Well, time to get back and help Nick work his way out of the problem. The nightmare on Silicon Street! He hoped that Nick had placated them with the partial payment he had mentioned!

Danny alighted from the plane at Logan in Boston at five p.m. EST thinking about time changes. He had left Zurich at 4:20 p.m. on a seven-hour flight. The jet lag was harrowing. It was April 18, over two weeks beyond the "drop dead date"! He hurriedly cabbed to the Waltham office building where Nick was waiting for him.

With reddened eyes and a weary face, sauntering after his jet lag, he walked into Nick's office and flopped into the soft leather armchair facing his boss. He pulled the deposit slip M75906J from his pocket and slid it across Nick's desk. "Mission accomplished, comrade!" Danny chuckled.

"Why comrade, Danny?"

"Because I met a Russian guy on the trip over who had recently defected from the Soviet Union. When I told him we had trouble with the Mob. I didn't use that word though. He said that the Russian mob was much more ruthless. They have no God! Only money!"

"I don't know how much tougher they are, but give me his card you're waving there." Nick perused it with interest. "Listen, Danny, while you were gone, ISCM Corp. called me. Johnson himself. The shit is hitting the fan. Unless we drop the rent to ten dollars per square foot and defer payments for a while they can't go on. They'll have to break the lease! That will drown us here, for sure." Danny was dumfounded. "Nick, ten dollars a foot will increase the already negative cash flow to a choke hold level. Fuck that!"

"What options do we have?" Nick wailed. "We'll just have to give them the reduction for now, I guess," Danny replied.

"That's one hundred twenty thousand dollars off the rent annually," Nick calculated. "It really sucks up cash flow. And, Our Prime Plaza lead tenant is having cash flow problems. Who knows how long they'll stay afloat? How can we survive? This building has been a major contributor to our overhead. Between this building and Prime Plaza our now reduced overhead has been covered to date. You know the Natick strip centers are just holding their own and the interest clock is ticking on the Waltham land loans! We have a serious problem! You and I will have to concede half of our salaries until things improve. And, they will eventually at some point?"

"Nick, what about the seven hundred thousand that you deposited in Coastal Bank in my name? Did you draw on the withdrawal authorization I gave you and make that payment to those people?" He shuddered to name any names. "No, Danny, I haven't, and I'm beyond their "drop dead" date of March thirtieth. I have no way of calling Mario. He did leave that number last month, but the phone is never answered. I might be OK until he calls again. I hope! But I'm drawing the five hundred thousand in cash in hundred- thousand-dollar incremental withdrawals beginning tomorrow."

"Will do, Nick. And don't forget that we still own all properties acquired or built except Arlington Square. It could be worse!" the always optimistic Danny pointed out."You're right, Danny, although I have to buy Arlington Square back and don't know where the other one million dollars payment is coming from. But like everything else, we'll work it out. Others are dropping like flies."

"OK, comrade, let's drink to that." Danny pulled a bottle of VO from Nick's credenza and poured a generous serving into two glasses. They tipped their glasses clinking together and drank to a turnaround in the future!"I'm going home, Nick. It's been a long two days. I'm drained."

As Danny sauntered out of his office, Nick yelled, "Thanks so much, Danny. We'll make it!"

CHAPTER 73

Danny left his office at Ford Plaza in Waltham and entered his car at 8:46 p.m. As he spun out of the lot the gray sedan followed closely behind on Route 128. He stopped at the Escadrille Cafe in Burlington for dinner. He was hung over completely from the jet lag, but was starved and he ordered a complete seafood dinner.

After he ate and relaxed a bit he left the Restaurant. Out in the parking lot he was approached by three men. Danny, acting fearless, said, "Good evening, guys!" With no reply, they quickly pushed him into the gray sedan which had been parked beside his BMW. He was beside two of them in the backseat while in silence the gray sedan drove off and wound down Route 3A toward Route 128.

Soon Carlo spoke, asking, "How much is in Zurich? And how much did you return with?"

Danny knew these men were bad, but didn't quite understand how ruthless they were. They were an extremely dangerous faction of La Cosa Nostra. Nick had never emphasized that fact too strongly to quell Danny's emotions. Even Nick didn't realize that to its fullest extent. He thought the slaying of his dog and his nocturnal imprisonment was probably as far as the intimidation would go. Fuck them! Scare tactics. A bunch of men pushing him into a car. Why me? It's Nick's problem?"Guys I don't have a cent in Zurich. I'm just a working class guy!"

"Well, let me re-phrase it, asshole," Carlo replied, as Angelo pistol whipped his face. "How much money does Packard have stashed there? You just came back from there, you know! Or are you brain dead?" "I have no idea. I went there to visit friends."

Relentlessly, Carlos rebutted "OK, names, addresses and relationships?" Carlo was intensive. He would not let up. This man is a liar he thought!

Danny replied with a quick, calm answer. "Hans Kliengdorf and Matilda Kliengdorf, his wife. They live at seventy-seven Rheinhold Avenue in Zurich. They are old friends from my days of traveling. When I lived in LA. It was Matilda's birthday and I went to a party for her," Danny lied.

Carlo almost believed him because of his quick, calm answer. Then he realized that no one would go for two days and travel half the time. He said, "Why only a few days? You're lying, asshole! Why are we listening to this bullshit?"

Carlo lifted a nine millimeter pistol to Danny's temple and said, "If you don't tell me the truth, then I'm going to pull this trigger, dickhead! Don't fuck with me. I'll splatter your brains in every direction! Tell me!"

Danny silently prayed to God for intervention while Carlo waited patiently for his answer. Danny had to decide what to say. If I continue with the birthday story it may bluff them and they may let me go. Or, they may torture me until I break? If I tell them about the deposit they may let me go because what good will they achieve from killing me? I could give them false deposit information? What a fucking nightmare!

Danny decided to reveal the deposit information. They couldn't get to it anyway, at least without the slip which he had given to Nick. His family and his life were far more important to him. "Look, guys, I had to deliver a deposit for my boss. I was only a delivery boy," Danny said nonchalantly.

"How much?" Carlo demanded to know. "Two hundred thousand dollars, in Bundesbank," Danny lied.

"Show me the deposit slip. That motherfucker spends more than that every week!" Carlo responded with exaggeration. "You're lying!" he screamed as he pushed the barrel of the pistol against Danny's temple. Pain permeated his head. He couldn't stand it any longer and broke with the truth. Carlos became more relaxed as the gray Sedan sped on toward the North Shore. He dialed for international information on the car phone installed on the console.

Carlo confirmed the existence of Bundesbank, then demanded to Danny "Give me the account number!"

"M75906J," Danny replied, thinking that the truth would save him. He then, guiltily, revealed every detail of the transaction including Hans, the manager's name, and the true amount. He knew that they couldn't get at it without the deposit slip and his proof of identity and sign off. He became more frightened and broke down to save his family and himself. He told them that Nick had part of "their "money to give to their boss, but wouldn't say how much!

The gray sedan continued on in the same direction.

"Will you please take me back now?" Danny pleaded.

"Yes, after one stop," Carlo responded.

Danny lay back in relief. After what seemed an eternity the sedan came to a halt at Good Harbor Beach in Gloucester. An eerie silence pervaded the moonless, night air. It was 11:09 p.m. and not a soul was in sight.

"All right, Levin. Get out," Angelo murmured. "We're going to meet a friend and you will tell him exactly what you told us. Then we'll take you back."

Danny, assuming they must be taking him to their boss, complied. Be cooperative and it'll save my ass!

The three men walked with Danny along the beach as the waves pounded with a stony-like rhythm. Angelo pointed a .45-caliber revolver from behind and emptied three cartridges into the back of his head.

Danny winced, then went blank! Forever!

A few days later Nick, while reclining in his office chair reviewing business documents and pondering Danny's no show for that time, received a call from Danny's brother, Conrad. He was in shock and could barely speak. The grim news was received. Clam diggers had found Danny's body face-down in the flats on a Gloucester beach. The mystical ocean movement had washed away a lot of the blood, but the cause of death was from multiple bullet wounds in the back of his head. Diane had called Danny several times over the few days and got no answer! "What happened? How long ago? Where's Suzie?" Nick asked in horror. "I don't know any details yet, but Suzie is with Mom and Dad in severe shock. I guess we all are! Nick,,do you have any idea why this might have happened? You've been closer to him recently. Please tell me if there was any trouble he was in that you know of ?" Conrad lamented.

"I have no idea," Nick lied. He knew what must have gone down. They followed Danny to Zurich or at least figured out where he was going through their long tentacles! What had Danny revealed? In the throes of threatened death he might have told the truth. I probably would have to save my life and family! This is like being thrown into a pit of coral snakes! Why Danny?

"I'm as shocked as you are, Conrad," Nick said bemusedly. "I'm going to pay for the entire cost of the funeral. Also, I'd like to donate one hundred thousand dollars to Suzie and Decky." Choked up, Nick went on, "And I believe that Danny had some accrued commissions due him. I'll see that they get paid immediately."

Nick hung up and sat for a long time in shock and sadness, then in fear. When he finally got up and walked around he recanted the news to Diane. She was in shock at first, then cried profusely.

Nick didn't know what to do! He paced his office relentlessly. I have to make a deal now with Mario for installments. But, how? I don't even know how to reach him. Why didn't I take care of this before! I never thought it would get this far. And, now it's out of hand!

At 3:17 p.m. the police visited Nick, asking many questions about Danny's activities in the days leading up to the murder. All Nick said was that Danny had been out of the office for a few days. He didn't know where, but never had to check on him because he was such a good producer. Nick sincerely had tears in his eyes when he spoke to them. He trembled at the details they gave to him. After receiving the exact same story from Diane, they left.

The telephone rang at 4:47 p.m. It was Carlo calling.

"Put him through, Diane."

With trepidation, Nick answered.

"Nick, Carlo P. Hold on for Mr. C." There was a long pause and finally Mario came on. "Nick, how are you my friend?" Mario was concerned about a phone tap and acted friendly.

Nick, holding back his animosity, said, "How can you be calling me now?"

"Nick, I just want to have dinner tonight and see if we can come to business terms." He was paranoid about the possibility of an FBI tap and was taking no chances. None at all. Other Mob characters had been under FBI surveillance lately which had come out in court proceedings. "I'll meet you at the Blue Moon Cafe in Danvers at eight thirty tonight. You know where that is, don't you?"

"Yes, I know the place, Mario. I'll be there," Nick replied. He reached into his bottom right hand draw and pulled out a .357 Magnum pistol which he had acquired a few weeks earlier. He had received a permit stating that his life had been threatened anonymously. When questioned further about that, he said that he didn't know who was making the calls. A crank? He didn't know. He made evictions and fired people over the years out of necessity. Who knows?

Nick decided that tonight was the end, no matter what happened. He would offer five hundred thousand dollars in cash now, which he had now drawn from Coastal Bank, and the remainder at two hundred fifty thousand bimonthly for the next four months. A total of the million and a half demanded. His fear controlled his rationality. He had no idea how he'd do that, but it would buy time. Prime cash was almost depleted and his personal cash was now in Zurich.

At seven thirty p.m. he left the office and drove his Mercedes along Route 128. It didn't matter what vehicle he was driving now. They were long past that stage. In a lucid moment as he was relaxing somewhat it hit him smack between the eyes. They were calling him in. As he had seen in the movies he had been "sent for." He was probably heading for the cemetery! They most likely knew that he had a large amount stashed in Zurich and maybe had a way to get it themselves? They had already killed his dog and now Danny! They are certainly capable of killing anybody!

He began to tremble and wheeled his car around at the Route 20 Sudbury exit and sped quickly back to Ford Plaza calling home on his new Motorola car console cell phone. "Noel, honey, listen closely. I'm in big trouble which might affect us all. Pack an overnight bag for you and Ali immediately and get out of the house. Drive the old jeep. Not your Mercedes. Come directly to my office. I'll tell you the whole story, long overdue, when you get here and I stress immediately!"What have you done, Nick?" Noel screamed.

"Just get here!" Nick yelled loudly.

Nick, then, called his mother and told her more gently. Overnight bag for a few nights stay. Will explain later. He said he'd pick her up within three hours. She yawned, but agreed. A little vacation. How nice.

Noel and Ali rushed frantically and were out the door in a little over an hour.

At 8:55 p.m. the gray sedan pulled into the driveway in Hamilton looking for Nick. Noel had just left a few minutes earlier frantically driving at fifty miles per hour down the winding driveway and taken a left on Route 1A. When the four men in the vehicle saw a dark house they got furious and doused it with gasoline on Carlo's orders. Carlo in a raging psychopathic fit lit a rolled newspaper on fire with his lighter and heaved it at the house. The flames instantly engulfed the house. Carlo watched intensively and laughed as the gray sedan backed out and turned away. He was one of the few psychopaths in the Mob that really enjoyed doing this sort of thing. Besides, Mario had wanted this, he reasoned. He would be pleased Carlo thought! The gray sedan made an exit with flames bursting behind it. And, behind the sedan were Nick and Noel's dreams fading to ashes!

The regional fire department worked for six hours straight to douse the fire and all that was left was a charred foundation. The Packard house had been razed to sheer ruins. It was a gruesome sight. The firemen struggled for hours trying to locate bodies but none emerged. The horses had been released while the barn was lit by Angelo. He did have a slight sense of humanity?

This was a horrendous act of vengeance. The crew

knew that, but Packard had fucked them royally! They had reasoned that Nick had transferred a losing property to them to shave off a huge loss. And, Mario had saved his life. Then Nick blatantly tried to hide money to foil them. Carlo mused, We are justified completely in doing what we've done. We'll find that motherfucker and make him bleed! And, we'll get that money in Switzerland, all of it. He probably took his family to a hotel. What's the closest? Marriott in Peabody. If not there we'll try his office!

"Angelo, drive to the Marriott in Peabody, now!"

CHAPTER 74

Noel drove ninety miles per hour down Route 128, praying while she drove. Ali was scared, even though she had no idea of what was happening. She was so tired and longed to be snuggled in her own little bed.

When they arrived at Ford Plaza Nick's car was the only one in the garage. She parked the Jeep in the garage and as she walked in the door of Prime Commercial Nick was hurrying out and grabbed hands with both her and Ali. He hugged them closely and breathed a sigh of relief. "Noel, we have to leave immediately. I'll tell you everything in the car!"

The Mercedes 560 SEL drove quickly out of Ford Plaza and onto Route 128 South toward Braintree. "Noel, I should have told you long ago, Mario Cavallaro is an evil character. More than you even know! He's worked his way into my life inextricably and is responsible for many terrible things which I'll tell you about shortly." He then said something to Ali to see if she was asleep in the backseat. She didn't answer. "Sit back and be prepared for a shock!" As he told the story softly beginning with Mario's demand "for saving Nick's life" at Ali's birthday party and then to Arlington Square and to Danny's death, Noel turned white and became more and more shocked as the story unraveled. They hadn't even learned of the destruction of their house in process at this point! "Noel, after Arlington Square took a downturn, the boss from New York demanded that I buy it back and give them a million and a half in cash. I didn't make their deadline, and then they found out that Danny took money to Switzerland and felt like I was deceiving them at each step, which I wasn't. Tonight I was going to give them five hundred thousand, and the rest over the course of eight months. But I realized while driving there that they probably would have taken the million and a half, and then come back for more, or whacked me in the end. I regret the day that I met Cavallaro and unwittingly told him about my success!"

"Oh, Nick, I can't believe this has happened. It's crazier than any movie I've ever seen. If only you had told me before?!"

"Noel, you wouldn't have been able to stand it and we would probably have broken up under all the pressure. I never dreamed it would escalate to this point! I promise you, honey, you and Ali are my life and I'll take care of you. They respect women and children, but we're taking no chances!"

He drove to Braintree and, fortunately, Frances was ready to leave. She questioned Nick again and again about where they were going. "It's a surprise, Mom. A surprise." She seemed happy.

The Mercedes left Braintree at eleven p.m. The gray sedan

was leaving Ford Plaza headed toward Braintree at about the same time. Nick's mother will suffer the consequences for that weasel son, thought Carlo. And, it will draw him to Braintree. We'll get him there!"

Nick drove hastily to Boston along Route 128 to Route 93 North and checked into the Westin Hotel in Copley Square. Ali woke up frightened while the valet entered into the car to get her overnight bag. Nick assuaged her, saying, "Sweetheart, we're going on a nice long trip. In fifteen minutes you can go back to sleep in a comfortable hotel room with us."

"OK, Daddy. Is everything OK?" Nick assured her that it was.

They checked in to two rooms and insisted they were adjacent to each other. He wanted everybody close together. Nick had the hotel manager unlock the door between rooms and he left it open. Nick lay on the left hand side of the bed while Ali jumped in and conked out instantly. Noel put her arm around Ali and hugged her tightly, finally falling asleep and saying nothing to Nick. She was in great shock, but also felt violated for not being informed all along.

When all were asleep Nick took the .357 Magnum out of his briefcase and placed it by his side under the sheets with the safety on! Nothing happened that night, but Nick stayed awake all night long in fear except for one hour of sleep. He was responsible indirectly for all this tragedy. He had to protect his family and map out a relocation plan for them in his mind. They had a wide latitude of choice. He had drawn out the five hundred thousand dollars and still had the cash in his large briefcase. Danny had done handstands explaining the need to the bank manager!

The following morning the sun shone brilliantly through the windows at the plaza Hotel. Nick had concluded his thoughts of the entire night about where to take his family and where to go himself. He was drained, but determined to move on.

He had decided to fly his family to Paris and get them situated there for an undetermined period of time. He would then secretly return to the U.S. by himself to handle his properties. Dispose of them and fly back to Paris to his family. He hoped Noel would hang in with him.

He knew that going back was a major risk for him and he did have the two million dollars in Zurich—he hoped. And he had the five hundred thousand in his briefcase, plus another hundred thousand left in the Coastal account. He had transferred the other hundred thousand from Coastal to Suzie using withdrawal slips signed previously by Danny. A fair sum of money, but his remaining real estate interests were prime and would be worth many times the amount of cash he was now holding in the future! He hoped that maybe he wouldn't have to dispose of them after all. Maybe he could hold at least on some of them long enough to reap the true value? How, was his guess?

Frances and Ali had gone to the restaurant for breakfast. Over breakfast in the room with Noel, Nick laid out his plan to her. She listened to it in its entirety without saying a word. Finally, she said, "Nick, I'm so disappointed in you. How you could have lead me to believe that everything was a bed of roses when you had such a problem. You could have told me a long time ago and we could have gone to the FBI for help! No, you had to treat it like a business deal. You really screwed up!"

"Noel, you have no idea what it's like being confronted by them. I thought a diplomatic settlement by me would have put it to rest. The shopping center conveyance would have been a score for them if the fucking depression hadn't set in. Maybe I was foolish, but calling in the FBI would have required witness protection and my business would have folded for sure. That I know!

Even dealing with the likes of them I had no idea all this could happen."

"I love you Noel. You and Ali are the world to me. They don't hurt woman and kids," Nick surmised.

"Nick, How do you know that? And, they do hurt and kill people. Look at Danny and Tommy. I can't believe it. And, Prancer even. I'll bet they did that!" Noel started crying vehemently.

"We'll go to Paris. But, I don't know what after that." She had no choice. It was survival!

Nick called American Airlines and booked a flight for four p.m. that afternoon. Four tickets. He was concerned that Mario's soldiers may start watching international flights. The sooner in the air the better. Nick charged $6,170 on a credit card for the tickets, then called Paris information and got a few Realty office telephone numbers. He needed two furnished apartments. Nothing was available. They'll get something when they get there, he thought.

He made one more call before leaving. The phone rang and rang at the office. No answer. He then called Diane at home. She was terrified. The news last night on the television about Nick's house burning down had startled her. And, then no calls from Nick. He choked and became silent for moments. "My house?! What happened?"

"You...don't know?! Where are you?" Diane cried.

"I'm taking my family on a trip. Diane,I've got major problems I'll fill you in on later, but please call maintenance at Ford Plaza and have our office padlocked and set the alarm. Redirect all mail to a post office box temporarily which I'd like you to set up and collect from. You stay far away from the office! You'll be OK, I promise! My house burned down? Fucking disaster!" They are as ruthless as those Russians Dimitri talked about he thought. He said a word to no one after the call and seemed in a daze.

Nick left his car in the hotel garage and they cabbed to Logan Airport. The crowds were thin and they made it through the checkpoint OK. Nick had left the .357 Magnum in the tire-well of the Mercedes parked in the Westin Hotel garage. He shouldn't need it until he returns, he reasoned. At 4:17 p.m. the plane lifted off the runway and was airborne. Nick uttered an audible sigh of relief.

Nick had chosen Paris because of the great love of the city he had enamored when he and Noel visited there in 1985. The grandiose style of the ancient architecture had mesmerized him. Everywhere a statue of Napoleon. The influence of that man made him a legend and he lived five hundred to six hundred years ago! The Opera House, the Louvre, Notre Dame Cathedral were so wondrous. And, then the Eiffel Tower with its amazing restaurant view. And, the building walls still riddled from Nazi bullets during the Occupation. The history was amazing.

He, also, enamored Paris because of the memory of romantic nights with Noel. Coffee at sidewalk cafes, fine restaurants and, most of all, nightly strolls hand in hand down the Champs D' Alisse and other avenues. They were permanently etched in memory!

As the flight glided on he thought about the news on his house. This on top of Danny's murder was almost unbearable. He must call the police or fire department in Hamilton to establish the fact that they are in Europe and will be for a while. Then, too, he must file an insurance claim. I'll do whatever I have to in order to protect my family forever and salvage as much of my holdings as possible! A new life in a new place. Those fucking animals will never get another dime from me!

CHAPTER 75

Carlo and the crew immediately drove to the Paradise Club in North Beach after coming up empty-handed from their chase which ended up in Braintree to find a dark house. They had picked the lock only to find Frances was not there. They were all apprehensive about the flaming inferno in Hamilton even though they had taken all precautions to cover them up as culprits of the fire. Nick would obviously no longer cooperate and he knew enough about them at this point to cause trouble. The FBI would bring heat if he contacted them! And, he probably will they concluded.

Packard had to be wasted! Their widespread tentacles now reached even wider. They'd get him in time, but all effort was made to get him quickly.

Mario met with his crew and others at North Beach. Carlo and Angelo were present along with Mio Ruggeri and six other made men, soldiers from New York City. The money which they thought was large,but didn't know because the real deposit,they thought, was never honestly revealed, would be split between whoever killed Nick and whoever got the money out of Zurich. The remainder would go to Mario and the New York bosses. Which would be much of it! They were all in high spirits and mean. Each one had visions of many dollars.

Mario, a powerful New England capo, made sure the club doors were locked and the area outside his office was empty before he raised his voice, saying, "This man, Packard—a slimy motherfucker—owes us a lot of money and has skipped out of town with his family. Mario went on to rehash Danny's trip to Zurich and Danny's admission of a two-million-dollar deposit. They had not seen the deposit slip. "I think there is a lot more than that there! I know he's worth better than fifty million dollars."

One of the made men from New York, Ronaldo Santori, suggested that he would go to Zurich and get the money. "If we know the deposit account number, which we do, I can say that we lost the slip M75906J and they'll produce it or else!"

Mario chimed in, "Ronaldo, there can be no trouble in Zurich. They can't be threatened. It would cause too much trouble for us. We can't be sure that Nick's puppet gave us the right number. We'll only have one shot at it and the number must be right. We have to get that deposit slip from Packard and finesse it through! That's the way it will work."

A contract was out on Nick's life everywhere the Mob controlled, but only after getting the deposit slip which stated the amount! "There's a lot of money at stake." Mario raised his voice to the soldiers. "Go get it!"

A relentless search was on! Orders…find Packard!

CHAPTER 76

American Airlines flight 739 landed at Orly in Paris. It was four a.m. and the Packards alighted from the plane. The jet lag from the time change discombobulated everyone. It was not the timing of choice, but Nick knew he had to stay ahead of the Mob if he wanted his money and life to stay intact. Eventually, in time, life would get back to somewhere, if not normal, at least livable. He prayed! The fact that his family was safe brought tremendous relief.

They took a subway to the main terminal. Orly was a huge airport. Noel hailed a cab and the family headed to the Intercontinental Hotel passing the Eiffel Tower and those buildings still riddled with bullets from the German occupation so many years ago. This city is fascinating. If only I could just get my money from Switzerland and come back here permanently with Noel and Ali. But I can't. My net worth has dropped from forty-one million dollars to now, what, two-point-six million or so in cash and maybe a few million from my Massachusetts properties and probably nothing from the insurance claim on my house after the mortgage is satisfied! I can't accept that. I worked too hard and I'm certain the value of my remaining real estate will increase substantially as the recession fades. I have to take action. Liquidate everything in time and retire with my family!

The cab stopped in front of the Intercontinental. A French speaking valet ushered them out of the cab while Ali impressively spoke her only known French phrase "merci beau coup".

"Ah, yes. You're welcome, mademoiselle," the valet replied. Nick and Noel managed a chuckle as they took Frances by the arm and walked inside behind the porter pushing the luggage cart.

Ali was excited, a new country! The family got settled that day and slept while the following few days were spent as tourists seeing the many sites. They visited the Louvre and viewed the Mona Lisa. A visit to Mont St. Michael fascinated Noel and Frances as did the many shops. Nick got bored, but never said a word. His mind dwelled on the trouble 98 percent of the time. Although he now had to watch the money, he spent three thousand dollars on them for clothes, meals, perfumes, and other things. They were worth it. Every cent and much more. He loved them dearly. He'd work things out and they would be financially sound all their lives. He hoped!

The time came for Nick to leave for Zurich to withdraw his cash. Too risky to leave it there now. Nick thought. He died his hair blond and put on horn-rimmed glasses he had purchased the previous day. He would take no chances. He donned a felt hat and wore a plain wool suit. Only an overnight bag was packed with essentials.

Before he left he asked Noel to sit down when they were alone and told her, again, how much he loved her and that when he worked his plan out they would have sufficient money for the rest of their lives. But, their life in Massachusetts or for that matter in the eastern part of the U.S. was over. When he told her that their house had been burned down she turned white as a ghost and her eyes opened wide. "Nick, tell me this is just a dream. Look what you've gotten us into!"

"Not by my choice." Nick exhaled. "We have to have a serious discussion when you return," Noel replied.

He didn't like the implications of that statement! He had to get everything back on track and soon! Nick double checked his bag for everything. He had a certified copy of Danny's will which bequeathed his bank accounts in Switzerland and at Coastal Bank to Nick and a death certificate that he had gotten from Conrad. He knew that he would need those and the deposit slip to get the money from Bundesbank. The will was produced by Nick and Danny had signed it before leaving Nick's office that fateful night to take all precautions. He wished that he had been able to bring the gun!

Nick opened his large briefcase, retrieving twenty-five thousand dollars in cash to take with him in the smaller case and gave the large case to Noel. It contained the remaining four hundred sixty-two thousand dollars in neatly stacked and bound piles of hundred-dollar bills!

"Everything now will be in cash," he told Noel. "Tuck this away and put most of it in the hotel safe. No checks or credit cards which are traceable. Tell Ali I went on a business trip and I'll be back in a few days. OK?"

"OK," Noel quietly answered as she kissed him on the cheek. He then departed for Switzerland.

Two hours later he boarded Swiss Air flight 71 and flew out of Paris as his anxiety level took a giant leap. The "smoking" light flickered on brightly as Nick drew a Marlboro from his suit coat pocket. He had just taken up occasional smoking under heavy stress. As the flight continued he walked back and forth in the aisles and received coy smiles from the passengers. He thought that he'd better hit the head and look at his face. Although he was not vain he looked pretty good and youthful. He decided to apply mascara that he had taken from Noel's bath and the black tone instantly added many years to his appearance. The smiles suddenly seemed to stop. Perfect.

Soon the plane taxied down the runway at Zurich. His heart pounded anxiously. This was a dangerous mission.

Nick alighted from the plane looking like a seventy-year-old man, with the soft felt hat and tired-looking eyes. His hair had been cut short like an older man. He purposely walked with an unsteady gait. His appearance had changed dramatically. He checked in at the airport hotel for an indefinite stay.

The next day Nick cabbed to a cafe a thousand feet down the street from Bundesbank. He paid the cab driver and went in for coffee, then meandered down the street to the bank with the unsteady gait. He didn't notice that eyes were upon him and everyone else in the area. Evil eyes! He was not yet a suspect in particular.

"Average-looking old man entering the bank," Ronaldo said on the car phone to Carlo Puglesi who was in a car on the street near the bank's entrance. Two soldiers stood outside the bank leaning up against the wall of the bank waiting for any sign from Ronaldo.

Nick entered the bank and bid "good afternoon" as he asked instructions for withdrawal while showing the teller the numbered deposit slip. She gave him a slip to fill out and he requested a full withdrawal of the bank's stated $2,001,356, which included interest to date. The teller went to Hans's desk for approval because of the size of the withdrawal.

Hans remembered the deposit, but not the face. His memory was photographic and he walked over to Nick."This account belongs to Danny Levin." Hans maintained a separate informal list of clients' names which showed nowhere in the records as was customary. "I can only give it to him!"

"Well, Hans, Danny died, and I have a certified copy of his will and a death certificate." Nick had obtained these right after learning of Danny's death. "He willed it to me as you can see here." Hans seemed sincerely upset for a moment, but then proceeded on in a business-like manner. Nick handed him a copy of the documents which Hans took into another room and was gone for what seemed like an eternity to Nick.

When Hans returned, he asked Nick for his license and passport, and studied both carefully. He looked at Nick, then at the license and passport, and then back to Nick. "This isn't you!" Hans stated earnestly.

"Oh, it's me all right. I've aged since those photos were taken over two years ago." He then produced his social security card.

Hans examined his face, then, folded! "We take our banking very seriously and even though accounts are numbered only we go to great lengths off the record to identify the person withdrawing. Thank you for your patience, Mr. Packard. Are you sure you want cash and not a check for this sizable amount?" I need a lot of cash for cash payroll on a sizable project I'm doing here. I might as well take it all in cash. At least seventy-five percent in U.S. thousand-dollar bills and the rest in hundred-dollar bills," Nick explained. He had decided to do all cash transactions indefinitely. It seemed those mobsters could trace just about anything!

He proceeded to sign more documents and set his glasses on the table beside him. Hans filled a large case with the cash. It was gratis from the bank. He was an important customer. Nick left the smaller empty brief case and his hat, inadvertently, beside the bank table and forgot about them. He was extremely nervous and his heart pounded like a jackhammer. Fortunately, he had left his now twenty-three-thousand-dollar balance of cash he brought with him in the airport hotel safe.

Nick, totally immersed in fear, walked out with just the large case. He smiled at the tellers as he passed them and went through the lobby out the front door. He looked quickly for a cab and didn't see one nearby. As he walked toward a cab stand way down the street he passed a black sedan. Inside Ronaldo and Carlo, now together in one car, were drinking coffee. Suddenly, Carlo noticed Nick and saw his unmistakable eyes. An older-looking blond man? But that's him. Those eyes and carrying a large case. Must be cash! "That's him! Get him and that case. We're way ahead, fuck the deposit slip!" Carlo wailed.

Two men from the backseat of the sedan jumped out and grabbed Nick's arms on each side. The one on his left was a shiny-black-haired thug whose grasp was iron clad. On his right a weasel-faced man stuck a .45 automatic into his side. Nick winced in pain, but held tightly on to the case. They moved him a few feet with ease without making it obvious to bystanders.

He thought this was the end and, in desperation and not realizing his own agility, stomped on the left foot of the weasel-faced man who grunted with pain and let Nick's arm go for a few seconds. Nick didn't know how, but he was able to grab the gun from him while swinging the butt of it smacking the face of the man holding the left arm who let go momentarily!

Nick backed up and saw Carlo aiming a gun at him from the passenger side window. He crouched down and fired the .45 automatic at the passenger side window just missing Carlo and Ronaldo. The bullet thrust through the driver's side window shattering it to pieces while the coffee splashed in every direction. Carlo jumped out of the car.

The people nearby were panic stricken and screamed while running for shelter! Soon many police sirens sounded nearby. Nick and Carlo met each other's stares coldly and Nick aimed the .45 caliber at Carlo. But, the encroaching blue lights of the police cars diverted him and he took off at a quick pace running down the street. He clutched the case!

Carlo jumped out of the sedan and quickly aimed and fired off three rounds. One hit Nick in the left rear shoulder. He was trying to pierce the heart a bit lower, but missed! All four mobsters frantically jumped into the sedan and sped off. Nick fell to the sidewalk, then picked himself up and hobbled with his shoulder drooping.

He turned down a side street and walked on, the pain in his shoulder searing beyond all imagination. He was losing blood and being drained of all energy. Crouched over and carrying the case with his right hand, he couldn't hold on much longer! His feet were dragging.

A cab came speeding from behind him. Nick turned and flagged it down, then staggered inside. When the driver noticed his shoulder which had obviously been shot, he said, "Get out of this cab. I don't want any trouble!" Nick pulled a thousand-dollar bill out of the case and mumbled, "For this you'll get me a doctor, with no questions. OK?" The driver hadn't earned near that all week and quickly assented to Nick.

The driver took the cab over back roads out into the Swiss countryside. Nick was hazy and near death! The driver stopped at a remote village where he was a cousin of the local doctor, Dr. Sam Bullard. He was only a local practitioner, but he knew how to remove a bullet and dress the wound properly. Due to the seriousness of the wound Nick had to stay at the doctor's house for three days to recuperate sufficiently. Upon leaving he gave Dr. Bullard three thousand dollars from the suitcase for his help and silence. They both thanked each other many times over.

Christian, the cab driver, drove Nick back to the hotel in Zurich at the airport. Nick gave him another thousand dollars. Nick was so thankful for this help which saved his life. To be safe he then moved from the airport hotel to a rooming house for two more days where he slept around the clock from weakness and nervous fatigue. God was with him!

CHAPTER 77

Alitalia flight 519 left Zurich at 7:16 a.m. three days later and Nick relaxed more than he had in a long time. He had to get to Madrid and settle down alone in his hotel room to rethink his strategy and make all necessary calls to the U.S. and to Paris. Also, the reason for going to Madrid was to deposit his cash in a bank there. He had changed his mind now that things were safer outside the U.S. He couldn't carry all this cash around and felt comfortable parking it, at least temporarily, in Madrid. The money was clean and a cash deposit wouldn't be a problem!

The landing gear lowered and the "No Smoking" sign lit as the Boeing 727 banked and descended into Madrid. A smooth landing ensued after which he cabbed to a second class hotel downtown which was recommended by Airport Information. His first call was to Noel who was relieved that he was safe after he recalled that getting the money was racked with agony, but that he had it and was safely in Spain. She talked a bit about the mundane life in Paris since he had gone. But, she didn't seem happy. How can she be happy? Her whole life has changed so dramatically!

The next call was to Diane at home. She answered after a few rings and was ecstatic to hear Nick's voice. "Diane, it's Nick. How are you?"

"Well, I've been better, boss! The mail has been pouring in. Bills, overdue notices, letters from your insurance company on your house fire, condolences on Danny!" She choked as she said Danny's name. "There have been many calls but I take them all on voice mail and call back only those that I know. Some callers don't leave voice messages?" "Diane, you're doing great. If you can keep the rent deposits and invoice payments going for now it will help substantially and keep up a log of telephone calls returning what you can. I'm going to wire five thousand dollars to your checking account today from my Coastal account and will take care of you with more cash later. Please stay with me, Diane?"

"Nick, what's going on? Please tell me!"

"I can't discuss it over the phone right now, but promise to tell you when I see you next which will be within a few weeks. You're it, Diane, all I have right now to support me in our company." He wanted to elevate her to his level of importance.

"You know I'll stand by you, Nick. I love you," Diane murmured.

"I love you too," Nick replied. Love is so broad, not always having romantic undertones! But I think she feels deeper!

Nick hung up and proceeded to call National Insurance Company. It had to be done right away to avoid any suspicion of arson. The fire was eleven days previous to his call. He reached an agent named Ms. Flaherty and first explained the reason for not responding right away. He was traveling in Europe with his entire family and didn't get the news until yesterday. Flaherty questioned Nick extensively, then demanded that he file a claim right away. Fortunately he had reported the fire of "unknown origin" verbally to the police who filled out the report for him. Nick promised to file the claim when he returned within two weeks. She reluctantly agreed to wait. This was a large residential claim for the company!

He, also, called Coastal Bank with reference to the Hamilton house mortgage loan and asked them to be patient. The insurance claim will be settled soon and they will be paid in full he assured the loan officer. He was cooperative and just asked to be kept informed of the progress of the insurance claim.

Finally, Nick called the lead tenants in each of his shopping malls and made agreements to reduce the rent in exchange for temporary management of the malls. This was fairly successful because of the times. The rent reduction was welcomed in most cases. The tenants were large enough to handle the management with existing employees. A crude arrangement, but he thought it would work for now.

He sat back in an armchair at the hotel room desk and was relieved that things were holding together for now. This nightmare has to end sooner or later. He reasoned. His mind wandered off in revelry. I've really been screwed and not by any wrongdoing? First Mario and his henchmen kill Tommy and extort a payment for Mario's "favor" and I gave him Arlington Square Plaza. Then, he drained it, but gets pissed off eventually because it tanks. They go for more! Huge amount of cash and kill Ali's dog and Danny because it isn't coming fast enough! Oh God, Danny! Still not enough, but they burn my house down, then attack me in Zurich trying to steal my savings! They must think I have tens of millions stashed!

Why me? I know many other real estate developers and other businessmen much wealthier than I who apparently have not been extorted from? The reason I think is that I was too much of a nice guy. I should never have talked so much in Santo Domingo and then should have ignored Mario when he called me at home! But, then again, if I shook loose of Mario would Tommy have had me killed for his dilemma while he was in prison? What I know for sure is that I will be their target in the future unless I and my family seemingly vanish from the face of the earth forever!

Around eight that evening Nick left the room after dinner and walked along an Avenue named Pero De Blanco. He veered off on a side Street which had a sidewalk and was easier to walk. Lights were flashing up ahead on signs over many buildings. One stood out, heralding La Chiquita Club. It seemed like it might be a relaxing place to chill out and he entered through the glass doors.

Inside he noticed gorgeous women dancing on a stage in different stages of nudity. A group of Spanish women at the bar stared at him but made no advances. He looked around the room and saw no men anywhere. It suddenly dawned on him that this was a Lesbian club.

As he turned to exit, two females, one butch and the

other very feminine, beckoned him over to the bar. "Have a drunk with us, senor," the butch said in broken English. Nick didn't want to insult them, and sat in an empty bar seat beside the feminine lady. What the hell, a drink and some talk. I need that.

They were pretty shattered as he could see. He said, "Hi, ladies. I'm visiting from Boston, Massachusetts, USA. You've heard of that place?" he joked.

"Ah, si. Usted es hermoso. Vamos a mi casa," said the pretty lady. He knew that she meant that she liked his looks and wanted him to go back to a house or apartment or whatever with her or them? Surprisingly, the butch lady shook her head in agreement.

Nick was at first flattered, but then reason set in. They probably had a scheme to roll him of his money. He had two thousand dollars cash with him in his pocket. He didn't answer the pretty lady, but, instead, asked about places to see in Madrid. He looked askance as the pretty lady wiggled on her seat until her panties were exposed below her dress line. When she proceeded to slide her panties down under the bar and then pull back far enough for Nick to see she stuck her middle finger into herself, moaning, he knew that he was being suckered.

She held his hand and tried to move it down so that he could do it to her! Nick pulled his hand back and said diplomatically, "I'd love to spend a night with both of you, but I have to catch a plane at five o'clock tomorrow morning. Maybe next time around!"

"Si, senor, vene aqui. Si?" the butch lady said.

"OK. Good evening ladies," Nick replied, as the pretty

lady tried one last time by rubbing his groin area. He pulled away and left. He loved Noel, but was very horny after that display!

Nick excitedly, hailed a cab and went back to his hotel room. He took a cold shower first and then relaxed turning on the television. He picked up a station in English and heard a news report about the shootout in Zurich, Switzerland and how police investigations had turned up nothing. It was believed that a group of men tried to steal a briefcase from a man exiting the Bundesbank, but none of the men including the man with the briefcase have been identified yet. Also, it is believed, that the man with the case was shot, but has not been found. Nick cringed at this news. It had been a close call!

In the morning Nick cabbed to the Banco De Espana and deposited an even two million dollars in cash to a savings account which he set up in his name. He thought that it was far enough removed from the tentacles of the Mob. He'd have to take the chance. He couldn't carry all this cash around with him any longer!

He, then, cabbed back to his hotel and packed. His flight was at two p.m. local time which would bring him home to Noel and Ali around five p.m. Paris time. He wanted to relax and not have to rush so he left right away for the Airport. Sitting in an orange plastic chair in the boarding area, he read a new issue of Forbes Magazine in English which he was surprised to find here. But, it was an international airport. He focused on the feature story

"Real Estate Real-ity Sets In." The gist of the article was that bricks and mortar have an exact value, but the major thrust of the U.S. real estate boom, location of property, was now succumbing to affordability. Those pricey houses and commercial buildings had simply soared too high. This, in the face of historically high interest rates,had evolved from the willingness of buyers to strap themselves to no end to own the American dream. The greater fool theory which had beset the stock market for the last ten years was now taking its toll. A serious recession had set in which toppled the excesses of the 1980s. It named many of the troubled giants such as Olympia & York. Prime Commercial Realty should be added to the list! Yeah, right, certainly not this list of behemoths!

The article went on to state that, where in the past real estate entrepreneurs could have borrowed from banks to stay afloat, the lending spigot had been shut off tightly. Failed commercial banks are being taken over by the FDIC and liquidated or sold to the conservative larger banks. A prime example cited was the acquisition of the previous giant New England Merchants Bank whose retail operations were acquired by Fleet Bank and its real estate loans assumed by the FDIC to be foreclosed or sold, then chase the deficiencies of defunct owners. Many were bankrupt or on the verge of it. The Resolution Trust was engaged in similar activity with the failed Savings and Loan Institutions. It was a bloodbath!

Over the speaker he heard "Air France flight seven twenty-one to Paris now boarding." The excitement rose in him. He was headed to what may turn out eventually to be the new home for he and his family. Probably not in the apartment, but in some nice modest house in the French countryside, permanently! He could, maybe, start anew here after he liquidated in New England.

CHAPTER 78

After two hours in the air, the stewardess announced the decent into Orly Airport and soon the Safety Belt sign lit up.

An hour later Nick alighted from a cab in front of the Intercontinental Hotel and slipped the driver 117 francs. He entered the hotel and took the elevator to the fourth floor and when he wrapped on the door of room 429 Noel opened it and casually embraced with Nick. They kissed lightly and she drew back a bit. She still is angry with me. I don't blame her. I'll do everything possible to repair the damage this has caused.

Ali ran to Nicks side and hugged him dearly. She was growing like a weed. Almost seven now.

The young girl prayed for a close and stable family again just about every night. She didn't know very much about what had transpired in the past, but she knew that something was wrong with them living in an apartment in another country! She sadly missed Prancer!

That night The couple slept together again, but only held each other for a while. He wanted to tell her about the gunfight in Zurich, but didn't because it would only sound crazier to her. Nick was aching for sex, but, Noel wasn't and rolled on her side eventually falling to sleep. He had covered up his wound with a T-shirt and said nothing to anyone about it.

The next day Nick took Frances and Ali to breakfast while Noel had a meeting. She was back working interior design consulting jobs for a French real estate developer named Phillipe. After she returned home the family decided to go look at apartments. It was time to get out of the hotel. They went to a Parisian Real Estate brokerage and were happy to find two recently vacated units at the sought after Rue De Seine townhouse complex. They were perfectly located two doors down from each other and faced the Seine River with ample deck space facing the river.

Nick offered 8,850 francs monthly rent for each unit, but finally closed on 9,440, or $1,600 U.S. each. Nick gave two U.S references, Suzie and Conrad back in LA. He didn't want any knowledge of his location with anyone else. Also, the Banco De Espana was used for a bank reference. They were accepted and Nick paid a security deposit and last month's rent on both units in addition to the first month's rent. They agreed to move in on May 1, a month away.

Nick was relieved with that settled. He would take the four hundred fifty-four thousand dollars Noel was still holding in the hotel safe and give her fifty-four thousand dollars of it in addition to the eighteen thousand he had left in cash which he originally took to Zurich. She was working for a good income to supplement that and he could wire cash beyond that as needed. Four hundred thousand would go back to the U.S. with him for working capital to liquidate his business and living expenses.

As a relaxing treat, Nick decided to take the family to The tour D'Agent Restaurant and to the Opera House for a musical performance. The Tour D'Agent was booked for a few nights in advance and Nick took the first available for three nights ahead. Fortunately he was able to get tickets to the performance for the same night. It all worked out well and Ali got excited. Nick beamed with joy to see her happy!

Nick and his family toured so much of Paris and the outlying countryside that the horrible situation in America became suppressed for Nick, at least temporarily. But, the anxiety churned within him. He knew that it was still very much alive!

The meal at the Tour D'Agent was superb. Those entrees with the famous French sauces were incredible. One of the best restaurants in the world and the breadth of the wine cellar amazed the adults. It was so extensive. Their conversation was endless and everyone, except Noel, seemed happy. Ali talked incessantly about the sights of Paris while Nick laughed admiringly and questioned her about the various buildings. She had been listening closely to the tour guides and was quite knowledgeable about them already.

Noel and Frances chatted incessantly. Frances was old, but still appeared to have a razor-sharp mind and made highly astute comments. The charm of antiquity at the Louvre occupied a significant part of the discussion. After dinner they all went to the famed Opera House and enjoyed a splendid French musical. The performers strutted out into the audience and sang directly toward Ali. She was in awe of this extravaganza. Nick and Noel hugged her tightly and were delighted for her. The multi-colored, plumed costumes glittered gleefully.

Two days later the time arrived for the return to Boston to liquidate his business and try to maintain his dignity with all business relationships. A huge task lay ahead. He was happy that his family was safe in Paris and OK financially for now, but, on the other hand sad that Noel had been so adversely affected by all the trouble. She was very indifferent and he prayed that would diminish soon. He couldn't help but wonder if she was being comforted and pleased by another man!

CHAPTER 79

At 3:05 p.m. local time Nick boarded American Airlines flight 847 nonstop to Boston. It was a smooth flight which landed uneventfully at Logan International Airport. From the moment he alighted from the plane he became paranoid. He knew that he wasn't imagining things and cracking up. It was a fact that he was in grave danger. They would torture him until he produced cash if they found him! And, if they were successful at that, then kill him!

He stopped at a phone area in the concourse and dialed Diane's telephone number at home in Somerville. She answered after a few rings and was delighted to hear from him.

"Diane I'm back and want to meet you tonight. Meet me at the place we've set up to meet. This evening at six p.m. OK?"

"I'll be there," Diane replied.

Nick cabbed to Dandelion Green in Burlington and met Diane. She was so happy to see him and hugged him for a long time finally kissing him on his cheek.

After they were seated at the restaurant he proceeded

to unveil the whole scene to her. He trusted her completely. He told her about the extortion scheme, but was careful to avoid the murders of Tommy and Danny. He didn't want her to have the knowledge and be guilty of any obstruction of justice. She knew about the house burning down and figured the Mafia took part in that as well as the murders. Nick let it go at that. When he told her of the gunfight in Zurich her eyes lit up with surprise. She even got excited. What a story she thought. He told her that he was back to liquidate everything and needed her help to do it. She would benefit greatly if she hung in with him!

He took a look around the room and saw no suspicious looking characters. "Diane, honey, I need you first to drive me to the Westin Hotel while I get something out of my car which has been there since I left for Paris at the end of march." He didn't tell her that it was the .357 Magnum. He, then, told her to call Fogel Leasing and tell them that they can pick up the Mercedes there in the Westin garage and that he can't afford it anymore. Further to tell them that he'll be in touch with them soon to settle up. She should say only that she's a friend and not give her name.

After a relaxing meal Diane drove Nick to the Westin where she waited in the car while Nick took the elevator down to the garage and retrieved the gun placing it in an empty briefcase. The car was in the same condition that he left it in. He went back to Diane and told her that he was staying at the Westin for the night and moving around in the morning. He patted her back through the driver's window as she offered to keep him company tonight if he wanted. He declined and said he would call her tomorrow to review the financial status of properties. She acquiesced and told herself to forget about any romance! She was embarrassed.

Lastly, he pointed at the briefcase resting on the car seat which he had brought back from Paris. "There's four hundred thousand dollars in that case, honey. I'd like you to take it home and hide it." She was speechless, but finally agreed. "I'll need the remaining ninety-five thousand dollars in Coastal Bank." He thought for a moment and then withdrew thirty thousand dollars in bills from the large case, tucking them in the briefcase. "I'll call and Coastal will give it to you. OK?"

"I guess," Diane responded.

In the morning Nick left the Westin Hotel and cabbed over to Beacon Hill . He strutted down Charles Street and went up the stairs of the MBTA Red line to cab over to Harvard Square. He was very nervous walking the streets especially with the .357 Magnum in his brief case.

Waiting on the platform he noticed a group of three men huddled together and talking low. Two of them stared at Nick while the other one said something and turned. Nick jumped back with total paranoia and opened his case pulling out the gun and making it visible. All hell broke loose and the three men scrambled running away in horror. There were a few screams from close bystanders as the train pulled in. Nick disappeared into the crowd and walked to the rear of the farthest car holding a newspaper in front of him to block his face. The train quickly sped away before there were any repercussions caused by the three men returning with the MBTA Police. He alighted from the train at the first stop sweating with nervous exhaustion, then waited on the platform for the next one to go on to Harvard Square.

At Harvard Square Nick got off the subway and had coffee in a coffee shop. He managed to calm down and realized that this was minor compared to the past events and maybe what will follow. He went directly to a real estate office which he had found the night before in the Yellow pages which specialized in leasing local apartments. There wasn't a huge inventory to choose from, but he focused on a furnished one-bedroom apartment on Mt. Auburn Street. Nick knew the area was nice and the room sizes were large. Besides, all this was only temporary. He hoped! He luckily thought it was very nice upon viewing and signed a six-month lease immediately to take it off the market. No time to be fussy! He gave the agent four thousand five hundred dollars for the first month, last month, and security deposit. Done in two hours!

He moved in the same day and then went on a shopping spree for new clothes. He wouldn't stray from the Harvard Square area feeling safe there. There wasn't much variety for clothes there, but what he bought was adequate for his work to follow. He also bought a new cell phone. Wireless technology had just come into play and although not the best service was available because of the sparse number of cell towers, they worked and these new devices were unlisted and couldn't be tapped. He decided to buy two phones . One for Diane which he'd give her next time he saw her.

Reclining in a large leather chair he called Diane. She had already handled the Coastal Bank situation. Nick's earlier call made that possible. That's all she said about money. She knew how to play the game. She was now holding four hundred sixty-five thousand dollars in cash, including the money she was withdrawing for Nick from Coastal Bank. He'd have to get some of that eventually to live on. For now he'd use the cash taken from the case.

The conversation switched to the properties.

"Diane please bring me up-to-date on the financial condition of…let's start with our office building. Ford Plaza." Diane was organized and had all the information at her fingertips.

"Well, the rents for May have been sent in for all but ISCM Corp. They're sixty-three thousand dollars in arrears. We haven't made the May first mortgage payment yet to Tri-Star. We're twenty thousand short to make the payment. There are about twenty-seven thousand dollars in overdue bills. Mainly utilities. We have fifteen thousand square feet of vacant space right now."

"I'll call Johnson and offer the requested rent reduction if he'll bring it current. Who's trying to lease the vacant space?" Nick inquired."Oh, Vantage Realty, and they have some interest, but who knows?" Diane replied.

"Prime Plaza has thirty thousand square feet empty and the mortgage is in arrears by one month."

"How about the Natick strip malls?""They're way behind on everything. Carl Johnson's company wants to assume management responsibility to protect his second mortgage position. The Tri-Star mortgage on the Waltham land is two months in arrears and they call twice a week! Doesn't look very good, Nick! Oh, and Carl's second mortgage is also two months in arrears."

"No, it certainly doesn't look good, Diane. And, I'm not using my money to pay these bills or we'll sink fast. We've got to get some of that empty space leased! Have there been any calls from National Insurance about the house claim?"

"Nick, a guy named Rudnick calls every other day and is pissed that you aren't communicating with them."

"I know, Diane, they suspect arson. I'm not sure how to deal with that yet?" It's pretty bleak, Diane. I wonder if it's all worth trying to salvage. I could just file for bankruptcy?"

"Let's not quit yet, Nick! Let's give it more time."

"Good call, honey," Nick responded. "I'll call you tomorrow. Bye."

He next dialed Carl Johnson's number. "Hi, Carl!" Nick tried to be upbeat."Nick, where have you been? I tried calling you last week a few times—no answer."

"I'll be straight with you, Carl. We're out there fighting fires!" Nick bellowed.

"It's tough out there, I know, but you've got to stay in touch," Carl warned.

"I promise that won't happen again. My house burnt to the ground a month ago and that has had me preoccupied."

"I'm so sorry to hear that, Nick. How did that happen?"

"Faulty wiring, Carl. I'm suing the electrical contractor." Nick had to lie."You nail him to the wall. Your house, what terrible luck!" Carl responded.

"Well, friend, I'm sure Diane informed you that I'm taking over the management and leasing of the Natick properties. I've got to be protected. Let's hope that this recession ends soon. For all our sakes!"

"Carl, I welcome your help, and will also send you fifty thousand dollars today for the overdue interest on the Waltham loan," Nick replied. It wasn't rational, but Carl was his best bet for any future business and would get priority!

As the day wore on the mood went steadily downhill. Things were really bad and getting worse financially. He called Diane again and authorized a fifty-thousand-dollar check to Carl. Funds should be transferred from all the property accounts in her possession to make the payment to Carl. This is top priority he commanded! A final call was made to Rudnick at National Insurance. He wasn't in and Nick left a message stating that,as he had told Ms. O'Malley last week, his family had gone to Europe the night of the fire and he had just returned. Please call.

Nick, finally, packed it in for the evening. On the evening news was a story of a lunatic waving a gun in the Red Line station in the Beacon Hill neighborhood. People scattered and some ran to the MBTA Police, but it was too late. The gunman escaped and is still being pursued. Anyone with further information should contact... Nick shook his head in disgust. If they only knew the real story!

CHAPTER 80

Mario was so disturbed over the news of the Zurich failure that he summoned a meeting and blasted the soldiers involved in the screwed up fiasco. He warned them individually with Sonny, the boss from New York, sitting behind him and saying nothing, thereby supporting him.

Mario spoke. "He's a smart man, but he'll fuck up sooner or later. Leave a trail somewhere. You have to find that trail and get all the money he has left on this earth. Then you will eliminate him and all discernible features. If you botch it up again your lives will get botched up badly and you all know what that means. Carlo, Ronaldo and the remainder of the crew involved in the Zurich fuck-up have forfeited thirty thousand dollars each from their earnings. Mild punishment compared to what will happen if another screw up is made. No more to be said about that!

That half-assed shopping center in Arlington. What a fucking losing deal and now we'll have to muscle Moriarty at the Pension Fund to erase the certain foreclosure deficiency and then must bankrupt the holding company, Oceanic

Trust. Arlington Square has been set for foreclosure in sixty days. Packard fucked us!"

He gritted his teeth as he talked. "But, not nearly as bad as we will fuck him up after we find him and get the money due us! And, that's just a matter of time!"

The situation had gone way beyond a Mafia business deal and turned to hatred! The fact that the Mob had already drained three hundred thousand dollars from the shopping center and would be able to erase the debt and any foreclosure deficiency seemed to be ignored. Mario would have had Nick killed even if he had received a large sum of money. He was so resentful and filled with hatred.

CHAPTER 81

August 1991

Nick had battled for survival for fifteen months, to no avail. The battle scars were multiplying. He had lost the Ford Plaza office building and The Prime Place strip mall to the auctioneers gavel. The resulting eleven-million-dollar mortgage deficiencies were staggering. Carl Johnson had ridden with him on the two-and-a-half-million-dollar second mortgage blanketing the two Natick Centers and the Waltham vacant land parcels ever since he made the fifty-thousand-dollar good faith payment fifteen months ago.

Mario and his crew had been searching for Nick, relentlessly, since the Zurich incident, but to no avail. Nick's cautiousness bordered on paranoia and caused him to hibernate and avoid being located by staying away from his properties. He knew that it wouldn't last and he longed to finish cleaning up in Boston behind the scenes and then get back to his family in Paris. He realized that he had to divorce himself completely from New England and thought that settling in Paris was the best solution.

The Natick shopping centers were "on their last leg"

at 71 percent occupancy, as Carl had referred to them in a recent telephone conversation. Carl had turned out to be his closest ally throughout the debacle. Nick was very grateful for Carl and would someday return the favor. However, Carl, the former real estate mogul that he was, couldn't manage or lease the Natick centers any better than Nick had. The condition of the economy overcame all expertise!

Nick wanted to file for bankruptcy, but was unable to because of the two million dollars plus accrued interest he had in the Bank of Espana and the four hundred sixty-five thousand in cash parked at Diane's house, consisting of the three hundred seventy thousand dollars given her upon return and the ninety-five thousand withdrawn from Coastal Bank. This money was for survival of his family. He would fight to the end to secure it! And, if he filed bankruptcy and tried to hide it he would be guilty of fraud and subject to criminal charges. He would have filed bankruptcy in a heartbeat otherwise because all he had left in the world was the two million four hundred sixty-five thousand dollars in cash plus a lot of accrued interest and the vacant lot in Hamilton where his home once stood! He was living modestly on cash ratcheted from his properties prior to foreclosure.

The only criminal threat hanging over him right now was the implied arson investigation of the house fire. Rudnick and Flaherty were relentless in pursuing the investigation while the mortgagee waited patiently for a payoff. It was a huge house casualty claim. The policy covered replacement cost up to one million three hundred thousand dollars, but Nick had stated that he would settle for the current balance due the mortgagee of one million eighty-seven thousand. He just wanted it settled. He had told them that Noel, coincidentally, left before the fire of unknown origin began. She was hurrying to meet him at his office building where they left the jeep and took Nick's car to Braintree to pick up his mother. They then drove to Boston to stay at the Westin Hotel for catching a flight to Paris the next day.

There was no real stated evidence of arson complicity, but the permanent stay by Noel in Paris and, of course, Nick's business problems were suspect. Nick had told the truth, except that regarding the Mafia involvement. But, their involvement was a surmise anyway. The investigation dragged on!

Noel and Nick had talked by telephone many times over the fifteen months since they'd been apart. Each time they conversed he sensed a spirit of indifference growing more and more over time. Each time, though, after Ali got on the phone her lovable personality lit up Nick's spirits.

Nick reasoned that Noel needed loving in all sense of the word and that if he returned to Paris for a while he could stroke her in every way. And, a promise of a calm and financially secure life—although away from America, or at least the East Coast—and their permanent reunion would bring it back together. Over fifteen months of celibacy would make anybody depressed. It hadn't left him in a good frame of mind! He decided to make a surprise visit to soothe it over.

On August 17 Nick booked a flight on American Airlines to Paris.

When he arrived at Noel's townhouse in the Rue De

Seine he wrapped on the door. It was opened by Ali who screamed "Dad" in sheer surprise. Nick hugged her firmly for many moments. The joy was monumental.

When the two of them walked into the living room there sat Noel and a man on the sofa fairly close together. Noel cleared her throat and moved away a bit. She quickly said, "Nick! What a surprise. You never told us you were coming."

"I thought a surprise would be nice," Nick said less than enthusiastically.

"Nick, this is Phillipe. I work for him as a design consultant. You remember me mentioning him before?"

"I do, Noel. Nice to meet you," Nick lied. It was fairly obvious what was happening.

Phillipe was quite handsome and sophisticated, but, was nervous and stuttered a bit when he talked. He also made very little eye contact. These were giveaways to Nick.

Noel ushered Nick into the kitchen at this point and was concerned that he hadn't given her notice of this visit. "What the hell is going on?" Nick implored.

"He's my boss and a friend," Noel replied.

"My ass he's only a friend," Nick speculated.

Noel squelched and would lie no more. "Nick, our life has been turned upside down and you've been gone so long. I needed male companionship! Can't you realize that? And, to come unannounced! Were you trying to catch me in the act? We've been together now for six months. OK, are you satisfied?"

Nick made an attempt. "Noel, we've had so much together in the past. I'm almost finished cleaning up my business affairs and will walk away with almost two-point-six million dollars in cash. I'll make it all up to you!"Noel wasn't impressed with materialism, and replied, "Nick, I love you, but am not in love with you anymore! I can't—no, I won't—leave Phillipe."

He was very saddened, but, held his cool and walked back into the living room, where he said to Phillipe again, "Nice to meet you. How's the real estate economy here, Phillipe?"

"Probably not much better than where you come from."

Nick grabbed Ali's hand and led her out the door to visit her grandmother two doors down. He stayed with his mother that night and left the next day for America!

CHAPTER 82

When he arrived in Boston he took the subway from Airport Station to State street,then the Red line to Park Street, then Green Line to Arlington Street and switch over back to Park Street where he hooked the Red Line again, but to Harvard Square. This was a diversionary tactic which he had been carrying on for some time. It was overkill mainly, but he couldn't be too careful. The paranoia had reduced somewhat overall. However, he knew the reality of it was that there will always be danger lurking. Life will never be the same again. The sun was setting as he walked down Mt. Auburn Street with tears in his eyes. He loved Noel truly.

A month slipped by during which very little occurred other than receipt of many deposition and supplementary process notices, summonses and all the other legal nuances. He did have to tend to them, though, to avoid Contempt of Court in many instances. Every day started with a call to his friend Diane if not only to check on her welfare. All rent receipts and project disbursements had been taken over by new owners and she just took calls at this point and basically shielded Nick. He allowed her to draw a salary off the four hundred sixty-five thousand dollars in cash and it was now down to three hundred seventy-five thousand dollars. Nick had been tapping the cash, too, in order to live. Their lifestyles were pretty meager at this point.

One day in late September lightning struck when he picked up the mail from his apartment mailbox. Included with many other envelopes was one from the IRS. Nick opened it and nearly fell over. In large print was an additional income tax assessment for the tax year 1989 of $2,011,037, including interest and penalties! How in hell did they get my address? I can't owe that much! It obviously includes a tax on the whopping big gain forced on me by those animals for Arlington Square, which I never reported. How did the IRS find out about that gain? And where I live? The paranoia returned big-time! The Mob found me in Zurich, although Danny probably admitted everything to save his life. Then they killed him anyway! Nick cringed in emotional pain as the guilt resurfaced.

The next day he called Agent O'Malley, whose signature appeared on the IRS notice. He called and made an appointment with O'Malley for the following week. O'Malley was rigid and hung up without saying good-bye! Let me put this into perspective. It's only the IRS. I've filed all returns properly reporting all income. There is nothing criminal about this one! Is there? But, I never reported the bogus extortion gain!

Two days later he got a foreclosure notice on the two Natick strip malls from Tri-Star Bank. How did they get my address? This place is certainly fading as a sanctuary!

A few days later he moved five blocks further down Mt.

Auburn Street into another furnished rental in an old 1930s brick building. The apartment was a dumpy studio and rented for $975. It was perfect for Nick's now completely anonymous lifestyle. Who would think that he lived in such a place. He secured the apartment giving very little personal information and gave a false Social Security number, which he knew wouldn't be checked in this place!

Nick went to his meeting with Agent O'Malley in Boston at the hodge-podge building in Government Center and proceeded to enter. Whoever designed this building was smoking grass!

He waited in the reception area for at least a half hour when finally a red-faced, heavyset man with tightly cropped blond hair appeared. He was abrupt and showed no smile when meeting Nick. But Nick wasn't intimidated by his demeanor. The IRS wouldn't kill him if he didn't pay promptly! And what was left to seize? Nothing on the surface. Diane was holding three hundred seventy-five thousand dollars in a briefcase hidden in her apartment storage locker and Banco De Espana had two million dollars plus interest of his hidden in their vaults. He had nothing! The hidden money could be used for something like this, but better to provide support for maybe a long time. It would stay hidden.

O'Malley's office was the typical government prototype. An eight-and-a-half-foot-by- ten-foot cubicle surrounded by six-foot partitions. Two government issue side chairs flanked his desk. Not much more would fit. Nick felt fairly comfortable in this situation compared to the past, but realized that he never reported the bogus sale to Oceanic

Trust where he received a second mortgage for five million dollars—never to be paid, but had to be included in taxable income to cover up the sham.

O'Malley ushered Nick into one of the chairs and began. "According to our records you failed to report a sale of real estate in the year 1989. You owe two million eleven thousand and thirty-seven dollars, plus interest for September." Nick acted dumb and questioned O'Malley as to its nature. The agent then slid a 1099-S across the table and said, "Is this familiar to you?" The form had been issued by Oceanic Trust to Nicholas A. Packard for a twenty-five million five hundred thousand dollar selling price on a sale of property with a copy to the IRS, as is required."How did you determine the taxable amount?" Nick whimpered.

"We computed the gain by assuming IRS cost guidelines for this sale with an average gain computed at five and a half million dollars. The two million eleven thousand and thirty-seven dollars is a tax on that amount, plus penalties and interest," the agent replied.

"How much is for penalties and interest?" Nick asked. He was trying hard to hold back his temper and be polite. It wasn't easy! "Let's see." O'Malley hammered away at his calculator and finally stated an amount of six hundred seven thousand dollars.

Containing his anger, Nick replied, "I've been hit by the real estate depression severely. Let's cut through it. There's no way I can pay that ridiculous sum. You must know what's going on out there. My contemporaries are dropping like flies! Besides, how could you know my project cost without my input?" O'Malley responded angrily. "You can settle this now by paying it, then filing an amended return if you are entitled to an overpayment refund or do nothing in which case the file will go to legal for further investigation! I assume you received the 1099-S form?"

I'm in deeper than I thought. Those bastards probably sent the 1099-S way back and it may have been buried somewhere in Rob's desk or it may have gone to my house directly and gotten lost and ultimately burnt! The chills ran down Nick's spine.

Nick's comfort level had dropped by 98 percent since he walked in the door. "Look," Nick said, "if you drop the interest and penalties, the tax due is one million four hundred and four thousand dollars. I might be able to borrow one-quarter of that, or about three hundred fifty thousand dollars, for a complete settlement." "That's not near enough. I have another appointment waiting for me. Good-bye, Mr. Packard."

Nick knew he had to cooperate. A criminal action for income tax evasion would be more than he could withstand and what were the ramifications of a further investigation into this transaction?

As O'Malley began to walk out the door, Nick said, "I will try to borrow more. Please be reasonable." He was at the mercy of this tyrant. "How much can you shave off?"

"You can set up an installment plan for the full amount, or settle now for one million two hundred thousand dollars immediate cash."

Nick was hard-pressed, and out of weakness came back again with eight hundred seventy-five thousand. "Mr. Packard, I have another taxpayer meeting, please!"

"Wait, Mr. O'Malley. Will you settle for one million dollars even?" Nick nervously replied.

The word million struck a chord with the agent. "If you pay it by the end of next week I will agree. Subject, of course, to approval by Management and Legal."

O'Malley left and Nick sighed with relief for a moment before it sunk in. He was desperate because of the tax evasion and further implications. In good times he could have negotiated a much better deal. Probably would have waited for an amended return to be prepared before any payment was made. The two million one hundred fifty thousand dollars in Spain, which included the calculated interest to date, just became one million one hundred fifty thousand in a flash! How much will it be next week? he feared.

The next day he wire transferred one million ten thousand dollars in funds from Madrid to the nominee trust account, HYZ Investors, he had set up in Coastal years back. Then a few days later, he wrote a check from HYZ to himself for one million nine thousand dollars and deposited it in a new account set up in his name at First Commercial Bank. He papered it over as a loan from HYZ and prepared a note with a phony lending agreement. He hoped the trail was adequately obscured. He even rented a vehicle to drive to First Commercial to complete the transaction.

A week later Nick called O'Malley and received approval of the agreement which called for payment within one week. Nick breathed a sigh of relief. He was beginning to feel beaten down and went back to his new apartment in Cambridge where he broke out a fifth of Crown Royal and drank himself to sleep. It was a welcomed get away after all the turmoil and he stayed in bed for two days.

Two days later he hand-delivered a check in the amount of one million dollars drawn on First Commercial Bank to Agent O'Malley and personally handed it to him after for which O'Malley gave him a copy of the release to be executed by the IRS after the check cleared. Nick was satisfied with the release language, but felt so vulnerable! He had been screwed!

He left the hodge-podge building in late afternoon and cabbed to Charles Street directly to the bar at the Charles Restaurant where he ordered a VO and ginger and sat in deep thought. I have been cut down substantially, but the bright side is that I have around one million one hundred fifty thousand dollars in the Banco De Espana, with the accrued interest, and three hundred seventy-five thousand left in cash at Diane's apartment. Although I have a lot of unpaid debts and serious mortgage deficiencies hanging over me, the cash is securely tucked away and I've committed no crime. No bankruptcy petition has been filed and I never lied in court .Yet! It could be a lot worse. That's financially, but the loss of Noel! He became very sad and consumed many drinks before he was asked to leave by the bartender. His words had become slurred and a sweeping hand gesture knocked over the drink of a man sitting near him at the bar.

He left the bar and hooked the Red Line to Harvard Square where he bought a six pack of Michelob and took a taxi back to his new apartment on Mt. Auburn Street. Sitting at his makeshift desk he tried to formulate a strategy to end all the craziness, but there was no legal solution. He had substantial debt far exceeding his approximate one and a half million dollars in cash. He recalled an article he had read about Donald Trump at the height of the real estate crash a while back which stated that he and Ivana passed a homeless drunk on the sidewalk and Donald said, "See that homeless drunk? He's wealthier than I am now! He's got zero net worth while mine's a large negative!"

Nick lost all interest in thinking about any solutions after a few more beers and thought "fuck it, what's the sense? The only way to get out of debt is by filing "down and out" chapter 7 bankruptcy. Then the cash would go because it is criminal to hide cash from the bankruptcy court!" He threw the pencil across the room and ironically it landed on top of a pile of cash on his coffee table. "At least I'm free." He had a claustrophobic fear of jail.

He picked up the telephone and called Noel in Paris. After seven rings she answered very softly. After trying to talk warmly to her, she responded coldly. Ali was sleeping and he ended the depressing call. She had told him that she and Phillipe were "doing well"! He drank most of the remaining beer and fell asleep.

At two a.m. Nick suddenly awoke. He was buzzed and went to the refrigerator. Two beers left. He had consumed many drinks since yesterday afternoon. While drunk when he fell asleep he was now mellow and felt extreme clarity he thought as he consumed the last two bottles. But, his judgment was impaired still and he dialed Noel again to apologize realizing that last night's call around eight p.m. was received about two a.m. Paris time. That's probably why she was so cold and abrupt. I'll apologize! His mind looked for any excuse to call her.

Ali answered the phone in her usual pleasant manner. She was now eight years old and still had a child's voice. "Hello, Ali speaking." She had been drilled by Nick and Noel never to recite the Packard name over the telephone. "Ali, it's Dad. How are you?"

"Oh, Dad, I'm so glad to hear from you. I'm doing fine, but how about you?"

"I'm OK. Working things out here at home."

"When are you coming back to Paris, Dad? I miss you so much and am worried about you being alone. Those bad men. Mama had mentioned something about trouble with them?"

"Honey, everything has been worked out and is fine and I'll be visiting soon." Nick was forced to lie and felt ashamed.

"Can you put Mom on for a moment and then get back on? What time do you leave for school?" She was being tutored by American teachers while also learning about French culture and how to speak the language fluently.

"I leave at nine Dad."

"Is it eight o'clock there now?" Nick inquired.

"Yes, eight oh-seven," she answered.

"OK, we'll be able to talk a while longer after I speak to Mom and, Ali, I love you."

"Oh, Dad, you're awesome. I love you too!"

Nick choked in tears. She really makes these tribulations worth struggling through!

Noel came on and acted much more pleasantly than the

previous night. Nick apologized for the absurd late night call and explained that the time difference threw him off. It was early evening in Cambridge. She knew different. He had been drinking and heavily at that.

"Are you getting by financially, Noel?" Nick queried. "OK, Nick, but it isn't very easy. I've been working, but you know the interior design business is sporadic. I could use more, but I've been frugal and getting by. Phillipe helps out, but it's limited." Nick felt pangs every time he heard that guy's name, but for Ali's sake he said that he'd wire some money which he decided to do through a series of account transfers from the Banco De Espana. He'd do it later in the morning.

"Noel, I'll send twenty-five thousand dollars later on today." He'd have Diane send the check. "OK?"

"Oh, thank you so much, Nick!" She almost slipped and called him "honey." The embers of her heart were still glowing.

"How's Mom doing? Every time that I call her she seems lucid and upbeat. The proverbial cosmopolitan woman. How is she in your opinion, Noel?"

"Let's cut to the chase, Nick, she's ailing and doesn't get out much now. After all, she was forced out of your old home in Braintree after fifty years and, what's more to a foreign country and language. She seems seriously disoriented quite often. We really should do something to help her! Maybe an assisted living housing development where she can be with other people her own age and receive in-house medical care which she'll need sooner or later."

"I think that you're right, Noel, and she should be

brought back to America. I'll call her tonight. Thanks for the heads-up, Noel."

He paused for a moment, then pursued the painful subject. "Are you and Phillipe serious?"

"Well, I'm seeing him still if that's what you mean?" She had feelings for Nick and didn't elaborate any further. "But, Nick, I will not live with him or let him stay over here all night. I don't want Ali to be exposed to that."

She didn't say anything about not staying overnight at his apartment though? Why are my torturing myself. Let it go!

"Nick, honey." She slipped. "I didn't plan it this way. It just happened."

"Noel, put Ali back on the phone, please."

Noel sighed displaying sadness in her voice. They had been through so much together."Hi, Dad. Listen to this…" She went on and on about school and her grades, new friends including a cute boy in their apartment complex, the neat CD player Mom had bought for her, and her new IBM personal computer. "Oops, Dad, it's eight fifty-five. I have to run. Call me a lot. Every night if you can. I love you." She made a smooching sound and hung up. God, he missed her so!

Nick decided not to make any more telephone calls to Paris from his apartment. It was too risky! There would be untold agony if either he or his family were located by the Mob. He shuddered to think of it. All calls will be from payphones in the future.

CHAPTER 83

November 1991

The days slowly passed and each dawn seemed to usher in a new set of problems. An occurrence in early November depressed Nick so badly that he started drinking more heavily. There was always a twelve-pack of beer in the refrigerator alongside the ginger ale. A quart bottle of Crown Royal was likewise consistently maintained in the kitchen cabinet. He never got completely drunk, but felt a good buzz most of the time. He thought that he needed this to save his sanity.

The calamity occurred on November 7. On a chilly fall morning with a crowd of people standing on a dew-covered ground the two Natick shopping centers went by the wayside of the auctioneer's gavel. The first sale went off at ten a.m. while Nick stood in the rear of the crowd disguised and watched. If only he were a bidder! They were still about 87 percent occupied and would be cash machines for the buyer when the recession ended which Nick assumed would happen eventually. He thought he saw Carlo Puglisi eying the crowd, but wasn't sure.

He wept silently as the gavel dropped at $6.7 million on the first mall, a meager portion of the acquisition price. He couldn't bear anymore and soon left in his rental car not bothering to stay for the auctioning of the second center. Fortunately he didn't because that went off for less. It was a steal for the hungry buyers. The existing tenants were national and most fairly secure.

Nick walked away that day being hit with a mortgage deficiency of ten million dollars. His mortgage deficiencies were now up to thirty-eight million. Still, he refused to consider filing bankruptcy because of the million and a half of cash he still had. And the lender's judgments were good for twenty years, if he could hold out. Although he'd have to swear in supplementary process under oath that he was broke. It was a quandary!

That evening Nick reclined in his armchair at his Mt. Auburn Street apartment sipping a cold Crown and ginger. It tasted so good and relieved the stress tremendously. He thought about the thirty-eight-million-dollar deficiency accumulated. It was so staggering that his overall negative net worth didn't matter anymore. The mortgage deficiencies could be a hundred million dollars. What difference did it make at that point? He was determined to let things slide and not to file for bankruptcy. He was desperately holding on to his cash!

He fell asleep early and stayed in bed for two days. He had a difficult time getting motivated and tried desperately to change his attitude by reading Donald Trump's Art of the Deal that Noel had bought for him years back when Trump was autographing this nonfiction book at Trump

Plaza on 57th Street in Manhattan. They had been staying at the Helmsley Palace Hotel at the time. Nick was in awe of this man and had wanted to build a business like his, although he never deceived himself by assuming he could come close to matching him. Those chances were quickly fading into obscurity.

When he finally dragged himself out of bed and now totally sober, Nick called Noel directly.

He had been calling Ali every two or three days, but not conversing with Noel. This time he asked for Noel, after telling Ali things were fine and that he missed and loved her dearly. Noel came on the phone and asked, "What's up, Nick?" That cold response disappointed him once again.

"Well, I'm calling to see how you are. Are you still seeing that silly Frenchman? What's his name? Phillie?" Nick asked with anger which had finally emerged. Noel got furious and replied, "No, Nick, his name is Phillipe, and he's living here now." She was reluctant to say that to Nick, but Nick was being an asshole. He knew it too!

"Well then, I must have dialed the wrong number. But, put Ali back on, you philanderer. He chuckled at his statement. "Phil-and-her-er." He hadn't intended the humor! When Noel hung up on him he realized that his anger had caused him to say such a mean thing. He called back with the intention of apologizing. Ali picked up and he conversed with her for an hour. At least Noel has enough dignity to spare Ali from the domestic heat!

CHAPTER 84

A week later Nick received a call from National Insurance Company agent Henry Rudnick who seemed very polite. He requested a meeting at his office. There were a few things to discuss before his company could settle the claim and payoff the mortgage loan on the Hamilton property. Nick inquired what the problem was and Rudnick replied, "We'll talk at our meeting. Say, next Monday at two p.m. in the Arlington office." Nick agreed and hung up the phone.

Memories of the Hamilton house, times with Noel and Ali all ran through his mind and made him extremely sad. Ali's birthday party. Beach trips. Santo Domingo. Loving evenings by the fire all pervaded his mind. He was in a state of denial. It'll come back and so won't Noel and the happy times!

He pulled himself together and changed his thought pattern to his sole remaining real property. The Route 9 Framingham land, the gem in the rough. If the crash hadn't occurred it would have catapulted his peak net worth when properly developed. Six hundred thousand to six hundred fifty thousand square feet of retail and office space. It would have been the flagship of Prime Commercial Realty and could have catapulted his net worth to around seventy million dollars, perhaps.

"Groan!" he mumbled, remembering his attorney's favorite word used when trouble occurred. Nick had always laughed at Mike's remark and way of saying it, but this time it wasn't funny. He frowned.

I owe Carl Johnson $2.5 million principal on the second mortgage loan and about seventeen months interest in arrears of about four hundred twenty-five thousand, and I owe Tri-Star eleven million seven hundred thousand on the land loan with about one million five hundred thousand in accrued interest. Whew! Tri-Star is ready to foreclose and Carl will get wiped out if that happens. Maybe Carl will take the property back and assume the first mortgage and settle with Tri-Star for substantially reduced principal and back interest Also, a reduced interest rate. It is probably wise for Carl given its future potential value, but he also could bid it at auction. I'll call him and ask if he wants a deed in lieu of foreclosure or to just bid it at auction? Or, maybe he's not interested in it anymore?

He dialed Carl's number and waited. "Hello, Johnson Enterprises." The new company name connoted a vast and diversified operation which it now was. Carl's interests in the computer industry were now much greater than in real estate unlike the 1980s. Johnson was now heavily invested in the software end of the industry, an emerging giant. Telecommunications was the major thrust now of his business. Nick's debt to Carl didn't rank high in his concerns. But, Carl did have to protect his interests. He wasn't Santa Claus. However, Nick surely felt like one of his elves!

"Is Carl available?" Nick inquired.

"Who's calling?"

"Nick Packard."

"Hold on, Mr. Packard, I'll see if he's in."

Nick waited, thinking how much he loathed secretaries obviously screening callers to ferret out only those worthy of speaking to the elite. Of course she knows if he's there or not!

"Hold on, Mr. Packard, I'll connect you with Mr. Johnson."

"Hey, Nick. How are you, buddy? Still toughing it out?"

"Well, physically I'm fine," he lied. And fortunately he was sober at the moment. "But business is horrendous. Nothing good happening in the real estate industry, Carl!" "I'm well aware of that, Nick. We shut down that end of our business around the time we sold our vacant land parcels to you and a few others. It was our core business for years. We've been out of it for, ah, two years."

Nick questioned Carl on his other business activities, and listened carefully and patiently while Carl babbled about the dawn of telecommunications. He spoke of the Information Highway, interactive TV and telephone, wireless communications, movies on demand, five hundred channels on TV. It was mind boggling. Then, he mentioned a new communication line called the Internet. Nick didn't wholly comprehend all that Carl was talking about. He "oohed and aahed" quite effectively, though!

A thought surfaced and raced through Nick's mind. After a few moments he suggested to Carl "You know, Carl, with all that activity about to take place it sounds like you'll need new sites and buildings. I could help you substantially on that end. You know that I've handled the site selection and acquisition process for practically every development project that I've ever been involved in. That's my forte."

"I know your talents full well, Nick! But, we've got a lot of surplus industrial property around the U.S. lying dormant right now that has and will be usable for our needs."

"But Carl, you must need some new property to fit the bill for your operations?"

"Maybe in time, Nick, but not at the moment. When a situation arises requiring new property I'd be glad to have you work for me." Nick knew that Carl was sincere about what he was saying.

"Well, Carl, this leads me to an extension of that thought. Given the present status of the residential and commercial real estate market around the U.S., I could ferret out and acquire some pretty attractive properties for you. When the market reshapes itself, which will happen sooner or later, in the future you could make windfall profits. I have good negotiation skills, as you know. A revival seems to be starting in places like Atlanta, Richmond, and Las Vegas, to name a few. Why not give it a shot, Carl?""I'll think about it," Carl responded. He smiled, but was noncommittal."Oh, and Carl." Nick had let the Framingham land matter go to the end to minimize it. "The Framingham land. Do you want me to deed it to you in lieu?" He skipped the "of foreclosure." It was too negative to finish the sentence. "I can't pay the interest in arrears now, and even if I could, I couldn't carry it forward."

"Nick, I was about to finish with that question." A long moment of silence ensued. Then, Carl slowly said, "I'll think about that too. It may be a good idea!"

Bingo, Nick thought.

"Thanks, Carl. I'll call you next week. Good-bye." He went to the refrigerator for a cold beer and drained it swiftly. He returned for many more that day. His anxiety level was off the charts. He might have made some progress with Carl—the first brief glimpse of sunshine in years.

CHAPTER 85

The following week, on Monday, Nick slept late into the morning. Having consumed a heavy quotient the night before on his jaunt to a few bars in Harvard Square, his head was heavy and felt like a wheelbarrow loaded with bricks. He remembered the first digit on the bedside clock flashing from two to three early in the morning when he flopped down to sleep.

After showering and shaving he donned a navy blue wool three piece suit and a red tie with blue dots. His thick black hair had grown somewhat long again and gave him a youthful appearance. At forty-six he looked as youthful and handsome as a decade ago, despite the cumulative stress.

He felt positive as he exited the building and hailed a cab for Arlington. He alighted from the cab in front of the headquarters of National Insurance Company. A huge brass eagle mounted above the entrance seemed to stare at him coldly, beckoning him to enter.

Inside the reception area he stated his business to a scrawny, googly-eyed receptionist with dark horn-rimmed glasses who instructed him to sit down in an orange plastic chair, one of three. She called someone on the intercom and announced the arrival of "Mr. Packard".

This certainly is a low budget operation, stately on the outside but very tacky inside. They probably fought every claim submitted to them. Where did I find this company originally? Oh, yeah, it was through Tommy!

True to his observation, Henry Rudnick appeared in a lime green polyester suit and white polyester dress shirt. His shiny blue tie completed the "Bozo" look. Nick would soon find out, however, that his looks were very deceiving!

Henry shook hands politely and ushered Nick into a small conference room with a plastic, laminated-top table. Another man dressed in the same fashion and Ms. Flaherty rose from their seats and shook Nick's hand, hardly smiling. He noticed the other man was the original investigator, Roland, who Nick thought had the same dumb-as-a-fox facade as "Colombo" in that old television series.

"Well, Mr. Packard. Your claim, now at one million one hundred ten thousand dollars, your present mortgage balance, is a large one," Rudnick proclaimed.

"It is what it is," Nick responded. "I paid the high premiums for the coverage, which, by the way, is one million three hundred thousand dollars, and replacement cost is in that range. I mean construction costs, not including the land. Isn't that what you're obligated to pay?"

"Ordinarily, yes, Mr. Packard. But not when arson fraud is suspected. We have established that you sped out of your driveway immediately before the fire started and then fled the U.S. with your wife and family."

"You bastard, I was willing to cut your losses by a few

hundred thousand to put this issue to bed. But if you want to play hardball, my claim will be for the full one million three hundred thousand, plus interest for the seventeen months you've dicked around with this claim!" Nick screamed. He had lost his cool, and to his detriment. He realized that."Mr. Packard," Rudnick chimed in, "are you reducing your claim as an inducement for us to drop the investigation?" He went on without waiting for Nick's response. "We intend to hand this case over to the Attorney General for further investigation and possible prosecution. You didn't file a police report and didn't report the fire to us for weeks after it occurred! Your wife and family, and you, leave at the time of the fire for Europe speeding out of your driveway as seen by neighbors. You're in financial straits according to all sources we spoke to and stand to walk away with your mortgage paid off and own the valuable land free and clear! Need I say more, Mr. Packard?"

Most of it was bullshit, Nick thought. But, they certainly had him cornered. It looked bad for him and he couldn't divulge the true story. They may look like "schlepps," but certainly have a lot of irrefutable and damaging facts.

"Most of your allegations are false, Mr. Rudnick. Please cut to the chase and tell me how your company proposes to settle this!" Nick retorted.

Then the bomb dropped and the sleazy executives let Roland, the lowly investigator, say it. "Of course, if you drop your claim down to six hundred thousand dollars and deed us the land, we might be able to settle. What do you think, Phil?"

"How the hell can I do that? I'd have to put up five

hundred ten thousand dollars in cash to pay off the mortgage. I'm broke!" Nick uttered.

"Well, Mr. Packard," Rudnick took over again. "Aren't you going to file bankruptcy?"

"You know full well that I can't convey the land without a mortgage release from the bank, and if that's in the bankruptcy court the land will go to the bank.""We might increase the claim, but, Mr. Packard, you'll have to come up with a substantial amount. You think about it and come back with a proposal."

This is positive because if they thought they had an airtight case they wouldn't pay anything. What sleaze bags. Talk about extortion!

Nick reluctantly agreed to get back to them, then stood and exited the room. Complete silence pervaded the room. As he walked by the secretary she winked at him. He didn't respond.

Outside, a Boston cab sped down the street and Nick flagged it down. He was frustrated and his face had become white. The friendly cab driver asked him if he was OK. Nick loosened up a bit and answered, "Yeah, sure. I'm just fighting the recession. It sucks!"

"How well I know, sir. My fares are down thirty percent from previous years."

"God bless you, friend," Nick said. "Be happy. My income is down ninety-seven percent. Not much left!"

The driver spoke compassionately all the way back and seemed very sincere. When the cab pulled up to Nick's door he slipped the driver a hundred-dollar bill plus the fare. "Good luck, friend." he exited the cab and patted Jimmy on the back. Jimmy was thankful and said, "Thank you. Thank you, sir, and blessings to you."

Inside his apartment Nick slid off his jacket and loosened his tie. He poured a Crown mixed with Ginger and fell into the recliner. Fuck them!

He dialed his mother in Paris. It was four p.m. in Cambridge and ten p.m. there.

"Hel-lo," she answered, sounding dazed."Mom, are you OK? This is Nick."

"Oh, Nick, honey. I'm so glad to hear your voice. My arthritis is horrible. My eyesight is getting worse. I feel sick to my stomach every day."

She needs attention. Friends and loved ones nearby. "Have you made friends, Mom?"

"There's a few in this building I chat with, but Nick, honey, when's Johnny coming home?"

Nick's heart filled with sadness and tears ran down his cheeks. "Mom, Dad is gone. You know that!"

"Oh, he is? When will he be back?"

That's all he needed to hear. "Mom, would you like to come home to America?"

"Oh yes, Nick. Can I?"

"Mom, you can do anything you want. I promise! I'll be there in a week to bring you back. OK?"

"Yes. Thank you so much, Johnny. Good night." She hung up.

Johnny. I haven't heard Dad's name spoken for a long time. This saddens me greatly. I wonder if Dad ever did the things that Mario has done? Who knows? He was cut from the same cloth! So the story goes. I love him, though, and so did Mom. She's still looking for him!

He decided it was time to bring her back to an assisted care facility for the elderly near him and he would visit as often as she wanted. He loved her dearly.

CHAPTER 86

December 1991

Having floundered for months Nick's only enjoyment was good food and alcohol. He felt some strength because he still had the now approximate one million one hundred sixty thousand dollars cash, including accrued interest, in the Bank of Spain, and three hundred fifty thousand remainder of cash resting in Diane's basement. He was pleased that he had been able to send twenty-five thousand to Noel. But, shell shocked from the calamities of the recent past he couldn't help thinking of all grave possibilities, mainly the safety of the cash at Diane's, not that Diane would ever double cross him, but that she'd somehow part with it! Like a fire at her house or God forbid something bad happened to her. He felt horrified about something happening to her because he loved her, not so much the money.

His paranoia proved real when he flipped on CNN one early afternoon and heard the news. Ironically, it was not about Diane. No, it was about the collapse of banks all over Europe. It named a few and as the devil would have it one was The Bank of Spain! He listened in shock! When he pulled himself together he dialed the bank's overseas telephone number. It was true, his bank had been taken over by a government agency similar to the FDIC in America. Was there deposit insurance? He had no idea, but even if there was, how much would that be? In the U.S. it was a hundred thousand dollars, he thought. All or most of his one million one hundred sixty thousand in cash was evaporating! Just like everything else!

He took two milligrams of Xanax and went to bed. As he mellowed out he realized that not everything was gone and things had to get better at some point. Life is cyclical. But, of this he certainly was apprehensive! The ensuing sleep soon became peaceful and took him far from reality.

He awoke late the next morning. I must retrieve the three hundred fifty thousand dollars in cash at Diane's house. All day long he waited nervously, then called Diane at six p.m. "Diane, honey, I need what you have!"

She knew what he meant, but wished that he meant something else. "Come over tonight at eight and get it," Diane softly refrained.

He left Cambridge in a rental car he had temporarily leased. He couldn't expose any plates registered in his name. In Somerville he rang Diane's doorbell many times before she appeared looking very sexy. "Hi, Nick," she replied. "You're looking good, as usual."

"Well, honey, you look even better!"

"Thanks, Nick."

"What's going on in your life, Diane? It's been a while since we last talked."

"Well, I am working for Antidote, a computer

troubleshooting company. I am assistant to the CFO. And, Nick I'm dating him." Diane wanted Nick to know that she was attractive to other high level executives of substance. Nick knew that quite well because he had been one step away ever since Noel left him. But, he was still in love with Noel and had no real interest in starting with someone else right away, especially with all the uncertainties.

"Honey, he's a lucky guy. If only it were me!"

"You know Nick that it could have been you. It probably still could be!"

"Diane, you're so beautiful and smart and lovable. I could go on and on. However, this isn't the right time for us. Maybe after the nightmare ends we could start off on a solid footing. Give it a try. I know what you just said about dating your boss. I'll have to take my chances." He was as sincere as possible.

This move to secure his cash was timely with Diane off on a new venture in life.

"Diane, may I have the bag? I need it to survive on now. Every missile shot by anyone has hit me. Can you believe that cash is just about all I have left."

"What about your land in Framingham? Any possibilities there?" she queried.

"That is so far under water that the best I can do is to deed it back to Carl Johnson, and he hasn't responded to me yet. He probably will just bid at auction for it next month. But you know, it's funny, Diane. Carl has let the interest ride for all that time and not harassed me. I think he liked me and would really like to see a comeback."

"Nick, I have faith that you will."

"Thanks!" Nick uttered.

She got up and walked to the stairs leading to the basement. He watched her graceful step and wondered if he should retract what he just said and give it a shot with her. Her beauty and angelic smile tempted him greatly, but he'd have to hold firm for now.

Moments later she ascended the staircase carrying the duffel bag. Nick took it from her and opened it. Not to count the money, but to take out twenty thousand dollars in hundred-dollar bills. He handed the stack to her and said, "Diane, this is to reward you for your loyal help all the way through this debacle. I'll never forget it!"

"Nick, I'm always here to help you. Thank you so much."

They talked for an hour about Diane's new job and her new relationship. Nick was relieved to hear that Ronnie, the CFO, wasn't married and just having an affair. He would never want to see Diane hurt!

He got up to leave at the end of the conversation. They embraced each other for countless minutes, then kissed passionately. "I love you," they both murmured spontaneously at the same time. Nick stroked her hair and then left.

On the drive back to Cambridge with the duffel bag on the front seat he watched the rear view mirror constantly. The fear of being followed by the North Beach crew permeated his mind. He knew that it was still a real threat. Did they know where Diane lives? He was afraid for her more than himself!

He pulled into his parking space at the Mt. Auburn Street building and carefully alighted from his vehicle looking around in every direction with the duffel bag swung over his shoulder. Everything seemed normal. A few cars passed slowly and he fingered the butt of the huge pistol under his coat. He had re-holstered after leaving Diane.

He entered the lobby and pressed the elevator button tensely. Time moved laggardly! "Oh, hurry up!" he barked at the elevator, as if it were a person. He was nervous!

When he reached his apartment door, he was sweating profusely. If it follows the pattern of the last few years something or someone will take this bag from me! He knew that was not paranoia, but reality! He entered the apartment and threw the duffel bag on the couch and sighed with relief. In the kitchen he mixed a tall Crown and Ginger and went back into the living room dropping his weary body into the torn Navy blue armchair in the corner. He lay back sipping relief from the glass.

After he mellowed somewhat he decided to hide the duffel bag in his storage bin in the basement and proceeded down in the elevator and stored it. Locked safely behind some boxes in the bin. He now had control of one of his few remaining possessions—three hundred thirty thousand dollars in cash.

When he went back upstairs he reclined on the couch thinking about Diane and that kiss. He soon fell into a deep sleep.

CHAPTER 87

The morning was clear, yet frigid, outside. Nick awoke with a hangover once again. His cell phone rang at eleven a.m. "Ni-ick, it's Mike. I hate to call you with more bad news, but missiles are flying. I've received six notices for supplementary process hearings relative to your mortgage deficiencies from various jurisdictions. But, hell you knew the missiles from your past mortgagees were headed your way eventually. Your house mortgage is included? Didn't your insurance company pay that off?"

"Mike, they're still dicking me around on that. The sleaze bags are still threatening criminal investigation, as far as I know. A few months back they were looking for me to kick in a ridiculous amount of about five hundred thousand dollars. I don't know where that stands. Funny, though, nothing has happened and the bank is totally bent out of shape. They foreclosed on the mortgage and received one hundred fifty thousand from the sale of the vacant land at auction. I still owe about a million or so before any insurance proceeds. I don't know. The fact that no one could locate me is positive, Mike."

Mike didn't quite understand the full impact of Nick's statement, but just acquiesced.

"I guess that I have no choice but to file chapter seven at this point," Nick moaned.

"That's right, Nick. Do you want us to file for you?" Mike queried.

"Not yet, Mike," Nick said. "I have a few matters to resolve before filing!"

"OK, Nick but you have to attend the supplementary process hearings in late January. I'll call you well in advance of the dates. I'll put the epistles aside for now. Call me and keep me posted on things. Good-bye." Mike's habit of calling documents "epistles" still made Nick laugh.

Nick lay back and pondered about repercussions from filing. He thought about many of his contemporaries and their mistakes about filing with hidden assets. The move made to decrease pressure from creditors for them ended in increasing criminal legal pressure. Much worse for them!

Some were doing substantial sentences in jail. A few of his friends and acquaintances had fallen into the trap. Nick felt sorry for them and was determined not to go that route. He was thankful that he wasn't guilty of hiding assets. Not yet, but after supplementary process or a bankruptcy filing that could change. Although, his only hidden assets were the three hundred thirty thousand dollars in the duffel bag and maybe some deposit insurance from the Bank of Spain. The cash in the bag he'd never reveal. The deposit insurance he'd have to!

He did still have a potential criminal charge from National Insurance Company. It was false, but, he couldn't prove it unless he wanted to reveal all to the FBI. That option had faded a long time ago with his guilt from criminal information withholding. He felt.

Nick had a few more crucial things to do before he could start a new life. He had to bring his mother back from Paris, Settle with Carl Johnson and with National Insurance Co.

He made a checklist and thought each task out, then began. First he called Johnson Enterprises. He got the same routine from the receptionist. "Hello, Johnson Enterprises... I'll see if he's in..."

"Carl, hi, Nick Packard. I have to tell you as a friend that your receptionist's greeting is very alienating. She never knows if you're in. It depends on who's calling. At least change it to he's in or not. And, on another line if you don't want the call!"

Carl's usual response came back. "I'll think about it Nick."

"Well, I don't think you need a board meeting to consider it, Carl!" Carl chuckled. He liked sharp wit. "Carl I've called to discuss the Framingham site. The interest is accruing and I never got a response back from you on the deed in lieu for the land."

"I'd hoped you were going to call and tell me you are rebounding and have plans at some time in the near future to resume the development process. Even a small retail section? Nick?" Carl responded.

"I wish my answer were affirmative, but it's not. I'm broke and my credit is mush. Only good thing left is my ability."

"No, Nick! Too many liens on the property now. I'll buy it back at the first mortgagee's foreclosure auction next month. I think that's the most feasible least cost route to take. I do want you to file chapter seven bankruptcy, a complete liquidation, to take the albatross of your neck."

Carl had no idea of the extent of Nick's problems, especially the alleged insurance fraud and, more so, of the grave danger still haunting he and his family from the Mob. And, he was guilty though of obstruction of justice from withholding vital information concerning extortion and murder! He was buried in albatrosses!

Carl had done Nick many favors in the past. He had originally sold the land to Nick below its intrinsic value. Nick knew that. It had been a winner in the pre-recession days. He would most certainly cooperate with Carl in the Tri-Star foreclosure proceedings and would not file until Carl had the property back. He promised this to Carl.

"Nick, I'm going to provide my attorneys for your bankruptcy filing in late January. Oh, and Nick, why don't we meet before Christmas to see how you can help me in acquiring distressed properties? Are you still interested?"

"I think we can wait until after the first of the year because of consulting work I have to complete for another client." Nick didn't want to seem desperate. Carl acquiesced and they set a date of January 5, 1992.

Nick decided to put National Insurance on the back burner for now. There was no smoke rising on the horizon at the moment.

He booked a flight on American Airlines to Paris in two days and when the day came he took the rental car to the airport, parked in the airport garage and flew out of Logan Airport at six p.m. direct to Orly. Once again no one followed him and he breathed a sigh of relief on the plane. He had thought that he would never go back because of Noel, but his mother needed him.

Ironically, he wished it was his last trip to Paris and that he would stay there forever with his family. It just wasn't in the cards though.

Anyway, he wasn't finished with the cleanup process in the U.S. and did have to start a new work career. It was a pipe dream to think of running away to Paris, especially with Noel out of the picture.

It was a smooth flight all the way to Paris and when he arrived he wasted no time and cabbed to the apartment building on the Seine River where Frances lived. He stopped by to make a surprise visit to Ali, but she and Noel were not home. Nick decided to come back later that evening. He and Frances were leaving in the morning to fly back to the U.S.

Nick walked down the hall to his mother's apartment and rang the doorbell incessantly. After fifteen rings she opened the door totally discombobulated. They hugged for a long time and she said, "I'm so glad to see you, Johnny!"

Nick replied sadly, "Mom, it's me, Nick."

"Oh, Nick. Why are you here? I thought you lived in Paris."

"Mom, we are packing everything and leaving in the morning!"

"Where are we going?" Frances queried.

"Mom, we're going back to a new house near your old Braintree house! Do you remember that?"

She laughed. "How could I not remember my house? Thank you for bringing me home! How far are we from there now, Nick?"

His eyes became watery as he answered, "A long ways away! I love you, Mom."

All afternoon they packed her clothes and a few other things. The furniture and furnishings were rented which made this move easy now. He'd deal with the landlord after the fact on the early termination fee. No notice had been made as of yet! Everything was beginning to change so fast!

That evening he and Frances visited Noel and Ali. Ali was so excited and wanted Nick to stay longer, but he couldn't. Noel was cordial and the visit was joyous. They all went to dinner on the Champs D' Elysee and had a nice time.

Early the next morning Nick had to, once again, explain to Frances where they were going and it took longer than expected to get her moving and make the flight on time. They barely made the early international minimum arrival time.

Riding down Route 93 in Boston with Frances dosing and leaning her head on Nick's shoulder, he looked out the window and thought he saw Carlo Puglisi in a black sedan to his right. He fingered the .357 Magnum hidden under his overcoat. He had left it in an airport locker at Logan Airport two days ago and retrieved it an hour ago. At one point as the sinister looking man in the sedan stared in his direction Nick almost pulled the gun thinking it was him. But, when the auto veered off on an exit ramp Nick made a major sigh of relief. His paranoia was growing again in leaps and bounds. Dear Lord, it's been a few years since any confrontation. I've got to stop it. Their probably extorting other people at this point.

The limo arrived at Brentwood where Nick checked his mother into the assisted living complex. He walked with her around the grounds of her new residence for a while and began to feel comfortable. It was a nice place and Frances met friendly people immediately.

When the time came to leave, Nick told her not to worry about money because she had four hundred eleven thousand dollars in her bank from the sale of her house, which Nick had arranged earlier in the year, and if that ran out he'd give her more. He didn't know how, but he would somehow. He promised to take care of her forever and vowed to visit her as much as she'd like. He took her new telephone number and made sure she had his in a convenient place next to the telephone. "It's nice to have you back, and remember, I'm very close by and will see you a lot. I love you, Mom. Thanks for coming back with me."

"I love you too, Johnny," she replied.

Nick left the premises. God, please bless her and give her peace and comfort.

CHAPTER 88

Christmas Eve 1991

Nick was alone for Christmas in Cambridge and sitting in the navy-blue armchair which he had purchased from a bankruptcy sale when he first moved into the new apartment. He had been thinking about his life's journey while sitting in the armchair and still couldn't believe what had transpired over that lifetime. A roller coaster ride of the greatest magnitude. Beside him on the table was a half-full bottle of Crown Royal and ginger ale which had maintained just enough of a buzz over the hours. Outside the howling wind blew the leaves in many directions. Snow was beginning to fall.

He had risen substantially at a very young age only to have the carpet pulled out from under him putting him into a tailspin falling in a downward spiral and experiencing what few people have in a lifetime. But, he and his family were still alive and healthy for the most part. To that he gave great thanks. He saw the glass as being half full. Well, at least one-third full! He hoped that he might be nearing the bottom. He prayed it to be so! He still had a sparkle about him.

In retrospect Nick realized he should never have offered the Arlington Square Mall to Mario. The mobsters may have killed him then, but that probably would have saved much danger which still lurks to this day. Look what had happened to everybody and everything around him. Torn to shambles! Danny and Tommy were murdered and his family was stripped of all wealth and their lives put in danger while he dodged bullets around the world and, then, lost his wife! And those still alive are hiding from the wolves! With hindsight he should never have bragged about his success while in Santo Domingo to Mario. Too late now.

He dialed Ali's telephone number in Paris. No answer. He left a Christmas message on the answering machine.

It was the night before Christmas and Nick was alone for the first time in his life. His Christmas tree dazzled with lights and reminded him of Christmases in the good old days. Tears flooded his eyes as he remembered those times with Frances and Chad as kids. Then with Mary Lou... Jacki...

Noel and Ali! He shut off the lamp to his side and fell fast asleep. The wind continued to howl!

Christmas Day 1991
Nick arose at ten thirty a.m. and called Ali again. She was so happy to talk to Nick and wished him a merry Christmas over and over. She apologized for not being at home when he called last night. She said that she would much rather have

talked to him than gone out to dinner with her mom and Phillipe. This made up for his being alone on Christmas. She asked when he would return to visit and talked a lot about how nice it was when he had come to take "Nana" back to the U.S. a few weeks ago. Nick wished Ali a merry Christmas and, after telling her that he loved her dearly, said good-bye.

Nothing social was planned for the day as usual so he began the excruciating process of gathering data for the inevitable bankruptcy filing. He filled out the many draft pages of the chapter 7 filing forms purchased from Hobbs & Warren in Boston. For hours he listed every debt he could recall, some actual figures and some estimates. Listing the personal assets was easy. His land in Hamilton sans the house: three hundred thousand dollars (estimate); his 1988 Ford Wagon purchased last month: eight thousand five hundred; clothes: four thousand; and jewelry: three thousand. When he listed the mortgagee deficiencies, all personal liability, he got depressed. They totaled forty-three million dollars, in addition to his other personal debts of two hundred sixty-one thousand. His stock in Prime Realty valued at zero. No duffel bag was mentioned in his asset section!

"Oops. I made a mistake. I forgot I don't own the Hamilton land anymore. It was foreclosed on earlier this month!" Within moments he threw the pencil once again and it landed on the navy-blue armchair and stuck between the cushion and the arm of the chair facing upward. Nick thought it was humorous and said aloud, "Anybody sitting in that chair gets it right up the ass!"

He closed the bankruptcy folder and opened the Crown Royal pouring it into a glass full of ice and ginger ale. Before long he suppressed the thoughts in his mind and lay back watching the traditional "Uncle Scrooge" on television. At least I'm not as bad off as that poor bastard. He's got a ton of money but is miserable!

CHAPTER 89

January 5, 1992

Carl and Nick met on a Sunny, spring like day in the dead of winter. It was unusual weather and they sat on the roof deck of Carl's headquarters in his office building. Sitting at a clean redwood table they exchanged limited stories about the "holocaust" of the last three years as they referred to it. Nick only spoke of technical real estate issues. Nothing else!

The FDIC and Resolution Trust were offering foreclosed properties at prices significantly below replacement cost all over the USA. In Texas some modern apartment buildings were offered as low as five thousand to ten thousand dollars per unit. These were the lowest prices Nick had seen in many years. He could remember doing a cost certification for a developer's apartment complex when he was in public accounting in the mid-seventies, almost twenty years ago. The total development cost was thirteen thousand per unit way back then. Replacement cost was now substantially greater.

"Carl there are tremendous real estate acquisition

opportunities everywhere. But, we shouldn't drag our feet. It won't last forever and you've got the buying power I assume? Don't you Carl?"

"It depends!" Carl said, not finishing, as usual. Nick knew what he meant. He had it, but wasn't going to spend it foolishly."I'm convinced apartments and retail strips should be our targets, Carl. The smart money is buying these properties now and has been for the last year. I've got a pretty good handle on the hottest areas in the country."

"How do you want to get paid? Do you need money now, Nick?" Carl inquired.

"Yes, a fixed fee arrangement, say, seventy-five thousand dollars per year and a reasonable equity percentage in each property acquired. Say, one-third ownership," Nick requested."That's too rich, Nick!" My son would do it for half that!"

"Come on, Carl. You know there's no comparison. I'll payback the seventy-five thousand annual fee easily because I'll co-broke for fifty percent of the commission from the seller and give it to you. I'll be your 'buyer's' broker.""Nick, fifteen percent is more reasonable!"

"I'll do it for twenty-five percent, Carl. When can I start?"

Carl didn't want to start the relationship leaving a sour taste in Nick's mouth so he acquiesced.

"Right away! I'll have Moriarty draft an agreement. I assume you want to receive a 1099 as an independent contractor?"

"Yes," Nick replied.

"You can start on Monday and I'll have an office set up

for you. Small, but sufficient. You'll be traveling a great deal. And, Nick, can you start searching in Las Vegas. There's a strong demand and captive market from what I can see."

"Sure, Carl. I'll get right on it!" They shook hands. A deal had been made and Nick now had access to a bottomless pit of cash. He was headed back into the "game "! He decided he would concentrate all his mind and spirit and make it work. Out to the limit.

CHAPTER 90

Nick and Carl exited the offices of Johnson Enterprises at New England Executive Park in Burlington and stopped at the Dandelion Green for lunch. Nick's fear still lingered and he inconspicuously watched all around.

After lunch and many ideas about Nick's quest, He left Carl and drove back to Cambridge.

Back in his apartment he yelled joyfully and danced around the room with an imaginary partner. It had been so long since any positive business opportunities arose. He was exhilarated and did the two-step and electric slide around the room as he blared country western music from his stereo radio. He felt like a ton of bricks had fallen off his chest. That feeling of relief after a long period of stress. He thought. Most people would say they had experienced it at one time or another, if not just in awakening from a gruesome nightmare.

Nick decided to move out of Massachusetts as soon as possible and fly in often to visit corporate headquarters and visit his mother. He still had to limit his exposure in Boston and the suburbs.

Nick pulled a cold Michelob out of the refrigerator and sipped on it while thinking about this new start over and over! He drained many more that evening and fell asleep on the couch at eleven p.m.

The new dawn came and Nicholas A. Packard began what he hoped to be a third and final shot at success. First as CPA, then a real estate developer and now an acquisition specialist, a hound dog sniffing out good values and artfully negotiating them. The progression seemed like going up and down a hill which it was. However, this run put him back in business and provided the best chance to gain wealth. Certainly real estate development was history, at least for now.

He felt alive again as he immersed himself into his work. He had immediately made many contacts in Las Vegas while the property listing sheets poured in from local Las Vegas brokers. Within three months Nick had a 160-unit apartment complex under purchase and sales agreement for $5.8 million, all cash.

Carl and he both believed this upscale complex had extreme potential. Due to apparent previous lax management it was only 83 percent occupied, but in spite of the 17 percent vacancy factor, the 13 percent capitalization rate made it a bargain. Carl invested one million dollars of equity into the deal and would earn an 18 percent cash on cash return which could skyrocket when and if the occupancy level increased.

The unit mix was pretty much equally one- and two-bedroom apartments. Nick had done much research through frequent trips to Las Vegas and via. the telephone. The rents were definitely below market rates. This provided even greater profit potential. Carl was quite pleased with Nick's efficiency and sharp negotiation skills. And, so Johnson Properties Inc, was off and running holding its first nominee trust, LV Properties I.

Shortly after he started and before the supplementary process hearings Nick had realized that he'd have to file bankruptcy before he could receive any ownership in Carl's properties. He had prepared the twenty-one-page chapter 7 filing forms with the help of Carl's attorney, Moriarty. Then, on a cold day in January he sauntered up to the Tip O'Neil Federal building in Government Center and took the elevator to the eleventh floor and entered the United States Bankruptcy Court. Upon the payment of the $110 fee, the clerk date stamped it and assigned a docket number. He was now legally filed and all creditors were stopped from actions for now. The supplementary process hearings, which Nick had been notified by Mike about, were canceled automatically!

The timing was appropriate. Tri-Star Bank had foreclosed on the Framingham land mortgage and Carl had bought the land back for $5.7 million and blown away about thirty million dollars in liens, many attachments for the other mortgage deficiencies had been filed against the Framingham land. Everything had been cross-collateralized.

One more major hurdle had to be cut down. The National Insurance Company claim had to be settled to pay off the bank and further to avoid criminal prosecution. The arson claim was ludicrous, but, of course given all his bad luck could not be disproved.

He picked up the phone in his office and dialed.

"Good afternoon, National Insurance Company."

"Yes, Henry Rudnick. Please. Nick Packard calling." "Yes, Mr. Packard?" Henry quizzed, seemingly hostile.

"I haven't heard from you for a while, Henry. In the meantime, my mortgage was foreclosed on and the deficiency is around one million dollars after the puny land auction?" "I know that quite well. We were served in a lawsuit for the maximum amount of one million three hundred thousand dollars, face value of the policy, yesterday!"

"You could have settled for quite a bit less months ago. I would have kicked in part of it just to settle and be rid of one more problem," Nick chanted.

"Well, it's too late now," Henry chimed. "We're not paying and will join the bank in a criminal action against you. And, don't worry the civil action by the bank will certainly not go away either, just because you filed chapter seven bankruptcy. Criminal actions aren't dischargeable. What's more, you may never be discharged of any of your debts in bankruptcy if proven guilty. Don't be surprised when the Sheriff knocks at your door. Mr. Packard you went well beyond your rights and obligations. The jury will determine whether you took part in the arson and total destruction of your house for gain.!"

"Fuck you, Rudnick!" Nick, in bad taste and uncontrollably, couldn't hold back. He was furious.

"Good day, sir." Rudnick hung up.

"Mr. Rude-nick," Nick mumbled to himself.

Nick was apprehensive the rest of the afternoon. What else can go wrong!

He booked a flight for a few days hence to Tucson, Arizona. A broker had called earlier with five apartment properties for sale that appealed to Nick. From there he was flying to Orlando, Florida to view a package of strip malls directly with the owner who Nick had found out through the grapevine was in deep financial trouble. After that he left for the day.

That night he tossed and turned in bed thinking about the insurance dilemma. However, he didn't drink and had quit when he began the job for Carl. He knew that had to stop and would only bring more disaster if he continued. He felt good about himself and confident. He had already buttoned down a 25 percent interest in the Las Vegas apartment complex and was now receiving a seventy-five-thousand-dollar annual salary. It wasn't the old days, but he was getting back on track and he was ecstatic about that. If only he could resolve the National Insurance case. If he didn't he knew that everything would blow up if he was criminally charged and on top of that maybe everything became non-dischargeable in the Bankruptcy Court. He just didn't know. There was much time to run before the court discharged!

Awake for hours, he flicked on the light of his bedside lamp. It was one thirty a.m. *I can call Ali now before she goes to school.* He dialed Ali's number in Paris. She answered, "Hello, Phillipe's residence." They had changed the greeting after Phillipe moved in. *Oh, isn't that cute!* He thought for a moment and decided that it was wise to have a man's name listed for protective purposes.

"Ali, honey, it's Dad."

"Oh, hi, Dad. Boy, am I glad you called. I was going to call you after school this afternoon."

"Anything wrong, honey?"

"You won't believe it, Dad! Last night…Hold on." She said annoyingly, "wh…aat?"

He could hear Noel speaking loudly and vehemently in the background. Noel grabbed the phone from Ali. "Nick, that asshole jerk. He's in jail now."

"Who's in jail, Noel?" He almost said honey, but caught himself."Phillipe," Noel went on. "He punched a man in a bar fight last night. The little man was a troublemaker from what I was told and probably provoked him. But, it was not self-defense. At least that's what the gendarmes said."

"Do you believe the police?" Nick asked.

"Yes, I do, Nick. Phillipe has changed so much since we first met. His temper has become animalistic and violent lately especially when he drinks and that's more often than not. He has pushed and slapped me on various occasions and even punched me once. Not too hard, but my eye was swollen for a few days after that."

"It sounds like you should dump him and fast. I'm concerned about both you and Ali!""Oh, he's fine with Ali. He's always nice and polite to her."

"Yes, Noel. Maybe for now, but he's already proven that he has the capability of physical abuse!"

"Yes, Nick, I'm finished with him. It's too much for me to endure!""Noel, get a restraining order if he comes near you again which he will. I assume he'll be released on bail soon?"

"That won't be necessary. He'll just move on to another

unsuspecting female with his superficial charm. He's too egotistical and prideful to try to hang on after I end it!" Noel responded.

"I pray you're right. Good luck, and call me if you need help. Anytime, day or night. Put Ali back on."

"Hi, Dad. Isn't he disgusting? Can you believe his temper? I am afraid of him! Mom's face looked like a Halloween mask for a few days."

"Why didn't you call me in Cambridge?" Nick queried.

"Well, Mom told me not to. She didn't want trouble and thought she might have gotten through to him about his drinking. But, I guess she didn't! She knew you'd be angry and might interfere. Now I guess it doesn't matter, because it's all over anyway!"

"OK, Ali. Do you know the French telephone number for emergency? Like our nine-one-one in the USA?"

"Oh, Dad, first of all he has no reason to touch me. But, I do know it and chill out he won't hurt Mom after her threat to call the police if it ever happened again."

"You're right, Ali, it's two a.m. here, which means you have to go to school and I need sleep." He didn't say anything about his new job. Too early yet! Not a sure thing! "I'll call tomorrow to see how things are going. OK?"

"OK, Dad. I love you very much."

"I do too." They both laughed. She knew what he meant! He was half-asleep.

CHAPTER 91

July 1992

Over the six months Nick had been working for Carl, he received a 25 percent interest in the 160-unit Las Vegas apartment complex and a 30 percent interest in a one-hundred-fifty-thousand-square-foot strip mall in Phoenix, Arizona. Carl had been so impressed with Nick's skills and acquisition prowess that he pushed the equity sharing percentage up.

The acquisition of properties had heated up substantially. The real estate economy was slowly improving and Nick's initial advice was pretty much "on the money". He and Carl had seen how the old adage was so true. "The man with the gold makes the rules."

During a hot summer's week in July the property offerings poured in from every part of the country. Nick had been quick to put out feelers everywhere to every known commercial and residential broker that he could muster up. His efforts were bearing fruit. His sense was that the market was turning around and that the deals should be made now!

Nick's intercom rang "Nick, it's Mr. Kensington on line three."

"Well, hello, Mike. How are you?"

"I've been better. Toby, our criminal defense lawyer came across something today at the Sheriff's office that you should know about." Nick cringed. Here it comes!

"Nick there is a warrant out for your arrest. The Essex County sheriff has been unable to serve it to you. The only address they have is ninety-one Silicon Drive, your old office, and, of course, your house. Apparently he's been looking for you for a fairly long time!"

"Mike, Silicon Drive was foreclosed on and my name completely divorced from that property quite long ago."

"I know, but that doesn't eliminate the problem. I think that you should turn yourself in and defend against the charge. I know that you had nothing to do with that fire. You have revealed much to me which I assure you is confidential, but I still don't know the extent of it!" Mike said.

"You don't have to. No one does. However, if I get any negative publicity now from the press it could jeopardize my new job. And, further, I'd have to reveal the whole story to the FBI and probably end up in witness protection. Then, bye-bye job! No, Mike, I will just let the warrant ride for now and have no idea how I'll duck it for too long, let alone resolve it!" Mike was cautious and didn't want to know any more!

At 5:17 p.m. on a hot summer's day Continental Airlines, with Nick Packard aboard, ascended nonstop heading toward Atlanta. Upon arrival he went straight to the Grand Sol Hotel and settled in early for the evening.

The next day was crammed with property viewings. As he began to slumber his last conscious thoughts were. My drink of choice at the restaurant this evening was Perrier water. Thank God I didn't get hooked on alcohol over the last few years. I feel ready to rejoin the race. I'm not guilty of arson and will resolve it! I hope!

In the morning he met Peter Driscoll, a local broker, to view the three properties. The first one, a ninety-thousand-square-foot strip mall, was constructed well and rather attractive. Even though it was only 50 percent occupied it might have had potential except that it was adjacent to a ghetto and many of the store fronts were boarded up with "white supremest" slogans painted on them.

They moved on to a well-constructed and 90 percent occupied apartment complex in a fine location. The firm price was set at fifty thousand dollars per unit. The numbers didn't in any way justify the price and the pair moved on.

In the late afternoon, Peter showed Nick another strip mall located in an upscale suburban community, two miles from downtown Atlanta. The two-hundred-seventy-five-thousand-square-foot mall had a good mix of retail tenants, with a 70 percent occupancy rate. It was priced at a 10 percent capitalization rate and listed with the broker for $19.2 million. Peter explained that the developer, Ron Fernandes, had gone belly up and the bank was in possession.

"It has been completely mismanaged. I have two prospective tenants now that I could lease fifteen percent of the space to," Peter proclaimed. "That's forty-one thousand square feet." Nick, of course, was leery of such a large number, and wondered why he hadn't already done it. Nick responded, "Peter, if I make an offer subject to obtaining thirty thousand square feet or delivering the property at closing with two hundred twenty-two thousand five hundred square feet occupied at nine dollars average per square foot or better, can you do it?"

Peter hemmed and hawed and said, "I'll try."

Nick returned to Peter's office and made an offer for the two-hundred-seventy-five- thousand-square-foot mall of seventeen million dollars, below the asking price. The offer was subject to receiving the mall with two hundred twenty-two thousand five hundred square feet leased under five-year or better terms with no leases in default for payment or otherwise. He gave Peter the offer with a twenty-thousand-dollar deposit check. The capitalization rate offered was just under 12 percent, which Nick thought was a good deal for this superb location. At this price Carl would have to put little money down. Maybe nothing. And, a hefty cash flow. Maybe!

CHAPTER 92

When Nick returned to the Grand Sol Hotel at 2:40 p.m. and entered his room he noticed the message light blinking. He was surprised, only Carl and Noel knew where he was. He had given Noel his travel itinerary earlier because of her possible need to contact him if any trouble occurred. Upon calling the front desk he retrieved three different messages from Noel. He became totally paranoid and dialed her apartment on the Seine in Paris.

"Hello, Phillipe's residence." Damn it! She's still saying it.

"Noel, it's Nick. Is everything OK? You and Ali?"

"We're OK, but that bastard came here earlier this evening. He had been released on bail yesterday. When I told him that it's over he should have known why, but didn't accept it. He broke down in tears and after a long glare at me he began to knock things over and swear vehemently. I mean he became violent and seemed ready to turn on me. Vengeance in his eyes!

Ali was in her bedroom reading and after she heard the commotion looked out and saw him standing in the living room ranting and waving his arms She quickly called the Gendarmes. Thank God they arrived quickly and cuffed him. His glare as they took him away terrifies me! Nick, honey, get us out of here, please! I want to see you again. I've made an awful mistake. You and I had it all, but things got so stressful that I couldn't cope with it."

"I know they did, Noel." But, Nick was leery of her intentions, her real feelings. She was desperate now and had left him before! However, his love and concern for she and Ali drove him to say "Pack up and leave tomorrow. The furniture is owned by the landlord and assuming no damage to your apartment the security deposit is all they're going to get. I'll call the management company after you leave. Book a flight to Orlando, Florida now and leave the flight information at this hotel for me. Take all valuables and only what you can fit in a few suit cases. I'm flying there and will arrive around eleven a.m. tomorrow. If you can fly out by eleven a.m. Paris time we will be there at approximately the same time. You understand that, right?"

"Nick, I do know about international time differences!"

"Of course you do. I'm just trying to cover everything. Just wait in your baggage area if I'm not there and I'll find you. OK?" Nick replied.

His heart was joyous and he started to say "I love you," but wisely held off. "Good night, Noel, and call the police if there is any more trouble. He might be out on bail!" Nick hung up. It was three p.m. in Atlanta and nine p.m. in Paris. Nick went to dinner and had a superb Filet Mignon, but couldn't even concentrate on the succulent taste.

Early the next morning the alarm rang at six. Its loudness awoke him abruptly and he jumped out of bed. The thought of today's events filled him with as much anxiety as any of the past debacles. He felt good though. No more hangovers. He dressed and was out by seven a.m.

Outside the hotel Nick flagged a cab and went to a meeting with Joe Morely, another local broker. Joe was a nice guy, but had crap to show and Nick cut it short at seven forty-five a.m. At eight he met Peter Driscoll at a Denny's restaurant where he was informed that Surfside Bank & Trust had accepted his offer for seventeen million dollars subject to the thirty-thousand-square-foot lease-up which Peter had given them comfort on.

"I have a meeting today with a client who will give a letter of intent for twenty thousand square feet. It's moving along at a ten dollars per square foot rental rate," Driscoll went on. Nick thanked him after receiving the written formal acceptance and, then, had to run to make his flight. He grabbed a cab outside to the airport. Another feather in my cap and potentially a sizable equity interest.

Nick arrived at the airport in just enough time to check in for Continental flight 659. Unbeknownst to him, he had just missed Carlo Puglesi who had picked up his trail from Cambridge. Their contact at the Federal building in the Bankruptcy Court had given them Nick's new Cambridge address from his bankruptcy filing records. The possibility of this happening had never crossed Nick's mind with all the confusion. They had found him at last and had been trailing him ever since he left Boston.

Carlo arrived at Denny's just minutes after Nick had

left. He was carrying a nine-millimeter Glock and would use it in a heartbeat if Mario didn't want him alive. As Nick arrived at the airport and was going through the metal detector framing, Carlo and Angelo couldn't quite get the chance to subdue him. Carlo had found his flight number to Orlando from his contacts, and called his associates in Florida to pick up his travel plan from there. That bastard Packard has the luck of an Irishman! But, our friends, the union baggage men, will find him! They'll know when he comes through!

CHAPTER 93

Luckily, Noel and Ali met Nick close to their time of arrival at the baggage area for American Airlines. Ali and he hugged for several minutes and Nick kissed Noel on the cheek. She returned the kiss and they hugged for many moments. It was like before the "storm "or more like "hurricane" had hit. If only it could return to the distant past. Nick prayed.

Noel was reserved, but Ali babbled on and on about the turbulence during the flight, things she did in Paris, her worrying about Nick and, of course could they go to Disney World?

Nick said, "I have to go to Boston early tomorrow on business, but on Saturday morning when I return we'll all go there. Even better, Mom can take you there tomorrow, Ali, also. Two days seems to be the minimum amount of time to do that place properly. Ali became excited and squeezed both her parents hands tightly with strong emotion.

Off at a distance Buster, a baggage handler with an identity description of Nick from Carlo in a call an hour ago, watched the Packards leave and hurried out to see where they were going. Buster walked over to a FLA cab and whispered something in the driver's ear while slipping him a twenty-dollar bill. The cab hustled up to the Packards and opened the doors. "Radisson Hotel," Nick told the driver while they got in, and the cab sped off!

They checked into the Radisson Hotel and were assigned two rooms on the seventh floor overlooking the massive pool clustered with little islands and rock formations. Nick had booked two rooms, one for Noel and Ali and one for him. He had to ease into this. He had no idea where the new relationship was headed.

That evening they dined at the hotel restaurant and conversed first about their life in Paris, especially more about Phillipe who was smart enough not to return again after bail the night before. Then, the conversation, of course, switched to Nick's life. He told them mainly about the now positive things. He spoke of his new job which was progressing well and could put him back into good shape eventually. He didn't mention that what he had already accomplished might prove to be worth a few million at some point. He did try very hard though to convey a positive attitude but out of necessity told Noel that his debts are in the process of being discharged. She knew what he meant and was happy.

"As to the bad guys, I haven't heard from them for a long time and am quite sure that's history now." He would not use the words mafia or mobsters around Ali. It was too frightful. Why would they spend any more time trying to find me, especially where I filed bankruptcy. They'd have to figure that they'd be wasting their time and they're not stupid. The money banked in Zurich is long gone. Of course, they don't know that, but might figure that I wouldn't lie on the bankruptcy filing? That's public record! He knew that he was being too optimistic, though.

"Noel, how about you? Have you been working the interior design consulting all along?"

"Nick, I was working for Phillipe up until six months ago even after he moved in. After that he supported us. I'll give him credit for that. However, the real estate crash over there was a disaster and his support grew thin. Thanks for the money you've sent for Ali from time to time."

"Noel, it was a mere pittance and someday I'll make up for it all!"

Around nine p.m. they took the elevator to their floor. Noel instructed Ali to go to their room and suggested watching TV or reading while she and Dad talked in Dad's room. She complied while she wrapped her arms around her dad. "I'm so glad we're with you again, Dad. I love you so much." This brought tears to his eyes. Had the tide turned back to him?

Noel said, "Ali, honey, you probably should get some sleep. We'll be very busy having fun for the next few days."

"OK, Mom, if I can order room service first."

Nick said, "Sure, if you can stuff anymore. That was a good sized dinner we had earlier." Nick and Noel knew that kids would always order room service because of the novelty.

The two former lovers strolled silently down the hall about twenty feet to Nick's room and entered. Nick doffed his navy blue linen blazer and neatly folded it resting it on an armchair sitting down at the round table in the corner of the room. Noel turned on the hanging lamp overhead adjusting it to a dim level of light while Nick loosened his tie.

"Well, here we are, Noel, together alone after two years."

"Two years, Nick? It hasn't been that long, has it?"

"Oh yes, it has, Noel. I took you and Ali and Mom to Paris in April of '90. Every time I visited after that we were never alone."

"What should we talk about?" She wasn't sure of Nick's intentions toward her after all that time?

"Ah, hummer, hummer, hummer!" Nick uttered. A perfect Ralph Cramden takeoff. Noel burst out laughing and Nick joined in. The tension had been lifted.

"Hey, Ralphie boy," she responded. Noel smiled sensuously with her wide lips. Only a few minor creases shown through. God, she looks great.

"Nick, when you left in 1990 it took me months to get oriented. Sure, you left me a fair amount of money, but you were gone. I lay in bed at night praying that you'd return to us, but, you didn't return to us. Yes, you showed love to Ali all along, but not to me! Of course, there was no sex for so long. I got so lonely and Phillipe filled the gap. At least temporarily."

Nick leaned back in his chair and agreed. He had no defense. "Honey I was fucked up, hiding from the Mob while trying to salvage my properties. My lifeblood, my work. But you were my life outside my work. I apologize, Noel."

Noel queried, "Do you still love me, Nick? Or have you abandoned that?"

"I only tried to forget you, Noel. Alcohol helped, but didn't erase. You were and are my life, honey. I'll never stop loving you."

"Phillipe was there when I needed male companionship. You were off fighting fires, I understand. But, Nick, you drove me to him and it worked for a while. It would have ended sooner or later. All I can say now is that I love you and have never stopped."

"So here we are again. Can we mend it, Noel?"

"I don't know. How many more fires are blazing?"

"Well, Noel, I think that the Mafia has given up on me and all my properties have been disposed of and all debts have been erased. But, the last thing I have to resolve is the claim by National Insurance Company alleging that I was involved in having our Hamilton house burned down. You remember leaving the house shortly before it happened?!"

"Of course I do, Nick. How did they blame you?"

"A neighbor saw someone driving our Jeep and flying out of the driveway, but didn't know who. It was dark and I was implicated in it, not you. The insurance company and the bank have jointly filed a criminal charge for arson. The insurance company was the instigator because they wouldn't honor their obligation. They haven't been able to locate me yet, but, will certainly in time. I could have revealed the story to the FBI, but that would force us into witness protection. We don't need that!"

"Nick, honey, I will stand behind you all the way. I

can testify against your involvement. I feel that I am now obligated to help resolve this."

"Honey, I want you back and will help fight this!" Noel replied. She seemed truthful!

Nick kissed her and she responded like years ago with a deep tongue kiss.

Noel pulled up her summer sweater and revealed her lacy bra showing ample breasts. She was intent upon sealing her promise and wanted to please Nick. She then unhooked her bra and showed Nick what he hadn't seen for years while rubbing her nipples into his hands. He fondled them for a long time. She proceeded to loosen her skirt and pulled it down to her knees. Her skimpy black panties aroused Nick and as he pulled the crotch section away he almost came as she kicked her skirt off. He crouched down and she moaned.

The reunited couple retreated to the bedroom and engaged in every kind of sex imaginable. Their love returned with a whirlwind. They embraced as if glued to each other for hours until the phone rang. It was Ali, stuffed with room service delights and inquiring when Noel would be back.

Noel said, "Nick, I have to go!"

Nick said, "I understand, Noel. Listen, honey, I have to take a final trip to Boston tomorrow, as you know. I have to retrieve my belongings." He never said that he needed to get the duffel bag full of cash, which was now at three hundred thirty thousand dollars. His belongings could be replaced easily if it weren't for the duffel bag!

In the morning, Noel, Ali, and Nick went to the beach and swam while in between they played checkers, old maid, fish, and polka. Nick made arrangements for Noel and Ali to move to a Marriott Hotel right after his departure. He told them that it was a classier hotel, but nothing else. He was being cautious. The next day the time came when Nick had to leave to catch his flight. Noel said, "Honey, get back as soon as you can. I'm so happy again."

Nick replied, "Ladies, I'll see you in a few days. I love you both. So much!"

Buster watched on a side street as Nick hailed a cab after Noel and he parted. He immediately called Carlo Puglessi now back in Boston's North Beach. His crew had traced Nick's airline reservation to Boston through their long tentacles!

CHAPTER 94

August 10, 1992

Delta Airlines flight 974 flew out of Orlando at 8:49 a.m. He thought that all he had to do was pick up the rental car reserved at Logan Airport and drive to Cambridge. He would load up his belongings in the car and, most importantly, pick up the duffel bag. He would make a three-way conference call to the bank and To Rudnick to give another shot at resolving the arson issue. Then, leaving no forwarding address anywhere and telling no one, he would leave Cambridge and drive back to Florida leaving that lonely apartment forever.

Nick's thoughts drifted to Noel and Ali. Once again he would sleep with his arms embracing his only true love while his precious daughter slept soundly in the adjoining room. He would never in a heartbeat let them slip away again!

Landing at Boston's Logan Airport a few hours later, he retrieved his single bag. At the Budget Car Rental counter he picked up the keys for a Ford mid-size vehicle and paid in cash. He was extremely aware of the need to remain anonymous. More than ever. Nick had a lot to lose once again!

He was totally unaware that eyes were watching him as he left Logan Airport in Boston. Buster had followed Nick to the Orlando Airport and watched him board the plane. A call was placed immediately to Carlo Puglessi!

Nick drove out of the airport and through the Callahan Tunnel. After entering Storrow Drive and driving a mile he exited to go over the bridge to Cambridge passing MIT. As he headed up Mt. Auburn Street he breathed a sigh of relief. I'm getting closer every minute to a restored life! At his apartment building he drove past and hooked a left on the adjacent side street. Instead of taking another left into the alley in back of his building, he pulled into the next parking area beyond a wooden fence. I may be paranoid, but this is all real. The Mob wants me dead and there is a warrant out for the arson charge. Whew! The arson charge is more apt to be the end of me than Mario Cavallaro!

Nick walked to the rear entrance and inserted his key opening the door. He carried nothing. His travel bag remained in the rental car. He didn't plan on staying long. It was now 1:38 p.m. If he acted diligently he could be on Route 95 South by four p.m. The traffic would be heavy, but so what, he'd be out of there!

The elevator ride to his apartment seemed like an eternity which made Nick uneasy because of his claustrophobia. His perseverance increased as he got closer and closer to forever parting from this place. Inside his apartment he looked around immediately to see that everything was in its place. It was. He proceeded to make a mental list of what to take with him. It was pared down to anything of real value which wasn't much. I didn't really have to come here except for the duffel bag! I'll take the few expensive items of clothing and jewelry. That's it! I must pull those together and call Rudnick now. Then get out of here!

Nick decided to call Rudnick to begin with. He thought about the possibility that Rudnick would have a tracer set up. But, he'd be out of Cambridge well before anyone could get to him and he would use his cell phone anyway! He punched in National's telephone number on his cell phone and the googly-eyed receptionist with the black horn-rims answered. Her voice was unmistakable.

"Hello, National Insurance. How may I direct your call?" When Nick asked for Mr. Rudnick and gave his name she became silent for moments. He could hear whispering in the background.

Finally she responded after Nick said, "Are you still there?"

"Yes, Mr. Packard. I spilled my coffee right after you spoke," she lied. "Hold on, I'll get him for you."

Again moments passed before Henry Rudnick answered.

"Well, well, well. Mr. Packard! A surprise call. From you? Where are you, Mr. Packard?" Rudnick questioned.

"Where I am doesn't matter! How we can resolve this does. Let me start off by saying that you've made a big mistake charging me with arson, sir." He remained cool and tried to be polite. "You have no positive evidence that I committed any such act. I have two witnesses that know I was at my office all day and well beyond the time of the fire.

What's more, the fact that I had financial problems isn't any kind of proof of guilt! We went to Paris to get away from all the creditors' attacks for a breather. What I would get from your insurance settlement couldn't chew off but a small corner of my debt. As a matter of fact, Mr. Rudnick, at that time, in addition to many real estate interests, I had cash of about three times my house mortgage," Nick responded.

"Mr. Packard, we have witnesses that saw one of your cars speeding away from the scene moments before the fire!" Rudnick was attempting to trace the call as Nick had assumed.

"It wasn't me, Mr. Rudnick. But, beyond that I have a story which will only be told to law enforcement and will clear the air! Now, let's cut to the chase. How much will I have to contribute to get you to drop the charges and pay the bank?"

"Oh, about one million dollars," the agent replied.

"Look, Mr. Rudnick, were you listening to what I just revealed to you? In order to get on with my life and not spend the rest of my remaining funds on legal defense, I can pay one hundred fifty thousand, tops!" Nick hopelessly said. He knew that the likes of this man might agree and take the money personally, which was OK with Nick if he got released.

"I have another call that I must take. Call me back in twenty minutes." Rudnick was gone.

The anxiety level was overwhelming and Nick felt like having a few drinks, but wouldn't give in to the thought. He was going to turn his life around and was making progress. He gathered up all jewelry and some clothes and put them in a travel bag from his closet. He, also, put the .357 Magnum and the cell phone in his pocket.

Nick walked out on to the balcony to breathe in the fresh air and relax a bit in the warm summer sunshine. He noticed a gray sedan parked on the street diagonally across from his building. He paused to stare at a man with shiny, slicked black hair and mustache sitting in the driver's seat and looking his way. He got nervous and considered leaving immediately. Within minutes another man walked up to the car and squeezed into the passenger seat.

Nick was stunned as his heart started to race. He remembered this face, the face of Angelo Bono, clearly. The man was an animal. It was he who threw me out of the limo at my office, then threatened me with the garrote in the North End! I've got to get out of here fast!

He opened his door to the hallway and looked out the front hallway window. He noticed a second nondescript car in which two men were laughing. He couldn't make out their faces the way they were sitting, but felt quite certain that they were all linked together. His heart thumped wildly as he took the travel bag and locked his apartment door. He ran into the exit stairway breathing heavily, taking giant leaps all the way down to the basement.

Unlocking his storage bin, he removed the duffel bag and looked inside. The cash seemed to be intact. There also was an old felt fedora that he had received as a Christmas present so long ago, but kept, for what he didn't remember. He donned the hat and opened the rear door, hopeful to get out the back way to his car parked behind the fence. As he stepped into the alley he saw a man on either end of the alley leaning against the building and looking askance. He slipped back inside immediately and took deep breaths, praying that he hadn't been seen.

It was then that he realized he was in serious trouble. He couldn't get out! He didn't know how far they'd make a search for him in the building. They might go to his apartment to kill him inside silently, but certainly wouldn't cause a disturbance with other tenants. That was too risky. They'd call the police. He was stuck down in the basement, but even that was dangerous. They might come down here looking for him!

His only chance, and it was slight, was to wait for nightfall and somehow sneak out the back then. He wanted to call the police on his cell phone, but the problems caused by that would be overbearing. No, he'd wait and take his chances. He sat still on a wooden box for a while as his heart pounded wildly. Oh, how he longed to be back in Florida with his loved ones. Was this the end? Nick feared.

Upstairs, Bono who was now joined by Carlo Puglessi knocked on Nick's apartment door with increasing force. When they got no response they picked his lock and gained entry. Puglessi muttered obscenities when he couldn't find him and trashed the apartment. The only thing other than closely watching all possible movements from and to the building was to check the common areas inside the building.

The crew was experienced at casing a building and could not be detected by the average person. They had done it all from heists to extortion to murders.

Carlo Puglessi ordered, "Angelo, get Santini and Rossi to

check for an attic and to comb the basement. The rest of the crew should continue to watch outside. The motherfucker is in here. That we know. Let's get him back to Mario and if he doesn't produce the cash we'll waste him. And, if he does produce the cash we'll waste him anyway! I'll be outside in the car making a few calls." Mario was ecstatic when he heard the news!

Nick decided to change his appearance and act like a janitor when nightfall came and just maybe he'd make it. He knew that he couldn't stay there and soon they'd be combing the entire building. Hastily, he removed his nice casual shirt and left his T-shirt and jeans on while he rubbed dirt on his face. Anything to change his appearance. He even took his keys which were attached to a leather strap and added more keys which he had loose in his storage bin. He attached the strap to his belt and looked more like a custodian. But, it was only 4:57 p.m. by his watch. Over four hours to dark.

He knew what he had to do now and it sickened him! Directly outside the back door, but not in view from each end of the alley, was a dumpster. He took the .357 Magnum out and tucked it into his belt. Then he lowered the travel bag and the duffel bag with the cash into the dumpster and got inside. He lay down and pulled the lid shut covering himself and the bags with trash. He gagged at first from the stench, then got claustrophobic. And that fucking rat and garbage in his face was too much! It was the greatest humiliation and torture caused by Cavallaro yet he thought! He loathed that man so much! He waited for hours in that rat-infested dumpster!

Nick snapped out of reverie after hours. His thoughts about his life over the last hours leading up to this moment had kept his sanity. It was now at least after eight p.m. He couldn't see his watch. He knew that darkness had fallen because he opened the dumpster lid slightly and saw the night sky from where he was. He brushed away the trash while feeling his carrying bags. He'd have to grab them and move fast. It was about forty feet from the outside edge of the dumpster alcove to the open-gated wooden fence, beyond which his rental car was parked. He fingered the key chain on his belt and felt the separated rental car keys. He checked his pants pockets and touched his license, which he had forgotten to put back in his wallet earlier. He was ready!

CHAPTER 95

He contemplated the situation for a moment. They probably either think I am waiting until very late to leave or have already snuck out. I guess it's now or never! They don't think I'm in here after they opened the lid earlier!

He fully opened the lid and pulled himself out brushing most of the debris off himself and donned the fedora once again which had been left near the door. After he lifted the two bags out of the dumpster he shifted them both to his left arm and fingered the Magnum with his right hand He began the slow walk beyond the alcove toward the fence.

Ten feet. OK! Twenty feet. OK! Suddenly, two drunks stumbled into his path. One put his arm around Nick and asked him for money while hiccuping. The other leaned against him on the other side, wobbling. "Get out of here! Now!" Nick softly warned, but, both were too drunk to comprehend fully and were oblivious to his words. They made Nick stumble.

This caught the attention of the men first on the right end of the alley, the end closest to Nick. Soon the men on the other end started to walk toward Nick. It was still dusk and Nick could see that at least two of them had guns drawn. Puglessi on the right end yelled at Nick ordering him to "stay right there!" He was under strict orders to bring Nick back alive to North Beach to reveal his millions in hidden cash.

Nick had no choice and drew the .357 Magnum, firing in rapid succession at the men on the right end. They dove to the ground. As he swung around he was too late and the men on the left end opened fire at Nick and the drunks. The night air resounded with gunfire as all hell broke loose. Bodies dropped to the ground as the gruesome scene unfolded. Loud noise and bright flashes were everywhere as blood spurted!

The men who were unscathed ran to their cars, deciding it was too risky to come after Nick and took off quickly. Two mobsters dragged a few bodies of their own crew to a nearby car and fled the scene. Within minutes sirens howled and police entered the scene, where they found two bodies blown apart lying in pools of blood, The face of one was completely torn up from some large-caliber weapon. The bodies were taken by ambulance to the hospital but there was no hope for them. They were DOA!

The next day the newspaper story read: TWO MEN WERE MURDERED GANGLAND STYLE LAST EVENING IN AN ALLEY OF AN APARTMENT BUILDING IN THE MT. AUBURN STREET SECTION OF CAMBRIDGE. ONE A HOMELESS MAN AND THE OTHER A FORMER REAL ESTATE DEVELOPER. NOTHING

IS KNOWN AS OF NOW ABOUT THE MOTIVE
FOR THE SHOOTINGS. JOHN THOMAS, WHOSE
RESIDENCE IS UNKNOWN, AND NICHOLAS A.
PACKARD, FORMERLY OF HAMILITON, MASS.,
GOT SHOT DOWN LAST EVENING AND WERE
DOA AT MT. AUBURN HOSPITAL.

CHAPTER 96

The North Beach crew drove back to the Paradise Club and met Mario in the empty parking lot in the rear later that evening. Carlo did the talking, he was in charge.

"Mario, we waited patiently for Packard to exit the building, but that motherfucker camouflaged himself pretty well until it got dark. We scoured the entire building for hours. He was hiding in thin air. He snuck out the back when it got dark and we weren't sure it was even him until we saw him talking to other men who appeared to be pretty drunk. Bums, a bad diversionary tactic, we knew it was him when he pulled a gun and started firing at us wildly.

I had tried to get him to surrender, but he wouldn't. We had to waste him and the others, which we are pretty sure we did. Two of the crew got shot, Bono died on the way back. No pulse now!"

Mario peered through the window of the gray sedan and looked at Bono's lifeless body. "Take him out to the point," Mario ordered. He was repeating an order given in the past which meant take him to a secluded beach on the North

Beach point and bury him! "And take Santini to Doc, he'll know what to do!"

Mario turned to Carlo and screamed, "Can't you orchestrate anything right? He fucked you in Zurich and now again in Cambridge. You missed him all down the line! The chance of getting his hidden cash may have died with him. We can't find his family anywhere. You'd better hope that he lived!

There will be a sit-down in two days with Sonny. You'll be there Carlo!"

And two days later, after the news of Nick's death became known, there was a sit-down with Sonny and two high ranking soldiers from New York. Mario made the call and Sonny sanctioned it. Carlo would be punished severely!

After Carlo was escorted out by the New York soldiers to his death, Mario said to Sonny, "Packard is dead. We missed out on a lot of cash. But look at it this way, we did get a few hundred G's from that half-assed mall he gave us and erased the mortgage! Now, listen, Sonny, there's a guy in Swampscott who we saved from the Chicago crew and he's very solvent. Much easier than Packard, we know that! He owes me big-time and…" Sonny listened, but was not convinced.

CHAPTER 97

Noel had waited for Nick's return and when he didn't come back she became extremely worried. He hadn't even called her or Ali, which was unusual. The news had been delayed. Noel didn't read the newspaper much nor watch the TV news. It was too depressing.

It turned out that she was right. The news about Nick's death would have floored her! But it had to come sooner or later. It came through the TV when, after becoming paranoid about Nick, she turned on the six p.m. news and heard the story being rehashed by a news commentator.

She and Ali were stunned and sat staring at each other for minutes. Then, the emotion set in. They both cried incessantly and hugged each other for a long time! The news report stated that John Thomas was a homeless man and had no family, known friends, or money. He was buried in a pauper's grave.

Nicolas Packard's last known address was in the Mt. Auburn Street apartment building where the shooting took place, as stated by the building management company. He was estranged from his wife and daughter whose whereabouts were unknown and had no other known family members alive. Sources revealed that he was a bankrupt real estate developer. He was also buried in a pauper's grave.

Noel knew what had transpired instinctively. That guy Mario had been the ruination of Nick! She had no control because she had no material evidence of anything. The Mob had reared its ugly head and got away free again.

Noel was relieved that the news had been delayed and the burial completed. It was not a selfish thing by any means. It was pure, good reasoning. She and Ali may have been in danger if they went to the funeral. Her obligation now was to the living, her daughter and herself.

Noel and Ali mourned for weeks and felt lethargic. They had no desire to do anything.

After a while Noel took some initiative to begin looking for an apartment. She had a small amount of money saved and would have to get a job soon. We will survive! Life will go on.

CHAPTER 98

October 17, 1993

Noel and Ali had been dragging their feet for weeks while in mourning and depressed. They had found an apartment in Boca Raton which was very desirable and close to the beach. They were scheduled to move in November 15th. Noel was a heartbeat away from landing an interior design position with a real estate developer who was on the road back to recovery. He was building a gated community attractive to retirees. Noel was his first choice for the position and was close to receiving an offer.

It was a sunny, warm day in Orlando and Ali had slipped a video cassette into the VCR. She sat down on the couch and curled up her legs. Suddenly, there was a knock on the door. She was very apprehensive because this was not a usual occurrence. Looking out the peephole before opening the door Ali went into shock. It was her father right outside the door!

She screamed, "Mom!" Noel ran from her bedroom. "What's wrong, Ali?"

"Dad's knocking on the door!" In disbelief, Noel looked

through the peephole. Sure enough, it was Nick. She opened the door and in he walked. Still in shock, but filled with emotion they all hugged together tightly. "Nick, you're alive!" Noel uttered. Ali beamed, "Dad!"

Nick quickly explained.

"When I went back to Boston the Mob had either picked up my trail somehow or knew where I lived. Maybe through some slip up on my part. Probably the bankruptcy filing! They surrounded the apartment building in Cambridge which I noticed, fortunately. When I tried to get away at nightfall, after hiding, I coincidentally was approached by two slobbering drunks looking for money. They drew attention. The Mob tried to capture me, but to hell with that, I opened fire with a .357 Magnum that I had acquired. They shot back at that point and killed the two drunks beside me. I dove to the ground as they took off to avoid the police. Everyone was confused in the gunfire.

"It just popped into my mind to slip my license, which fortunately was loose in my pocket, into one of the drunk's pockets and high-tailed it through the fence to where my rental car was parked. God was with me because that drunk with my license was unidentifiable. They had blown his face off and undoubtedly left no opportunity for a dental match. I fortunately had no blood tests available anywhere because of my good health and they couldn't locate you, Noel, for DNA evidence or visual identification. They could only assume that it was me from the license in the drunk's pocket. Apparently the poor drunk had no identification or family anywhere and must have been about my size! My attorney helped me piece the facts together.

"I ran away with my duffel bag in hand but left my bag of other belongings on the ground which I think further substantiated the dead guy as me. Three hundred thirty thousand dollars cash inside the duffel bag. I threw it inside the rental car as I managed to drive away!

"I had to stay in Boston to meet secretly with Carl Johnson and tell him the story. He was shocked when I walked into his office and amazed at the story which I told him in its entirety. As I expected, though, he had to terminate our relationship. He couldn't risk being connected with me and I understood full well. Hell, I'm dead and still a Mob target. How could I stay there anyway? He promised me that his lips are 'zipped', I trust him."

Nick hesitated and pulled something out of his shirt pocket. It was a check from Carl for two million five hundred fifty thousand dollars, made payable to a straw, Winwin Realty Trust, a nominee trust controlled by Nick.

"I set the trust up after the shootout! Carl was fair in settling what I earned working for him. Extremely fair! He wants me to make a comeback. I held off telling you about these earnings until I had them secured. There may not be a future with him, but I do have a future starting with this money and of course the contents of the duffel bag. I'll have to work low-keyed in the future and can never receive any publicity because after all I am dead! I'll have to change my name, though. Beyond that, I'll have to take some risk of not being recognized by those involved in the Massachusetts fiasco!"

They all breathed a sigh of relief.

"What about the arson charge against you? Ali knows

about it and understands you are innocent, so don't get nervous."

"Oh yes, the charge has been dropped, and logically so. A death certificate has been filed!

You know, Noel, I've been dancing on the edge all my life and now have the opportunity to sit back and relax. I'm a free man! I'm positive that the Mob has given up. Why wouldn't they? The Boston newspaper article declared me dead. It's a new start for us. Well, almost, because I am dead!" Nick laughed.

They all smiled and hugged each other again, tightly, as the sun shone through the windows.